AMANDA SCOTT

The Secret Clan

Reiver's Bride

WARNER
FOREVER

WARNER BOOKS

An AOL Time Warner Company

If you purchase this book without a cover you should be aware that this book may have been stolen property and reported as "unsold and destroyed" to the publisher. In such case neither the author nor the publisher has received any payment for this "stripped book."

WARNER BOOKS EDITION

Copyright © 2003 by Lynne Scott-Drennan

All rights reserved. No part of this book may be reproduced in any form or by any electronic or mechanical means, including information storage and retrieval systems, without permission in writing from the publisher, except by a reviewer who may quote brief passages in a review.

Cover design by Diane Luger
Cover art by Franco Accornero
Hand lettering by David Gatti
Book design by Giorgetta Bell McRee

Warner Books, Inc.
1271 Avenue of the Americas
New York, NY 10020

Visit our Web site at www.twbookmark.com

An AOL Time Warner Company

Printed in the United States of America

First Printing: September 2003

10 9 8 7 6 5 4 3 2 1

ATTENTION: CORPORATIONS AND ORGANIZATIONS:
Most WARNER books are available at quantity discounts with bulk purchase for educational, business, or sales promotional use. For information, please call or write: Special Markets Department, Warner Books, Inc. 135 W. 50th Street, New York, NY. 10020-1393.
Telephone: 1-800-222-6747 Fax: 1-800-477-5925.

APPLAUSE FOR AMANDA SCOTT AND HER MARVELOUS THE SECRET CLAN SERIES

ABDUCTED HEIRESS

"A vivid Scottish setting, an engaging battle of wits, and a dash of fantasy all come together beautifully."
—*Booklist*

———

"Totally engaging...highly charged romance, snappy repartee, memorable characters, and some wild adventures...a non-stop read."
—*Romantic Times*

———

"Ms. Scott soars through her story with excitement."
—*Rendezvous*

———

"Filled with adventure, fantasy, and the wonders of love."
—**TheRomanceReadersConnection.com**

HIDDEN HEIRESS

"An exciting work of romantic suspense...a wonderful novel."
—*Midwest Book Review*

———

"Sensual...a well-written, recommended read."
—*Romantic Times*

Please turn this page for more praise...

"Amanda Scott has done it again!…This is the perfect combination of reality and legend."
—*Rendezvous*

"Vivacious…fluid and lyrical…a whirling, twirling read that's as haunting as the beautiful skirl of bagpipes."
—www.RomanticFiction.com

"Doesn't miss a beat…plenty of intrigue, suspense, and romance…a very satisfying and entertaining read."
—TheWordonRomance.com

"Scott's fans will be glad to see this one."
—*Southern Pines Pilot* (NC)

The Secret Clan

Reiver's Bride

OTHER BOOKS BY AMANDA SCOTT

To Sue B. Steele, Lady Peel, and Kay Cole,
whose comments and attitudes continue to inspire me.
Thank you, now and always.

Everything that deceives may be said to enchant.

—PLATO

Author's Note

For readers who enjoy knowing the correct pronunciation of the names and places mentioned, please note the following:

Buccleuch = Buck-LEW
Ceilidh = KAY-lee
Dunsithe = Dun-SITH-ee

Prologue

The Scottish Borders, Ellyson Towers, July 1541

Lady Anne Ellyson gazed despairingly at her dying father, the third Earl of Armadale, as he struggled weakly to raise himself in his bed. The bedchamber was stuffy, too warm, and redolent with myriad odors of a sickroom. She gestured to the earl's wiry manservant to help him.

Slight of build as Anne was, and standing beside her father's huge bed, she felt smaller and more vulnerable than usual. She wore an old robe over her nightshift and had slipped her feet into fur-lined mules when her woman had wakened her. Her auburn hair hung untidily down her back, and her gray eyes were somber. Her throat felt tight, and as she watched the earl, her stomach clenched with fear.

"Pillow," Armadale muttered.

Without argument but with visible disapproval, his manservant helped him shift his wasted upper body forward and shoved a plump pillow behind him.

"He tires easily, my lady," the man said with a speaking look.

Wearily, but in a stronger voice than before, the earl said, "Go away, John. I would be private with her ladyship."

"Aye, my lord." Turning, he said quietly, "I'll be just outside, Lady Anne."

She nodded, her attention fixed on the glowering figure in the bed.

It was four o'clock in the morning, and although she had left him asleep only two hours before, he seemed to have lost even more weight, strength, and color in the meantime. His usually ruddy complexion was gray, his eyelids drooping. The pale blue eyes behind them, however, still showed much of their usual spark.

Armadale, like most men of the Scottish Borders, was a man of less than middle height but one born to the saddle and possessed of a strong sense of independence. Until the previous fortnight, he had enjoyed a healthy, muscular body and a vigorous life. His formidable power had derived not only from his rank and his energy but also from his domineering spirit and legendary temper. Now all that lingered of that power and spirit was the grim look he bestowed upon his sole surviving child as the door shut behind his servant.

Anne automatically braced herself, but his first words made it clear that what anger he felt was not directed at her.

"I've failed you, lass. By God's feet, I have."

Shocked to hear him admit such a thing, she felt unfamiliar sympathy stir as she said, "You have not done any such thing, sir. Moreover, you should not distress yourself by fretting about such matters but should try instead to go back to sleep. I warrant you will feel much better after you rest."

"Faith, but I'm sped, like your mother and two small sisters afore me. And I'll rest soon enough. Whether I'll feel better when I do must depend upon the Almighty and where He sends me. I've not much hope of heaven, for I've not led a pious life, but I can't mend that now, either. The good thing is, wherever I go, I'm bound to find most of the men I've dealt with over the years who passed on before me. We're all much of a muchness, after all, whichever side we've served."

Hastily crossing herself, Anne said, "You must not talk like that!"

A glimmer of a smile touched his dry, cracked lips. "God kens me through and through, Anne-lassie. What I say or how I say it won't vex Him now."

"Still—"

"Hush, lass. I've no time or strength left for fratching. Indeed, I do not know where I've found the strength to talk, for I swear I could barely open my mouth afore now to sip water when it were offered me. Still I mean to make the most of it, for there be things you should know before I leave you alone in this world."

"I can learn what I must from your man of affairs in Hawick," she insisted. "He knows your wishes, does he not?"

"Aye, Scott kens my mind on most subjects. On some there be nowt I can do in any event, with your brother gone as he is."

He fell silent, his eyes taking on the faraway look Anne had seen so often since the day nearly a year before when the terrible news had reached them that Sir Andrew Ellyson had fallen in a brief but fatal skirmish after troops of England's Henry VIII had crossed the line near Carter Bar to harass the Scots.

The earl had withdrawn from his family then, in mind if not in body, and the passion he had previously displayed for his lands and his people had diminished noticeably. He had not shirked his duties, but with Andrew dead, the fire inside his lordship had nearly died, too.

A few lingering embers had glowed briefly upon learning two months before that his countess was once again with child, but that glimmer of hope had died six weeks afterward with her ladyship and the wee seedling bairn inside her.

The fever that had swept through the Borders, particularly Roxburghshire, was fearsome, wiping out whole families and decimating villages. But its strength had waned, and they had thought the worst over when it struck Ellyson Towers.

Determined to recall the earl to the present, Anne said, "What must I do?"

"You must not stay here," he said, his voice losing strength again.

"But I thought . . ." She hesitated, reluctant to admit that she knew, or thought she knew, how things would be left.

"Ellyson Towers will be yours in two years, Anne, when you reach twenty-one. In the meantime you'll have an adequate allowance from the rents, even with England's wretched Harry wreaking mischief wherever he can."

She nodded, for she had learned as much from her mother before the countess's death. Blinking back tears at that unhappy memory, she forced herself to concentrate on her father's words, for his voice had weakened again, frighteningly.

"Scott will write to inform Thomas . . ."

"Thomas Ellyson?"

"Aye. He is the heir now to my titles and the Armadale estates in Stirlingshire." He drew a rasping breath. "Still, the inheritance will surprise him."

"But surely you wrote to him when Andrew died."

"Och, aye, but he did not bother even to reply, doubtless believing I still had plenty of time left to produce an army of sons. You must write to him, lass. 'Tis the proper thing to do, for he will be head of the family when I'm gone."

"He won't expect to look after me, will he?" Anne asked. She remembered their distant cousin Thomas Ellyson fondly from her childhood and the one or two occasions when he had paid them a visit, but the thought that a near stranger might call the tune for her dancing did not appeal to her.

The earl's parched lips twitched slightly. "You are to do as I bid you, lass."

"Aye, sir, but I'd prefer to remain here."

"Nay, you must not, for we lie only three miles from the line and English Harry's troops. Our own King Jamie's nobles are gathering armies nearby too, to support him, and there be little to choose betwixt one fighting man and another where an unprotected lass is concerned. Don't count on Jamie to protect you, either. For one thing, he is not here. Moreover, he has troubles enough, just trying to determine from one day to the next who is with him and who is against him."

"But I—"

"It's settled," he said. "You'll go to your aunt Olivia at Mute Hill House."

"Mute Hill House?" Anne scarcely remembered the place, for her aunt Olivia, Lady Carmichael, and Armadale were not close, and Anne had not visited Mute Hill House since her early childhood.

"It won't be bad," the earl said. "You will be only ten miles from home. Moreover, the house is large and well fortified, so you'll be comfortable and safe. You can help support your aunt's spirits, too, for she will pretend to miss me, especially since she plunged herself into grief after her husband died two years ago and apparently refuses to emerge from it. She's a tiresome woman, but you may find a friend in your cousin, for although you are older, you have much in common, including the fact that you were both named Fiona Anne after my mother."

"But I—"

"It's settled," he growled. "You'll go to Olivia."

Anne sighed but nodded, saying, "At least living at Mute Hill will be better than traveling all the way to Stirlingshire to abide with Cousin Thomas."

"If Thomas Ellyson has married, he has not had the courtesy to inform me," the earl said with a hint of his customary testiness. "And if he has no wife, although he is years older than you, it would be most inappropriate for you to live with him."

"I suppose it would."

"I warrant you'll not stay long with Olivia in any event, lass. After all, with the Towers and your mother's fortune, plus what more I shall leave you—which includes your little sisters' portions now, as well as your own—you will be a wealthy woman even if English Harry does take the Borders—or takes all Scotland, for that matter—so you will doubtless marry well."

"If that is true, sir, I cannot imagine how you have failed me."

"My dear child, you are nearly nineteen years old! You should have married long since, but what I meant to say is that your aunt Olivia will most likely see to that business quite easily. She's a fool and thinks too much about herself, but she did manage to get that lass of hers betrothed to Sir

Christopher Chisholm of Ashkirk and Torness, which was no mean feat. Indeed, I should think—"

But what he thought she would never know, for his words ended in a gasping cough as his voice and frail body failed him at last. His eyes widened, a sharp spasm wracked his body, and a moment later, his eyes closed.

Anne heard one last rattling breath, and then he was gone.

A wave of desolation swept over her. In less than a year—no, in barely a fortnight—she had gone from being a member of a happy, vigorous family to being alone in the world. And although she disapproved of her father's arbitrary disposal of her future, it was his right to command her and her duty to obey. In any event, she knew she lacked the fortitude to defy his wishes, even now.

As soon as he was buried in the little cemetery just outside the castle walls, she would pack her things and go to Mute Hill House.

Chapter 1

Six weeks later

Twenty-eight-year-old Kit Chisholm swallowed hard as he and his two silent companions reached the top of a hill pass a few miles southeast of Moffat and a salty tang in the soft Border breeze brought a rush of memory and stirred a familiar longing in his soul. The three had left Lanark early that morning, the first sunny morning in a sennight, and had already endured eight hours in the saddle, following four equally long, wet and dreary days before this one, journeying south from the Highlands. They were tired, but all three were Border bred, and Kit knew that Tam and Willie must be feeling much as he did.

Before them, beyond the wide, low-lying forest of Eskdale, lay the homeland of his childhood, the steep, rolling hills and deeply cleft river valleys of Roxburghshire. There, wandering mountain streams divided thick woodlands from occasional patches of arable land as their waters rushed to spill into the greater flow of the Teviot, the Ewes, the Liddel, and other powerful rivers of their ilk.

The deep, aching homesickness that his memories stirred

seemed only to strengthen with the knowledge that he was almost home again. Six long years had passed since the angry day he had left Hawks Rig Castle for the Highlands, when he had declared that he would never be homesick. But he had been wrong. Indeed, the feeling now was as strong as it had been during the fifteen months he had spent as a prisoner aboard the *Marion Ogilvy*, a time he remembered as endless, lonely months of helpless, often seething rage punctuated by periods of uncharacteristic despair.

Now that he was nearly home, it seemed to him that his yearning to be there should be easing a bit. Perhaps, he mused, it was simply safe now to acknowledge the homesickness and recognize how deeply it had affected him. Perhaps, too, he had simply grown up.

He had no idea what lay ahead. His father, the late Laird of Ashkirk and Torness, had died during his absence, so the estates and Hawks Rig were Kit's now, but the first thing he had felt at hearing the news had been fury, fury with the old laird for dying before they could reconcile their differences, and fury with himself for not growing up sooner.

"How far would ye say Hawks Rig lies from here?" young Willie Armstrong asked him, breaking the long silence.

Kit frowned. "I'm not sure," he admitted. "Ten miles or so if we could fly, but since we must ride, I'd say a half-day's journey. But 'tis only an hour and a bit from here to Dunsithe."

"That's good, that is," the older, stockier Tam said in his deep, gravelly voice. "I'll be glad tae slip off this saddle for a good night's rest."

"I wonder what they'll think of our news," Kit said, smiling at last.

Near Dunsithe Castle

"Riders!" Twelve-year-old Wee Jock o' the Wall raced barefoot across the damp, grassy hillside, shouting, "Riders approaching the castle, laird!"

Wild Fin Mackenzie, Laird of Kintail, and his constable and best friend since childhood, Sir Patrick MacRae, both turned in their saddles. They had taken advantage of the first dry day after a sennight of intermittent rain to go hawking.

Kintail yelled, "How many, Jock?"

"Three o' them," the boy yelled back. "Ye can see for yourself an ye look beyond them trees yonder."

"Go ahead, Fin," Patrick said. "I'll call Zeus in and be right behind you. Whistle up the dogs, Jock."

"Aye, sir," Jock replied, putting two fingers in his mouth and producing an ear-splitting shriek to which the three spaniels responded with tongues lolling and tails awag. The giant deerhound, Thunder, loped after them, showing far more dignity but soon outpacing the smaller dogs to catch up with his young master.

Patrick whistled the goshawk's recall signal, whereupon the great bird raised its wings and swooped toward him from the high branch where it had perched to survey nearby fields for its next unsuspecting prey. When the bird's talons met Patrick's leather glove, he caught its jesses and gave it a quail's wing. As Zeus tore flesh from bone, Patrick spurred his horse and caught up with Kintail.

"Three, just as the lad said," Kintail told him. "They carry no banner."

Since Patrick's distance vision was nearly as keen as the hawk's, he had already noted the lack of a banner, and other details as well.

"Faith," he muttered. "My eyes must be deceiving me."

"They rarely do," Kintail said, "but what makes you say so?"

"Because if they do not, we're about to offer hospitality to a dead man."

When Dunsithe Castle came into view at last, squatting solidly atop the highest hill in the area, its gray square towers and rounded turrets outlined starkly against the clear blue sky, Kit pointed it out to his companions.

"'Tis a fine looking place, that," Willie Armstrong observed. "Wonder how many kine they run in the hills hereabouts."

"You will stifle that reiver's soul of yours whilst we're here, lad," Kit ordered bluntly. "Besides being my friend, Kintail is a bad man to cross, and his constable, Sir Patrick MacRae, can take down a stag at four hundred yards with a single shot from his longbow."

Widening his blue eyes, Willie said, "I'd never lift beasts belonging tae anyone ye speak for, Kit. Ye should ken better nor that, should he no, Tam?"

The older man merely grunted.

Indignantly, Willie said, "D'ye think I'd lift beasts from a friend, Tam?"

"In sooth, lad, I think ye'd lift the featherbed from under your own mother, did a more lucrative use for it occur tae ye," Tam said.

Kit chuckled, and although Willie cast him a darkling look, the lad wisely let the subject drop.

"Someone ha' seen us," Tam said.

"Aye," Kit agreed, already watching the two men riding toward them.

The two of them, despite being Highlanders as tall and broad-shouldered as he was, rode like Borderers bred to the saddle. One carried a large hawk on his fist, and the bird lifted its wings now and again, not in protest but as if it simply enjoyed the sensation of wind beneath its wings.

Smiling, Kit said, "You are about to meet our host and his constable." He drew rein and waited patiently for Kintail and Patrick to close with them. As they did, he noted a lad and four dogs racing uphill toward the castle.

Tam had seen them, too. "Likely, we'll soon ha' a host of armed men descending on us," he said grimly.

"More likely, the servants will be setting extra places for supper," Kit said.

"That's no so likely as spears and arrows," Tam said, "for they can scarcely ha' seen who we are yet. Mayhap if they be friends o' yours—"

"They know who we are," Kit said, raising a hand to return a similar greeting from Patrick.

"How could they?" Willie demanded.

"Sir Patrick's long vision is even keener than mine."

Nodding, Willie said, "Aye then, I'll believe ye. On the ship, ye always could make out sail or landfall long afore the rest of us could."

Tam looked narrowly at Kit. "I ha' seen ye wi' a sword in your hand but no wi' a bow. Still, wi' that long sight o' yours, I expect ye've a fine eye for a target."

"Sir Patrick is more skilled, but I can give him fair competition."

"From what we ha' seen hereabouts and in the Highlands, I'd wager ye might soon ha' the chance tae show your skill," Tam said. "They say Henry's army lies ready tae attack somewhere between the line and the English city o' York."

The approaching riders had slowed and were waving them forward.

"Come on," Kit said, spurring his mount.

He laughed with boyish delight when Kintail clapped him on the shoulder and Patrick cried, "Kit Chisholm, by all that's holy, we thought you were dead!"

"I nearly was, I can tell you," Kit said. "I spent fifteen long months in hell, at all events. These are my lads, Tam and Willie," he added before Kintail or Patrick could demand further explanation of his absence.

The men shook hands all around, and then Kit said, "Whatever gave you the notion that I was dead? 'Tis true I was out of the country for longer than I'd have wished, but as I'd been in the Highlands four years and more before then—"

"Faith, is that how it was?" Patrick demanded, his eyes narrowing. "I heard what happened before you disappeared, you know. Fin knows, too, although I hope I don't have to tell you we didn't believe a word of what they said of you." He glanced at Tam and Willie, then back at Kit, raising his eyebrows as he did.

Easily following his thoughts, Kit said, "They know more about the murders than you do, so we can talk freely." For Tam and Willie's sake, he added, "I've known these two since my schooldays. You can trust them as you do me."

Kintail said, "Then we may assume the matter was settled sensibly and the authorities know now that the charges against you were false."

"You may," Kit said, sobering.

"But how did you manage to disappear for over a year?" Patrick asked.

"For that I can thank the Sheriff of Inverness. His men assumed I had committed two murders, but they feared a jury might disagree with them, so they simply arrested me and handed me over to one of Cardinal Beaton's ship captains as a convicted criminal. My protests of innocence and the fact that I had never had a trial being utterly ignored, I served as the cardinal's involuntary seaman for fifteen months before Tam, Willie, and I escaped and I was able to prove my innocence."

Patrick looked curiously at Tam and Willie, as if he would have liked to ask what crimes they had committed, but then, visibly collecting himself, he said to Kit, "I'm glad you were cleared, but like it or not, my lad, the official position is that you are as dead as our last Christmas goose."

"Dead!" When Patrick nodded, Kit added, "The *official* position? But how can that be when anyone can see that I'm alive?"

Raising a hand to stop Patrick's explanation before it began, Kintail said, "Shall we ride on to Dunsithe to discuss this? You'll stay the night at least, Kit. Molly and Beth will both want to meet you and hear any news you've brought."

"Molly and Beth?"

"Our wives, of course," Patrick said, adding as his eyes lit with pride, "They are both presently in a delicate condition, so mind how you behave."

"My congratulations to you both," Kit said. "I do bring news, too, particularly from your sister and mother, Patrick."

Clearly surprised, Patrick said warily, "How do they fare?"

"Excellently," Kit replied. "As a matter of fact, your sister recently married my cousin, Alex Chisholm."

Patrick's jaw dropped. "Why have I heard nothing of this?" he demanded.

Kit chuckled. "I expect Bab wanted to punish you," he said.

"He can tell you all about it on the way," Kintail said sternly. "By now our lads are lining the ramparts, trying to decide if all is well, and if we do not return soon, our wives will be riding out to join us."

Accordingly, as they rode up the hill to Dunsithe, Kit described what he knew of Barbara MacRae's marriage to Sir Alex Chisholm.

"So it was all my mother's doing," Patrick said when Kit reached the end of his tale. "How astonishing!"

"You may say so, but you helped," Kit said, grinning. "From what I heard, you had suggested the match often enough to make it seem unnecessary to apply for your permission."

They continued to discuss the wedding and other news of the Highlands until they rode through the open gates into Dunsithe's cobbled courtyard.

Two young women, both beautiful and bearing a strong likeness to each other, came hurrying to meet them.

"We thought you would never come back," the elder one said accusingly to Kintail. She had clouds of red-gold curls hanging nearly to her hips, and when he leaped down to gather her into his arms, Kit easily deduced that she was his wife.

The other woman, despite the strong resemblance, had smooth, silvery blond hair and an air of serenity that Kintail's wife lacked. She waited patiently while Patrick handed the hawk to a waiting gilly and dismounted, but then she walked into his embrace, returning it with fervor. Both women were visibly pregnant.

Introducing them as Molly and Beth, Kintail added as Kit dismounted, "This gentleman is Sir Christopher Chisholm, Laird of Ashkirk and Torness."

Molly frowned. "But did we not hear that . . . that is . . ."

When she hesitated again, Patrick said with a chuckle, "Aye, Kit's dead. I informed him of his demise only moments ago, however. He did not know."

Kit said to Kintail, "Perhaps we should postpone the rest of this conversation until after we eat, when we can speak more privately."

Molly Mackenzie cast her husband a silent but speaking look.

Kintail's eyes twinkled as he said, "We'll discuss it as privately as you like, Kit, but you should know that you will be condemning Patrick and me to certain inquisition and torment if you refuse to let us tell our lasses what's afoot. Still, if you want the discussion to remain private, we'll keep it to ourselves." He met his wife's gaze, and although she wrinkled her nose impertinently, she did not argue.

"I have no reason not to trust them," Kit said, "but I'd as lief the discussion not be a gift to all and sundry, so mayhap we should wait until after we've eaten."

Smiling in a way that lit her whole being and showed Kit how she had fascinated Fin, Molly said, "I'll tell them to serve us in my solar, sir. Our personal servants will wait on us there, and they know better than to speak of anything that happens thus privately at Dunsithe."

She glanced at Kintail, who nodded his approval, whereupon she caught up her skirts and hurried back inside with Beth at her heels.

Watching until they had disappeared inside Kit said, "Are they sisters?"

"They are," Patrick said, "although they lost track of each other for many years until by good fortune, I met and married Beth. We'll tell you all about that another day, but first let us get you and your lads settled and find you some food."

"Now, will one of you please explain to me how I've come to be officially dead?" Kit said an hour later when their meal had been served.

Tam, sitting beside him, said bluntly, "Aye, pray do, for I dinna ken how officialdom can enter into it when the man involved is plainly no dead at all."

"But where were you, sir?" Molly asked Kit. "How is it that your people lost track of you long enough to assume that you had died?"

When Kit hesitated, Kintail said, "He was away, lass, due to a misunderstanding betwixt himself and the Sheriff of Inverness-shire."

Kit grimaced at the memories the words evoked. "Suffice it to say, my lady, that I was out of the country."

When Molly turned to her husband, Kintail said, "Two of Kit's cousins were murdered in the Highlands a year ago last Easter, and Kit was falsely accused of killing them."

Patrick nodded, his gaze fixed on Kit as he said, "His disappearance afterward lent credence to those rumors. I think you should have known, my lad," he added with a grin, "that to tell two women smart enough to marry Fin and me that you were simply 'out of the country' would not satisfy them."

"Certainly not," Molly agreed. "Surely you could have

got word to someone amongst your friends and family, to let them know where you were."

"Faith, I did not know where I was a good part of the time," Kit muttered, exchanging looks with Tam and Willie. This part of the tale was not solely his to tell, but he could reveal to the women as much as he had to their husbands. "I was a prisoner on one of Beaton's ships," he said, "but I'm here now, the true murderer was caught, and there are no longer any charges against me in Inverness."

The servants returned, and conversation became desultory while they served the next course. But when the little group was alone again, Kit said abruptly, "You still haven't explained how I came to be officially dead. Surely, a mere lack of communication for less than a year and a half was not sufficient reason, especially since the lack cannot have disturbed anyone until my father died."

Patrick and Fin exchanged looks, and then Fin said, "Have you managed to glean any knowledge of the present political situation here?"

Kit nodded. "I know that Henry, having wrested control of the Church in England from Rome and his holiness, the pope, now wants to take command of the Scottish Kirk as well."

"In truth, that villain would control all Scotland," Tam said.

Patrick glanced at the older man and nodded. "That is true," he said. "Some time ago, Henry invited our Jamie to meet with him in the city of York to discuss the Scottish Kirk. Fortunately, he put it to Jamie that he was just a kindly uncle offering to help his young nephew understand the benefits of distancing himself and his country from Rome."

"Henry is no one's kindly uncle," Kit said. "Moreover,

James would have to be a fool to journey so far into enemy country to confer with anyone."

"And our Jamie is no one's fool," Patrick said. "He has been careful not to defy Henry outright, though. First, he told him quite plausibly that he could not leave whilst the queen was about to produce his second child. Then, of course, the tragic deaths of both young princes less than a month later, doubtless of the same pestilential fever that next swept through the Borders, made it possible for him to defer the matter even longer. But Henry grows impatient."

"And the deaths of the princes make the situation more dangerous than ever," Kintail said. "Without an heir to the throne, Jamie's position becomes fragile. He has offended most of his Border lords at one time or another, so he can't count on them to fight Henry, and many of his more ambitious nobles would like to unseat him, making them all easy prey for Henry's manipulating. And Cardinal Beaton—"

"Yes," Kit said evenly, "do tell me about the good cardinal."

Patrick's eyes narrowed thoughtfully, but he said only, "He too advises Jamie to strengthen Scotland's ties with Rome, of course."

"Aye, well, I cannot say either side of that debate appeals to me," Kit said, "but what has any of it to do with my being declared dead?"

Kintail said, "Political instability and the need to protect Hawks Rig and your other estates was the excuse your uncle, Eustace Chisholm, offered after your father's death to persuade the magistrate in Jedburgh to declare you officially dead as soon as you'd been missing a full year. That allowed Eustace to take control of your estates immediately and to assume your titles in April when the year was up."

"The devil you say!" Kit exclaimed.

"The villain!" Tam said in the same breath.

Willie sat wide-eyed, looking from one to the other.

"I have heard only rumors, of course," Kintail said. "But you know how swiftly news travels when armies gather. They say Eustace is calling himself Ashkirk and has done so these past few months and more."

Patrick said, "As the eldest of your father's brothers and the only one to survive him, Eustace Chisholm would be his legal heir had you truly predeceased him, would he not?"

"Aye, that's true," Kit admitted, "but it's damned cheek nonetheless. If my uncle ever sought information about my whereabouts in the Highlands I heard nothing about it, and I've just come from Torness. My steward had received no word from Eustace, although he did know that my father had died, thanks to my cousin Alex, who also took it upon himself to look after my Highland estates. If anyone tried to interfere with them, Alex would have known about it, I'm sure."

Kintail frowned. "Then I'd advise you to tread lightly, Kit. You would be wise to learn exactly what Eustace Chisholm has done and how matters stand before you show yourself at Hawks Rig."

"Aye, 'tis good advice," Kit said, suppressing a surge of disappointment at the thought that he would have to delay his return home a little longer. "In truth, I have not the least notion how my father left his affairs, but if he thought I was dead, they may have become a trifle complicated."

"Your uncle was astonishingly quick to take the reins," Patrick said.

Tam made a sound of disapproval, much like a growl.

"Eustace is a cunning bastard," Kit said. "I've never liked

him or trusted him. Although we rarely saw him, he stirred much of the trouble between my father and me with letters filled with seemingly casual gossip and criticism."

"Then you'll certainly want to learn his intentions and how he has situated himself before you confront him," Kintail said firmly.

Thoughtfully, Patrick said, "Did I not also hear that you had become betrothed shortly before your cousins were killed, Kit?"

"Aye, my father wrote some such thing to me," Kit said, grimacing.

"Ye never told *us* about any lass," Tam said, clearly surprised.

"Well, I own the matter has been of concern to me, but since I had no chance to reply to my father's message, I assumed that other arrangements had been made. Even if they were not, if I'm officially dead now, doubtless she is betrothed to someone else. In truth, I'm much more concerned about Hawks Rig."

"But she may still be grieving for you," Molly protested. "She certainly must wonder what became of you."

"She may wonder," Kit said with a wry smile, "but I doubt she has grieved much. We've never even met. My father arranged the match with her mother. As I said, I'd only learned of it just before . . ."

"Who is she?" Molly demanded. "Do we know her?"

"Her name is Fiona Carmichael," Kit said. "As I recall it, her mother is some connection of Armadale's."

"Lady Carmichael is Armadale's sister," Patrick said. "I've been constable here at Dunsithe only a short time, but Armadale's name is as well known hereabouts as Scott of Buccleuch or Maxwell of Caerlaverock. In any event, I took interest in Armadale's kinsmen because Armadale married a Gordon. Although Molly and Beth never knew her, she was a cousin of theirs."

"Was?"

"Aye, she died of the fever that swept through the Borders a short time ago. It killed Armadale, too, and since his only son died last year in a skirmish with English Harry's lads, the title goes to some unknown cousin from Stirlingshire."

Molly turned to Patrick. "Did I understand you to say that Kit's Fiona is a cousin to Beth and me?"

"She's not my Fiona," Kit protested. "At least, I'm sure that if I'm supposedly dead, and have been for nigh onto eighteen months now, the betrothal must have been annulled or whatever one does to overset betrothals."

"She is not your cousin in any event, sweetheart," Kintail said. "Fiona's mother is no kin to the Gordons except through Armadale's marriage, so neither is her daughter."

"Then that's all right," Molly said, smiling at Kit. "Perhaps your encroaching uncle will have been kind enough to take her off your hands along with your titles and estates."

The others laughed, but Kit said, "He's welcome to her, although I should think he'd be years too old for her. I'll choose my own wife, thank you, but in any event, first I mean to reclaim what is mine."

His friends understood and sympathized and they discussed the matter at length, with Kintail holding firm that Kit should proceed with caution.

"Fin's right about that," Kit said later when he was alone with Willie and Tam. "I need to learn more before I confront my uncle, but in truth I scarcely know where to begin, other than to discover who handled my father's affairs."

Tam said, "I ken a few folk in these parts. If ye can manage without me for a few days, I'll nose about some. I've matters o' me own tae look into, for all that."

"I should think you must have," Kit said, clapping him on the shoulder. "You and Willie have been overly patient with me and my troubles. I should command you both to abandon me and deal with your own long-neglected affairs, but I confess I'll be grateful for any information you can glean."

"I've got a better notion than just waiting about for Tam," Willie said with a twinkle. "My lads will doubtless ken all that's happened hereabouts over the past year and longer. Verra little happens wi'out they hear o' it."

"Your lads?" Kit exchanged a look with Tam.

The latter frowned heavily, saying, "Ye'll no be mixing Kit up wi' that scurvy lot o' yours if ye ken what's good for ye, me lad."

Willie grinned. "Ye'll admit I speak true, though. There isna much the reivers dinna ken about who's doing what in the Borders, either side o' the line."

Kit agreed with Tam that mixing with the reivers might prove foolhardy, particularly since he had been away for so long and knew little about their activities. Nevertheless, the thought of action, any sort of action, appealed strongly to him.

So it was that when he took fond leave of his friends at Dunsithe, promising to send word as soon as he learned how things stood, he parted for the first time in a year and a half with Tam as well, to ride off with Willie Armstrong under a gray sky heavy with spitting clouds, in search of Willie's reivers.

Chapter 2

Elsewhere and in their own time

Maggie Malloch was in a temper and in a rare quandary as well—rare, because she never found herself in situations she could not handle, and a quandary because the few choices open to her were choices she wanted to reject out of hand.

Never before had she felt so powerless or so certain that failure must not be considered. Had it been anyone else who needed her, she believed her mind would be clear, the proper course of action obvious. But her own son was missing, and she was at a loss to know what, if anything, she could do to find him.

Nearly every other member of the Secret Clan who knew of the situation firmly believed that she wasted her time even thinking she could do anything.

"He's dead, and ye'll no get from that, Maggie," their high chief told her bluntly. "Ye've your own duties tae attend, no tae mention the wee task the High Circle set for ye long since, about which ye've done little that anyone can see."

"I've told ye, the bickering betwixt two feckless tribes be

o' small concern tae me in the face o' Claud's disappearance," she said.

"Sakes, woman, 'twere no a mere disappearance! Your Claud were blasted tae bits by a lightning bolt flung by the hand o' the Clan's mightiest wizard!"

"Exactly so," Maggie retorted. "But that shape-shifting villain Jonah Bonewits be as powerful as I be myself—or nearly so," she amended.

"But, Maggie, that be just my—"

"Whisst now, will ye whisst? I'm telling ye how it is. Ye ken as well as I do that Jonah never meant tae strike our Claud, for Claud be his son as well as mine."

"Aye, I ken that fine, although I'd point out—no tae put a fine point on it—that a sore disappointment the lad were tae Jonah."

"Nevertheless, and villain though Jonah be, I canna believe he would kill his own son, even an he thinks Claud be nobbut a witless dobby."

"Ye're certain Jonah didna mean tae do it?"

"I were there wi' that slut Catriona from the Merry Folk," Maggie reminded him. "Jonah ha' hoped tae lure Claud tae follow another feckless wench—that Lucy Fittletrot wi' the dancing feet—but Claud were sorely smitten wi' Catriona. I'd venture tae guess that ye do recall Catriona," she added sardonically.

"I do," the chief agreed, his eyes glowing. "She'll be the poor wee lass from the Merry Folk that ye persist in maligning every chance ye get."

Maggie made a rude noise. "Ye men! At least I'll say this for that Catriona. She cares about what happened tae my Claud!"

"She should. As I recall the matter, ye said yourself that

Claud threw himself into the path o' yon lightning bolt because it were flung at Catriona."

"Aye, and had it struck her, I'd ha' lost little sleep over it, for on that subject Jonah and I be in full agreement."

"Now, Maggie . . ."

"Pish tush, dinna 'now, Maggie' me. Ye ken what I think, and I'll no keep me thoughts behind me teeth now when I ha' always spoken me mind afore."

"Ye have that, but what d'ye aim tae do, woman? Ye've power enough for most things, but bringing a member o' the Clan back tae life when he's been blown tae mist be more than even ye can do."

"Aye, well, if he were only mist, 'twould be easy, but ye'll agree, will ye no, that Jonah's fury has nowt tae do with either Catriona or Claud."

The chief nodded. "'Tis yourself who infuriated the man, as always. Did ye no spoil his plans yet again and cause him tae lose his place in the High Circle?"

"He lost it through greed and by interfering in mortal affairs!"

"Aye, but ye interfered, too," the chief reminded her. "It wasna Jonah who took a common serving lass, clad her in a grand dress, decked her wi' jewels fit for a queen, and sent her tae a royal ball."

Maggie dismissed that incident with a gesture. "Nobbut good came o' that. However, Jonah employed black arts and shape-shifting tae keep rightful mortals from finding a treasure his own Lord Angus wanted, no tae mention his other, more recent wickedness."

"Aye, 'tis true," the chief agreed.

"Still," Maggie said, "'Tis me Jonah blames for what's

happened tae him, and he willna rest till he's bested me. That be why I believe he didna kill our Claud."

"Then who did?"

"Nae one."

"But Maggie—"

"Jonah be the most powerful wizard in our Clan. Ye said that yourself."

"Aye."

"And when we o' the Secret Clan pass on, 'tis sometimes tae dwell in the mortal world, is it no?"

"Aye, on rare occasions," the chief said, frowning.

"Then I believe Jonah altered the course o' that lightning bolt at the last minute and instead o' sending Claud tae fly wi' the Evil Host for all time, as he would ha' done had he struck Catriona, he hurled him into the mortal world."

The chief was silent, his eyes smoldering as he thought over what she had said. "'Tis possible," he said at last. "But 'tis a vast world, that o' the mortals. How would ye ever find him?"

"I willna rest till I do, that's all. Ye see—"

"Whisst yourself now," the chief commanded. "Ye still need tae mediate the troubles between them two tribes ye call feckless, and afore our next meeting, too. D'ye fail, ye'll lose your own seat in the High Circle. We ha' lost Jonah Bonewits, and we canna seem tae replace him. I dinna want tae lose ye, too."

"Ye'll no lose me," Maggie said confidently. "We've had nae trouble from the Merry Folk or the Helping Hands since our last meeting, and I ha' the word o' both their chieftains that they'll keep this truce until Catriona succeeds or fails tae restore her mortal tae his proper place and assure his happiness there. I'll find Claud well afore that, because Catriona still must—"

"Phui, woman, ye needna tell me what Catriona must do. Were I no sitting in me long black robe a cat's whisker from ye when ye made the bargain? Surrounded, I'd remind ye, by all ten o' the others, several o' whom still be determined tae restore Jonah tae our midst?"

"Aye, ye were."

"I was, and ye promised no tae break any rules whilst ye settle the debate betwixt the Merry Folk and the Helping Hands over who should look after mortal Highland clans that ha' their ancient roots stuck deep in the Borders."

"Aye, and I'll settle it, too, for the Merry Folk will soon see that if we ha' tae send Border members tae the Highlands whenever a Highland mortal marries a Border lass and takes her north, we'll soon be as populous there as they are."

"But in the meantime, ye've set the lovely wee Catriona tae look after a lad from one o' them Highland clans so rooted in the Borders that he's coming home tae roost, whilst your Border-bred Claud were set tae look after a Highland lass."

"Which he did do, and very well, too."

"Aye, he did. But, still—"

Interrupting him, Maggie said firmly, "I'm going tae find him and bring him home again. If ye mean tae be obstreperous, I canna stop ye, but if ye'd like tae help, ye'll see to it that the Circle doesna meet again too soon."

The chief grimaced but nodded abruptly as she vanished.

Mute Hill House, Roxburghshire

"Turn about slowly, Fiona, and let me see how you look," Olivia, Lady Carmichael said as she fanned herself with a limp hand. She was a handsome woman in her late thirties, fashionably if mournfully dressed in dark purple with black lace trimming, but any onlooker would swiftly see her strong resemblance to the slim, fair-haired girl standing in the center of the elegantly appointed bower.

Obediently, seventeen-year-old Fiona Anne Carmichael turned, anxiously observing the expressions of her mother and the room's two other occupants as all three watched with critical eyes.

Fiona was stunningly beautiful, and the elegant sky-blue brocade gown she wore became her. But then, everything Fiona wore became her.

Sunlight chose that moment to emerge from the clouds outside and pour through the tall leaded windows flanking the hooded fireplace, but that sunlight was no more golden than the soft shining curls that tumbled over Fiona's shoulders to her waist. Her blue-gray eyes were large and luminous, their thick lashes so dark they looked as if she had blackened them. Her eyebrows arched delicately. Her rosy lips were full and eminently kissable. Sadly, though, her tip-tilted nose bore a dusting of freckles across the bridge, a detail that her cousin Anne Ellyson had learned soon after her arrival was one that Lady Carmichael deplored as the sole flaw in her daughter's otherwise perfect complexion.

Anne had decided before the end of her first sennight at Mute Hill that she'd have been wiser to remain at Ellyson Towers despite her father's decree. Watching narrowly now, she decided that Fiona looked worn to the bone, and considering that the poor girl had been standing and turning, dressing and undressing, and listening to her mother's criticism and complaints for the better part of two hours, Anne could not blame her. For her own part, she wanted only to escape, and she knew exactly where she would go as soon as she could slip away.

"What do you think?" Olivia asked in the faint tone she affected these days in all but truly private conversations.

Knowing the question was not directed at her, Anne turned her head toward the fourth person in the room.

Her aunt Olivia's waiting woman, Moira Graham, was short and plump, and looked as if she were made of soft, stuffed pillows. As she pursed her lips and narrowed her eyes, she reminded Anne of a cloth doll that she had had when she was small. Even Moira's frilled white cap was similar to the doll's.

Moira turned to her mistress, saying, "It will do nicely, I think, my lady."

"You don't think it could bear to nip in a bit more at the waist?"

"It must be as you wish, of course, madam," Moira said, "but to my mind, taking it in will spoil the way that fabric drapes over her hips."

Anne agreed. She thought the dress looked fine and much as it had an hour before when Fiona had first put it on, before all the nipping and tucking. Had Anne chosen the fabric, however, it would not have been sky blue but a shade more suited to her cousin's misty eyes. Better yet would have been the pale pink that was Fiona's favorite color. A girl's wedding dress, after all, ought to be the color she liked best rather than a lesser one chosen by her mother.

At least Olivia had not insisted that her daughter wear the

dark purple mourning she favored for herself, but somehow she had got it into her head that Fiona's intended husband, Sir Eustace Chisholm, Laird of Ashkirk and Torness, fancied sky blue, and so sky blue the dress had had to be. No one argued with her, because one never knew what the result would be if one even hinted at opposition.

"Anne dear, pray fetch that lavender lace scarf from the table yonder and drape it over your cousin's shoulders."

"Yes, Aunt Olivia," Anne replied, moving with her customary calm grace to obey. As she approached Fiona with the filmy lace scarf, she encountered a look of such abject, pleading misery that she felt an impulse to gather her into her arms and attempt to soothe her fears and frustration.

Ruthlessly stifling that impulse, Anne smiled instead and said to her aunt without looking away from her cousin, "It must be nearly noon, Aunt Olivia, and the Laird of Ashkirk is rarely behind time. I warrant you will want me to help Fiona change into something more suitable to receive him."

"Yes, of course," Olivia said with a sigh. "But first we must see to this business. Their wedding, after all, is only two days away."

"If I could just sit down for a minute," Fiona said in her soft, breathless voice, "I'm feeling a trifle faint, but I am sure the sensation will soon pass."

"Don't talk like a noddy," Olivia said with more spirit than she usually revealed. "You cannot sit in that gown or you'll muss the skirt, and in any event, you cannot possibly be as tired as I am. Why, I've scarcely enjoyed a night's repose since your father died. What with the shock of Sir Christopher's death and then his father's, followed so soon afterward by that of my dear brother, Armadale, I can assure you my grief knows no bounds. And grief, my dear Fiona, is far more exhausting than simply standing to have one's wedding dress fitted, so I do not want to hear another word of complaint from you."

Tears sparkled in Fiona's eyes, doubtless at the mention of her father's death, but Anne knew they would do her no more good than if Anne were to mention her own several losses over the past year. It seemed to have altogether escaped Olivia's notice that she shared her bereavement with others.

Anne smiled encouragingly at Fiona and murmured, "Just a few more minutes, love."

Since her back was to her aunt and Moira, she knew they would not hear or see that she had spoken, but when Fiona's eyes welled with more tears, she could have kicked herself for offering sympathy.

"There now," she said in a louder, brisker tone as she draped the lavender lace over her cousin's shoulders. "Is that how it should look, Aunt Olivia?"

"Stand away so I can see," her aunt said plaintively.

Obeying without further comment, Anne hoped she would see for herself that the lavender shawl did not improve the gown. Little could detract from Fiona's ethereal beauty, but the fine lavender lace draped over the heavy sky-blue brocade was a near thing. Without it, at least the gown bore distinctive elegance.

Olivia frowned, but whether at the effect of the scarf or because she had detected Fiona's tears Anne would not know, for at that moment pandemonium erupted in the great hall adjoining her ladyship's bower.

Dogs barked and men shouted. Other less easily identified sounds accompanied these, as plump Moira hurried to open the connecting door.

Her mistress cried out to her not to do so, but it was too late. As the door cracked open, a small bundle of red fur hurtled through the opening, followed moments later by six large, baying hounds.

The door crashed back against the wall, nearly to the undoing of Moira, for although she snatched her skirts out of the path of the pursuing dogs with one hand, she failed to release her hold on the door handle with the other and was nearly flung against the wall when the door banged back.

Fiona shrieked and snatched up her skirts. Olivia cried out again to Moira to shut the door, but two large men trying to follow the dogs blocked the way, becoming entangled when they tried to push through the doorway together.

Anne stood where she was, noting first and with relief that the dogs took no interest in the shrieking Fiona, and then that the small bundle of fur, which she had taken for a cat, was in fact a terrified fox. When she saw it dash through the opposite doorway toward spiral stairs leading to the upper and lower levels of Mute Hill House, she caught Fiona by the shoulders and gave her a gentle shake.

"Hush, love," Anne said. "Those dogs care only about the fox. See, they have already run away after it."

The exhausted Fiona burst into tears.

Holding her, listening to the fading sounds of men chasing the dogs chasing the fox, Anne turned to her aunt and said, "I am going to take her upstairs, madam. She should wash her face and rest before she dresses to receive Eustace Chisholm."

"Where did those damned dogs go?" bellowed a familiar masculine voice from the great-hall doorway, where Sir Toby Bell, Lady Carmichael's uncle, filled the opening nearly as completely as the two men before him had. Huffing, he turned himself slightly so as not to catch the jamb with the dress sword he wore and entered, hooking his thumbs in his sword belt as he glared across the room at his niece, clearly expecting an answer.

"Your dogs have no business in this chamber, sir," she said, her voice weak again, her posture limp and pathetic. "Everything is still wet outside from the rain, so they've surely tracked mud all over the floor. You know how they distress me!"

"Shouldn't have opened the door then," he said with a mocking smile. "I warrant my dogs didn't distress you as much as they distressed that witless fox, though. Would you believe it, the beast was just strolling up the avenue toward the entrance as mild as you please. Front door was shut, of course, until my dogs began barking and that fool man of yours opened it to see what the din was about."

"Please go and collect them," she said, putting the back of one hand to her brow. "You know how the least little disturbance oversets me in my grief."

"God's wounds, Olivia, it's been five months and more since that fellow Ashkirk died."

"I grieve for my husband, sir," she protested indignantly.

"Fiddle, lass, you grieve for your lover. Stephen died nearly two years ago, and after Kit Chisholm's disappearance and supposed death spoiled your plan to marry Fiona into that family, you set your own cap for Ashkirk. 'Twas his death that cast you into this stupid melancholy of yours, for Stephen's death scarcely affected you. I should know," he added. "Came to live here directly after Stephen died, to lend you the consequence of having a gentleman in the house, didn't I? I tell you, you were as right as rain until Ashkirk popped off."

Anne was not surprised to see tears well in Olivia's eyes, for she had quickly learned that, like Fiona, her ladyship could produce such tears at will and without in the least disturbing her fine complexion.

Olivia said faintly, "You are cruel, uncle."

"I am honest, Olivia, that's all."

"I shall mourn Stephen's death until I die," she said with a tearful sniff.

"Bosh," he retorted with a chuckle. "Now where did those damned dogs go?"

Anne waited no longer, swiftly taking Fiona from the room and upstairs to her bedchamber before anyone could think to stop her. It was another three hours, however, before she was able to make her own escape.

Elsewhere

After her meeting with the Clan's chief, Maggie retired to her private parlor to consider how to proceed. She dared not trust Catriona. If anything was certain in this world or the mortal one, it was that Catriona was not dependable, although, to be fair, she had behaved well since Claud's disappearance. When she had accepted the task of serving the Chisholms, she had taken that task to heart despite opposition from her tribe and fiendish interference from Jonah Bonewits.

Thinking about the troublesome, shape-shifting wizard seemed to bring him right into the room. She could almost see his harsh features in the flames dancing in her fireplace. Blinking away the annoying hallucination, she returned her thoughts to Catriona and the sacrifice Claud had made for the wee strumpet.

Maggie knew it was unfair to blame only Catriona, but blaming her had become second nature because of the ease with which she manipulated Claud. Of course that, Maggie had to admit, was Claud's fault as well, thanks to his predilection for falling into lust with any beautiful lass who flitted past him. Still, the plain truth was that if Catriona had not been there when Jonah . . .

Here, fairness intruded again. Catriona had been at the site of Claud's mishap because her charge had been there, and in serving her charge, she had enraged Jonah and nearly lost her life. Maggie could not blame her for enraging Jonah, however, since Maggie herself had frequently enraged him.

The flames shot higher and seemed again to depict his features. Indeed, they seemed clearer than before. Suddenly, she realized what was happening and the fury that had smoldered since Claud's disappearance suddenly erupted.

"Show yourself properly, ye meddlesome knave, or I'll make that fire too hot tae hold ye," she snapped, flying to her feet. "Ye needna hover about, trying tae read me thoughts, for I'll tell ye tae your villainous face just what I think o' ye."

The shape in the flames oscillated as if the energy producing it faltered, but then, with a whooshing sound, an orange-gold cyclone of sparks whirled out of the fireplace to the hearth, where it lengthened upright into the outline of a tall, long-robed man, and then solidified until Jonah Bonewits looked as he always did.

He wore a long gray robe, and his hair was dark at the roots and fair at the tips, radiating from his head like rays of the sun. His long, narrow face was not remarkable unless one counted thin yellow, green, red, and blue streaks on each cheek, but his dark eyes gleamed and his smile was mischievous.

Fluttering the six, heavily ringed fingers of one hand, he said, "Well, Mag?"

"It is *not* well, ye shameless murderer. What ha' ye done wi' my Claud?"

His laugh sounded both eerie and menacing. "Woman, *our* Claud is a fool. Did ye have half the brain in your head that ye think ye do, ye'd no miss him at all."

"Where is he?" she repeated, fighting to control her temper.

"I thought that brilliant mind o' yours had worked it out for ye."

"Ye've been spying on me, is that it?"

"I have and all. Ye're too smart for me, Mag."

"Ye've fooled me often, Jonah Bonewits, but I ken ye fine, and I hold by what I said tae the chief. Ye'd no kill our Claud an ye could avoid it, nor would ye send him tae fly wi' the Evil Host, for he'd be as lost tae ye in either instance as he would be if ye'd let that lightning bolt kill him. So ye . . ."

She hesitated, unwilling to put the thought into words again lest he instantly prove her wrong and end her mission before it began.

As often happened, though, he read her thoughts easily. "Ye're not usually such a coward, Mag," he said. "Ye'll no find him, though, seek ye how far."

Relieved to hear him admit that Claud still lived, she said shrewdly, "'Twould ruin the game for ye did I ha' nae chance tae find him, so I'll wager ye've put him somewhere in plain sight, did I only ken where tae look."

He grinned. "Aye, well, mayhap ye're right, lass. But consider that if I did such a thing, I might add a trick or a trap to the plan."

"I ken that, too," she said.

"Ye won't ask what they might be, will ye?"

She did not, knowing he would refuse to tell her and declining to give him that satisfaction.

"Very well, to prove ye're wrong about me, I'll give ye one wee clue. He's where ye think, in plain sight, but ye'll never recognize him as our Claud."

"So ye've made him mortal."

Jonah shrugged. "In a manner o' speaking, I've melded him."

"Melded? What mean ye by that?"

"Just that I've bound our Claud's entity to that of a mortal, that's what, and that's where he'll stay."

"Unless ye intervene," Maggie said, eyeing him narrowly.

He did not reply.

She shook her head at him. "Ye'll no cozen me into believing ye did this melding business without leaving yourself a way tae alter things if ye want to, Jonah. Ye'll always keep control o' your mischief."

"Mayhap ye give me powers more credit than they deserve."

"Nay, for I believe ye want summat, and ye ken fine ye'll no get it wi'out summat tae bargain in return."

"Ye ken well what I want, Mag."

"Ye want me tae fail at making peace betwixt the Merry Folk and the Helping Hands. Ye've made that plain from the start."

"Only so ye'll lose your place in the High Circle and see

how it feels. Ye can make your silly peace if ye resign. But I'll want me own seat back when ye go."

She frowned, thinking furiously and exerting herself as she did to hide her thoughts from him. He might suspect what she was thinking, but she could keep him from actually reading her thoughts now that she knew she must.

"They willna let me resign until the peace be made," she said. "I'd ha' nae authority over them obstreperous hill folk were I no a member o' the Circle."

"Then settle their peace."

"Ye ken fine that that triple-turned slut Catriona has a duty first tae the Chisholms tae restore their lost lad tae his proper place, settled and happy. After she does that, I can easily create a permanent truce."

"Then ye'd best help your wee slut do her business, Mag."

His voice was smooth, almost oily. She could read nothing in his expression.

"Ye'd best leave her be, Jonah, if ye want tae reclaim your seat."

He was about to depart, for his shape was losing definition as he said, "Ye're no fooling me, lass. Ye'd never give up your place in the Circle, even for our Claud. Take care o' yourself, though, until we speak again."

With that, he was gone, taking with him the energy from her little fire. Only a few glowing embers remained until she flicked a finger to restore it.

Dunsithe had barely passed from view when Willie said, "We'll speak tae me cousin Sammy, Kit. He'll ken where the lads be and what mischief be afoot."

"I'm not looking for mischief," Kit said, but Willie only laughed.

An hour later, they were in a tidy cottage beside a swiftly flowing stream, being sized up by a truculent fellow whose name, despite his obviously normal eyesight, appeared to be Blind Sammy Crosier. Since Blind Sammy's response to Willie's introduction had been a gruff, "We'll be naming nae names if ye please," Kit had not asked for an explanation of the nickname.

Willie quickly put Sammy in possession of their need for information, whereupon the older man grunted again and favored Kit with a long look.

Kit met that look silently.

At last, Sammy said, "There'll be moonlight tonight."

Kit glanced at Willie and saw twinkling astonishment in the lad's expression.

"But . . . but . . ." Willie's sputters halted when Sammy shot him a fierce scowl, but a moment later he found his tongue again, saying, "Ye canna do it, Sam. Kit's nae reiver but a gentleman born, as ye can see for yourself."

Sammy snorted. "Bless ye, lad. Full three-quarters o' the gentlemen in these parts rides wi' the reivers whenever they've a mind to. Think o' Buccleuch!"

"Aye, but Kit's nae like Buccleuch or us. He weren't born tae the reiving."

Kit realized that Sammy was watching him narrowly, so he said, "I'm interested in information about Hawks Rig and Eustace Chisholm, nothing more."

"Aye, perhaps, but ye want tae glean your information from our lads, and some willna want tae talk tae a man who could bear witness against them did some'un bring a grievance for the reiving. So if ye'd speak wi' us, ye'll first ride wi' us, and like I said afore, there'll be moonlight tonight."

Again Kit glanced at Willie, but this time the lad's eyes

were full of mischief, and Kit felt his sense of humor stir. Something else stirred, too, something he had not felt in years—his boyhood sense of adventure.

Turning back to Sammy, he said, "So you want me to incriminate myself before you will trust me to speak with your men."

"Faith, sir, reiving's nae crime," Sammy said. "The plain truth be that it's nobbut our ordinary way o' life, so we'll say rather that if ye ride with us, ye'll be less likely tae bear witness against us if any mean-spirited folks should lay a grievance, come next Truce Day."

"Do you intend to cross the line?"

Sammy shrugged. "That's as may be, but there be cattle aplenty nearer than that, because more than one master fell tae the recent fever, leaving none but his land steward and a few lads tae guard his herds. Since they ha' more cattle than they need, whilst we ha' too few, the solution tae such an imbalance be plain tae see."

"It does seem obvious, put like that," Kit said, amused despite himself. "I don't suppose you'll tell me exactly where you intend to seek this overabundance."

"Not just yet. Are ye with us then?"

"I am."

"Ye ken fine that do we find them cattle unfairly well guarded, we'll be looking elsewhere. Our need be sharp set just now wi' winter coming on."

"I do understand," Kit said, smiling. "I'm astonished to admit that I'm looking forward to this foray with some eagerness."

"Ah," Willie said, grinning. "We'll do now. Just see if we don't!"

Chapter 3

Elsewhere

Having kept a close eye on Kit throughout his journey from the Highlands to the Borders, Catriona took advantage of his stay at Dunsithe to scan the area for potential trouble, and then to fly off in search of the papers the late laird had sent to him at Torness. Finding them proved easy, and studying them, she concluded that her problem was well on its way to being solved.

All she had to do was arrange for him to fall in love with his betrothed.

She was sure it was what Claud would have done in the same situation, and Claud's plans, while never appearing to be brilliant, always worked out in the end. Before being ordered to look after Kit Chisholm, she had not taken her duties to any mortal seriously, so she was sadly inexperienced at this guardianship business. But if her success could help rescue Claud, she was determined to succeed. Kit Chisholm would marry Mistress Fiona Carmichael, and that was that. So, before returning to Kit, she made a quick visit to Mute Hill House.

The discovery that Mistress Carmichael was well on the way to marrying someone else was a setback, but Catriona knew that Kit felt no more loyalty to his uncle than the uncle apparently felt toward him. Therefore, one had only to determine the best way to overset Eustace's wedding plans.

Kit's lack of interest in his betrothal created a greater obstacle, especially since he clearly did not intend to visit his betrothed and was unlikely, in any event, to do so before her marriage took place.

When Catriona returned just in time to hear Kit agree to ride with Willie's reivers, she considered that plan for possibilities, but the only one that occurred to her was that she might somehow redirect them toward Mute Hill House. The certain chaos that would result if a band of reivers rode into the yard there dissuaded her, however, and she was at a loss as to how to proceed.

Perhaps, she decided, the answer still lay at Mute Hill House. While she waited for her charge and his new companions to get organized, she could at least have another look at the place.

The midday meal proved to be even more of a trial than Anne had feared. Fiona seemed no more rested after her brief nap, and despite Anne's attentions and those of Fiona's own devoted maidservant, she looked wan and far from her best.

Olivia was quick to notice her daughter's lack of color when Anne and Fiona made their curtsies to her.

"Pinch your cheeks, girl, or by heaven I'll pinch them for you," she hissed as Fiona stepped forward to kiss her cheek.

Hastily, Fiona obeyed, managing to produce more color

by the time she turned to greet her intended with a tremulous smile.

Eustace Chisholm was a tall, boney man with a nose too large for his face and eyes that bore such an intensity of expression that Anne felt as though they looked through people. He always dressed fashionably, and had chosen to wear a pale green satin doublet and trunk hose slashed with darker green-and-gold striped silk. A heavy medallion embossed with the Chisholm crest hung round his neck, making him look wealthy and important, if not particularly warm or friendly.

Responding to Fiona's murmured greeting, he chucked her under the chin, saying in a jovial way, "How now, puss, no need for pinching those pretty cheeks of yours, for I'll gladly put color in them for you. Not that they require more color, for I'm partial to ivory skin, and yours is perfection, as I've told you many times. Now you may thank me for my pretty compliments with a kiss, for I swear I've thought only about the touch of your soft lips all the way from Hawks Rig."

Seeing flames of embarrassment leap to Fiona's cheeks, Anne thought cynically that even Olivia could not complain of a lack of color now, but she took no satisfaction in the sight.

Fiona stiffened as he pulled her into his arms, and Anne saw her eyes widen with dismay, even fear, when he held her chin and kissed her hard upon the lips.

Eustace could not have failed to notice her reaction. Indeed, Anne was as certain as she could be that he had noticed and that Fiona's reluctance only added to his pleasure, because he held her even closer and gave her another great, smacking kiss on the lips.

When he released her, Fiona stepped back so quickly that she nearly tripped over her skirt. She raised a hand as if she would wipe away the kisses, but catching her mother's stern eye, she clearly thought better of it, and quickly let the hand fall to her side again.

Olivia said with a faint laugh and a twitch of her purple-net fan, "You anticipate your husbandly rights, Sir Eustace. I pray you, sir, restrain your passions until the child is yours, lest you frighten her witless before then."

"Faith, madam," he said with a loud chortle, "since it was not the lass's wits that attracted me to her, she may lose them with my goodwill. 'Tis her soft skin and bright eyes—aye, and other attributes, as well," he added, looking Fiona up and down with a leer that fairly turned Anne's stomach.

Sir Toby Bell entered just then, and for once she was glad to see him. In general, she found him too loud and merry for her taste, but his pleasure at seeing Eustace, and his instantly expressed desire to tell him all about the fox that had cut up everyone's peace, came as a welcome interruption.

"Blasted creature must still be somewhere in the house, too," he added after describing the uproar the fox had caused by its precipitous entrance into Olivia's bower. "I've had lads searching the place, but no one has seen hide or hair of the beast. The dogs won't go outside without being dragged, either, so they believe it's still in the house. Don't worry, my dear," he added when Olivia put a hand to her forehead. "I've shoved the whole lot of them outside."

"But the fox!"

"Oh, aye, but he's most likely gone to earth somewhere or other, and if you leave him be, he'll leave you be. I say, Ashkirk," he added, "what do you say to a few games of Cent after we dine—penny a game?"

"I had it in mind to spend some private time with my lass," the other man said, throwing Fiona a look that cast her into visible tremors.

Anne wanted to shake him until his teeth rattled in his head. It seemed to her then that he delighted in terrifying the poor girl.

Rescue came from an unexpected source when Toby said firmly, "Can't allow that, my dear fellow. Time enough for all the privacy ye want wi' the lass after Parson Allardice has said the proper words over ye. Time is short, so ye'll not expire in the meantime from unrequited lust."

"I believe Malcolm wants to announce dinner," Anne said hastily, having noted the entrance of her aunt's house steward, Malcolm Vole.

A slight man with a habit of lacing his fingers at his waist and otherwise carrying himself as if he were lord of Mute Hill House, he made the announcement, whereupon they adjourned to the high table in the hall to eat their noonday dinner.

Anne sat at the opposite end of the table from Fiona, making it impossible for them to talk, let alone for Anne to offer her any comfort, so it was fortunate that Olivia maintained a stream of languid conversation about the wedding plans.

Calling Eustace "Ashkirk," she submitted each detail for his approval, and when he said testily that he was sure she had everything in excellent order, she replied with a beseeching smile, "But I want everything to be perfect for you, sir."

"For Fiona, too, I imagine," Anne said blandly.

"Yes, yes, of course. How absurd you are, my dear, when you know how I have fretted myself to flinders to ensure that my darling's wedding is just as it should be. But gentlemen always know exactly how everything should be."

It was tempting to suggest that the groom was scarcely what he should be, let alone anyone who should be advising her about wedding details. Anne only wished she had the courage to point out that Eustace was not only old enough to be Fiona's father and far more interested in her fortune and beauty than he was in her heart or mind, but that he was also a man who enjoyed frightening her. But Olivia had long desired alliance with the Chisholms, and sacrificing her daughter to Eustace clearly was not—in her mind, at all events—too high a price to pay for the connection.

By the time the meal ended, Anne was itching to escape. She was extremely fond of her cousin and grateful for her aunt's hospitality, but the longer she stayed at the huge, fortified manor house, the more she longed to murder someone.

Not that anyone would have guessed it, for since childhood she had cultivated a serenity of manner that had long since become habit. Nevertheless, the moment Olivia arose from her chair, Anne did likewise, saying quietly, "Come, Fiona. You know we promised your Molly that we would allow her to practice the new arrangement Aunt Olivia suggested for your hair."

Fiona turned to her with a startled look, but although she was not quick-witted, neither was she simple.

"Oh, yes, of course," she said. "Pray excuse us, everyone."

Eustace scrambled to his feet, and the expression on his face told Anne as plainly as words that he meant to object.

Hastily, she said, "Malcolm, Sir Eustace's goblet is nearly empty. Please have one of your lads refill it."

"At once, my lady," the steward said smoothly, but she did not miss the look of resentment he shot her.

Suppressing a sigh, she ushered Fiona from the chamber. Malcolm Vole had been sending resentful looks her way from the moment of her arrival at Mute Hill House, and she had long since given up hope of changing his opinion of her.

Accustomed as she was to managing the earl's large household at Ellyson Towers, she had not hesitated to make herself useful to her aunt and Fiona at Mute Hill. However, she had soon come to realize that although Malcolm prided himself on his position as house steward, he had accepted his orders from Sir Stephen before that gentleman's death, and afterward had simply taken it upon himself to run things according to his own notions of what Sir Stephen would have desired.

Toby Bell was unequal to the task of supervising the steward, but Anne had quickly seen that Malcolm did a poor job of running the household. Her first, tactful attempts to instill a more orderly system had failed miserably, because Malcolm had taken umbrage, whereupon Olivia, without discussing the matter, had taken his side.

"Because men always understand things better than women do, my dear, and Malcolm understands my needs perfectly. Although I am sure that your odd notions answered well enough at home, Ellyson Towers is much older than Mute Hill House and not nearly so modern in its ways. You must trust Malcolm, as I do, to know exactly what will suit me best."

After that, Anne had resorted to more subtle methods, but she did not expect Malcolm's attitude, or Olivia's, to change.

Although Malcolm clearly resented her request now to

attend to Eustace, the diversion served its purpose and she took Fiona from the room without opposition.

"I loathe him," Fiona muttered.

"Then tell your mother you will not marry him," Anne advised practically.

"You know I cannot do that." Fiona wrung her hands. "She would be so angry, Anne. You know she would."

"I expect she would," Anne agreed, "but it is less than useless to complain to me if you will not take a stand against marrying him."

"But don't you think he is dreadful?"

"What I think butters no one's bread."

"But, truly, Anne, don't you?"

"I think someone should have drowned him at birth," Anne said.

Fiona giggled.

Anne added bluntly, "But it does not matter what I think, because no one did drown him, and so if you are determined to obey your mother—"

"It is my duty, Anne. You know it is. Besides, one cannot say no to her."

Anne knew that Fiona, at least, could not. "Then you must reconcile yourself to the marriage, if that is the only choice that remains for you."

"You know it is." Tears spilled down Fiona's cheeks. "What am I to do?"

"I have already given you the only advice I have, love, but I'll try to think of something else that may help," Anne said. "In the meantime, I believe you are exhausted, and although you did lie down for a short time before dinner, I know you did not sleep. I mean to ride this afternoon to shake the fidgets from my mind, and as always, your mother will be occupied with her own concerns after dinner—"

"She naps, usually," Fiona said.

"Exactly," Anne said with a smile. "So you can enjoy a nice long sleep and no one will disturb you, for I mean to ask my Peg Elliot to keep watch, and you know Peg can rout anyone who may try to disturb you."

"Very well, I'll try to rest, but I keep thinking about how close the wedding is. Two days from now, I shall be Lady Chisholm, and I don't think I can bear it."

"Hush now, and come to bed," Anne said soothingly.

Fiona obeyed, but by the time she was settled, Anne's patience had nearly expired and the hour was far more advanced than she had hoped. Taking only enough time to send a lad to the stables to order her favorite gelding saddled, she hurried to her bedchamber to tell Peg what she had promised on her behalf and to change into her riding dress. The sky was still overcast, but even if it opened up and poured forth in a flood, she was determined to have her ride.

Before going out to the stable, she made certain that, despite Eustace's continued presence, Olivia had taken to her bed for her usual postprandial nap. Reassured on that point, Anne was soon on her way.

An intoxicating sense of freedom filled her as she rode down into the dale and left Mute Hill behind. It was not by any means the first time since moving that she had made the ten-mile journey between her aunt's house and Ellyson Towers. The track was well defined, her pony was swift and sure, and she was an excellent horsewoman who had come to know the way well over the past weeks.

Not that Olivia approved of her solitary ventures. Indeed, the case was otherwise, and she would doubtless scold as she always did when Anne rode to the Towers alone, but Anne knew she would do no more than scold her, so she could submit calmly to the lecture and then go about her activities as usual.

Turning her thoughts to her cousin's trouble, she tried to think of a solution, but none occurred to her. She disliked Eustace, who was possessed of a licentious nature, too old for Fiona, and in Anne's opinion, a man who would do anything he had to do to increase his position, power, and wealth, and who would trample anyone in his path to achieve those goals. His recent inheritance of the great Chisholm estates had, she believed, only whetted his hunger for more. And she did not think Fiona would satisfy his other, more fundamental appetites, especially since he delighted in leering at or accosting maidservants or even young women he merely suspected of being maidservants.

She certainly did not approve of forcing Fiona to marry him just to ally the Carmichaels with Chisholm wealth and power. For Olivia to scheme with the previous Laird of Ashkirk to marry her daughter to his son was understandable, and doubtless many would say it was therefore logical to want Fiona to marry Ashkirk's heir, but at least Sir Christopher Chisholm had been of a suitable age. Anne had never met him, but one had only to suffer the leers and other unwelcome attentions of his uncle, as she had, to be certain the nephew had to have been a better man.

Such musings made the time pass swiftly, and as she neared the Towers, a break opened in the clouds, and slanting rays of the sun sparkled on the grassy slope leading to the massive castle. It looked formidable from below, but Anne felt only the comforting peace of homecoming.

Admittedly, the sun was lower in the sky than she had

hoped it would be, allowing her a scant two hours to visit before she would have to return. With such a short rest, her pony would still be tired, so she would not dare push it on the return trip as she had in coming. Perhaps she should allow herself even less time at home.

When Catriona saw Lady Anne ride out alone, the answer to her problem presented itself. Anne wanted to stop her cousin's wedding to Sir Eustace, so Kit just had to meet Anne.

He would identify himself to her, whereupon she would take him directly to Fiona, and that would put an end to the wedding. The plan was excellent, better than any of Claud's, because Catriona would leave no room for error.

Anne's intentions were admirable, but it had been a fortnight since her last visit, and she was eager to talk to everyone, to be sure that all was well.

Rumors still abounded, as they had for months, that the English king's armies hovered dangerously near, and that invasion was inevitable, and she knew Ellyson Towers lay too close to the line for safety or comfort. But despite everyone's fears, the area had remained generally peaceful, with only a few armed forays taking place and those far from their part of the line.

Therefore, Anne had stripped off her gloves and cloak and lingered happily, enjoying familiar, pleasant conversation and the company of folks who had looked after her home for her entire life. Her father's steward having received no word yet from Thomas Ellyson, despite messages sent to his family seat in Dumfries and to his house in Stirling, things marched along much as they always had.

She was still sitting in the kitchen, enjoying a comfortable chat with the steward's wife, when the steward put his head through the doorway and asked if she intended to spend the night. "Because if ye dinna mean tae stay, mistress, ye'd best be going soon. Darkness be a-coming earlier these days."

Rising reluctantly, Anne said, "I know, and I should not have stayed so long, but in truth, I do not want to go. Were it not that my cousin would suffer from my absence, I'd be tempted to stay here. Indeed, once she marries—"

"Nay, mistress, ye mustna move back here even then," the steward said. "It isna fitting for a young lass tae live alone in a place as vulnerable as the Towers be tae English Harry and his ilk, especially when we dinna ken friend from foe these days. Ye'll be going now, and I'll send some o' the lads along tae look after ye."

"No, don't do that," she said firmly as she always did when he made such a suggestion. "I enjoy the solitude of these rides, for I get too little of it at Mute Hill. Nearly everyone in these parts knows me, so I'll come to no harm."

"The clouds be thinning, and the moon be likely tae draw out a few reivers," he warned. "They come from all parts, reivers do."

Anne smiled but got up obediently and let him help her don her cloak. As she picked up her gloves, she said, "I'll not worry you by staying longer, but it is still too early for reivers to be riding, and I shall reach Mute Hill before moonrise."

He shook his head at her but did not argue. Danger abounded in the area, but all the servants at the Towers knew that Lady Anne, despite her calm demeanor and ready smiles, always took her own path. Even the earl had rarely curbed her, and the plain truth was that although her impulses often seemed foolhardy to others, she had never yet come to harm.

Catriona sighed with vexation. Everything was in train, and she had been gently encouraging Anne to linger, hoping she would stay long enough at the Towers to suit the excellent plan. However, the steward's influence was strong, and she dared not interfere further. But it was not nearly late enough yet.

Anne's luck was out. Thoughts of Fiona's upcoming wedding still intruded upon her peace, and in pondering how she might persuade her aunt to postpone that event, she failed to pay proper heed to the track ahead. Thus, and with dusk rapidly descending, her mount stepped into a rabbit hole and came up lame.

Dismounting, she carefully examined the horse's leg and hoof.

It did not seem badly hurt, but even a slight injury would be compounded if she continued to ride. With a sigh, she glanced around, trying to determine exactly how far she had come and how much farther she had to go.

The clouds had dissipated, and although it was still light, she could see a scattering of first stars. The moon would not rise for two hours or more.

"Here now, what d'ye think ye're a-doing?"

Since her attention was focused on Anne, Catriona nearly leaped out of her skin at the sound of an unfamiliar masculine voice. Whirling to face the speaker, she stared in amazement, because the angry fellow she confronted was unlike anyone she had ever seen before. Although she was in alien territory, she had met other Border folk, including Maggie Malloch, and none of them had had bodies through which one could see.

He was not transparent, exactly, but he was certainly diaphanous, for as he moved, she could see the outline of the brown grassy hills behind him.

He seemed astonished, too. "Faith," he exclaimed, "who are ye?"

"My name is Catriona," she said, recovering her wits and smiling at him.

His eyes opened so wide that his eyelids nearly vanished. "But ye're lovely."

"Thank you."

"But why did ye lame me lass's pony?"

"She was going too fast."

"But she must get home!" He flicked a finger toward the lame gelding.

"What are *you* doing?"

"Fixing him, o' course. Ye canna be going about laming ponies. We ha' rules against such as that."

"Who are you, and why do you care what I do?"

"Me name's Fergus Fishbait," he said. "Hereabouts everyone kens me."

"I don't care if they do. I do not want her to ride, and in any event, since she does not know that you fixed the pony's leg, she will still walk, so that's all right."

"I'll just put the notion in her head tae try it then."

"She knows the pony stepped into a hole. She'll not chance further injury." She had taken his measure and was certain she had more power than he did, but it would not help her cause if he complained to the High Circle about her tactics. She stepped nearer, smiling again as she said, "It's gey important, you see."

"Why?"

"Because Lady Anne does not want her cousin to marry the man they are forcing her to marry, and I can help her stop that."

"Aye? Ye can do that?"

"I can if you will help me. You are her guardian spirit, are you not?"

"I am," he said, regarding Anne thoughtfully. "'Tis true she doesna want her cousin tae marry him, and I dinna like the man much m'self."

"Then you'll not stop me," Catriona said happily as she flitted over to the gelding and settled herself comfortably in its mane. "Come along, Fergus Fishbait," she said, patting the place beside her. "There is room for two, and you will not want to miss what happens next."

Grasping the reins high at the bit, Anne plodded on, muttering imprecations at herself for her carelessness both in lingering so long and in not paying attention to her path, until she saw a thicket ahead in the gathering dusk. Remembering that the track skirted the trees for a time before fording a brook at the foot of the hill, she realized she still had at least three miles to go and sighed again at her foolishness.

Patting the horse's nose, she muttered, "Walking serves me right, I expect, but I'm sorry that you have suffered, too."

Ten minutes later, as she approached the ford, a noise from the thicket startled her, and before she could gather her thoughts, mounted men galloped out of it and surrounded her.

"Sakes, lass, *now* see what ye've done," Fergus exclaimed in dismay.

"Hush," Catriona said. "Watch now, for this is just how I planned it."

Anne peered at the men through the fast fading light, trying to find at least one among the half dozen or so whom she recognized. They were a ragged lot, though, and she could not make out any familiar face.

"'Tis a fine looking pony, that 'un," one of them said, sliding from his saddle to catch her by an arm.

"Unhand me," Anne said firmly. "You would be foolish to harm me without first learning who I am."

"Faith, lass, I dinna mean tae harm ye," he said with a chuckle. "However, if ye'd like tae favor me wi' one wee kiss, I'd go tae me bed a happy man."

Anne stood still, giving him look for look. Her horse twitched nervously, but she maintained her steady gaze until the man blinked and glanced uncertainly at his companions.

"Let go of her."

The deep, calmly authoritative voice came from none of the men gazing down at her but from nearer the trees amongst which they had hidden.

The man gripping her arm released her at once. Looking anxiously past the other horsemen as they made way for the one who had spoken, he sputtered, "I didna mean the lass nae harm, sir. Ye ken fine, we wouldna—"

"Step away from her."

"Aye, I'm steppin' straightaway," he said, suiting action to words as he added, "but ye'll agree that that be a fine piece o' horseflesh she be riding."

"Take yourselves back into the trees, lads. I'll deal with the lass," the newcomer said evenly.

No one argued. The riders vanished back into the thicket, leaving Anne alone with her unknown rescuer.

"Who are you?" he asked, still sitting at his ease in the saddle.

"Anne Ellyson," she replied, gazing up at him as she stroked her horse to soothe it. She could see little other than his shape and size. He seemed very tall, though, especially on horseback, and he was broad across the shoulders.

"Ellyson," he said thoughtfully. "Would you be kin to Armadale?"

"He was my father."

To her surprise, a choke of laughter escaped him before he stifled it and said soberly, "I am truly sorry for your loss, Lady Anne, but although you may not realize it, this situation contains an element of humor."

"I thought your men were reivers," she said.

"They are." He dismounted, standing much too close to her.

He seemed somehow even taller than before. Anne frowned at him, feeling as if she had to look a very long way up to do so. "But you speak like a gentleman."

"Some say that I *am* a gentleman. I used to be one, anyway." With a slight bow, he added, "My name is Christopher Chisholm. My friends call me Kit."

Chapter 4

Shock swept through Anne. "But you can't be Sir Christopher. He's dead!"

"I've heard as much from others," he said, "but I assure you, I'm no ghost."

"Faith, but this is marvelous then," she exclaimed. "If you are truly Sir Christopher Chisholm, you are the solution to our greatest problem!"

"I doubt that, my lady. I have problems of my own with which I must deal, not the least of them being my promise to help those lads yonder in their mission tonight. As soon as the moon rises—"

"Do you truly mean to help them steal someone's cattle? But whose?"

His amusement plain now, he said, "Why, yours, Lady Anne."

"Mine?"

"Aye, for we were told that with Armadale having passed to his reward, Ellyson Towers has no master, so the reiving will be particularly good there."

She stared at him, bereft of words.

"It is time you returned home, I think," he added blandly,

putting a hand to the small of her back. The sensations his touch stirred in her addled her thoughts. For once in her life, she was unable to think of a single thing to say.

"Willie," he said sharply, "lend me your horse. I'll see her ladyship home."

An unhappy voice muttered, "*My* horse?"

Anne said swiftly, "There is no need for you to do any such thing, sir. I can see myself home."

"You were going the wrong way," he pointed out gently.

She felt no fear of him, but something in his manner made her wary, and she wished she could read his expression more clearly in the fading light. Nonetheless, she stifled her annoyance and said reasonably, "I now reside with my aunt, Lady Carmichael, at Mute Hill."

He was silent for a long moment, but when his man rode up to them through the shadows, he repeated the name Carmichael thoughtfully.

"Yes, that's right," Anne said. "Lady Carmichael of Mute Hill House."

"Why d'ye need me pony, Kit?"

Anne could not make out the lad's features, but he was much shorter and slighter of build than Sir Christopher. He also sounded younger.

Sir Christopher said, "I'm going to put her ladyship on my horse, because I know his manners are more what she is accustomed to than that beast of yours."

Before the lad could reply, Anne interjected, "But, really, sir—"

"Don't argue with me, my lady," he said in a tone stern enough to put her forcibly in mind of her father.

"But—"

"If you mean to tell me that you will be perfectly safe by

yourself, I'd advise you to save your breath for a more useful purpose. Even if that horse of yours had four good legs under him, we have already proven that you are not safe on your own. Moreover, I'm in no mood for fratching."

"But what about my horse?" she asked.

"We'll lead it, of course. It can easily keep up if it need not bear weight."

"What about me?" the lad demanded. "What am I tae do?"

"You will await my return here with the others, if they still want me to ride with them," Chisholm said. "Talk to Sammy. The moon won't rise for another hour or more, and I should return shortly after that. If the others decide to ride on, you wait here and try to persuade Sammy before he leaves to let me meet with him and his lads later to have our talk."

"Och, aye, but he willna like it," Willie said. "As for me sitting here in the dark waiting for ye if the others ride on, I'll no like that. There be boggarts about!"

Quietly, Anne said, "You might tell your friends that despite what they have been told, the cattle, sheep, and horses at Ellyson Towers are well guarded."

"Are they now?" Willie said. "And how would a slip of a lass like yourself be knowing aught about that?"

"Because they are my beasts."

"Are they now?"

"They are," Sir Christopher said, chuckling. "She is Lady Anne Ellyson, Armadale's daughter."

Willie gave a low whistle. "An ye do say, m'lady, that . . ."

He fell tactfully silent, but Anne did not hesitate.

"I say there are plenty of men guarding my beasts," she

said, "and prime sleuthhounds as well, eager to catch the scent of any reiver foolish enough to think my father's death might have undone his careful guardianship. Would you have dared to attack the Towers whilst Armadale lived?"

"Nay, never!" Willie exclaimed.

"Then have a care now," Anne said.

"Aye, your ladyship, I'll tell them. Thank ye kindly."

As they watched his shadowy figure dash back and disappear into the thicket, Sir Christopher said on a note of laughter, "I commend your methods, lass. You handled that with great aplomb. Are your cattle truly so well guarded?"

"Do you think I would tell you if they were not?"

He chuckled, and she realized she had been hoping to hear the sound again. Before she was aware of his intent, two strong hands caught her around the waist and lifted her to his saddle, leaving her feeling strangely breathless.

"Can you settle yourself, or do you require further assistance?" he asked.

"I'll manage," she said. "Your saddle is larger than mine, but I've often used my father's or brother's saddle."

He swung onto Willie's horse, steadying it as he did. "You have a brother?"

"Sir Andrew Ellyson was my brother," she said. "He died last year at Carter Bar in a clash with some of King Henry's men."

"So you are doubly bereft," he said, all humor gone.

She swallowed, caught off guard by a wave of grief. "M-my mother and two little sisters d-died, as well, of the same horrid fever that took my father," she said, striving to keep her voice under control even as she wondered what had stirred her to reveal so much.

He was silent for a long moment before he said quietly,

"I have a notion that I'd risk offending you if I expressed my sympathy as strongly as I'm feeling it, lass. Likewise, instinct warns me that I'd be wiser not to say that I think you must be a remarkable young woman."

The warmth in his voice nearly undid her, and she drew a deep breath, trying to ignore the tears pricking her eyes. Exhaling slowly, she said with commendable calm, "Thank you for your sympathy, sir, but many hereabouts lost their families just as I did, either to the fever or to Henry's soldiers. Our king and queen lost their precious sons to the fever, too, before it swept its way south. So although my losses affected me sorely, I cope by trying to make myself useful to others."

"Good lass," he said. "I collect that Henry of England is becoming a damnable nuisance in these parts."

"Aye," she said, accepting the change of subject gratefully, "although it has been peaceable enough in this area for these past few months at least."

He nodded and turned his attention to the track ahead.

The horse she rode had excellent manners, and she easily guided it toward the ford in the brook, glad that she would not have to get her feet wet. The night was turning chilly.

Chisholm led her lame horse, and as they forded the brook, he watched to be sure the animal's bad leg would cause it no problems on the slippery stones. Then, safely on the opposite bank, he turned toward her and said, "Are you sure you know the track well enough to follow it by starlight?"

"Aye, and you will not have difficulty finding your way back, either," she said. "It is the only real track betwixt here and Mute Hill."

He was silent again for a few moments before he said, "Does no one hold you to account, mistress?"

"I cannot imagine how that can concern you, sir," she said, raising her chin.

"Suppose I should prove to be even less of a gentleman than your brief acquaintance with me has already suggested?"

A shiver raced up her spine at his grim tone, but she suppressed it, saying in her usual calm way, "I am an excellent judge of character, Sir Christopher. I believe I can trust you to see me safely home."

"You can trust me," he agreed, "but you are a fool to trust your instincts in such a case, lass, and if you were my daughter or sister—"

"Have you got a daughter or sister?" she asked curiously.

"No, but that is not the point."

"That is precisely *my* point," she said. "You have no authority to scold me, sir, and none to force me to your will. We should do far better, I think, to discuss a matter of greater importance that does concern you."

"What matter is that?"

"Why, my cousin, of course. Since you are betrothed to her—"

"The devil I am!"

Anne swiftly crossed herself. "There is no need to swear. Surely, you must know that you are betrothed to Fiona Carmichael. Indeed, I am sure that you do, because I saw how you reacted when I first spoke my aunt's name."

"It is true that I was apparently betrothed to Mistress Carmichael at one time," he said. "My astonishment is due to the fact that you seem able still to consider her betrothed to a man that everyone hereabouts believes is dead."

"But you *were* betrothed," Anne insisted.

"My father certainly wrote to inform me of some such arrangement," he said. "But that was over eighteen months ago, and I never replied to his letter, so how anyone can have thought—"

"But what kind of son fails to reply to such a letter?"

"You should not interrupt me," he said. "Surely, your parents taught you better manners than that."

"They did," she admitted, "but I grow impatient when I want to know something and the other party persists in . . ."

"In what?"

His tone seemed ominous, but she replied calmly, "Well, in truth, I was going to say 'prevaricating,' but I have no evidence that you are doing that, so perhaps I should say when the other party appears to be avoiding a direct answer. If your father informed you of your betrothal . . ." She paused tactfully.

"If you must know, he commanded me to return so that the matter could be formally completed, or to understand that he would attend to the details by proxy."

"You did not come home, however."

"No, because circumstances intervened that were beyond my control. I have been unable to return until now."

"Nonetheless, the arrangement between your father and my aunt was a legal one, was it not?"

"One must suppose so, although I was scarcely a minor at the time. Nor did I ever sign anything."

"Still, your father, as head of your family, had full authority to act as proxy, I should think. My aunt and my cousin certainly believe the betrothal was legal."

"You appear to be well versed in the matter," he said.

She did not miss the undertone of sarcasm but said tartly

nonetheless, "Do you think women cannot understand complex matters, sir?"

"I never said that. I warrant you must be of greater age than I first judged you, however."

"I am nearly nineteen," she said. "My birthday is two days after Christmas."

"Then I wonder that you are not yet married with a family of your own," he said. "You certainly seem eligible enough, and despite your tartness when you misunderstood me, you do not seem to possess a shrewish disposition."

"I apologize if my tone seemed disrespectful," she said sincerely. "I cannot think what made me speak as sharply as I did. As to my single state, my father was indulgent enough to allow me to reject suitors that presented themselves if they did not appeal to me. None did."

"Indulgent, indeed," he agreed. "I wish that my father had been so indulgent. Still, I reckon your suitors were numerous. Are you so particular?"

She nibbled her lower lip, hesitant to say the words that sprang to her tongue, but when he waited patiently, she decided to risk it. "In truth, sir, I do not want a husband who would marry me solely for my family name and connections. I'd prefer one who would value my opinions, but although I have heard that such men exist, I have never met one." She did not mention that, deep in her heart, she harbored a wish to meet one who would give his life, if necessary, for love of her. Such wishes, she knew, were merely self indulgent and unworthy of her.

He was silent again, this time for so long that she wondered if he hoped to end their conversation.

"I'd prefer to talk about Fiona," she said quietly.

"Surely, you must know that if I am officially deceased,

all legal documents and contracts to which I am a named party have become moot."

"Not all of them, surely," she said. "Your last will and testament, for example, would certainly not be moot."

He chuckled again, and she found that the now familiar sound was not only strangely reassuring but warmed her, as well.

"If I had had the prescience to create such a document, I suppose you would be right," he said. "Are you never at a loss for an argument, my lady?"

"This matter is of grave importance to me," she said.

"Is your cousin so desperately in need of a husband? I trust she has not gotten herself—"

"Do not say such a thing! Even if it were possible for her to get *herself* with child, as I suppose you were about to say, she has done no such thing."

"I beg your pardon, but your insistence that I am the hope of her soul did prompt me to wonder."

"It is not just a husband she requires. Indeed, she is to be married soon, as it is, and therein lies the problem. I thought you must have heard as much."

"No, how would I? Still, I cannot be amazed. If my father thought she would make a suitable bride for me, she must possess many excellent qualities."

"She is stunningly beautiful and a great heiress," Anne said.

"Ah, then she need have only those two excellent qualities. I stand corrected. But if she already has a husband in the offing—"

"Do stop being so heartless. My aunt intends Fiona to marry your dreadful uncle, and we must not let that happen."

"Now you do interest me," he said with a definite edge to his tone.

"I thought I might," she said bitterly.

"Is he truly dreadful?"

Surprised, she said, "Don't you know him?"

"I have not laid eyes on him in six years, so I cannot claim to know him well, but I do know that I did not like him when I was a lad."

"Fiona is afraid of him."

"You interest me more than ever now. Much as I disliked him personally, I would not have thought him the sort of ogre who goes about frightening innocent maidens. How old is your cousin?"

"Don't you know that either?"

"I have a lamentable memory at the best of times," he said but then added on a note of obvious sincerity, "In truth, I paid little heed to those papers my father sent me. If they bore any mention of her age . . ."

"She was only fifteen when my aunt agreed to that betrothal," Anne said. "But although she is seventeen now, she seems younger to most people."

"Ah, now I see how it is. The lass is simple."

"She is not!" But hearing the echo of her own words, she could not blame him for thinking so. Still, she wondered if he might be purposely casting flies to see if she would leap to his baiting.

"Fiona is exceptionally biddable and a little shy," she said. "My aunt wants her to marry your uncle, and therefore she will do so if we cannot prevent it. She simply has not got it in her to defy Aunt Olivia."

"No spirit, eh?"

Clearly, he was baiting her, but much as she would have

liked to deny the accusation, honesty forbade it. Instead, she said, "Fiona is a dear, loving girl. The man who weds her will delight in her if he is kind and does not frighten her."

"Then we will simply tell my uncle that he must cherish the lass."

"Unfortunately, Ashkirk—" She broke off, offering him a rueful smile. "Mercy, he's not Ashkirk, is he? I usually call him Eustace, which irritates Olivia, but I was trying to be respectful, because he is your uncle."

"Oh, don't be swayed by that. I told you, I never liked the fellow."

"Well, I expect it is you who are Ashkirk now, in any event, but I cannot wrap my mind around calling you that when . . ." She hesitated, thinking it would be less than diplomatic to tell him that she had thought of the name with loathing from the moment she had first met his uncle. "What should I call him?"

"I can think of several things," he said, "but I don't think I'd like hearing any of them from your lips. I don't object to your calling him Eustace, but you may more properly call him Sir Eustace Chisholm—if you admire propriety. He holds a knighthood in his own right, although I've never understood why he should."

"Well, he is perfectly well aware of my cousin's fear of him," Anne said. "Indeed, I'm afraid he cultivates and takes delight in it."

"I see. Clearly, you know him better than I do. What other pleasing attributes does he possess?"

"I don't see them as pleasing or as attributes," she said.

"I spoke in jest."

She eyed him speculatively. "You did not sound as if you were jesting. There was a definite edge to your tone."

"Perhaps, but I'll wager you can tell me more about him."

"Very well," she said. "I dislike him, because he enjoys pinching young women's cheeks and making ribald remarks calculated to shock them, and because he is the sort of man who catches and kisses maidservants on the stairs."

"Just how do you know that?"

"Because, to my misfortune, he kissed me, having mistaken me for my cousin's maid when he called on her shortly after my arrival at Mute Hill House."

"I see."

This time the grimness of his tone made her wish she could read his expression, but the deep dusk had darkened to moonless night and the starlight was barely enough to give a faint indication of the track ahead.

She felt no concern that they might get lost, for they had covered more than half the remaining distance and would soon reach the crest of a hill overlooking Ewesdale, from which they would be able to see the lights of Mute Hill House.

He did not speak again for some time, and she was content to remain silent, because the silence now was comfortable and gave her a chance to consider her odd reaction to the man. For it was certainly odd that his presence gave her comfort when she scarcely knew him and had little reason to think him wiser or more reassuring than the reiver she had seen when first they met.

To be sure, he had a certain aura about him that instilled confidence. She had the distinct feeling that even if the English army should descend upon them at that moment, Sir Christopher would rout them single-handedly, easily, and without a blink. The notion was foolish, of course. Logic told her as much, but the confidence she felt remained undiminished.

She felt as if she knew him, not factually, as in the details of his life, for she knew next to none of those. But the essence of him, his inner spirit, was another matter. The comfort she felt with him riding silently beside her was the comfort of riding with an old and trusted friend. And regardless of his warning earlier, Anne trusted her instincts.

She had long realized that she possessed a gift in her ability to read people, to know good ones from bad, and the trustworthy ones from the untrustworthy. Her mother had called it intuition. Her father had called it other things, particularly after a ten-year-old Anne had told him that a man with whom he was about to enter a contract was a bad man. Armadale had punished her for her impertinence and ignored her to his cost. After that, although he was as likely to tell her to mind her place and to pretend to ignore her opinions, he took greater care and occasionally even sought out her estimation of people who had approached him.

That experience and others like it assured her that she could trust Sir Christopher. Without a qualm, she dismissed his warning that she should not.

"There, you see," Catriona said, pleased with the progress of her plan. "She trusts him, although I cannot think why she should when she does not know him."

Fergus wriggled beside her in the thick mane of Anne's mount, looking anything but pleased or comfortable. "He is a good man, is he not?"

"Aye, but how would she know?"

"She has a gift, o' course."

"I have heard that some tribes bestow such gifts upon

their charges," she said, remembering that Claud had told her as much.

"I'm thinking ye're no from around here," he said grimly.

"Of course I am not," Catriona replied. "Do I *look* as if I were from here?"

"Nay, for ye're even more beautiful than the women o' me own tribe, so I'm thinking ye must be a pixie from one o' the hill tribes. I ha' never seen one afore, but I'm told they be the only lasses more beautiful than ours."

"Well, I have not met anyone like you before either," Catriona said.

"Aye, well, although we bestow gifts, we dinna do things like ye just did," he said righteously. "Ye canna go about these parts interfering in mortal business."

"But we have a duty to look after them."

"Aye, sure, but only in small ways," he said. "Banishing nightmares when they threaten, soothing harsh feelings, easing worries, and such like things."

"But that cannot be all you do," Catriona said. "Your aura seems so powerful, not like that of a brownie or a dobby with no power to speak of. What fortunate tribe can boast of having you as its member?"

"I be an Ellyl," he said, preening himself. "Me tribe's called the Ellyllon."

"I fear I have never heard of them," she admitted. "What manner of folk are they exactly?"

"They be the Forgetful People is what they be," Maggie Malloch snapped, materializing between them in a puff of mist.

"Maggie," Fergus exclaimed. "What be ye a-doing here?"

"I ha' business here," she said. "If it concerns ye, Fergus

Fishbait, I'm that sorry. Form yourself properly, so the wench doesna take the notion that ye always go about half baked, or fear that ye'll fade away altogether."

Clearly startled, Fergus looked down at himself. "Och, I forgot!" he exclaimed, snapping into a solid form at once. "I were that stunned by what ye were doing that I forgot tae finish producing m'self."

"But how can you stop halfway?" Catriona asked.

"Never mind that," Maggie said, giving her a stern look. "What did ye do tae stun the man so?"

Catriona smiled. "I merely arranged for my lad to meet the cousin of his betrothed, that's all. With luck, and if Fergus Fishbait can stop arguing with me at every turn and trying to prevent—"

"But we're no tae interfere wi' them," he protested. "That be the rule!"

"Dinna heed him, lass," Maggie advised. "Likely, he'll forget about it soon. Ye've heard o' the Holy Grail?"

Catriona blinked at what seemed to be a non sequitur. "Aye," she said doubtfully. "That is, I don't remember what it was exactly, but did it not go missing centuries ago?"

"It did, because it were in the charge o' the Ellyllon," Maggie said with a severe look at Fergus. "They were tae keep it safe, and they swore they hid it in a perfect place. But when time came tae let the mortals find it again, the Ellyllon couldna produce it, and so they ha' been called the Forgetful People ever since. Ye'll find their members everywhere, and sithee, they canna help forgetting. It be their nature, just as it be your nature tae—"

"I dinna forget things," Fergus interjected crossly.

"D'ye recall my Claud?" Maggie asked.

"Aye, o' course, I do," he said.

"Well, he's gone missing, and we've got tae find him," Maggie said. She glanced at Catriona. "The case be just as I expected, lass."

Catriona grimaced. "Jonah Bonewits cast him into the mor—"

"Aye," Maggie said, cutting her off before she could finish the sentence and casting an oblique, warning look at Fergus. Then she stared. "Here, Fergus, ye're fading away nearly tae nowt," she scolded. "Pull yourself together, ye foolish man."

Clearly struggling to obey, he said, "Did the lass say Jonah *Bonewits*?"

"Aye, she did. What d'ye ken o' Jonah?"

Fergus was trembling. "He doesna like me."

"Jonah dislikes everyone," Maggie said. "That be *his* nature."

"Aye, but when he were last vexed wi' me, he said I'd forget me head if it were no tied on, and he threatened tae prove it did I vex him again," Fergus said, nearly in tears. "If ye mean tae cross him, I dinna want tae be near ye."

"Ye poor wee man," Catriona said, patting his knee.

"Pish tush," Maggie said. "Ye've nowt tae fear. I can manage our Jonah."

Chapter 5

"Tell me more about this wedding," Sir Christopher said abruptly.

Anne smiled, certain he could see no more of her expression than she could see of his.

"Why does such a simple request amuse you, lass?"

Startled, she looked sharply at him. "Can you see my face?"

"I have excellent night vision," he said. "My long vision is likewise very good. Why did you smile?"

Still surprised, because she could make out only the strong lines of his profile against the starlit heavens and nothing more, she answered honestly, "I am just pleased that you are curious enough to want to know more."

"My uncle has had me declared dead and has usurped my lands and titles. Now I learn that he intends to marry the woman to whom I was betrothed. Surely, you will agree that I am entitled to a certain measure of curiosity."

"To be fair, sir, he does believe that you are dead."

"Does he?"

"Why, yes, of course. He must." As she said the words,

though, his question stirred thoughts deep in her mind. Could Eustace know that his nephew was alive?

Sir Christopher did not speak. It was as if he knew that his curt question must stir her to think and was giving her time to do so.

"Where were you," she asked, "to make everyone think you had died?"

"Away."

"It is over a year, sir, nearly eighteen months by your own count, since anyone in these parts had word from you. There were rumors, too. My aunt does not speak of them, nor my cousin, but I did hear that . . ." She paused, biting her lip.

"Go on. What did you hear?"

"Only that something dreadful had happened, that you had done something wicked and that many believed that, in your guilt, you had taken your own life or died of remorse." She watched him as she spoke and saw him nod. "Is that so, then? I mean, clearly, you did not die, but did you disappear voluntarily?"

Instead of answering the question directly, he said, "If I told you that I had done nothing dreadful or wicked, would you believe me?"

"Yes."

"Just like that?"

"Yes, of course. You can have no cause to lie to me."

"Perhaps I would lie merely for the sake of lying, or because it is expedient."

"Many people do that, I know, particularly if by 'expedient' you mean you might do so to protect yourself. But I do not think you are of that ilk."

"A man never knows what he is capable of doing until the time comes to do it," he said bitterly.

"Perhaps." She waited a beat, but when he did not continue, she said, "I know that such curiosity is unbecoming, sir, particularly since you have already snubbed me twice, but I would like to know where you were. Your uncle, after all, is not the only person who believed you were dead."

"Are you going to tell me that your cousin was cast into black despair?"

"No, for I do not believe that is the case. She has scarcely ever mentioned your name, but I can tell you that she was saddened and disappointed."

"She did not even know me."

"Had you never met, not even once as children?"

"You say that she is seventeen now. I'm eight-and-twenty, and I've not set foot in the Borders in more than five years. We might have met at Stirling one of the few times that I accompanied my father to court, but I do not recall meeting her."

"I do not think Fiona has been to court," Anne said. "Her mother meant . . . that is, she *means* to present her after her marriage."

"I do recall that her father died before mine arranged the betrothal. Do you three women live alone at Mute Hill House without masculine protection?"

She knew that, once again, he was attempting to divert her from the subject of his whereabouts, but she said, "Aunt Olivia invited her uncle, Sir Tobias Bell, to live with her after Sir Stephen's death. As to whether Toby counts as protection, I have my doubts, sir, but he certainly lends us a certain consequence if one does not mind the occasional fox hunt through the great hall."

He laughed. "Does he really hunt foxes indoors?"

She smiled. "Not purposely, I suppose, but he does have a knack for creating havoc. That was one reason I felt such a strong urge to escape to the peacefulness of the Towers today. First, Aunt Olivia tortured poor Fiona for two hours whilst she satisfied herself that the wedding dress is as it should be, and then, a poor little fox darted through, pursued by a half dozen hounds. You cannot imagine the uproar."

"What happened to the fox?"

"It headed for one of the stairways, and that was the last I saw of it. I took Fiona upstairs afterward, so that she could rest."

"I collect that Toby Bell is not what Lady Carmichael hoped he would be."

"In truth, I think she relies more on her household steward than her uncle. Toby is as fat as a brood-sow and jovial. He enjoys childish pranks, good claret, and the company of men he meets in alehouses and other such places. He is forever bringing one or another of them home with him, and he tells Aunt Olivia he does so in hopes of providing her with an eligible suitor of her own."

"I should think you would applaud that notion. If her daughter is only seventeen, Lady Carmichael must enjoy excellent prospects for remarriage."

Anne bit back a gurgle of laughter, saying, "She would not thank you for saying so, nor does she appreciate Toby's efforts. She prefers to . . . to concentrate on her bereavement."

"To wallow in it, I expect you meant to say." When Anne did not contradict him, he added thoughtfully, "Sir Stephen must have been dead now for more than two years. Surely, she has not kept herself secluded all that time."

"Oh, but—" Anne bit back the words before they leaped from her tongue.

"Don't stop there, lass. What else were you going to say?"

She hesitated and then said stiffly, "She also mourns my father and mother, sir, as I think you must realize."

"Now, that was neatly done," he said approvingly. "Puts me tidily in my place and is calculated even to make me squirm a bit for forgetting that their deaths might have affected her. But it won't serve. You would not have broken off so abruptly to avoid mentioning your father and mother. So what was it?"

Anne bit her lip, wishing that she had foreseen the pitfall earlier.

"Come now," he urged. "Coyness does not suit you, and I've a notion the bit you're not telling me somehow concerns me."

"Not really," she said. "At all events, it is certainly no business of mine to be telling tales. I have grown comfortable with you. 'Tis the darkness, I expect."

"Tell me."

He did not raise his voice, but with those two words, she realized that it might not always be comfortable talking with him. He was clearly accustomed to commanding others and to having his commands instantly obeyed.

"She mourns your father, too," she said.

"I must remember to thank her for her sympathy, but why should she?"

Anne resorted to silence again.

"I see," he said. "I expect that does much to explain my betrothal. Lady Carmichael must be nearly as beautiful herself, though, because my father always had an eye for a pretty face. Did she imagine he'd marry her?"

"That is certainly not for me to say," Anne said.

"God's feet," he muttered, "what a coil you lay before me!"

"Well, I did not create it!"

"I know you didn't, but I'll wager you expect me to unravel it."

"You must," she said. "You cannot allow your uncle to marry Fiona under false pretenses. Indeed if he knows you are alive—"

"I cannot imagine how he would, nor do I mean to tell him until I have a better understanding of what he has already done and what he means to do."

"But—"

"Is that our destination yonder?"

"Aye," she said, for they had reached the top of the hill and could see the lights of Mute Hill House half a mile away.

"Why do they call it Mute Hill?"

"It was the site of an ancient moot court," Anne said. "Sir Christopher, with respect, you may change the topic of conversation as often you like, but I'm afraid that at best you cannot keep your secret longer than one more day."

"Do you mean to betray my presence here?"

"I hope I shan't have to. Your uncle expects to marry Fiona two days from now, on Friday. You must not let that happen."

She saw him shrug. "Despite your understandable dislike of him, I am not persuaded that I should interfere in his wedding," he said. "To do so would only make things more complicated for me, and I don't want to marry anyone until I know how the rest of my affairs stand. Moreover, since I'm legally dead, I do not see that my interference would matter at all. What if my uncle simply orders the parson to continue the ceremony?"

"Your being alive would certainly matter to Fiona," Anne said. It would also matter to Olivia, she knew, but she was certain that it would not help her cause to point out that Olivia was interested only in marrying her daughter to the Chisholm wealth, titles, and power. So she said only, "Perhaps it has slipped your mind, but Fiona is a great heiress. Moreover, I should think that you are morally bound to her, and bound likewise in the sight of God. *He* certainly knows you are not dead."

He sighed. "How was my funeral, by the way?"

Although she was growing accustomed to his abrupt changes of subject, the non sequitur surprised and amused her. Nevertheless, she said matter-of-factly, "I do not know, because I was not here. That is irrelevant now, in any event."

"Not to me," he said. "Hush now. I want to think."

Anne remained obediently silent until they had crossed the dale and were halfway up Mute Hill. Then she said, "If you won't tell me where you were all that time, will you at least tell me why you were riding with reivers tonight?"

He said lightly, "I was tempted by a call to adventure and by some small hope of learning exactly what mischief my uncle has been up to. A good friend assured me that the reivers know everything that occurs in the Borders."

"Well, I hope when you return to them you will not let them steal my cattle. Let them do their lifting properly, from some scurvy Englishman."

He chuckled, as she had hoped he would, and soon afterward, they rode through the gateway into the torchlit yard at Mute Hill House.

Stable lads came running to help with the horses, and Sir Christopher dismounted, handing the reins of his horse and the one he had been leading to the first lad. Then he moved to help Anne before any of the others could.

As he gripped her firmly around the waist and lifted her down, she gazed curiously at his face, finding it strong and handsome, golden in the torchlight. His eyes seemed curiously golden too, and a lurking twinkle met her searching gaze. She liked the twinkle, but even as that thought crossed her mind, the twinkle deepened into something warmer and more intense.

That intensity was unfamiliar to her and oddly disturbing.

He set her on her feet but did not release her.

"I will see you again," he said.

She dampened suddenly dry lips. "Well, of course you will, sir. Fiona is—"

"Never mind Fiona," he said, raising a hand to cup her chin. "I saw the curiosity in your eyes, lass, and I confess to feeling curious about you, too. What's more, I may never have this opportunity again," he added, bending toward her.

His lips captured hers before she fully recognized his intent, and right there in her aunt's stableyard, in front of who knew how many servants, he kissed her hard, as if he had every right to do so. The hand that still clasped her waist slid to the small of her back, pressing her body against his in a most unseemly manner.

For a long, amazing moment, she did not react, but when she felt her lips move against his as if to taste him, and realized that she was savoring his strength and a strange sense of being possessed, she put both hands to his chest and pushed.

He released her at once, but her right hand had already shot back, and without a thought for reason or consequence, she smacked it hard against his cheek.

Grabbing the offending hand in a bruising grip, he pulled her close again. With his lips a tantalizing inch or so from hers, he murmured, "Before you strike a man, you should know him well enough to be sure that he will not strike back."

"A woman is always entitled to defend herself against unwelcome liberties," she retorted, struggling to control her sudden and quite unexpected fury.

"Ah, but a woman who wanders about unprotected *invites* liberties," he said. "You told me earlier that I have no authority to take you to task, Lady Anne, and you are certainly right about that. Nevertheless, if you are wise, you will not let me find you out without appropriate protection again, particularly after dark."

Angry now, she said, "By heaven, if I could shoot a gun—"

"Aye, that would make a difference," he agreed. "If you like, I will teach you, but you should not ride out alone even then, not unless you want to risk my learning about it."

"I cannot imagine how you think you can stop me," she snapped.

"Don't tempt me to show you," he said. Then the twinkle returned to his eyes, and he stepped back. "Go on inside, lass. If your aunt has any sense she will give you a fierce scolding and send you to bed without your supper."

In a vain attempt to retain her dignity, she tried to meet his gaze, but she feared her expression more nearly resembled childish resentment than any semblance of dignity. She did not fear Olivia, but she was by no means so certain now what she thought about Sir Christopher Chisholm.

As he took the reins of Willie's horse from the lackey holding it and swung onto his own saddle, she remembered that she did have one way to strike back.

"Tell me where you were all that time everyone thought you were dead," she said, "or I swear that the moment I walk inside I'll tell them you are alive."

He glanced around at the curious gillies, and then, leaning closer to her so that his voice would not carry to the others, he said, "I was on a prison ship, my lady, sentenced to remain aboard her for life. Think of that before you urge me further to renew my betrothal to your simpleton cousin."

"Sakes, listen tae that," Fergus said in disgust. "Wha' manner o' man ha' ye brought tae Mute Hill House? Likely, he's a thief or a murderer who will endanger the entire household!"

"Whisst now," Maggie said before Catriona could reply. "I'll give ye me word ye ha' nowt tae concern ye on that head, Fergus. Ye'll no doubt me word, will ye?" she added with a menacing look.

"Nay, nay," he replied hastily. "But what if he falls in love with her? As dear as she is, any man might!"

With a laugh, Catriona said, "Nonsense, have you seen her cousin?"

"Aye, o' course I have, and she's gey beautiful, tae be sure, but my lass be worth two o' her sort any day."

Maggie snorted. "A mortal man—aye, or one from our own world, for that matter—rarely sees worth if beauty catches his eye. Ye'd best study men more carefully an ye mean tae protect your lass, Fergus Fishbait."

"But—"

"Cease your nattering, and follow her. Likely, she'll need your help when she faces her aunt after being away so late."

"Aye, 'tis true," Fergus agreed, flitting away after Lady Anne.

When he had gone beyond earshot, Maggie said, "I didna want tae say more tae him wi'out speaking tae ye first, Catriona, but I'm thinking we'll ha' tae take him into our confidence."

"But what if he forgets that he must not tell others what we are trying to do?"

"I'll see that he doesna speak out o' turn," Maggie said.

"But why tell him at all?"

"Blame yourself for that. 'Twas your bright notion tae bring his lass into it."

"But even had I not, Kit Chisholm was bound to mix with the Carmichael household eventually, so we'd have encountered Fergus anyway," Catriona retorted.

"Aye, that be so," Maggie agreed. "That dratted Jonah set me temper afire, and it hasna cooled yet. But ye've set your own finger on why we must tell Fergus."

"Why?"

"Because he can help us. He'll ha' been watching his lass, so he already kens much about that household."

"D'ye think Claud is there?"

"He may be," Maggie said. "He's near, because I can sense his presence and Jonah wants us tae find him. It wouldna be any fun for him otherwise, and he thinks we canna help Claud even if we do find him, so likely he's melded him tae some'un in the Carmichael household or at Hawks Rig. We'll just ha' tae learn who."

"But how?"

"I'm thinking that being tied tae my Claud would alter any mortal," Maggie said with a wry smile. "We'll watch for traits that seem more in keeping wi' his personality than wi' that o' the mortal, but tae do that we'll ha' tae find which one o' them has recently changed his or her ways."

"*Her* ways?"

"Aye, sure, Jonah could ha' put Claud anywhere."

"I never thought of a woman," Catriona said. "What if no one has changed?"

"Then we'll try summat else, but we'll no quit till we find him. And then Jonah Bonewits will rue the day he did this. On that, ye ha' me promise."

"Fergus was right about one thing, Maggie. Jonah *is* dangerous."

"Aye, he is, but so am I. Now, follow that lad o' yours. I want tae think."

Catriona obeyed, but as she went, a tear spilled down her cheek. What if they never found Claud?

His body, or whatever was left of it, stirred abruptly as if Catriona had touched him, and something inside him strengthened at her touch. He had sensed her presence in the air for some time, but the sensation had been vague at best.

At the time of the incident, he had felt as if a bolt of burning fire surged through him only to be doused when he plunged into icy water. From there, water nymphs had transported him to a doorway filled with light. Passing through it, he had felt an extraordinary sensation, as if his spirit had died, taking all desire with it and leaving him exposed to what lay on the other side. He had heard that death meant losing one's sense of self and one's desire, primary traits that members of the Clan shared with the mortal world, and so he had believed that he was dying.

Apparently, that belief had been wrong.

Earlier, he had felt lonely, certain that Catriona had forgotten him and already had other affairs on her mind. In the dense gray light he had inhabited for what seemed eons, he had feared he would never again see her lovely face.

But suddenly, he had seen all three of them, and he could hear them, too, but he could not speak and obviously they could not see him.

Who was the scoundrel with Catriona, and why did she flutter her lashes at him? Never before had he felt such helpless frustration.

As Kit rode away from Mute Hill House, his usual sharp wits threatened to abandon him and he found himself shifting uncomfortably on his saddle. Half-formed thoughts collided with one another before any could fully form itself or make much sense. His lips burned, and for some distance, his body's reaction to the woman he had just kissed made sitting difficult and his ride thus a penance.

He had never met a woman like Lady Anne Ellyson, but the same independence of mind and spirit that attracted him had stirred him to take liberties that no gentleman should take with a lady. On the other hand, had he not kissed her, he might well have shaken her for taking such dangerous risks with her life.

What if he had not been there when she chanced upon the reivers? The thought made him shudder. At the least, Sammy and his lot would have taken her horse and left her to walk the rest of the way in the treacherous darkness. At the worst . . . But he refused to entertain thoughts of the worst. Reivers were guilty of many things, but rarely did any of them harm innocent women or children.

Of course, any innocent, sensible young woman would have relinquished her mount to any band of reivers that demanded it, but he had no doubt that Lady Anne would have continued to raise a fuss had he not been there to intervene. What had her people been thinking to allow her so much freedom?

Other men than reivers stalked the Borders, after all, including English and Scottish soldiers and the vermin that skittered in their wake. Moreover, nothing that he had heard about Armadale led him to believe the earl would have approved of his daughter's behavior or that he would have countenanced such goings-on whilst she lived beneath his roof. Clearly, Lady Carmichael, although born into the same family, was not cut from the same bolt as the earl.

The tip of a quarter moon peeked over the eastern horizon, spilling more light onto his path. Urging his horse to a trot, and satisfied that Willie's beast would follow, Kit continued to try to impose order on his scattered thoughts.

His primary course remained the same, for it was more important than ever now to learn what his uncle was up to and to decide exactly what he himself must do to sort out his affairs and reclaim his rightful lands and titles. But he could no longer ignore his erstwhile betrothal while he looked into those things.

Certainly poor Fiona, in the belief that he was dead, was

being led to the altar unwillingly and under false pretenses. Whatever else she might believe about Eustace Chisholm, both she and her mother clearly believed that by marrying him, Fiona would become Lady Chisholm and reign as mistress over the vast Chisholm estates. As for his greedy uncle, evidently the man was not satisfied to have usurped the estates and titles but was determined to carry off the heiress, too.

However, they were all acting without considering Lady Anne, and Kit had the feeling that left to her own devices, her ladyship might come up with a way to stop the wedding. Even as that thought formed, it stirred an appreciative smile, although he knew she had little chance of success on her own.

If she were to declare that he lived and should be the one to marry Mistress Carmichael, they would doubtless dismiss her assertions and clap her up securely for the duration of the ceremony. Then, even if he should step forward afterward to reclaim what was his, Eustace would already have his heiress bride. If one believed Lady Anne's description of her cousin, as he did, Mistress Carmichael would not defy her mother's wishes by taking a firm stand and refusing to marry.

Kit had meant it when he said that he would seek Anne out, and he meant to do so soon, because he looked forward to crossing verbal swords with her again. Her cousin, by comparison, sounded like a lass who would blush, bridle, and agree with whatever a man said, as so many innocent young women did. Commendable behavior, he supposed, but he suspected that such submissiveness would grow tiresome before long. In fact, the meek Fiona sounded like a dead bore.

Lady Anne, on the other hand, was a woman so cool that one longed to warm her up, so calm that one longed to agitate her. He had wondered if she ever lost her temper, and it had afforded him a certain satisfaction to learn that she did, although admittedly, the behavior that had provoked her was outrageous. Still, her shocked look after she slapped him assured him that the temperamental outburst was a rarity.

His body relaxed at last, and riding grew easier. He continued to think pleasantly about Lady Anne until it suddenly occurred to him that if he freed Fiona from his uncle, an unfortunate but natural outcome would result unless he could persuade them that her betrothal to Eustace had abrogated the one to him or that his supposed death had rendered it moot.

By the time he rejoined Willie, Sammy, and the others, he had decided that no matter what he might learn about Eustace from the reivers, he would attend the wedding. Few if any guests were likely to recognize him, and certainly, Eustace himself would not, for in the past six years, the Kit Chisholm that he had seen so infrequently had changed from a stripling to a man, adding height, girth, and muscle. His face had lost the soft curves of youth, and the past year and a half had added harshness to his features and a hard, sinewy strength to his body.

Lady Anne might recognize him, of course. Despite the dim, flickering torches in the yard, he knew she had studied his features carefully, as he had studied hers, and he did not want her to spoil his surprise at the wedding by blurting out the fact of his presence. She would be concerned with her cousin and would have little time to peer about at the guests, but even so, he would take care to avoid her until he decided exactly what, if anything, he meant to do.

If he let the wedding run its course, which he was still strongly inclined to do if only to eliminate what was presently only a minor problem, he could walk away unseen and without fear that Lady Anne might confront him and take him to task.

That thought, however, brought another smile. Perhaps he would let her catch a glimpse of him, *after* the ceremony.

Chapter 6

For several moments after Sir Christopher had ridden out of the yard and through the gateway, Anne stood where she was, still stunned by his kiss and her reaction to it, and trying both to understand what demon had possessed her to make her slap him and to make sense of his parting words to her.

To think of him as a man knighted, undoubtedly for bravery, by the King was hard. To think of him as plain Kit Chisholm, Border reiver, was far easier. Not only did his behavior suit her notion of a reiver but also she knew that many bands of reivers on both sides of the line included men of even the highest stations.

Armadale had not approved of such unseemly behavior amongst his peers, but some of the greatest and most powerful names in the Borders—Scott of Buccleuch and Scott of Hardin, along with the heads of the Maxwell, Johnston, and Armstrong tribes—all were known frequently to lead their own reiver bands. It was said that when a Scott wife thought her stores had fallen to an unacceptable level, she uncovered a platter before her formidable husband, revealing a pair of spurs where the meat should be, thus suggesting that it was time for another raid. Indeed, the motto of the Scotts of Buc-cleuch was "let there be moonlight," and other branches of their family and others boasted similar maxims.

She could not believe that she had struck Sir Christopher, great though the provocation had been. Her lips still burned, though, and she had to exert self-control to keep from rub-bing the sensation away. But she knew that the stable lads were watching and knew, too, that their opinion of her be-havior would doubtless reach Malcolm Vole's ears before long and her aunt's soon after that. Moreover, she had en-joyed that kiss and the astonishing sensations it had stirred within her. Not that she could admit that to anyone, she re-minded herself firmly. Just thinking of what she had done by kissing the man who was still, despite his denials, betrothed to her cousin sent heat into her cheeks.

Drawing a deep, steadying breath, she lifted the front of her skirt enough to keep it from touching the ground and turned toward the house. As she had expected, several lads were watching. All but one looked hastily away, but that one stepped forward, saying diffidently, "Beg pardon, me lady, but I thought ye'd want tae ken that the gelding's fetlock be scarcely swollen. Wi' a day's rest, he'll be fine."

"Thank you, Teddy," she said with a rueful smile. "It was through my own carelessness that he stepped in a rabbit hole, so I am glad he is not badly hurt."

"Aye, well, seein' it were dark and all—"

"Not then," Anne said. "It happened in broad daylight, I'm ashamed to say. I had walked a good way before Sir . . . before someone came along who was kind enough to help me." Mentioning Sir Christopher's name now, she realized, would only complicate matters more.

"A good thing he come along," Teddy said. His curiosity

was plain, but Anne was certain he would not so far forget his place as to demand her rescuer's name. Peg Elliot would not be so reticent, however. Nor would Olivia. Before either event occurred, she would have to decide how much or how little to tell them.

As she walked around to the front of the house with her usual brisk stride, she briefly savored a mental image of herself walking into her aunt's bower and announcing to Olivia and anyone with her that, contrary to what they believed, Sir Christopher Chisholm, true Laird of Ashkirk, was alive and eager to reclaim what was his. Such an announcement so near Fiona's wedding day would eliminate any need to endure another scold, for in the uproar that followed, Olivia would certainly forget her irritation over Anne's solitary excursion. Even the information that Sir Christopher was disturbingly handsome and admirably large and broad-shouldered would weigh little with her, although it might impress Fiona.

Anne wondered as she approached the entrance if Sir Christopher expected her to make such an announcement. He had not asked her to keep silent, but neither had he expressed anything resembling delight at learning that Fiona, although betrothed to his hateful uncle, had not yet married him.

Oil lamps on short posts lit the extensive garden paths, telling her that her aunt had entertained guests at supper, for they did not waste the oil when the family supped alone. Anne took note of the detail subconsciously, while her thoughts remained fixed upon her erstwhile protector.

She did not know much about Scottish law. Even so, it seemed odd to her that titles and estates, especially ones of so powerful an entity as the Laird of Ashkirk and Torness, should change hands so quickly without positive proof of Sir Christopher's death—which Eustace Chisholm clearly had not been able to produce. How, she wondered as she entered the house, had he managed it?

Her eyes had scarcely adjusted to the brighter light when a familiar, high-pitched masculine voice said tartly, "One would think that before disappearing for hours without a trace, a well-bred young woman would take a moment to consider the upset such behavior was bound to cause those who care for her."

Malcolm Vole stood with his arms crossed over his thin chest, glowering at her. Clearly, he had been on the lookout for her return and had exerted himself to be the first to greet her.

Anne returned his look as she calmly stripped off her gloves and said, "Is my aunt sitting in her bower, Malcolm?"

"Aye, and where else would she be, with supper over this half hour and more, and with Ashkirk kindly bearing her company. You should be—"

"Thank you, that will be all," she said as if she had not realized he meant to say more. "I shall go to her at once." She gave him a straight look, and although he met it, he made no further comment as he stepped aside to let her pass.

Conscious of his quick, mincing footsteps behind her, she paused when she reached Olivia's bower and waited for him to open the door. Instead of holding it open for her, however, he slipped through ahead of her.

He did not so far forget himself that he let it close in her face, as she half expected, but said pompously as he held it for her, "Here is your errant niece, my lady, returned to us at last."

Anne indulged in a brief fantasy of drawing a pistol from

her cloak and shooting him. From that vision, it was a natural leap to wonder if Sir Christopher would actually teach her to shoot. Perhaps after he and Fiona were married. . .

Swiftly recalling her wandering wits, she said, "Good evening, Aunt Olivia. I apologize for missing supper."

"Mercy, Anne, where have you been?" Olivia demanded querulously. "I have been so dreadfully worried that dear Ashkirk felt obliged to remain and take supper with us, which means that he must now spend the night."

"That was thoughtful of him, madam, but you need not have concerned yourself. As you see, I have returned safely."

Eustace, lounging in an armchair with his legs sprawled before him and a pot of ale on a small round table conveniently nearby, stared balefully at her, but when she gazed back, affecting mild surprise, he remembered his manners.

"Here, Malcolm," he muttered as he got to his feet, "bring more ale, for I'm parched. That fish tonight was too salty. As for you, lass," he added as Malcolm left, "you should know better than to distress your aunt so. You won't mind my putting a word in, my dear Lady Carmichael. You may be sure that such behavior will cease forthwith after Fiona and I are married."

"Do you intent to reside here at Mute Hill, sir?" Anne asked innocently.

"No, no, of course I don't, but her ladyship knows she can call upon my services whenever she likes. She has allowed you—and doubtless Fiona, as well—entirely too much freedom."

"Where is Fiona?" Anne asked, turning to her aunt.

"She went to bed right after supper," Olivia said wearily. "She said she had a headache, but it was thoughtless of her to leave me to entertain Ashkirk by myself. Not that you present any difficulty, dear sir," she added gracefully. "I am sure no one could ask for a more pleasant companion."

"I am sorry if no one told you I had ridden to the Towers, madam," Anne said. "Malcolm, Fiona, and my own Peg Elliot knew that I had."

"Yes, yes, Fiona did say something," Olivia said, "but I could not imagine you would do such a thing with Ashkirk still in the house, so I paid her no heed."

"You would scarcely have expected me to entertain him by myself."

"When one is a dependent in a kinsman's household," Eustace said as he sat down again, "one does not form an intent or act upon it without permission."

Anne glanced at him, more strongly tempted than ever to tell him his nephew was alive and meant to reclaim what was rightfully his. Only the certainty that Sir Christopher would not thank her for forcing his hand prevented her from speaking.

Had anyone asked how she could be so sure of his thoughts on the subject, she could not have told them, but she was certain he would be annoyed if she revealed his intent before he was ready to do so himself. Indeed, the gleeful pleasure that she knew she would feel if she revealed all to Eustace right now was pleasure that Kit Chisholm had every right to enjoy for himself.

A lackey entered with a pitcher of ale, and silence reigned while he refilled Eustace's mug, but when he had gone away again, Anne said, "Is there anything you would like me to do for you before I retire, Aunt Olivia?"

"No, no, my dear, but you mustn't run away just yet. We

don't want the servants carrying tales about my sitting alone with Ashkirk," she added archly.

"In truth, I was surprised to find only the two of you in here," Anne said.

"I should have been more careful, I expect," Olivia said, "but Moira has just gone to fetch a new canvas to stretch on my frame. Perhaps you will be so obliging as to help her sort my threads, although I warrant you must be starving."

"If you will accept my advice, my lady," Eustace put in with another, more challenging look at Anne, "you will send the lass to bed without her supper."

Anne thought again of his nephew, and a smile touched her lips, but noting a flash of anger in Eustace's eyes, she quickly lowered her gaze.

As she removed her cloak, tucked her gloves inside, and folded it over a stool, she said quietly to Olivia, "I did not intend to be so late, but my horse stepped in a rabbit hole and came up lame. I was forced to walk a good part of the way."

Eustace launched into another lecture, but as Anne adjusted the candles near Olivia, replacing one and trimming two wicks, she paid him little heed other than occasionally to glance his way so he would not realize she was ignoring him. One such glance produced a sudden, startling awareness that his gaze was far too intense for a gentleman merely scolding one whom he regarded, however inaccurately, as in his charge. Although he clearly sought to dominate her, his expression was strangely possessive, even flirtatious, and it made her uncomfortable.

Moira entered then with linen for Olivia's tambour frame, and Anne had no more time for private thought. In the hour that followed, she learned that Eustace had decided to remain at Mute Hill House until the wedding, having sent his servant to Hawks Rig to collect what he required for the ceremony.

It was Olivia, of course, who had persuaded him to stay. "For it will give me such assurance to have a strong-minded gentleman to support me," she explained, gazing limpidly at him in a way that made Anne want to shake her.

He said, "'Tis my pleasure, madam, but surely your uncle is an excellent man and one upon whom you must place great reliance."

Olivia sighed. "Would that it were so, sir, but you must see that Uncle Toby has been a sad disappointment. He spends much of his time in alehouses with men of low repute, several of whom he has actually invited to Mute Hill House."

"God's wounds, to what purpose?"

To Anne's astonishment, Olivia lowered her eyes and blushed. "Why, sir," she said coyly, "I fear he quite fails to comprehend the depth of my bereavement and hopes to provide me with an eligible suitor."

"Poor lady," Eustace said, patting her hand. "You must suffer grievously."

Anne suspected him of mockery, but Olivia smiled warmly and said, "You are so kind, sir. My dearest Fiona—*our* dearest Fiona, as I should say—is much luckier than she knows."

"'Tis I who am the fortunate one," he said.

Anne stood up more abruptly than she had intended but said with carefully controlled calm, "Pray excuse me, madam. There will be much to do tomorrow, so I should sleep whilst I can. Good night, Sir Eustace."

Scarcely awaiting permission and ignoring his look of irritation at being addressed as Sir Eustace instead of Ashkirk, she left them and hurried upstairs, where she found Peg Elliot in possession of her bedchamber.

"At last!" Peg exclaimed. "Like a cat on hot bricks Mistress Fiona is and will not rest until she speaks with ye. Pray, go tae her at once."

"I thought her asleep this past hour and more," Anne said.

"Not her. Fretting, she is, over what's tae become o' her. If she were a pony, mistress, I'd say she were ripe for bolting."

"I am sure she never had such a wicked notion in all her life," Anne said. "She is the least likely person I know to go against her mother's wishes, let alone dare to snap her fingers at a man as domineering as Eustace Chisholm."

"Aye, but she's so frightened o' him there be nae saying what she'll do."

Anne sighed. "I know she is frightened, and they are cruel to force her into this marriage, but we may yet find a way out, Peg, if only the Lord proves willing."

"I canna think how," Peg said.

"Nor may I tell you," Anne said. "The possibility involves others for whom I must not speak, but if all goes as I hope . . . Well, just pray that it does, that's all."

"Aye," Peg said, eyeing her skeptically. "Likely, ye're up tae some mischief, and we'll all of us land in the suds."

"When have I ever landed anyone in the suds but myself?"

Peg grinned. "Aye, butter wouldna melt in your mouth, would it? But I could tell a tale or two, were I of a mind tae do so."

"But you won't," Anne said confidently. "I shall go to Mistress Fiona, so if you have laid out my things, you may go to bed."

"Oh, aye, I'll go," Peg said with another chuckle, "but if Mistress Fiona disappears afore she walks tae her doom at that wee chapel, I willna ha' far tae look for the one who stirred the notion in her head."

Anne considered Peg's words as she hurried to her cousin's bedchamber but dismissed them before she reached it. Even if by some miracle she could persuade the timid Fiona to defy both Olivia and Eustace, she had not the slightest idea how she could remove her cousin beyond their reach. Surely, they would find her and force the marriage anyway, and then Anne would face punishment herself for encouraging such rebellion.

The thought of her own fate was the least of her concerns, but she had taken Eustace's measure and that of her aunt. Olivia was a woman who believed in the superiority of men over women to such an extent that she submitted to the wishes not only of her uncle and Eustace but also of her absurd house steward. And while she held Toby in mild contempt, Anne had long realized that the contempt arose from his singular lack of interest in exerting authority. Toby took no responsibility, generally behaving in the manner of a favored guest.

Because Olivia would submit to nearly any decree Eustace issued, Anne knew that both she and Fiona would have to tread carefully. He had so far behaved in a civil if lecherous manner, but Anne sensed that beneath his civility lay a more primitive, even violent nature.

These thoughts passed through her mind in the few minutes it took her to reach Fiona's room, but their remnants evaporated when she entered to find her cousin pacing back and forth before her fireplace, wringing her hands.

"Oh, Anne, you've come! I've wanted you for hours!"

"Hush, love, I'm here now. But what are you thinking to

be striding about in that thin bedgown without so much as a shawl to fend off the chill?"

"I couldn't sleep, and I cannot sit still. Oh, Anne, I cannot marry him! All through supper he gazed at me like a wolf contemplating a lamb feast!"

"Then tell your mother you won't marry him," Anne said as she opened a chest and found a soft, pink wool shawl.

"I couldn't! I should be in such disgrace, and it would be utterly dreadful. Just the thought of it curdles my stomach."

Anne shook her head but smiled as she draped the shawl around Fiona's slim shoulders. "I expect I could tell her for you if you like," she said.

Fiona shook her head, making her long hair ripple and gleam in the candle- and firelight. "She would be so angry. I couldn't bear it. You *know* I couldn't!"

Anne hesitated, then said gently, "Something may yet happen to prevent it."

Fiona brightened. "You could take my place! Oh, Anne, it is the very thing, because every woman needs to marry, and you are not afraid of him. I know you are not. And he is a very good catch, my mother says—so rich and powerful. He counts Cardinal Beaton and even the King amongst his friends, you know, and others nearly as powerful. Some of the gifts they have sent are utterly splendid, but I shouldn't mind a bit if you have them," she added. "They say," she added, lowering her voice, "that Ashkirk has powerful friends even in England."

Anne chuckled again. "My dear Fiona, surely you realize that every powerful man in the Borders has friends on both sides of the line. Why, one of my father's best friends was the late Lord Dacre of Naworth, warden of the English western march. He—my father, that is—said the only way to hold one's own was to know all that the other side held dear and to treat every opponent with respect."

"See, that is just what I mean," Fiona said, "you will understand him much better than I ever could. Oh, do say you will, Anne. No one need ever suspect."

"Silly, they would know at once. We are much the same size, but our hair—"

"I am to be veiled, Mama says, because of your papa's so-recent death."

"The veil must come off at the end of the ceremony, however," Anne reminded her. "Such talk is nonsense in any event, for I've no desire to wed Eustace Chisholm. Indeed, I am sure I would murder him at the first opportunity."

"Anne, you wouldn't!"

"I am very sure I would," Anne said.

"You should not call him Eustace, you know. Mama said we must always call him Ashkirk."

"I just always think of him as Eustace Chisholm," Anne said. "You will be Lady Chisholm, after all, not Lady Ashkirk, because your title derives from his knighthood, not from the property. But never mind that now. Just get into bed, love, and enjoy what sleep you can, for tomorrow will be a long day. And do not despair. I have a premonition that everything will turn out well."

Fiona eyed her uncertainly but then, in her usual fashion, submitted to Anne's stronger personality. "If you say it, it must be so," she said, snuggling under her quilt and allowing her cousin to tuck her in.

As Anne bade her goodnight, it occurred to her that were Sir Christopher the man Fiona had begged her to marry, she might not have refused so quickly or so firmly. Her lips burned again at the thought, almost as if he had kissed her again, and chastising herself for thoughts that any right-minded person would roundly condemn, she reminded herself that he was betrothed to Fiona and would make her a much better husband than Eustace would. "And arranging *that*," she told herself, "is where your duty lies, my girl."

Kit's thoughts likewise kept returning to that kiss, but although thinking about Lady Anne Ellyson made his return journey seem swifter than expected, he told himself the impact he experienced was due to nothing more than having suffered through eighteen months without touching or kissing any woman. Still, it was pleasant to think of Lady Anne and to wonder how she had fared with her aunt.

He found Willie and the other men easily despite new clouds that kept drifting across the moon and dimming its light, but it was not easy to persuade Blind Sammy and his lads to seek their prey elsewhere. While waiting impatiently for his return, they had thought only of the cattle at Ellyson Towers. Not until one of the others remembered an estate just over the line, the owner of which nearly always penned his kine in the same place, did Sammy agree to pass up the Towers.

So agreeable did he become thereafter, however, that Kit decided to send an anonymous warning to Lady Anne's steward to take particular care of the Ellyson herds during the next fortnight or two.

Sammy and the others seemed happy enough with the cattle they collected without incident from the English estate, and as Willie had promised, the men were talkative afterward and proved extraordinarily well versed in the news of the area.

"Och, aye," Sammy said when pushed for information about Hawks Rig. "Sir Eustace—or Ashkirk as he's been calling hisself these past six months or so—be a wily fellow and guards his cattle well, just as the auld laird did afore him. He be none so generous as the auld man, though."

"The previous laird was a generous man?" Kit had never thought of his father in such terms.

"Och, aye," Sammy said, shooting him a speculative look. "Ye've the look o' him, ye ken. Ye'll no wander these parts long afore folks take note o' that, lad."

"Do you know who I am, then?" Kit asked, concealing his surprise, for he had not given his name but had depended on their accepting him as Willie's friend.

"Och, aye, 'tis plain ye be the auld laird's son. What I dinna ken is if ye be young Kit rose from the dead or one we ha' never heard tell of afore."

Glancing at Willie, who shrugged, Kit smiled wryly. "I am Kit Chisholm," he admitted, "but I'd as lief you tell no one else just yet about my being here."

"As ye like," Sammy said. "We'll be mum as the fleas on me auld hound."

"Can you tell me just when Eustace claimed the estates?"

"Straightaway, he did," Sammy said. "Arrived less than a sennight after the auld laird's death. Canna blame him, though, if he thought ye was dead."

Kit nodded. "What of our people? Does he look after them well?"

"He does not, for he's turned off most o' them. Some went tae live wi' family, but some ha' disappeared. Sir Eustace ha' brought in his own men, who dinna be from these parts, and they keep themselves tae themselves."

Such news was unsettling. If his uncle had entrenched himself at Hawks Rig and surrounded himself with his own men-at-arms, Kit knew Fin Mackenzie was right. He would have to move cautiously until he knew what he faced.

It occurred to him that he might not enjoy the luxury of choosing his time to confront Eustace. If Lady Anne somehow managed against the odds and before the wedding to persuade her aunt and the unfortunate Fiona that he lived, Eustace would immediately learn the truth, and he should prepare himself for that.

He was wondering if he should just ride to Hawks Rig and have it out with his uncle at once when Sammy, who had turned to speak to one of his men, turned back and said, "D'ye ken that Sir Eustace be about tae wed, sir?"

"Aye, on Friday, I'm told."

"The lad here tells me the wedding's tae be at Mute Hill, and your uncle be there now and might stay if her ladyship invites him. Sir Eustace would liefer eat his beef from someone else's larder any day than from his own."

Frowning, Kit said, "So the wedding will be at Mute Hill?"

"Aye, but their chapel will hold a good many folk for the mass, and the gardens will be open, so anyone who wants a peek at the wee bride can see her."

"I want to be there," Kit said, wondering if he could escape Anne's notice at such an event. "I don't want anyone to recognize me straightaway, however."

"Aye, sure," Sammy said. Even in the dim moonlight, Kit saw the other man's eyebrows rise nearly to his hairline. Clearing his throat, Sammy added, "If that be how it lies, sir, ye'd best attach yourself tae someone who were invited, I'm thinking. Them at Mute Hill be unlikely tae heed an extra gentleman after everyone crowds inside, even one as big as what ye are."

Kit hoped he was right, although he could not imagine whose party he could succeed in joining without comment.

Catriona gave a crow of delight. "Thank the fates," she exclaimed. "Now he will see Mistress Carmichael and fall in love with her."

Maggie grimaced. "Ye're as bad as that Fergus Fishbait."

"I'm no such thing!"

"Well, dinna be so sure o' yourself. What makes ye think he'll love her?"

"You've seen her, Maggie, and you said yourself that all men fall flat for beauty. Fiona is an heiress besides. No mortal man could fail to love her."

"We'll see," Maggie said. "Until then, we must watch them all carefully and try tae determine which is Claud's mortal."

"What be the pair o' ye up tae now?" Fergus demanded, popping into view.

"Ye should be watching your lass," Maggie said.

"I was, but she's sleeping, and ye two be up tae summat, Maggie. I ken ye well, and I could see at once that this lass here wants summat o' young Chisholm."

"I just want him to marry Mistress Carmichael," Catriona said. "That is what Lady Anne wants of him, too, and now he's going to see how beautiful her cousin is, because he means to attend the wedding."

"What good will that do? Mistress Carmichael be marrying his uncle."

"Nay, for when Kit Chisholm sees how beautiful she is, he will tell them he's alive and still betrothed to her."

Fergus looked skeptical. "That be all ye want?"

Catriona glanced at Maggie, who said, "That's only part of it, but I'm no so sure I should tell ye the rest."

When Fergus bristled, Catriona said, "You said yourself that we must tell him, Maggie. We need his help, and as smart as he is, we'll need his ideas, too."

Preening now, Fergus looked expectantly at Maggie.

"Verra well," she said. "What I didna tell ye is that Jonah Bonewits ha' melded Claud wi' a mortal, likely one o' them at Mute Hill or Hawks Rig. We ha' tae decide which one, so we can rescue him."

"How?" Fergus asked, clearly scared again by mention of Jonah.

"We'll seek mortals wi' characteristics o' my Claud," Maggie said.

"But I dinna ken what he's like."

"The first thing ye'd notice is that he falls in lust at the twitch o' a lass's hips," Maggie said with a slanting look at Catriona. "He'll be impulsive, too, and thoughtless, and he willna like following rules. It shouldna be difficult."

"Aye, sure," Catriona said, "but he'll be kind, Claud will, and he'll be frightened, too, and yearning to come home. In sooth, Fergus, we do not know how he'll affect the mortal he's bound to, so we must watch them all and try to learn who has changed recently—women as well as men. Isn't that so, Maggie?"

"Aye, it is," she agreed. "Use your brain, Fergus. Catriona seems tae think ye've got one."

He shot her a resentful look but then smiled at Catriona. "We'll find him," he said confidently. "Ye'll see."

Maggie nodded, satisfied that she and Catriona might make a good team after all. At least, the lass understood how to manage the likes of Fergus Fishbait.

Chapter 7

During the night, the rain began again, pouring down in gusting sheets that slammed against the closed shutters of Anne's windows and created such a din that it awakened her. It was not the first time she had wakened, either, for Sir Toby had come home late, as usual, and had either brought friends as he so often did, or had roused Eustace to join him in his revelry. Anne had not cared which it was. She had just pulled her pillow over her head and ignored the noise.

The rain was a different matter, however, for she could not remember if Fiona's shutters were open or closed when she had visited her earlier. The younger girl frequently slept with her windows unshuttered, and since only the upper halves of the windows at Mute Hill House were glazed, if she had not shuttered the lower halves, rain would be blowing right into her room.

Knowing she would not go back to sleep if she did not check, Anne got up, put on her robe, and slipped her feet into fur-lined mules. Then, her way lit by low-burning night candles set inside porcelain water basins at each end of the gallery, she hurried to Fiona's room, quietly opened the door, and stepped inside.

As she had feared, wind was whipping the curtains about wildly and rain pelted the floor. Shutting the door to keep it from banging, and taking care not to slip in the puddles, she hurried to shutter both windows. Fiona's bed curtains hung half open, and she could see her cousin sleeping peacefully despite the noise of the storm outside or the sudden muting of it when the shutters were closed.

Smiling, Anne crossed the room again and opened the door.

Eustace Chisholm stood just outside it, his hand stretched toward her as if he were reaching for the handle. He stared at her in astonishment. Even with distance still between them, she could smell wine on his breath.

Firmly suppressing both her shock and a flash of anger, she gazed stonily at him, knowing she would be wiser not to say what she was thinking, which was that someone really ought to have drowned the detestable lecher at birth.

He straightened with the abruptness of a man not certain of his control over his movements and snapped, "W-what the devil are you doing here?"

"I came to be sure that Fiona had closed her shutters," she said icily. "She frequently leaves them open."

"Foolishness," he said. " 'Tis raining fit to flood all Scotland, and even on an ordinary night, open windows invite danger. I'll soon put an end to such nonsense, I promise you." When Anne did not reply but continued to gaze directly at him, he said stiffly, "I came to be sure the storm had not frightened her."

"This is her home. She has weathered many storms here."

"Oh, aye, but a man likes to protect his lass, you know," he said. "I expect it is no more than any man about to wed would do."

From the other end of the gallery, startling them both, Malcolm Vole said, "Dear me, what is all this? It seems a very odd time and place for an assignation."

"Mind your tongue, sir," Eustace snapped.

Malcolm stood straighter, his eyes narrowing as he said in his haughty way, "This is a gentleman's house, sir, even though its master has long passed to another world. I want to know what you and Lady Anne mean by this unseemly meeting."

Anne's temper threatened to overcome her, but before it could find purchase, the look of dismay on Eustace's face altered her emotions considerably and nearly served as her undoing instead, for she suddenly had all she could do not to laugh. If humor was inappropriate, it served nonetheless to steady her, for even her foolish aunt would not think for a moment that she had arranged to meet Eustace or that he had arranged such a meeting with her outside Fiona's door. Only Malcolm Vole was fool enough to imagine such an absurdity.

To his credit, Malcolm was clearly unimpressed by Eustace's blustering denial that he had had any such unseemly intention.

"Not that I must answer to you, but my meeting Lady Anne here was entirely unexpected," he said. "As to *my* presence here, I thought I heard Mistress Fiona cry out and feared that the storm must have terrified her."

"Indeed," Malcolm said dryly, raising his eyebrows in patent disbelief.

At that moment, Anne almost liked him.

Eustace did not. "You . . . you are offensive, sirrah," he said.

Anne had had enough. "Now that we both know Fiona is

safe, Sir Eustace, Malcolm will show you back to your chamber. I'll warrant he is up for the same reason that we are—to see that the storm stays outside where it belongs—and the route from this gallery to the one where your room is can easily confuse anyone."

Eustace scowled but did not attempt to argue with her, and as she watched the two men walk to the other end of the gallery, she decided that whatever he had been drinking with Toby had addled his mind. Even the ever-foolish Malcolm would not believe Eustace had heard Fiona cry out from a room at nearly the other end of the house from his own.

Maggie had barely settled in her parlor when Fergus hurried in, his face alight with purpose.

"I ken who be melded wi' your Claud!" he exclaimed.

"Do ye now," she said dryly. "And which one d'ye suspect?"

"It's no suspicion. It be that varlet Eustace Chisholm."

She frowned. "Why d'ye say so?"

"He were trying tae get into Mistress Fiona's chamber, that's why. Me lass had gone in tae shut the windows, and she walked out bang into the wicked man."

Maggie frowned harder. "Are ye saying ye suspect Eustace because he lusts after Mistress Fiona?"

"Well, ye said Claud falls in lust at the twitch o' a skirt," Fergus said defensively. "That be just what Eustace ha' done."

"Ye'd best think again," Maggie advised him. "Claud does fall in lust more than be good for him, but he'd no trouble a lass who didna want him, and sithee, Eustace ha' been hot for Mistress Fiona for more than a year now."

"Aye, but Eustace flirts wi' anyone in a skirt, and I wager

he'd take any willing lass tae his bed," Fergus said. "So I still think he would be the most likely one for Jonah Bonewits tae meld wi' your Claud. 'Twould be gey smarter than putting him wi' someone who'd seem suddenly different tae everyone."

"Ye've a point there," she said. "Still, it willna do tae leap tae conclusions wi'out more proof, so we'll continue tae keep our eyes skinned, me lad."

"Well, I'm sure it's Eustace, and I mean tae watch him," Fergus said.

"Ye do that," Maggie said kindly, ushering him out.

She returned thoughtfully to the fire, which had died down a little, and flicked a finger to refresh it.

"That lad's not even warm, Mag."

Whirling so quickly she felt dizzy, she found Jonah behind her, leaning at his ease against nothing in particular, arms folded across his chest, his eyes twinkling mischievously. She had not been aware of his presence before he spoke, which meant that Fergus's suggestion had distracted her more than she had realized.

"What d'ye want now?" she demanded, exerting effort to conceal her surprise.

"Why, I just wanted to hear what the lad had to say," he said innocently.

"Ye're tae leave him be, Jonah," she said. "He told me what ye said ye'd do an he vexed ye again. Ye're tae leave his head where it belongs."

Jonah shrugged. "Ye should ha' thought more on this matter, Mag."

She looked him in the eye but said nothing.

"Apparently there be one detail ye've forgotten," he said. When he did not continue, she knew he was baiting her, but curiosity defeated her determination to remain silent. "What?" she demanded.

He rolled his eyes, and their depths changed to myriad, multicolored rings that resembled spinning archery butts.

Holding her tongue firmly behind her teeth, she waited, because just as he had known she could not resist asking, she knew that he was dying to tell her.

Softly, he said, "What'll ye do if ye do find him?"

"I'll bring him home, o' course."

"How?"

She hesitated. He had warned her that his plan contained traps, but she had concentrated on finding Claud, and now that she was certain of his approximate location, she knew it could be only a matter of time before she determined which mortal contained his entity. Then she would . . .

Her imagination lurched. If she knew how Jonah had created his so-called meld, she could undo it easily, but she had no idea what he had done.

"Ye see, lass. Like I said, ye should ha' thought more."

"What ye ha' done, I can undo," she said confidently.

"Aye, perhaps, but it willna be so easy as that."

Something in his tone warned her that he intended his words to have more than their usual meaning.

Frowning, she said, "Ye've done summat awful then. What is it?"

"I doubt it will trouble ye, Mag, as brilliant o' mind as ye be, but ye'll want to get it right the first time. Ye see, I've put a wee spell on him to make the game more interesting."

"What sort of a spell?" she asked, his confident air unsettling her at last.

"Why, 'tis the merest thing, lass. To free Claud, ye must kill the mortal I melded him to."

This was it, then, the moment toward which he had so deviously drawn her. If she killed a mortal, any mortal, she would sacrifice much more than her place in the High Circle. She would sacrifice, for all time, her membership in the Secret Clan, and that, in turn, would expose her to be swept up by the Evil Host.

Members of the much-dreaded Host were spirits of mortals and others who had died sinfully. They flew about in great clouds like starlings, sweeping up folks who had betrayed their own or broken the laws of the Clan. The Host forced those poor souls to fly with them to atone for their sins, and since only the Host could decide how much time was required to satisfy their requirements, that effectively meant forever. Maggie knew of no one who had won free of their control.

"What if someone else kills the mortal or the mortal dies a natural death?"

"Then Claud will die, too, I'm afraid. There's a wee bit more," he added.

She glowered, pressing her lips tightly together.

"If ye kill the wrong mortal, ye'll still free the lad from his bond, but since his freedom will come at such cost, both o' ye will ha' to fly wi' the Host."

Maggie winced. Claud's greatest dread had always been that the Evil Host would take him. Jonah knew that as well as she did. What a dilemma he had set her!

But when she opened her mouth to tell him what she thought of him, he vanished in a whirl of multicolored sparks.

As Anne walked back to her bedchamber, she wondered just what Eustace had intended to do in Fiona's room. Nothing she could imagine made her think anything but the worst of him. He was truly a despicable man.

However, within moments, her thoughts had returned to the intriguing Sir Christopher. Even as she decided that she must forget how intriguing he was and do all she could to end his horrid uncle's hopes of marrying Fiona, the memory of Sir Christopher's parting words to her in the yard struck hard.

No man would lie about having been condemned to a prison ship for life, so what had he done to deserve such a fate, she wondered, and had he escaped or been somehow set free? And what was she thinking, to want him to marry Fiona?

Even as these thoughts passed through her mind, however, she rejected them. Although she had barely met him, had barely been able to make out his features in the dim light of the courtyard, and knew little more of him than what he had told her, she had liked his infectious chuckle and his warm, deeply vibrant voice. And she certainly could not deny, to herself at least, that she had also enjoyed that amazing, too-brief kiss. Every instinct told her she could trust him, and she had long since learned to trust her instincts.

By the time she finally fell asleep, she had come to no understandable or logical conclusion, nor did any occur to her upon waking the next morning, but her resolve to put a spoke in the dreadful Eustace's wheel had definitely intensified.

When Peg bustled in to help her dress, Anne said, "Have we any additional visitors in the house today?"

Taking her meaning easily, Peg said with a grimace, "Nay, thank heaven, we have not. Sir Toby came home late with a couple of new friends, to be sure, but that Ashkirk were still up, and he sent them packing. One o' the lads that looked after them told me Ashkirk said Sir Toby were a fool to think Lady Carmichael would accept any such drunken louts as eligible suitors. But he and Sir Toby were both laughing, the lad said, and then they sat down and played Cent at a penny a game together whilst they drank two whole pitchers of ale."

Anne's disgust matched Peg's, but she was glad that on the day before Fiona's wedding they would not have to deal with men of the sort that Toby usually brought home with him. Although he said his purpose was to find a new husband for his niece, one had only to witness Olivia's reaction to the would-be suitors, and Toby's glee, to understand that his behavior reflected only his devotion to mischief.

As soon as Anne had broken her fast, she went in search of Fiona, knowing that Olivia would demand their presence soon and would have lists of tasks for each of them to perform before day's end.

Fiona was awake but still in bed, evidently having no interest in rising or dressing. Her woman greeted Anne's entrance with relief.

"I fear she may be ailing, m'lady," she said in an undertone.

Casting an experienced eye over her cousin, Anne replied, "She is exhausted, Molly, that's all. 'Tis my belief that she should rest again today, but I suspect my aunt will disagree with me."

"Her ladyship has already sent for her," the maidservant said.

Anne nodded. "Leave her to me, then. I'll send for you if I need you."

"Thank you, my lady. I'll just be in the next room, where

we be packing up her things tae send along wi' her tae Hawks Rig."

As soon as Molly had gone, Anne turned her attention to the bed, where Fiona lay with the covers pulled up to her chin and her eyes squeezed shut.

"It is of no use to pretend to be sleeping," Anne told her. "I know you are awake, and if you do not want to get up, I don't blame you, but you must if you are to get any breakfast."

"I don't want any," Fiona said weakly. "I'm dreadfully ill, Anne. I'm sure I must be coming down with that awful fever everyone died from."

"No one hereabouts has contracted the fever for weeks now," Anne said as she pulled the bed curtains all the way open. Gray light came through the windows, for although the night's storm had passed, a light drizzle continued.

Fiona lay where she was, eyes still shut.

"Come now," Anne said more firmly. "Your mother will descend upon us the moment anyone suggests to her that you are ailing, and I am sure you want to put some clothes on and fortify yourself with food before you must see her."

Fiona's complexion paled, and her eyes opened, but the look she cast Anne was resentful. "What would you do in my position, Anne?"

"I would send Eustace to the right about and ask Aunt Olivia to find me another suitor."

"You make it sound so easy, but you know that it is not, for whenever I try to behave as you say you would, I come to grief. Indeed, if I am not sick now, I can promise you I soon would be if I were to attempt such a daft course."

Anne had seen it happen before, whenever her cousin had tried to run contrary to Olivia's wishes, so she knew that

Fiona did not exaggerate. Nevertheless, she wished her cousin were stouter of heart.

Knowing that nothing else would stir her from the bed, she said, "Then you had better get up, love, and prepare to obey her. Molly said she has already sent for you, so you will have to see her soon."

Sighing, Fiona sat up and threw back the covers.

As Anne helped her dress in the simple but elegant lavender gown Molly had laid out for her, the younger girl muttered, "I should just run away. I could enter a nunnery. Indeed, that is exactly what I should do."

Anne tried and failed to stifle a bubble of laughter. "Yes, indeed, that would be the very thing," she said when Fiona eyed her resentfully. "Certainly it would put a stop to the wedding."

"Well, it would."

"You precious ninny, you are an heiress of the first order, so although I warrant that any nunnery would be elated to accept you, they can do so only if your trustees will agree to hand your inheritance over with you. And since your mother counts herself as one of your trustees, that will not happen."

"Are you plagued with trustees, too, Anne?" Fiona asked, sitting on a stool so Anne could brush her hair.

"Well, I've got two of them, if that's what you mean, but they don't plague me," Anne said as she undid Fiona's golden plaits and began to brush them out. "One is Ben Scott, my father's man of affairs in Hawick, and the other is the new Earl of Armadale, who has not deigned to recognize my existence since I wrote to inform him of my father's death. In any event, Mr. Scott told me that most decisions require only to be authorized by one of them, and he never tries to act the guardian over me. He knows me for a sensible lass, he said, so I've only to let him know what I want and he will see to it. I don't imagine the new earl will make difficulties either when he finally wakes up to his position."

"But you must be as much of an heiress as I am," Fiona said. "Surely your father had as much wealth as mine, or even more."

"I don't know if he did or not, but it does not affect me," Anne said, setting down the brush to braid her cousin's hair into a single thick plait that she could then wind into a knot at the nape of Fiona's neck. "Most of what my father left automatically goes to his successor, you see, along with his titles and all the Armadale estates. I inherit only Ellyson Towers, which was part of my mother's marriage settlement, along with sufficient income to maintain the place and myself. Mr. Scott told me the sum is sufficient to keep me in the style to which I am accustomed, but he clearly expects me to assure my future by marrying well."

"And so you shall, I'm sure," Fiona said, inspecting herself in the glass Anne held. "As soon as I am married, Mother said she would see to finding a husband for you. She said that your being an earl's daughter would make the task an easy one."

"With all due respect to your mother, who is an earl's daughter herself, if one's father is deceased and the new earl barely known to one, one must lose a certain amount of desirability," Anne said, exerting herself to conceal her dislike of the subject. "Moreover," she added in what she felt was an understatement, "I doubt that your mother's taste would suit me. Are you ready to go downstairs?"

"I suppose."

Anne said no more, grateful only to have stirred her cousin to dress and agree to break her fast. Accompanying her down to the hall, she sat beside her at the high table and watched as Fiona examined a basket full of manchet loaves and the soft white rolls known locally as baps. Selecting a bap, she spread it with honey, and nibbled daintily. When she called for claret to drink, Anne signed to the lackey to water it well.

Fiona glanced at her wryly. "Are you afraid I might grow tipsy, Anne?"

"I'm just thinking it would be as well to give Aunt Olivia no cause to complain about either of us today," Anne said.

Her hope was dashed within moments of entering her ladyship's bower, however, for her aunt took instant exception to Fiona's attire.

"You must change that drab gown before you greet Ashkirk, Fiona," she said as she gestured to Malcolm Vole to refill the goblet on the table beside her. "You look pale and insipid today and should try more to show off your beauty."

Seeing tears well in her cousin's eyes, and annoyed that Olivia would take her to task in front of Malcolm, Anne attempted a diversion, saying, "Fiona is still very tired, Aunt Olivia. Surely, she can change her gown later."

"I believe I am the best judge of what suits my daughter, Anne. In any event, it is not your position to offer me advice."

Stiffening but managing to speak calmly, Anne said, "If I sometimes overstep my place, madam, 'tis doubtless because I have acquired a habit of command that is difficult to set aside. My mother and I, like most Border women, often found ourselves alone at the Towers whilst my father and brother were away, and thus I am perhaps too well accustomed to managing a large household." She did not add that her ladyship's lassitude was often the force that drove her.

Olivia fanned herself more energetically than usual as she

said, "I vow, I do not know how I shall contrive to find you a husband if you display such a strong-minded attitude to every gentleman I produce, but I shall do my best as soon as my dearest Fiona is off my hands. Perhaps Ashkirk will have someone in mind. Pray, Malcolm, go and see if he requires anything," she added, turning her head toward him and thus sparing Anne the need to reply, which was just as well.

Fairly choking as she sought to repress a declaration that no one Eustace Chisholm suggested could possibly find favor with her, she fought to recover her calm as the steward left the room to attend to his mistress's request.

Olivia watched him go with a fond smile. "If only Malcolm were of suitable breeding and I not plunged so deeply into mourning," she said with a light laugh before the door had quite shut behind him, "I declare, I would be tempted to marry him, for he is exactly the sort of man who would suit me best as a husband."

"Mama, you don't mean that; you couldn't!" Fiona said with a shudder.

Anne watched as the door, which had stopped moving, shut silently behind the steward. Then she said, "Malcolm serves you well, madam, to be sure."

"Yes, he does," Olivia said. "And who knows how custom will have changed by the time I emerge from my mourning—if ever I can bring myself to do so!"

Fiona stared, but Anne diverted both women's thoughts by asking what, if anything, Fiona wanted her to do for her before they returned to the hall for dinner.

"You should more properly ask me, my dear," Olivia said, just as Anne had expected her to. "If Fiona has broken her fast, she should hold herself ready to take a turn in the garden with Ashkirk, and perhaps if she does not wish to change her dress yet, she can wear that gray cloak with the fur trim that becomes her so well."

Anne glanced out the nearest window at the gardens beyond. The drizzle had stopped, but puddles lay everywhere and the shrubbery glistened damply.

"It is too wet to walk in the garden," Fiona said.

"Then you may stroll along the hall gallery with him," Olivia said, adding with narrowing eyes, "Pray, do not cry again, Fiona. You will find that gentlemen dislike women who constantly weep at them."

Anne put an arm around Fiona's shoulders. "I'll help her change, madam."

"Yes, do."

Practically pushing her cousin from the room, Anne asked a maidservant emptying flowers from an urn to take Fiona to her room. "I'll come up soon, love," she said. "Just rest until I do."

"Where are you going?"

"Back to speak to your mother again before her Moira returns or Eustace appears. I want to see if I can persuade her to let you rest a bit more today."

"Oh, if only you can," Fiona said.

Anne returned to her ladyship's bower, where Olivia had drawn her tambour frame near and was examining the progress she had made on her new design.

"I beg your pardon for disturbing you again," Anne said when Olivia looked up, "but I feel obliged to point out to you that if you truly want Fiona to marry Eustace tomorrow, you would be wiser to let her avoid him today."

"You are being impertinent, Anne. Fiona will do as I bid her."

"Yes, generally she will," Anne agreed. "However, she is

beside herself with fear of that awful man, and I believe that if you push her to accept more of his lecherous attentions before the wedding, she will faint at the altar or find some other means to avoid her part in the ceremony."

Olivia frowned. "Is she really so terrified of him?"

"You must know she is. I believe it is cruel to make her marry him."

"Yes, well, your beliefs do not hold sway here, fortunately. Fiona is a foolish girl without enough sense to know what is best for her. Once she is married to Ashkirk, she will quickly lose her fear, as I know from my own experience. It may surprise you to learn that I was not overjoyed to marry Sir Stephen. I did so only in obedience to my father's will, but you certainly know by now how very deeply I came to care for him."

"Yes, but my uncle was a kind man," Anne said. "Eustace is not."

"You should more properly call him Ashkirk, as I am sure I have reminded you daily," Olivia said. "He is every inch a gentleman, and even if he should prove otherwise, do not forget that he controls the Chisholm power in the Borders. As Lady Chisholm, my Fiona will attend court and be known as a woman of import."

"Aye, if she marries the Laird of Ashkirk, she will be all of that," Anne said, deciding to leave it at that in order to persuade Olivia that Fiona needed to rest.

Matters having reached a point where Maggie suspected she would soon have to take a more active role, she decided to see for herself how carefully the others were watching their charges, and popped into Mute Hill House in time to see Fergus flick a hand toward Lady Carmichael.

"What are ye doing?" Maggie demanded.

He turned with a start, the picture of guilt. "Dinna sneak up on a body like that," he exclaimed. "Ye could cause damage tae me spell that way."

"I'll damage *ye*, ye forgetful maw-worm. Answer me question."

Grimacing, he said, "Lady Anne wants her cousin tae rest. That's all."

"Her cousin isna wi' them," Maggie pointed out.

"Nay, she's upstairs, but me lass were trying tae persuade her mam tae let her sleep. I just helped her a wee bit is all. Ye'll no tell me I canna do that much."

"Nay," Maggie said. "I've a notion we'll all be doing things we'd as lief no ha' tae explain tae the Circle afore this business be done. Where's Catriona?"

Fergus shrugged. "Wi' her charge, I expect."

Maggie nodded. She would see how Catriona was faring, tell her about Jonah's latest revelation, and then decide how much Fergus needed to know.

But first, she would seek a private moment with Anne Ellyson.

Having at last persuaded Olivia that her plan for Fiona could only benefit by keeping her separated from Eustace as long as possible, Anne went upstairs to find her cousin fast asleep and Molly watching over her.

"Keep everyone else out of here, Molly," Anne commanded. "If her ladyship sends someone to demand Mistress Fiona's presence for the noon meal, tell them she puked up her breakfast and looks like puking again at the least mention of food. That should keep them at bay until suppertime. I've seen enough of Sir Toby to be sure he will have a plan to entertain our chief guest afterward, so I warrant Mistress Fiona will come to no grief then by putting in her usual appearance at supper."

Anne was still worried about what Olivia would do, but at noon she learned her worries were groundless.

Olivia scarcely waited for her carver to carve the joint before explaining to Eustace that Fiona was indisposed. "Sheer exhaustion, through wanting everything to be perfect tomorrow," she said, "but I promise you, sir, her usual vivacity will be completely restored by then."

"Faith," he said, "does she mean to sleep all afternoon, too?"

Anne said with forced lightness, "If not to sleep, sir, at least to rest. She is worn to the bone, and we do not want her to become ill. Only think how shocking it would be if she were to fall ill at the altar before she takes her vows."

"Aye, well, that would not do, I agree," he said, eyeing her narrowly. "Are you sure she means to present herself at the altar?"

"Oh, yes," Anne said in the same light tone before Olivia could speak. "I will see to that myself, sir, I promise you. Fiona is very obedient, as you know. As long as she is properly rested, she will carry off her part without a single error."

And, Anne thought, *with luck, she will walk away with a more desirable husband.* She wished she could be certain that Sir Christopher would be there, but if he did not show up at the wedding, perhaps another solution would occur to her.

Chapter 8

Arising early the next morning, and knowing she probably would not have another moment to herself for the rest of the day, Anne dressed quickly and decided to take the roll Peg had brought her outside to eat in the garden. She had no wish to enter the hall, where servants were setting up tables for the meal they would serve to the bride and groom and their honored guests after the ceremony.

The high table would provide food now for any family member or guest who wanted to break his or her fast. However, in general, the several guests that had arrived the previous afternoon and slept at Mute Hill House would take small, cold repasts in their bedchambers. Thus, they would not interfere with Malcolm's preparations for the wedding feast. Both bride and bridegroom would remain in their respective bedchambers until they set out for the chapel.

Anne used the service stairway near Lady Carmichael's bedchamber, hurrying quietly past it in case her aunt was still inside. She did not want to be summoned yet, for she knew Olivia would have tasks for her to perform, and before the bustle began, she wanted time to think.

Outside, despite days of intermittent rain and a sky the

previous evening full of threatening thunderclouds, Fiona's wedding morning had dawned golden with sunlight. The air smelled fresh from the rain, and the brook that divided the garden lengthwise in two splashed through it in merry spate.

As she followed the path to the narrow, arched stone bridge that spanned the brook, Anne saw several gardeners doing last-minute pruning and trimming so no guest should think the gardens untidy.

Taking the first fork that led away from the chapel in the hope of finding privacy, however brief, she drew a deep breath and tried to focus her thoughts on finding a way to help Fiona avoid marrying Eustace if Sir Christopher did not come. The nearer the ceremony drew, the more difficult such an undertaking would be, because interference of any sort would create uproar. Interference by Lady Anne Ellyson would likely launch the matter into the annals of local history.

"Why would it be so bad if ye believe your cousin shouldna marry the man?"

Stopping short, Anne looked around for the source of the unfamiliar voice.

"Here I be, up here."

Looking up, she saw a plump little countrywoman in a long gray cloak over a green dress, perched on the lowest branch of a tall beech tree. "Faith, who are you, and how did you get up there?"

"Me name's Maggie Malloch," she said, "and I'm up here because I didna think it wise tae pop up right in front o' ye. I can come down closer if ye'd like."

"Yes, please, but do be caref—"

She broke off when the woman vanished.

"Will this do?"

The voice came from behind her, but whirling, she saw no one.

"Here, on the bush!" A slight movement drew her gaze to a nearby rosebush, where the little woman—much, much smaller now—waved at her from a leaf upon which she sat in apparent comfort, a bit lower than Anne's eye level.

Anne gasped. "What did you—? That is, how . . . ?"

"This be much better, dinna ye agree?"

The hairs on the back of Anne's neck prickled, and her mouth felt dry. "What manner of creature are you?" she demanded. "Am I still asleep and only dreaming that it is morning already?"

"Ye're no dreaming, and ye ken verra well what I am if ye'll but let yourself believe it, but ye've nae call tae fret, for I dinna mean tae meddle. However, I were that curious tae hear why ye'd fret about doing what ye believe tae be right."

"Are you one of the wee folk?"

"I am, but we'll no talk about me. We'll discuss your troubles instead."

"But you must somehow have intercepted my thoughts, for I am quite sure I did not speak them aloud."

"Whisst now, dinna prattle. Tell me why ye canna interfere."

"Because, as horrid as the man is, one simply doesn't," Anne said. "I suppose it would do no good to point out that this is none of your business."

Maggie dismissed that with a gesture. "Chatting about a dilemma often helps tae resolve it," she said. "D'ye fear I'll tell others what ye say tae me?"

"No, I cannot imagine that you would," Anne said, relaxing. She had never seen one of the wee folk before and had thought them creatures of folklore, but for no discernible reason, she decided she could trust Maggie Malloch. "What made you ask me about it if you can simply listen in on my thoughts?" she asked.

"I wanted a dialogue, o' course. Moreover, it takes much more energy tae read thoughts, and some mortals get flustered and upset if I try tae carry on me dialogue in their heads."

"Can you do that?"

"Oh, aye, but it generally counts as interfering."

"And you are not interfering now," Anne said dryly.

"Nay," Maggie said, chuckling.

"I see. Well, it might help me to talk about it. Which was the last of my thoughts that you heard, or read, or whatever it is that you do?"

"That interfering would launch the affair into the annals o' local history. What d'ye mean, it isna done?"

"It just isn't. People don't go about interfering in other people's marriage plans. I mean, parents do, of course, because they arrange them, but once they are arranged, one doesn't try to overset them. And it would be worse if I did it—"

"Because ye're *Lady* Anne?"

"Well, that would draw attention, but also, at least a few people would say I was doing it out of jealousy or because I want to marry Eustace myself."

"But ye dinna want that."

"Of course not. He's a dreadful, lecherous creature, and one moreover who probably wouldn't be above killing me for speaking up. Even if he didn't, my aunt very well might. She would certainly insist that I leave Mute Hill House. Not that that would be any great penance." She hesitated, hearing the bitter echo of her words. "I should not have said that, but— Look here, may we walk on? Someone is bound to see me and wonder why I'm standing here talking to a rose-bush."

"Aye, sure," Maggie said, plucking a bit of thistledown from a nearby leaf and flicking it into the air.

To Anne's astonishment, the thistledown grew to the size of her fist, floated a few feet in front of her, and suddenly Maggie appeared on it, sitting comfortably upright in the down as if it were a large cushion, her booted feet crossed neatly at the ankles, her plump hands folded in her lap.

"Now ye can walk, and we'll talk at the same time," Maggie said.

Fascinated, Anne said, "Your voice stays the same, no matter how large or small you are."

"Aye, why would it not? Now, go on, lass, and dinna fret about what ye say. Ye're just speaking your thoughts, and I ken well that ye'd like tae return tae your own home, King Henry or nae King Henry. 'Tis only natural, that."

"You do understand."

"I know ye think that at best ye've few choices in this matter, and that as far as ye can tell, nary a one o' them be guaranteed tae do aught but make a scandal."

"If I tell my aunt that I met Sir Christopher— I expect you know about that, too. You seem to know all about me."

"I've only just begun tae watch ye, but I ken more than ye might think. Ye seemed right taken wi' the man, though."

"Oh, no, not real—"

She broke off when Maggie shook her head with a knowing smile.

Anne frowned. It was disconcerting to think one was being watched, and she certainly did not want to think about her own reaction to Sir Christopher, as strong as it had been.

But even as the thought crossed her mind, it vanished and a warming sense of comfort replaced it. "Did you do that just then?" she demanded.

"Aye," Maggie replied. "Ye've nae need tae worry. We'll do ye nae harm."

"We?"

"I'm no alone, mistress, but sithee, few o' me clan can make themselves seen tae mortals that dinna possess the gift o' second sight."

"Can the others with you also read my thoughts?"

"Nay, verra few can do that. Anyone in the Clan can tell how ye're feeling or the mood ye're in, but it takes powers near as great as mine tae ken your thoughts."

"I see," Anne said, although even that much was disconcerting.

"As tae the matter at hand," Maggie said, "ye fear your aunt willna believe ye if ye tell her Sir Christopher be alive, because she willna *wish* tae believe ye."

"She'll say that if he were alive, he would have presented himself at Hawks Rig, if not at Mute Hill House, as soon as he learned of his father's death."

"And ye'd ha' tae explain tae her why he didna do that."

Anne's imagination boggled at producing the scene that would follow any such explanation.

"Ye fear she'd prefer tae marry her daughter tae the fiendish Eustace even if he's no the rightful Ashkirk than tae marry her wi' a man who'd been condemned tae life aboard a prison ship," Maggie said, easily following her thoughts.

Anne regarded her narrowly. "What did he do to deserve such a sentence?"

"Nay, I canna tell ye that," Maggie said. "Giving ye that information would be interfering for sure."

"But I do not know how you can avoid that," Anne said. "Is it not interfering merely to reveal your interest?"

"Aye, it is, so mayhap I should go."

"No, not yet!" Thinking swiftly, Anne said, "Can you at least tell me what a man *might* do to deserve such a fate? I've thought of little else since I met him, and I cannot imagine him committing a crime evil enough to warrant such punishment."

The thistledown shot into the air and drifted down again. When it had returned to its former place, Maggie said evenly, "Dinna ask such questions, for I canna answer them. Nor can I tell ye if the lad will be at yon wedding, because I canna predict the future. I only wish I could," she added fervently.

Anne sighed. "If you cannot help me, I am at a standstill, for they would lock me up if they so much as suspected I might try to stop the wedding. Even if I wait to speak when the parson asks if anyone knows why they should not marry, Eustace or Olivia need only order me taken away, and the parson would just continue."

"Could they get away wi' that?"

"Yes, because most of the guests are their friends, not mine, and many are powerful men who would be happy to restrain a young woman who had clearly lost her senses. For so it would seem if I were to make such a spectacle of myself."

"Who will be there?"

Anne shrugged. "Numerous Armstrongs, of course, because as you must know, that wild tribe counts the Carmichaels as their allies and has few scruples about anything. They have only to desire a thing to take it, only to disapprove of someone to destroy him. Scott of Buccleuch and

Branxholme will be there, too, because his first wife was a Carmichael."

"But she's dead, and his second wife be nae connection."

"If you know this already—"

"Pish tush, ye're the one wha' needs tae think out loud. Go on."

"Well, they say that Buccleuch's second wife, Janet Kerr of Ferniehirst, is proving tiresome and that he already has his eye on a new one called Janet Beaton. He would marry her instantly, they say, if he could arrange to do it legally."

"Aye, and he's gey powerful, is Buccleuch."

"Yes, and like the Armstrongs, he would side with Eustace and Olivia. The present Lady Scott, on the other hand, might prove an ally for Fiona."

"A verra dubious one," Maggie pointed out.

With a sigh, Anne said, "Even if anyone should listen to me, no one would act in opposition to Aunt Olivia's wishes, certainly not quickly enough to stop the wedding. The ceremony is quite short, you know."

"Aye, ye've the right of it, I'm thinking, so it all depends on Sir Christopher—if he shows himself and if he chooses to speak up."

"Can you not talk to him as you have to me?" Anne asked. But a gardener came around a turn in the path just then, and Maggie Malloch vanished. The bit of thistledown, reduced again to its normal size, drifted slowly to the ground.

"What d'ye think ye were a-doing, talking tae me lass like that?" Fergus demanded the instant Maggie had removed herself from Anne's view.

Maggie had been aware of his presence while they

talked, because he had been following Anne as usual, and had been bouncing up and down and flitting around, issuing protest after protest, all of which Maggie had easily ignored.

Now, however, she turned on him angrily. "I dinna answer tae ye, Fergus Fishbait, so if ye want tae continue speaking in me presence, have a care!"

"But ye've nae business—"

When his words ended abruptly and involuntarily in a high-pitched squeak, his eyes widened in horror, but Maggie said grimly, "Now mayhap ye'll listen politely whilst I explain. Will ye listen, Fergus? Quietly?"

He nodded vigorously.

"I care only about finding my Claud," she reminded him. "And though I ha' sensed his presence in the area, I canna find him. We can watch these mortals all we like, but we'll no learn enough just by watching, and since neither ye nor Catriona can make yourselves visible tae them— Here now, show yourself properly!"

He was nodding and shaking his head, so agitated that his figure kept disappearing. Hastily, he reformed himself but pointed to his mouth, his expression pleading with her to let him speak.

She flicked a finger. "D'ye mean ye can make them see ye?"

"I can," he said, gasping.

"Och, aye, I remember now that ye bring it tae mind that the Ellyllon can show themselves occasionally, but ye canna make them hear ye speak, can ye?"

Fergus shook his head.

"Well, that may prove useful in the end, but I'm thinking I may want tae talk tae more mortals, too. We'll see. I've fixed it so the lass will soon forget our talk, and I'm sure she kens nowt tae help us learn which one be melded wi' Claud."

"I tell ye, that be Eustace Chisholm," Fergus insisted.

"Ah, bah," Maggie snapped, silencing him again. But as she turned away, she remembered that Jonah's last appearance had been just after Fergus had first made his suspicion of Eustace known to her. And at the time, Jonah had made a point of telling her that Fergus was not even warm. That, in itself, made her wonder if she might be wrong to dismiss Fergus's suspicion.

Wondering if the little woman had ever been there at all or had simply been a figment of exhaustion and an overactive imagination, Anne walked back to the house, deciding unhappily that she would have to hold her tongue if Sir Christopher did not attend the wedding. Only then did she realize that she had not told him where the ceremony was to be held. Common sense stirred then, however. He would have no difficulty discovering that for himself if he desired to know.

In any event, she had tarried long enough, for Fiona would surely be awake, and would have begun the ritualistic dressing that tradition demanded of all brides. Having promised to help, Anne went at once to her cousin's room, where she found something less than the mad bustle she had expected to find.

At first, she saw only Molly, smoothing out Fiona's sky-blue wedding dress, which lay on the high bed, because Fiona was having her bath behind a screen near the fireplace. Olivia had not yet arrived.

"Her ladyship sent word to advise her before Mistress

Fiona begins to dress," Molly said when Anne asked about her absence.

"I see," Anne said, moving toward the bed.

From there, she could see Fiona in a deep, high-backed tub by the hearth where a fire fended off the chill and the screen shielded her from anyone in the doorway. Her golden hair was piled in soft curls atop her head, and the skin of her shoulders and breasts glowed rosily from the hot water. Thanks to the French soap she used and a bouquet of pink and white asters and pale blue rosemary in a jug on the table near the bed, the air was redolent of flowers.

Gesturing at the bouquet, Anne said, "You must have been up before I was, Fiona, if you gathered those for your bridal bouquet and chaplet."

"I didn't," Fiona said. "I did not want to chance meeting *him* in the garden with no one else about, so Molly picked them and brought them to me. I did help to arrange them though," she added.

Anne did not have to ask what she meant by "him," nor was she superstitious enough to believe that Fiona's failure to gather her own flowers would result in bad luck. Indeed, she believed that, unlikely as it was that Eustace would have risen any earlier than necessary, the only bad luck for Fiona would have been if she had gone outside alone to find her flowers and had found him instead.

To her relief, her cousin did not seem inclined to further complaint, apparently taking interest only in her bath. Anne had feared another scene such as the one the previous day, and since she had thought of no way yet to stop the wedding, such a discussion would have been both fruitless and painful.

When Fiona said no more, Anne went quietly back to Molly. "Should you not be helping her?" she asked.

Molly shook her head. "She's hardly spoken a word since she got up, but she did say she didna want me tae fuss over her. There will be enough o' that presently, she said."

"Yes, for more guests will be arriving soon," Anne said. "Doubtless, many of the women want to take a part in her dressing."

"Aye, and her ladyship must be growing impatient," Molly said. "The ceremony willna begin for yet another two hours, but folks will fill the gardens near the chapel long afore that, I'd wager, tae watch for the bridal procession."

"Then we should get her out of that tub," Anne said. "She will be more comfortable in her shift than if they descend on her whilst she is still bathing."

"I can hear you, you know," Fiona said from behind the screen.

Anne smiled as she said, "Then it is fortunate we said nothing we did not want you to overhear. Are you ready for your towel?"

"Yes, please."

"I'll take it to her, Molly. Find someone to send to her ladyship, or go yourself, and tell her that Mistress Fiona will be ready in a few minutes to dress."

Handing Fiona a large towel and then her soft cambric shift, Anne pulled a back stool near the fire and gestured for her to sit on it so she could brush her hair. However, she had done no more than remove the pins that held the soft curls atop Fiona's head when the door opened and Olivia entered. Four other women followed her, chatting and laughing. They greeted Fiona and Anne cheerfully, but Olivia stopped a short distance from the door and looked critically around.

Instead of the stark black or deep purple she usually wore, she had framed her still lovely face with a white barbe and soft folds of a long, white silk veil that draped down her back to within a foot of the floor. To be sure, her ladyship's gown was black, albeit fashionably cut, laden with expensive black Naples lace, and included a gold-link belt hung with golden trifles and a jeweled pomander.

Hoping to divert her from words of censure clearly hovering on her tongue, Anne said mildly, "I see you have decided to ease your mourning, madam."

"Certainly not," Olivia said. "Not on this of all occasions, when memories of my beloved Stephen fill every chamber. White is the color French royalty wears for mourning, you see, so it is entirely appropriate for an earl's daughter."

"It is a most elegant dress," Anne agreed.

"Why have you not sent for someone to remove that tub?" Olivia asked. "It is very much in the way."

"Molly will see to it," Anne said, continuing to brush Fiona's hair.

"But you are not dressed, Anne. How will you be ready in time? I expected you to attend to yourself before you came to help Fiona."

Sensing Fiona's increasing tension, Anne rested her free hand on her cousin's shoulder as she said with a smile to Olivia, "I hate to think what you would have said had I spilled something on my gown or wrinkled it whilst helping her."

"Oh, yes, only think how tedious that would be," one of the other women said. "So likely, too, and doubtless a great stain right in the middle of the bodice."

Glancing toward the voice, Anne recognized Lady Scott. She had met her before, more than once, because her husband, Buccleuch, was one of several powerful Border lords whom Armadale had exerted himself to know.

Changing the subject, Olivia drew a pair of gloves from a hidden pocket in her dress, saying abruptly, "Ashkirk has sent you these as his gift for your wedding, Fiona. Just look at the exquisite embroidery."

The other women gathered around to admire the gloves, and although Fiona showed small interest in them, she responded politely to one comment and then to another. Seeing her thus satisfactorily occupied, Anne left her to the women's care and hurried to her own bedchamber.

Peg Elliot was waiting, and with her help, Anne quickly changed from her ordinary day gown to a splendid one of rich emerald green velvet trimmed with gold-embroidered black bands. The black French hood that concealed her hair was similarly adorned, but its veil at the back softened its severity, being fashioned from the same green velvet as her gown. Bands and hood declared that she still grieved for her father, but Armadale had not approved of long mourning. In fact, he had not approved of mourning at all, saying it was just another fiendish whim of the Roman Kirk, in that august body's determination to control every aspect of people's lives.

"That gown becomes ye well, Mistress Anne," Peg said. "The green makes your eyes look green, too."

"I am glad you approve," Anne said with a chuckle, "but you are the only one who will see me, Peg. Everyone else will have eyes only for my cousin, which is exactly as it should be."

"Aye, she's a lovely lass, is Mistress Fiona, and will make a splendid bride."

"She must be ready by now," Anne said. "I'd better go."

Still she hesitated. Time was too short. In less than an hour, the ceremony would be over.

Gently, Peg said, "It will be well, my lady. Things happen as they should."

"Sometimes, Peg, but not always." Nonetheless, she felt comforted, and her thoughts turned to Maggie Malloch who seemed even more of a dream creature than before. Although Maggie had said she would not meddle, perhaps she could still find a way to help. Deciding to hope for the best, Anne went to join the others.

As she expected, Fiona was nearly ready, and by the look of things, had resigned herself to her fate. She stood in the center of the room in the sky-blue gown, looking rich and elegant with her hair flowing down her back in soft curls to her hips. The darker-blue-and-white-ribbon points that connected her sleeves to her bodice, as well as others attached about her slender person, hung invitingly loose to serve as favors for male guests who would leap forward to snatch them from her the moment the ceremony ended.

Olivia greeted Anne's return with relief. "Perhaps now that you are here at last, Fiona will don her veil and we can go downstairs," she said. "Ashkirk must have departed for the chapel by now, and everyone else will be standing in the garden, watching for her arrival. Don't muss her hair, Molly," she added, as the maidservant moved to drape Fiona's waist-length veil over her head.

Fergus flapped his hands wildly, so Maggie let him speak.

"The lass mustna cover her face," he exclaimed. "Lady Anne will want that lad tae see how beautiful Mistress Fiona be—if our Catriona can just get him here."

"Aye, he must certainly see her," Maggie agreed, realizing she would have to wait at least until the festivities were over before she could satisfactorily discuss Jonah's latest revelation with either Catriona or Fergus.

Anne suddenly realized that Fiona's nearly opaque veil was a mistake.

Unlike Olivia's, which merely framed her face, the many folds of sky-blue lace hid Fiona's and hung to her waist, overpowering her slender figure. If Sir Christopher did chance to be in the garden, he would be far more likely to intervene if he saw how lovely she was. But instead of looking ethereally fair as usual, she looked rectangular and sky blue from top to toe.

Taking the plunge, she said quietly to Olivia, "That veil looks more cumbersome on her than I thought it would."

"Anne is right, madam," Lady Scott said, tilting her head to observe Fiona. "Such a lovely bride should not hide her beauty."

Austerely, Olivia said, "I must say, although the custom of veiling has come into high favor of late, I agree that everyone would prefer to see Fiona. Take the veil off, Molly. She can wear the chaplet alone."

Obeying, Molly set the gold circlet entwined with fresh flowers on Fiona's head, and the ladies who had helped her dress applauded the decision.

"Slip your pattens on, my dear, and take care that you do not let your skirts touch the ground," Olivia said. "You do not want to soil your hem."

"I'll be careful," Fiona murmured. She did not look at Anne and was clearly maintaining her poise only with effort.

Brides were often interestingly pale, even scared, as

Anne knew from what small experience she had of weddings. After all, most brides knew little of what lay ahead of them. Nevertheless, Fiona's tense demeanor worried her.

Downstairs they found many others waiting to accompany the bride on her journey through the gardens to the chapel. Sir Toby stood with them, regally attired in a dark blue doublet, puffed hose slashed with white satin, and sporting a gold medallion on a chain around his neck. He was to serve as Fiona's escort, and as they set off, the entourage was merry if the bride was not.

The ceremony itself would occur at the chapel door before the nuptial mass took place inside, because that was the tradition on both sides of the line for rich and poor alike. When Anne had asked Sir Toby if he knew why that was so, he had grinned in his usual impish way and said, "Sakes, lass, you cannot think the parson would commit the indecency o' granting permission *inside* the church for a man and his woman to sleep together!"

She had chuckled, as he had clearly intended, but a memory stirred of Armadale telling someone he believed the tradition arose from nothing more complicated than folks' desire to keep the Kirk out of their lives as long as possible.

Two little girls led the procession, strewing rosemary and flower petals from gilded baskets, followed by a boy carrying the rosemary- and ribbon-bedecked silver bridal cup from which the bride and groom would drink their communion wine at the nuptial mass, and Anne followed next as Fiona's chief attendant. Fiona and Sir Toby walked behind her, followed by the rest of their entourage.

Many of the younger women wore sheaves of wheat in their hair to encourage fertility in the bride, or carried bouquets of roses and rosemary intermingled with wheat straws.

Three minstrels strummed lutes near the chapel, their music filling the air as the procession approached the arched stone bridge.

The bridge boasted neither parapet nor railing, and as Anne reached its center, her curiosity as to whether Fiona and Toby could cross side by side without mishap made it impossible to resist glancing over her shoulder.

With Sir Toby's bulk, the undertaking clearly was not easy, but putting an arm around Fiona, he drew her close, and they managed it safely if not elegantly.

On the other side, as Anne walked along the petal-strewn path to the chapel porch, where Eustace waited with his best man and the parson by the makeshift altar, she searched the crowd for the face she had hoped to find.

Feeling mixed disappointment and frustration that Sir Christopher was nowhere in sight, she went up the shallow stone steps and took her place at the opposite end of the porch from Eustace. A light breeze stirred the pair of red and green Carmichael banners that flanked the altar.

From where Anne stood, she had a slightly better view of the crowd and realized that many had ignored the paths and stood in flowerbeds or knot gardens.

As if to accompany the minstrels' lutes, birds chirped in the trees and shrubbery, and garden scents mixed with other odors that wafted from the murmuring sea of humanity.

Anne swiftly scanned the crowd again, seeking that one barely remembered face, but if he was there, she did not see him. Remembering how tall he was, she had been certain he would stand out easily and that her own instinct would draw her gaze straight to him, so her disappointment was sharp.

A sudden lull in the murmuring drew her attention to the bride.

Framed by her uncle's huge body now behind her, Fiona had paused at the foot of the steps, clearly reluctant to proceed.

Evidently warned to expect some reluctance, and without losing a jot of his composure, Toby put his arm around her slender shoulders again and urged her forward until she stood in her place between Anne and Eustace, her head bowed.

"Look up," Anne muttered for her cousin's ears alone. "Whatever you decide to do, you cannot want all these people to see you behave like a sullen child."

The crowd remained silent.

Anne glanced at Eustace and was not surprised to see him frown at Fiona. She was as certain as she could be without looking that Olivia was frowning too.

Fiona drew an audible breath, raised her head, and glanced back at the assembled crowd. Then she straightened and turned fully around to face them.

She had gathered her dignity, and she stood now with her head as high as any royal bride, the gold flowered circlet adding to the illusion of royalty. Her beauty had never been more arresting.

Chapter 9

Kit had been trying to decide if the elegant-looking young woman in green velvet who had preceded the bride to the altar was Lady Anne Ellyson. He suspected it was she, because his instincts cried out that it was, but the lass he remembered had had dark curls flying wildly around her face, and had been dressed much less fashionably.

The bride's chief attendant stood calmly, hands folded at her waist, her eyes scanning the crowd until the bride reached her side. Since her hair was covered, it was that searching look more than anything else that made him think it must be Anne, because he believed she was searching for him.

He saw the bride pause at the bottom of the steps, and he saw, too, that the enormously fat man who accompanied her seemed to push her forward until she stood between Eustace and the young woman in green. When the latter murmured something to her, she straightened, visibly collecting herself, and turned.

Kit gasped, for her beauty was truly stunning. An air of fragile vulnerability surrounded her, making him feel as if he should exert himself to protect her, and he was certain that every other man in the place must feel the same way.

Before the woman in green velvet had approached the porch, he had watched his uncle, thinking Eustace looked more arrogant than he remembered. The older man gazed steadily at his young bride, and Kit found himself wondering if Eustace felt protective, too, or even really loved her, if only for her incredible beauty.

What he saw in his uncle's eyes, however, was raw desire, not tenderness. The hungry look was startling, almost as if Kit had caught him in a private moment and ought to apologize for seeing what he had seen. It made him feel a little sick.

Realizing he had dropped his guard, he glanced again at Anne and saw with relief that she was watching the bride's mammoth escort step down from the porch.

Her green eyes looked enormous, and her full, soft-looking lips reminded him of how she had tasted when he kissed her. Remembering how quickly she had smacked him for that impudence, he smiled.

Willie Armstrong stood beside him on tiptoe, watching as avidly as everyone else. His recalling a kinsman certain to be invited to the wedding had resolved Kit's problem of how to arrange his own attendance. The kinsman, a chieftain of the fractious Armstrong tribe, took a large entourage wherever he went—what the Highlanders called a tail—and although Kit had doubted that he would allow them to join him, after Willie spoke to him, Armstrong told his men simply that they were coming, and that had been that.

They stood near the rear of the crowd amidst a scattering of Carmichaels, to whom the Armstrongs were more closely akin than to the Chisholms, and for that Kit gave thanks. As he had expected, Anne paid more heed to a group of Chisholms near the porch, evidently believing he would mingle with his own. In truth, though, he saw few kinsmen and wondered if Eustace had offended other members of the family with his dubious actions.

It did not matter, of course, because Kit was just as glad not to have to run a gantlet of Chisholms, lest he meet one who would recognize him.

The music stopped, and the parson began the ceremony with a brief prayer. When he commended Mistress Carmichael and the Laird of Ashkirk and Torness to God's keeping, Kit was tempted to shout out that he was grateful for the thought but that the parson erred if he believed the man in front of him was that laird.

He held his peace, however, still undecided as to his course. The bride looked so small next to Eustace, and it was not necessary to recall Anne's words to see that Mistress Carmichael was reluctant if not afraid to marry him. That she was doing so because her mother believed falsely that Eustace was Laird of Ashkirk made matters worse, for only a scoundrel could allow such a fraud to continue.

That awareness did not make his choice easier, however. Wresting control from Eustace, if he was indeed entrenched at Hawks Rig, could prove very difficult. He was certainly not the first man to usurp a title and estate, nor could Kit believe he would back down simply because the rightful man had returned to claim them.

Other Chisholms might help him, but he needed first to learn who sided with Eustace and who did not. In the meantime, embroiling himself in Mistress Carmichael's problems, even for the sake of getting to know Anne Ellyson better, would only fetter him and make maneuvering more difficult.

In any case, if he remembered correctly, a good bit more of the ceremony remained before the point where he must speak or stay silent.

Catriona saw Maggie and Fergus and waved at them to join her on her branch not far from Kit, where she had perched to keep watch over him.

"As you see, he is here," she said. "But he cannot decide. Do you think I—"

"Nay," Maggie said. "If he be the man ye say he be, he'll do right by the lass. If he does summat else, ye'll ken ye were mistaken in him. But keep an eye on them others, too. I feel Claud's presence gey strong here today."

Catriona pouted at the refusal, but as Maggie's last comment sank in, she perked up and obediently turned her attention to the wedding guests.

Catriona was so near he could almost touch her, almost taste her lips and feel her soft breasts and silken skin. His body ached for her, and his frustration grew stronger with each passing moment.

He had been floating in dense grayness, and then suddenly he had seen them again, the three of them together, and heard his mother say she felt his presence. He could feel hers, too, and another one, stronger and far more malevolent.

Clearly, his father was nearby, and he wondered if Jonah merely taunted him by letting him occasionally glimpse what he had lost. That thought stirred an anger greater than any he had ever known.

"Dearly beloved," Parson Allardice began, "we are gathered together under the sight of God and before this company to join together this man and this woman in holy matrimony, which is an honorable estate instituted of God in the time of Man's innocency, signifying unto us the mystical union . . ."

Certain words in the text shouted at Anne, specifically "honorable" and "innocency." Although Fiona certainly qualified as innocent, Eustace was wicked, and the whole business was less than honorable, including Anne's own part in it.

She had to stop it. No matter what happened to her or even to Fiona as a result, knowing what she knew, it was simply wrong to let the ceremony proceed. Sir Christopher might think his reasons for holding his tongue were good ones, but she could not hold hers any longer. In truth, she did not even know that he was who he said he was, but she believed him, and Fiona did not deserve to be shoved into marriage with a wholly despicable man who had presented himself falsely to her.

The parson paused and looked out at the assembly as he said, "If any o' ye here present ken cause or just impediment why these two persons should not be joined lawfully in holy matrimony, speak now or forever after hold thy peace."

Heavy, dramatic silence greeted his invitation.

Drawing breath, hoping she had courage enough and that Eustace or Olivia would not order her dragged off and locked up while the ceremony proceeded, Anne turned to face the priest. "Wait," she said, but her voice emerged as a croak.

"Therefore," the priest said, "do I require—"

"Wait!" shouted a voice from the back of the crowd. "I will speak. I must!"

"Thank heaven," Anne said, turning to see who had spoken just as Fiona gasped and fainted away at her feet.

A path opened before Kit as he strode to the front of the crowd. He had seen Anne drop to her knees beside the fallen bride, but his attention was fixed on Eustace, who glowered fiercely at him.

He could not be certain Eustace recognized him, but it did not matter, because he would see the matter through now, wherever it led. Willie had melted into the crowd, so Kit was alone, and every eye but Anne's was on him as he neared the steps to the porch. Then she looked up, and as their eyes met, he felt himself relax. Whether he was doing the right thing or not, she clearly believed he was.

"Who are ye?" the priest demanded. "State your name and business."

Meeting the angry cleric's gaze, Kit told himself it was time to strike the fierce, as the Chisholm motto commanded. "I am Christopher Chisholm," he said in a clear, carrying voice, "the true Laird of Ashkirk and Torness."

Behind him, the chorus of gasps and murmurs sounded like the stirrings of a windstorm.

The priest frowned. "Are ye, indeed?"

"I am."

"And the cause or just impediment ye believe exists would be what, then?"

"I should think that must be plain to everyone here," Kit said. "You have named my uncle incorrectly as Laird of Ashkirk and Torness, and thus he stands ready to claim Mistress Carmichael as his bride under false pretenses."

"I do not know you," Eustace declared loudly. "I doubt that any Chisholm here will recognize you as a kinsman. At least," he added sarcastically, "I doubt that any would claim you as my brother's legitimate son. With your height and that chin, I don't doubt that you could be one of another ilk, however."

Kit's temper could be ferocious when aroused, but he had learned to control it through bitter experience. He met Eustace's scowl steadily but said to the priest, "I am indeed Sir Christopher, as I can easily prove, given sufficient time."

The priest nodded, taking in the prostrate Mistress Carmichael and Anne's anxious attempts to arouse her. He turned toward the bride's mother and erstwhile buffoonish escort. Clearly dismissing both, he gestured to a young man in the front row and said, "Prithee, step forward, sir, and help Lady Anne take Mistress Fiona into the chapel where she may more easily recover her composure."

Anne looked up at that moment, and he nearly smiled at her, but something in the way she regarded him warned him against it. It would do neither of them any good to let others know yet that they had met before. Casually, he returned his attention to the parson but kept a wary eye on Eustace.

When the man who had served as his uncle's best man took a step toward him, Eustace put a hand out to stop him but otherwise remained where he was without moving or speaking.

Having seen Mistress Carmichael safely inside the chapel, the parson turned to Kit and said, "I will not ask why ye didna speak up afore, lad, on any o' the several occasions when I published the banns for this union."

"I will tell you nonetheless, sir, that I heard about this wedding only two days ago. My intention then was not to intervene, but I came to realize where my duty lay, and so I came here today."

The parson's gaze shifted to a point behind Kit as a feminine voice said curiously, "Are you really Sir Christopher Chisholm?"

Turning, he found himself facing the bride's mother. Despite her obvious state of mourning and a certain limpness of manner, she was a woman nearly as beautiful as her daughter, and one to whom he knew his father would have been strongly attracted.

Politely he said, "I am indeed Christopher Chisholm, my lady. I am sorry to interrupt these proceedings, but I hope you can manage to forgive me."

"My dear sir, of course we forgive you, but you did not mention the primary impediment." Turning to the parson, she said, "We all thought he was dead, you see, or my daughter could never have been betrothed to Sir Eustace, because she was already betrothed to Sir Christopher."

Kit grimaced. He had purposely not mentioned the betrothal, hoping to learn more about it first.

The parson looked from Lady Carmichael to him and back again, still frowning. "Clearly, we must talk at length before this ceremony can go forward, if ever it can," he said. "I fear ye must send your guests home for today, my lady."

"Nonsense, nonsense," the bride's erstwhile escort said cheerfully, stepping forward and extending his hand to Kit. "Toby Bell at your service, sir. Sir Tobias Bell, if we must be formal, and since this is—or was—a wedding, formality does seem appropriate to the day."

Lady Carmichael said faintly, "Uncle Toby, please, not now!"

"Sakes, lass, when if not now? Think of all that food!"

She stared at him.

"Just so," Sir Toby said, grinning. "I'll see to everything, so you've no need for you to bother your head about it. Matters like this soon sort themselves out." So saying, he turned to face the still-murmuring crowd, raised his hands, and shouted, "Hear me, all o' ye! The wedding feast will take place, wedding or no wedding. Someone's got to eat that food, and whilst I may look as if I can manage it all alone, I assure you there is far too much even for me!"

Laughter greeted his words, but the guests willingly let him shepherd them toward the house, leaving Kit and the parson alone with Lady Carmichael, Eustace, and the best man.

"Sir Eustace," Lady Carmichael said, "is it not wonderful that your nephew is not dead after all?"

When Eustace did not reply, clearly not sharing her sentiments, Kit decided to make the first move. Extending his right hand to the older man, he said, "Come now, sir, surely you remember me well enough to recognize me if you will but take a moment to do so. Although I've thickened and grown a bit, I'm only five years older than the last time we met."

"I do not know you," Eustace insisted. "I think your behavior in pretending to be my nephew is unconscionable. He is dead, as everyone here knows well. My dear Lady Carmichael, surely you do not believe this scoundrel!"

She opened her mouth as if to debate the matter, but when he scowled at her, she quickly submitted, lowering her lashes and saying weakly, "You surely must know better than I, sir, whether he is or is not a member of your family."

But the priest was having none of it. "Beg pardon, my lady," he said, "but if an agreement cannot be settled between these gentlemen, a court of law must decide that point. However, if this young man is indeed Sir Christopher—"

"He is not!" Eustace snapped.

". . . and if a betrothal exists between him and your daughter and—"

"It does not!"

"Please, Sir Eustace," the cleric begged.

"But I do not please," Eustace snapped. "There was no betrothal, only the beginnings of one. My brother had written to his son, but his son never replied, so the appropriate papers concluding the arrangement were never drawn up or signed."

"Nevertheless, if the old laird, as head of his family, made the agreement with Lady Carmichael, and the lass thus believed herself betrothed—"

"She did, I'm afraid," Lady Carmichael said with a sigh. "So did I, for the late laird assured us that no more than a proxy exchange of vows was necessary."

The priest nodded. "That is true. You see, sir, it is as I feared, and Sir Christopher's arrival stirs many questions that we must answer before your union with Mistress Carmichael can go forward, if it ever can. I was not aware that a former betrothal of any sort existed, but if they exchanged vows, even by proxy, it was more than the barest beginning. If such is the case, she was betrothed to your nephew according to the laws of the Kirk and thus of Scotland, as well."

"This is nonsense," Eustace said angrily. "I command you to continue."

The parson shook his head. "Even if your nephew were truly dead, as you say, you must realize that your close kin-

ship with him places you within a forbidden degree of consanguinity and thus precludes your being allowed to marry
her without papal dispensation or, at the very least, a special
license granted by a bishop."

"Then, by God, I'll arrange for a special license," Eustace declared.

"You will have to apply to the bishop, sir. I cannot help
you with that."

"Bishop!" Sir Eustace made a rude noise. "I have resources more powerful than mere bishops, I promise you."

Lady Carmichael put a hand on his arm, saying, "Pray,
sir, do not fly into a temper. As my uncle has said, this will
all resolve itself in time. I trust you will not leave Mute Hill
House before we have discussed it all thoroughly."

He looked at her, and when she gazed soulfully into his
eyes, he patted her hand. "I will not be so uncivil, certainly
not to you, who have always been kind to me. Moreover,"
he added, "your uncle is right. We should not waste all that
food."

"Thank you," she said, clearly relieved. Turning to Kit,
she said graciously, "You must stay, too, Sir Christopher, at
least until you have had an opportunity to prove that you are
who you say you are."

He was tempted to refuse, feeling as if he were being invited, however kindly, to enter a slaughterhouse. Neither her
attitude nor Eustace's sudden affability made sense to him,
so he did not reply at once, trying to collect enough of his
wits to compare his previous beliefs with his new position.

Just then, Anne emerged from the chapel and smiled at
him, making the decision an easy one, after all. "I'll stay,
and gladly, madam," he said. "Thank you."

"Oh, this goes very well," Catriona said, rubbing her hands together.

"Aye," Fergus said, gazing raptly at her. "Ye're a clever one, lass. I'll grant ye that. O' course, that other one—Mistress Fiona—she'll ha' tae play her part too."

Catriona laughed. "Oh, she will. You just watch. How could she not find him singularly attractive after that fiendish man she just got rid of?"

Maggie shook her head. "Ye'd best learn no tae count things as done until they are done, Catriona. 'Tis only a matter o' time before summat happens that ye dinna expect."

"Not this time," Catriona said confidently. "Watch."

When the lad who had carried Fiona into the chapel left, Anne had all she could do not to leave her cousin drooping in the family pew and rush back out to the porch to see what was happening. There could be no question of that, however, until Fiona recovered her senses, if not her color and her composure.

When she finally opened her eyes, she sat up too abruptly and looked around dizzily and in panic. Finding herself alone with Anne, she said, "Is it true?"

"If you mean is the gentleman who interrupted the ceremony really Sir Christopher Chisholm, then yes, I believe he is, love. You will not have to marry Eustace after all."

"No," she said doubtfully. "You did say that something might happen, and it has, but shall I have to give back all the presents now?"

"Goose," Anne said, repressing an impulse to laugh, "you should have more important matters on your mind than that."

"Yes, but perhaps I need not give them back, for if I must

marry Sir Christopher instead of his uncle, is it not much the same thing? I mean, after all, they are both Chisholms, so cannot the same presents count for either one?"

No longer feeling an urge to laugh but experiencing instead an unfamiliar desire to shake her cousin, Anne took a deep breath and said, "I think you should rest quietly here for a few moments whilst I go see what is happening outside."

"Don't leave me alone!"

"Compose yourself, Fiona. No one will harm you here in the chapel with Parson Allardice, your mother, and the others just outside the door."

"But what if *they* come in?"

"I won't let them. Moreover, I will return as soon as I believe it is safe for you to return to the house without meeting anyone who might demand answers you are in no condition to provide."

"Oh, no, I couldn't!"

"Then sit here quietly and collect your composure. You know perfectly well that I can look after things for you, do you not?"

"Oh, yes, Anne. You are always so good."

"Then wait here. You need worry no longer about Eustace. Your betrothal to Sir Christopher must supersede any such arrangement with his uncle."

"He . . . he will not want to be married straightaway, will he?"

Knowing that Sir Christopher did not want to marry at all made it easy for Anne to say, "No, love, I'm sure he will not want to rush into anything. But surely you would prefer to marry a man nearer your own age than Eustace is."

Fiona shuddered. "I don't care how old he is, as long as it is *not* Sir Eustace."

"Then let me see what they are doing," Anne said, patting her shoulder. "I shan't be long, I promise."

And with that, she hurried out in time to hear Sir Christopher agree to stay at least overnight at Mute Hill House.

Eustace was looking daggers at Olivia, so Anne had no need to wonder who had issued the invitation, but Parson Allardice was beaming.

" 'Tis the very thing," he said approvingly. "We'll sort things out much quicker if everyone can sit down all together and discuss the matter."

"Well, you can sort them out without my help," Eustace said. "I've agreed to stay for this nonsensical feast of Toby's, but I'll have nowt to do with any discussion of a never-existent betrothal."

Anne glanced at Sir Christopher and discovered he was looking directly at her, almost as if he expected her to speak. The intensity of his gaze reminded her of his kiss, and feeling her lips burn at the memory, she was sure she must be blushing. So determined had she been to produce him and thus stop Fiona's wedding to Eustace that she had taken no time to consider her own position, or her feelings, if Fiona married Sir Christopher. Nor, however, could she consider them now.

Gathering her wits, she said quietly, "I thought I should let you know that Fiona is nearly herself again, Aunt Olivia. Still, I think it would be wise to take her up to the house as quickly and unobtrusively as we can. She does not want to meet anyone or answer questions just now, as I am sure you will understand."

"Yes, oh, yes," Olivia said. "But I'm sure I do not know

how we can get her across the bridge and up to her room without meeting any number of people."

Sir Christopher said quietly, "Is there an entrance that is less used than the others, my lady?"

Olivia looked at him with dawning appreciation. "Why, yes, a postern door between the kitchen and bakehouse. Anne, you must take Fiona in by that way. I warrant you will not meet anyone there who would dare to ask questions of her."

"Yes, madam, but we still have to negotiate the gardens, and it is possible that everyone is not inside yet."

"I'd be happy to accompany you, Lady Anne," Sir Christopher said.

"You are singularly well informed, sir," Eustace snarled. "I do not recall that anyone has made you known to her ladyship."

Anne felt fire in her cheeks again, but if Sir Christopher was caught off guard, he did not reveal it by so much as a twitch.

Smiling ruefully at her, as if she were an injured party, he said, "I beg your pardon, my lady, but when you called Lady Carmichael 'aunt,' I knew you must be her niece. Your presence here at Mute Hill House is known throughout the area, but I should not have presumed to speak to you without a proper introduction."

"You need not apologize, sir," she said. "I am grateful for your offer. Fiona is rapidly recovering her composure, but I doubt that I could protect her by myself against anyone encroaching enough to invade her privacy. You, on the other hand, are large enough to daunt the most determinedly curious."

"You cannot intend for this impostor to accompany you

and Fiona to her bedchamber," Eustace exclaimed, looking scandalized by the thought, just as if he had not been caught on the brink of entering Fiona's room in the middle of the night, which in Anne's opinion was far more scandalous.

"Have mercy, good sir," Olivia said, clasping a hand to her bosom. "I am sure Anne had no such improper intention."

But Eustace was staring grimly at his nephew.

Parson Allardice said crisply, "I am sure we are all grateful for your assistance, young man, but ye'll go only to the kitchen door wi' the lassies."

"I had no other intention," Sir Christopher said.

Olivia turned again to Eustace and held out her hand. "If you please, sir, you may escort me into the house now. I vow, I weary of this discussion."

"It will be my pleasure," Eustace said. "Do you join us, Parson Allardice?"

"Aye, for I dinna mind admitting I'm that famished," he said.

Kit touched Anne's elbow, and she looked up to see him smiling. His features were harsh, his nose aquiline, but his teeth were white and strong, and she thought him very handsome. The hair she could see beneath his hat was a lighter brown than she had thought it, and his eyes surprised her. She had imagined they were dark, but they were light blue with dark rims to the irises, and his lashes were dark and unusually long and thick.

She did not want to look away, but when he nodded toward the chapel entrance, she remembered Fiona.

"Pray, let me go to her alone first, sir," she said. "It will be better if I tell her you are to escort us than if you suddenly appear."

"Of course, mistress. When you want me, just speak my name. I'll hear you."

"Thank you," she said with, she was sure, far more sincerity than he would think the occasion warranted.

She hurried back to Fiona, saying as she approached her, "We are going into the house, love, so you must get up now and straighten your dress. We have a stout protector to accompany us, and you must not let him see you looking so mussed."

"Who?" Fiona demanded, her eyes wide with apprehension.

"No one to frighten you, I promise. Only Sir Christopher, who will escort us as far as the kitchen door to assure that we get into the house unmolested. May I call him?" When Fiona nodded, Anne raised her voice, saying, "You may come in, sir."

He stepped inside but showed the good sense not to approach Fiona.

"Are you really Sir Christopher Chisholm?" she asked shyly.

"Yes, mistress. I am sorry to have spoiled your wedding day."

"That does not matter," she said. "May we go into the house now, Anne?"

Anne exchanged a look with him but said only, "Of course, love."

They made their way through the gardens without encountering anyone except a disinterested gardener near the rustic plank bridge that crossed the brook near the stable. Stopping at the postern door, Anne said, "If you will wait here, sir, I'll return quickly and walk with you to the hall.

You have been very kind to do this, and you should not have to confront that crowd alone."

"With respect, mistress, you should perhaps stay clear of me for the present." Slanting a look at Fiona, he added, "My uncle seems to suspect that we have met before. If I enter the hall with you on my arm, it may cause trouble later."

"You are being absurd, sir," she said, barely stopping herself from touching his arm to emphasize her point. "If you do not wait for me, I shall have to enter the hall alone, which would not suit me in the least."

"I'd venture to guess you would manage quite well, however."

"Yes, I would, for I have done so before, but your escort would lend me consequence. Besides," she added in a burst of honesty, "I don't want to miss anything, so pray do not go until I can go with you."

He chuckled. "I see. Very well then, I'll wait, but don't tarry, or my uncle will doubtless send someone to fling me into the nearest dungeon."

"Mute Hill House has no dungeon," Fiona said.

"Take her upstairs, my lady," he said, rolling his eyes, "and hurry back."

Anne's intentions were good, but it was only by hardening her heart against Fiona's pleas to stay that she was able to get away, and by the time she did, she was certain that he must have gone. Nonetheless, she hurried down the service stairs and out the postern door.

Chapter 10

Sir Christopher was leaning against the wall of the bake-house—arms folded across his broad chest, black hat tilted over his forehead—watching the kitchen doorway. When he smiled lazily at Anne, she noted again how handsome he was, but to attract Fiona she decided he would need some furbishing up. His hair was too long, his clothing sadly out of fashion. The hat was too large, too, and his russet-colored doublet and hose lacked the heavy padding, slashing, and puffing of current styles, although they certainly showed his splendid physique to advantage.

"Do I meet with your approval, my lady?"

She realized she had been staring and collected herself, saying, "I was just thinking you look as if you've been out of the way of fashion for some time."

"Ah, my clothing. My cousin already took me to task for my sad lack of style, so you may rest easy. I promised him I would order new things soon."

"Your cousin?"

He nodded, straightening as he did and offering her an arm.

As she placed a hand on it, noting instantly how warm

the sun had made the russet-colored cloth, she said, "Does your cousin live near here, sir?"

"Curiosity is an unhappy flaw in a female," he murmured.

"Yes, so I have been told," she said, smiling up at him. "Nonetheless, it is the only way to get answers to one's questions."

He put his left hand atop hers on his forearm and gave it a squeeze. "Are you never at a loss for words, lass?"

"I have not given you leave to speak so informally to me, Sir Christopher."

"Very true," he agreed, idly stroking her hand with a fingertip. "And we have seen, have we not, what a stickler you are for the proprieties."

Feeling flames in her cheeks at the memory of their first meeting and her insistence then that a young woman riding alone at night was no occasion for comment, Anne said no more about informality and hoped he would take the hint.

Evidently he did, for he did not press the issue, saying instead, "The cousin I mentioned lives in the Highlands. His father is Lord Chisholm of Dundreggan, and serves as the Sheriff of Inverness-shire."

"I collect, then, that you returned to the Highlands before coming here."

"I did, but only because I knew I'd be welcome there. I did not yet know my father had died, you see."

She looked up again sympathetically. "That must have been hard, learning you would have no opportunity to say goodbye."

"Or to make my peace with him," he said. "We are being observed, lass, so try not to rip up at me for the next few minutes or so."

They had rounded the corner of the house and were indeed within sight of the main entrance, where a small group of guests had gathered. Several heads had turned their way, so Anne resisted the temptation to scold him for his mockery.

She had no more to complain about in his behavior, however, for he escorted her inside and through the crowd to Olivia, who sat regally acknowledging the many guests who approached to commiserate with her at the wedding's failure.

"Thank you for your assistance, sir," Anne murmured politely to him.

"It was my pleasure, my lady." He turned to Olivia, adding, "May I ask, madam, when you believe we can further discuss the question at hand?"

She gazed at him in apparent confusion. "But my dear sir," she said, "surely you cannot expect to discuss such an important matter in the midst of this revelry!"

"In fact, madam, I had hoped we might retire to some more private place." If Olivia detected the sardonic note in his voice, Anne saw no sign of it.

To her surprise, Olivia fluttered her lashes and tilted her head coyly as she said, "My dear Sir Christopher, you must know that what you suggest is most improper. You should never ask a woman in mourning to be private with you."

Sensing the shift of his emotions from irritation to annoyance, Anne said hastily, "I believe Sir Christopher assumed that Parson Allardice, Eustace, and perhaps your uncle Toby would be with you, Aunt Olivia. Surely, you must see that the sooner this tangle is unraveled the better it will be for everyone."

"Indeed, I do see that, Anne. I am not a noddy, for

heaven's sake. But you might show more concern for my nerves. Today's events have created a shattering ordeal for me. As for Sir Eustace, he has made his position clear, and if he is furious, I am sure no one can blame him."

A manservant approached with a silver salver and hesitated expectantly. At Olivia's nod, he moved forward, saying, "Pray, forgive the intrusion, my lady, but a letter has arrived for Lady Anne."

"Mercy," Olivia said, taking the missive from the salver. "Who can be writing to you on Fiona's wedding day, my dear?"

"I am sure I do not know, madam."

Glancing at the wax seal, Olivia exclaimed, "Why, that is Armadale's seal! I'd know it anywhere. But who can have had the effrontery . . . Mercy on us!"

Anne, realizing then who must have sent the letter, said, "I believe Mr. Scott, my father's man of affairs, sent the earl's personal seal to Cousin Thomas, madam." To Kit, she added, "Thomas Ellyson of Dumfries and Stirling is my father's heir—to the earldom of Armadale, that is."

"I understood that," he said, smiling at her so warmly that she looked quickly back at her aunt and tried to ignore responsive warmth spreading deep inside her.

Breaking the seal and unfolding the letter, Olivia muttered, "But why should he write to you and not to me? He has always been the most inconsiderate person, and elevation to the earldom clearly has done nothing to alter that. Naturally, I sent him an invitation to Fiona's wedding, but he did not even deign to reply. Although I suppose I should be grateful now that he did not attend it."

"I barely remember him," Anne admitted. "Is he truly so horrid?"

Scanning what was apparently a brief message, Olivia shrugged. A moment later, she looked up and handed the letter to Anne. "You may read for yourself what he has written," she said.

The letter consisted of only a few lines, so Anne read swiftly.

Olivia said, "As you see, he merely apologizes for not having written when he received word of your father's death, and says he will come to see you as soon as he attends to some few, lingering matters of business pertaining to the estates."

"Yes," Anne said, feeling a surge of resentment as she read the last line, "and he also writes that until such time as he is able to discuss my future with me, I am to consider myself under his guardianship and to make no decisions regarding the disposal of Ellyson Towers or myself without first acquiring his permission."

"Well, I am sure I do not know why that should surprise you," Olivia said. "You are underage, after all, and so Cousin Thomas—mercy, I must remember to call him Armadale now, mustn't I? Well, it is Armadale's business to look after you until you marry."

"I would be more willing to accept his authority if he had had the courtesy to write when he first learned of my father's death," Anne said. "Whatever else he may be, he is clearly not a man who attends promptly to his duties."

"Aye, he was ever a heedless man," Olivia said, yawning behind a hand. "Mind, I haven't seen him since I was a girl, and he is much older than I am."

Sir Christopher bowed, saying, "Doubtless you would prefer to abuse your relative in privacy, madam. Mayhap

Parson Allardice will have a suggestion as to what we should do next."

Olivia shrugged. "You must do as you please, of course, but I do not see how this business can be settled in an afternoon, sir. We do not know yet that you are who you say you are, after all, and Sir Eustace insists that even if you should prove to be his dead nephew come back to life, it will not alter his betrothal to Fiona."

"I wish you will believe that I have no desire to run counter to your daughter's wishes or yours, my lady. Surely you can understand, however, that I could not allow him to marry her whilst she believed him to be Laird of Ashkirk."

"Oh, yes, I suppose you had no choice, and I am glad to know that you did not die, of course. But pray, do go away now, sir, for I must rest. I do not want to think about this dreadful business any more today."

Sir Christopher walked away, and the din of laughter and conversation in the hall, augmented by music from the minstrel's gallery above them, suddenly became more than Anne could bear. She felt as if her world had been turned on its ear, and the thought that the new Earl of Armadale might arrive at any moment to tell her how she should go on in a life she had hitherto lived very successfully without his guidance only made it worse.

Deciding that she would soon do something to destroy her long-established reputation for serenity in the face of calamity if she did not find a private place to collect her thoughts, she took an orange from a fruit basket on the high table and slipped out of the hall before it occurred to anyone to stop her.

Making her way outside and around to the yard, she decided to order a horse and go for a long, solitary ride, telling herself that anyone who thought she ought not to go alone could just keep his opinion to himself. However, the bustle in the yard and stables, where servants tended guests' horses as well as those belonging to Mute Hill House, dissuaded her, and she turned with a sigh toward the gardens.

Following the path from the stables away from the house and across the plank bridge, she saw no one else. The gardeners had moved to other duties, and all the guests were inside. In some undefined distance, she heard birds chirping and the cheerful, tumbling rush of the rain-swollen brook. Nearer at hand, she heard only the crunch of the pebbled path under her feet.

That path meandered away from the brook, past flowerbeds quickly passing their prime, and through the shady copse of tall beech trees. From there, the path skirted the knot gardens that Sir Stephen had laid out with his own hands after drawing their patterns on sheets of foolscap that he had afterward framed and hung in the garden hall. Tall boxwood hedges screened that part of the garden from all but the uppermost windows of the house, protecting plants from the ever-present Border winds and creating an illusion of privacy for anyone who walked there.

Coming to a wooden bench where one could sit and contemplate the central and largest knot garden, Anne sat down and peeled the orange she had brought with her. The garden was at peace, presently occupied only by myriad wild creatures and a tawny stable cat that stalked a magpie while she ate her orange. When she had finished, she wiped her fingers with her handkerchief, carefully wrapped her orange peels in it, and carried it with her to discard at the house.

The sound of the brook grew louder as she neared the narrow bridge. Soon after she crossed it, her peaceful idyll would end, so to prolong her sense of freedom, she kept her gaze on the pebbled path, knowing when she left the shelter of the hedges only when a line of sparkling sunshine met the deep shadow they cast.

A few steps further, and the stones of the arched bridge lay before her. As she stepped onto it, a singular large shadow shifted in front of her. Startled, she looked up at last and saw Sir Christopher standing at the crest of the arch, barring her way, his hat tilted rakishly over one eye now and his hands on his hips.

His obvious delight as he took a step toward her put the polite words that had sprung to her tongue out of her head. An unfamiliar but pleasant sensation stirred in her midsection, her mouth felt dry, and she could not think of a thing to say.

"I couldn't find you, and so I wondered if you had come outside," he said.

His deep, vibrant voice reached out to her, stirring chords within her in a way that kept her silent and made her wish her heart were not pounding so hard in her chest. She resisted the temptation to look down and see if one could see it pounding. Surely, it must be evident to anyone who looked.

The thought of him looking at her breasts sent flaming heat to her cheeks. He was too close, but she would not step back, certain he expected her to do just that and not wanting him to think she was so predictable or so easily intimidated.

"Have you decided never to speak to me again, lass?"

"No," she said. Pleased that the word had come out calmly, she darted a glance at his face.

He raised his eyebrows. " 'No,' as in you will never speak to me again, or 'no' as in you have *not* decided to take such a cruel course of action?"

She licked her lips, wondering how it was that the man could so easily disconcert her. The brook gurgled and splashed below, its water level—thanks to a sennight's worth of rain—nearly even with its banks.

Behind her, the cat must have flushed its magpie at last, for the bird or another like it emitted a clamor of shrieking protests as it flapped wildly into flight.

"Well?"

She drew a breath and let it out before she said, "I think you understood me plainly, sir. Perhaps you do not realize that you are barring my path."

"Am I?" The teasing look in his eyes told her he knew exactly what he was doing and that his behavior disturbed her.

"Are you flirting with me?" she demanded.

"What if I am?" A smile tugged the corners of his mouth, but he suppressed it. The twinkle in his eyes remained undiminished, making her wish briefly that her conscience would allow her to respond in kind.

"You should not flirt," she said, her tone sharper than she had intended. "Such behavior is inappropriate when you are betrothed to my cousin."

"But I am not betrothed to her," he said. "My uncle insists that naught has changed. Moreover, even if he is wrong about his own position, her subsequent betrothal to him must release me from any contract my father made."

"That has not yet been determined," Anne said. "It seems clear to me that Sir Eustace's contract cannot be binding, since its foundation—which is to say, his assurance that you were dead—is patently false."

"I'll not deny that it's still the devil of a coil," he said, smiling. "I think you and I ought to discuss it at length."

"I have no say in the matter. You must discuss it with my aunt and with Parson Allardice."

"But your aunt does not want to discuss it, and the parson is presently drinking more claret than is good for him whilst exchanging amusing stories with Toby Bell," he said. "In any event, I'd rather discuss things with you."

"We should not even be standing here alone together," she said. "Please stand aside and let me pass."

"What if I were to demand a forfeit first?"

"That would be most unchivalrous of you, and impolite as well."

"But I have not been a gentleman for a year and a half. As I mentioned the first time we met, I fell into bad company—rough sailors and their ilk—and I am afraid I acquired some of their worst habits."

"You are being absurd now," she said. When he did not move, she tilted her head thoughtfully. "What sort of forfeit would you demand?"

"A kiss, of course, what else?"

"Now you step beyond the line," she said, ruthlessly suppressing a nearly overwhelming temptation to pay the forfeit. "Pray stand aside at once, sir."

"Do you never lose that devilish equanimity of yours?" he demanded.

Certain that she would be wiser not to answer such a question, particularly since she would rather die than tell him the truth, Anne glared at him, but if she had hoped to shame him into moving, she had sadly misjudged the man.

He grinned, and after a long moment at this impasse, he hooked his thumbs in his belt, clearly challenging her. "You bring out the worst in me, lass. You have two choices now.

You can turn round and follow the path back the way you came or you can pay my forfeit and cross this bridge."

Anger flashed, and without thought, she snapped both hands up to his chest and gave him a mighty shove.

Although his strength far surpassed her own, she caught him by surprise. His hands flew from his belt, his boot caught a stone at the edge of the bridge, and he staggered and fell. He was agile and managed to land on his feet, but the stones were slippery, the swollen brook swift, and neither foot gained solid purchase.

To Anne's dismay, his feet shot out from under him, and he sat down hard in the middle of the brook. Bits of orange peel that had flown from her handkerchief floated past him, and as she watched, his hat slid down over both eyes.

Clapping a hand to her mouth, she hesitated between blurting out how sorry she was and offering him a hand, or pointing out triumphantly that in the face of stupid ultimatums one frequently had other choices.

However, meeting his angry gaze as he struggled awkwardly to get to his feet only to slip again, she realized that if she were wise, only one choice remained.

She snatched up her skirts and fled across the bridge toward the house.

"Well, this is a setback," Catriona said in disgust.

"I warned ye," Fergus said. "Lady Anne be worth a dozen o' Mistress Fiona, but no tae worry, lass. As clever as ye be, ye'll think o' summat."

Having decided to keep Catriona company while she kept an eye on Kit, Maggie had hoped to find an opportunity to tell her Jonah had said they must kill Claud's mortal to free him. However, although she could easily have created the opportunity, she had not done so, fearing that the news would terrify Catriona as it would Fergus to the point where they would both abandon Claud to his fate. Thus, Maggie had fallen victim to her own thoughts and had not noticed Fergus until he spoke. Nor had she seen what Anne had done to Kit. However, a swift glance at the man in the stream and another at the lass running up the hill to the house with her skirts held up out of her way put her in possession of all she needed to know.

"I warned ye, Catriona," she said. "Things never be as tidy as they seem, and nae plan goes off without a hitch."

"We'll think o' summat," Fergus said, patting Catriona's hand. "Me lass wants him tae marry her beautiful cousin, so she'll help all she can. Ye'll see."

Catriona smiled at him and reached to stroke his face. "Ye're a kind one, Fergus Fishbait, and no mistake."

Maggie watched them both with narrowing eyes.

His anger stirred and deepened to fury. Did that fellow Fishbait want to die? And as for Catriona . . . but just thinking about her stirred him as it usually did, and those feelings combined with his anger put him in such a black mood that he decided Fishbait was lucky that he was on the far side of whatever divided them.

Managing at last to stand and hold steady in the rushing water, albeit with effort, Kit straightened his hat and watched the lass run up the hill to the house.

His first furious impulse was to run after her, to catch her, and to give her what she deserved for the trick she had served him, but three excellent arguments raged in his mind against such a course. First, the pair of them would be in sight of anyone who looked out a window from the house, and even if the watcher made no objection to his putting the lass across his knee, in his sodden state he would look ridiculous. Second, he knew that if he attempted to leap for the bridge or the bank with too much haste and too little care, he would slip again. The third and most persuasive argument, however, was that he had richly deserved his damp fate.

What was it about Anne Ellyson, he wondered, that stirred him to take such liberties with her? Even as the question occurred, however, he knew the answer. She fascinated him far more than her lovely cousin did. It was her damnable calm, of course. Some demon inside him—doubtless having dwelt there since his childhood—tempted him to poke at her, to see if he could get a reaction. The realization did not make him think better of himself, however, for he knew that if a son of his ever teased a lass the way he had teased Anne, it would be the son, not the lass, who went over his knee. A wetting was less than he had deserved.

Because he was soaked to the skin and had seen no sign of Willie since the lad had vanished into the wedding crowd, Kit decided his best course would be to call for his horse and leave, much as it went against his nature to do so.

"Nay, nay," Fergus protested, "he canna leave! We must stop him."

"Aye," Catriona agreed, looking warily at Maggie. "Everyone concerned will want him to stay until the business of the betrothal is settled. Moreover, it will be easier for us to watch them if they all stay in one place."

"I'll see tae that," Maggie said, "but we need tae talk, the three o' us, just as soon as ye can both manage tae do it without abandoning your charges. Go on now and follow your lass, Fergus. Ye've nae need tae linger here wi' Catriona."

"Aye, I'm going," he said. "She's only just got to the door, after all."

By the time Kit climbed back onto the bridge, the lass had disappeared into the house. He noted with relief that no guests were near the entrance now to witness his predicament.

As he stood there, a warm breeze stirred the leaves on nearby shrubbery and trees, making the air feel more like summer than autumn. At least he would not freeze while he decided what to do next.

Remembering that the path on the chapel side of the bridge would take him to the stables, he set off that way, ignoring a lingering temptation to follow Anne. She'd had good reason to run, he decided, knowing she had recognized his fury. Before that moment, he had seen only dismay in her expression, and he wondered if she might have been about to apologize. A second's consideration made him decide she would have done no such thing, and the thought made him smile.

The lady was one of a kind.

His walk through the gardens was surprisingly pleasant. Birds chirped, and a tawny cat emerged from undergrowth in a copse he passed through and followed at his heels. When it meowed at him and rubbed against an ankle, he paused, bending to stroke its soft fur. Instantly, it rolled onto its back, inviting him to rub its tummy.

"What do you make of all this fuss and to-do, Madam Puss?" he asked. "Doubtless, things in your world are more easily dealt with. A mouse here, a rat there, and one's needs are met. Oh, and a handsome tom or two, as well, I'm sure," he added as the cat began to purr loudly.

Straightening, he realized to his amazement that his clothing was nearly dry.

He took off his hat and turned it in his hands. It was dry. Of course, it had been only splashed, he reminded himself, not soaked like the rest of him.

Pushing a hand through his hair, he looked at his boots. That morning, he had thought them far from fine enough for such an occasion but had donned them because he had no others with him. Now they looked like fine, well-polished leather, as if the water of the brook had been exactly the tonic they had needed. He bent down and felt them. They, too, were dry, and by the time he straightened, he could find nothing about his person that was even damp.

He stood for a long moment, gazing around. To be sure, the breeze was warm and brisk, stirring dry leaves to dance along the path, but no breeze could dry a velvet doublet so quickly. Deciding his reverie must have lasted longer than it seemed, he continued along the path until he came to the plank bridge near the stable yard. Ongoing bustle there told him that at least some guests were leaving.

The sun had well begun its downward journey to the western horizon, and since he was dry, he decided to return to the hall. Nothing would go forward until Parson Allardice and the others had talked things over and decided what they wanted to do, and it certainly behooved him to be present when they did, if for no other reason than to keep an eye on Eustace.

When he entered the hall, he found that many had gone. None of the few Chisholms he had seen at the wedding remained, nor had any approached him earlier, so they were clearly taking their cue from Eustace. He saw no one he recognized except Lady Carmichael, who sat with three other ladies at the high table near the fire at the far end of the hall. In the lower hall, a few guests still ate and drank, and the musicians still played, but the crowd and general noise had diminished considerably. It was easy to see that Anne was not there.

Wending his way among trestle tables and benches to the dais, he stepped onto it and approached Lady Carmichael.

"Forgive me for interrupting your ladyship, but I wonder if you have decided yet when it will be convenient for us to meet with Eustace and Parson Allardice."

Putting the back of one hand to her brow, she said, "Pray, Sir Christopher, can this not wait? I have been trying to get away this past hour to lie down and rest, and I promise you, I have such a headache that I could not discuss anything sensibly. As to my uncle, although he is the one who invited everyone to this feast, he has disappeared, and I believe he must have taken Parson Allardice with him."

"I have no wish to distress you, madam, so I will go, but perhaps you would like me to send for Lady Anne first to assist you to your chamber."

"I cannot think where she has gone," she said pettishly. "I saw her come in, but she went straight to the stairs, and she has not come back."

"Little coward," he murmured.

"What's that, sir?"

"Nothing, madam. Shall I send someone to fetch her?"

"No, no, that is not necessary. Nor should you leave Mute Hill House," she added, sitting up straighter.

"I dislike trespassing further on your hospitality."

"Nonsense, Sir Christopher, you have barely met Fiona,

and if your betrothal to her stands, you will soon marry her. I should think you might at least spend the night as I had planned and try to get to know her a little. All these people should depart before supper, for they cannot require more food or drink after this, and I have invited no one to stay." Raising her voice, she said, "Malcolm, I want you."

"Yes, madam?"

"Pray, show Sir Christopher to a bedchamber," she said. "Malcolm will see that you have everything you need, sir."

"Thank you, madam," Kit said, thinking that this would repay Anne Ellyson. He could hardly wait to see her again, if only to see the expression on her face when she learned he would remain an overnight guest despite his ducking.

Lady Carmichael said abruptly, "Where has my uncle gone, Malcolm?"

"I believe that he, Sir Eustace, Parson Allardice, and others left some time ago, madam. He suggested that Sir Eustace must be bored with the wedding feast since he would win none of the fruits of . . . that is to say since there had been no wedding," he amended swiftly. "I believe they went out riding."

"Nonsense, you know that Toby never rides a horse if he can help it."

"Just so, my lady," Malcolm said, darting a quick glance at Kit.

Lady Carmichael said, "My uncle travels in a specially made pony cart, Sir Christopher, and since the ponies refuse to carry him any great distance, I warrant they will have gone no farther than his favorite alehouse in the village." Fluttering her eyelashes at him as she had once before, she added in a tone more suitable to a demure innocent, "I shall certainly scold him for neglecting you."

"Unnecessary, I assure you, madam," Kit said. "If we are not to discuss this odd situation in which we find ourselves, I shall welcome a good night's rest."

"Put him in the blue room near Sir Eustace, Malcolm."

"Yes, your ladyship."

Although Kit was by no means sure that he wanted to sleep so near his uncle if that gentleman was presently indulging himself at the local alehouse, he followed the steward obediently and soon discovered that Mute Hill House resembled a rabbit's warren. They passed several stairways before coming to one that apparently met with Malcolm's approval. At the first landing, Kit followed him down a gallery, assuming that his room would be somewhere along it. Instead, Malcolm led him to the far end and up a second stairway.

They went up only one more flight. This time, the gallery where they found themselves faced a bank of windows overlooking the gardens.

"A splendid view," Kit said.

"Aye, sir, we like it," Malcolm replied, as if the house were his own. "Sir Eustace is in that chamber at the end," he added, opening a nearby door.

Kit stepped into a pleasant bedchamber and strode across it to open the shutters in the lower section of a window overlooking a central courtyard he had not seen before. As he peered down, he heard the steward moving briskly about the room behind him. Turning, he saw the man peer into the ewer on the washstand and touch the towel on the rod, as if to be sure that all was in order.

"Thank you," Kit said. "I see that this house is even larger than it appears."

"It is a good size, which suits us, for Sir Stephen was accustomed frequently to entertain large parties, and her lady-ship enjoys company, too," Malcolm said. "I'll send up a lad with hot water, sir, and despite what her ladyship said, I assure you supper will be served in the hall as usual, although not until eight o'clock."

Glancing out at the sky, Kit was surprised to see how late it was, for the sun was low and the light had begun to fade.

"Faith, but it must be nigh onto five already," he said.

"Aye, sir. Shall I shut that window now?" he asked as Kit stepped away.

"No, leave it," he said. "I've spent much of my life in the open air, and I dislike being shut in unless it's raining hard or snowing. As for that hot water, I'd prefer you to send it up when I retire for the night."

Malcolm nodded and left.

Under ordinary circumstances, Kit would have had clothes to change and a personal servant with whom to chat. Since he had neither but did have three hours to spend before folks would gather in the hall for supper, he decided to go outside again and see if he could learn where Willie had gone.

Returning to the hall proved easy, but although he usually had a keen sense of direction, he was not sure he would as easily remember the way back to his bedchamber. However, he decided to worry about it only if he got lost.

Chapter 11

Anne was hungry. She had eaten nothing since breakfast other than the orange she had taken into the garden, and the thought of that orange reminded her that its bits of rind were now floating in the brook, doubtless well on their way to Ewes Water. Instantly, her imagination produced the picture of Sir Christopher, sitting in the swiftly flowing water with his hat tilted over his eyes.

He undoubtedly wanted to murder her. As she changed from the green velvet gown into a more informal one, she wondered unhappily when she would see him again. So certain was she that he had gone rather than face anyone in his sodden state that it came as a shock to find him at the high table when she went down to supper. It was even more surprising to find Olivia smiling and chatting with him, but Olivia's smiles were soon explained by her flirtatious manner.

Turning to Anne, she said lightly, "Where is Fiona? I was sure she would come down with you."

Guiltily, Anne admitted that she had assumed the opposite and thus had not even gone to Fiona's room.

"Well, you must go and tell her I want her here. She has

hidden away too often of late, and with Sir Christopher spending the night, she has a duty as one of this household to make him feel welcome."

"Yes, Aunt Olivia," Anne said, intensely aware of Sir Christopher but avoiding his eye by the simple tactic of keeping her gaze riveted to Olivia.

Glad to escape before she had to see the anger he undoubtedly still felt toward her, she hurried to her cousin's room, wondering if there were any way to send Fiona downstairs without accompanying her. The thought had barely passed through her mind, however, before she rejected it. Not only would Fiona refuse to go without her but she would despise her own cowardice if she avoided him. She owed him an apology, and she would simply have to get it over with.

As she had expected, Fiona did not want to leave her bedchamber, insisting that she would send Molly to fetch food for her when she grew hungry.

"Which I'm not now, Anne, I promise you. I don't want to see anyone!"

"Don't be a goose. You must go downstairs, or your mother will be up here in the twinkling of a bedpost. Kit Chisholm is spending the night, and she wants you to get to know him."

"Mercy, do you call him Kit?"

"No, of course not," Anne said, annoyed with herself. "I don't know why I did just then. But that is not important. You must come downstairs, Fiona."

"But I don't want to."

"Then tell your mother so when she comes to fetch you," Anne said, turning back toward the door.

"Oh, very well, but if Sir Eustace is there, I'll turn right around and come back if I have to get sick all over the floor to prove to them that I must."

"Eustace and Toby have gone to the alehouse," Anne said. "And you know that your uncle will not leave it until someone rolls him out the door to his cart."

"Good," Fiona said, turning more cheerfully to let Molly straighten her dress.

Downstairs, Anne felt only relief to see that her cousin was shyly polite to Sir Christopher and that he was charming to her. The conversation that ensued was desultory, even boring, so when she took a sip of her claret and chanced to catch his eye over the rim of her goblet, his teasing expression startled her into a smile.

He was still looking at her when Olivia said, "You should more properly ask him questions about himself, my dear. Men like to talk about themselves."

Startled, Anne turned toward her aunt, only to realize that she had addressed her remark to a deeply reddening Fiona.

"Oh, I couldn't," Fiona exclaimed. "I don't know what to ask him!"

"I am sure we'd all like to know where he has been hiding himself," Olivia said, turning to Kit. "We're eaten with curiosity, sir."

"I have been many places," he replied with an easy smile. "I have been to Italy and Spain, and sailed the Mediterranean Sea, and I've seen Ireland, too. I know little about what has transpired here in my absence, however. Perhaps you can tell me about life in Roxburghshire. For example . . ."

Anne watched with increasing admiration as he adroitly led Olivia away from a discussion of his activities and deep into Border gossip, flattering her one moment for her keen

insight into her neighbors and friends, and affecting astonishment the next at the vast extent of her knowledge.

Just as deftly did he draw Fiona into the conversation,
and within moments, Anne saw her cousin begin to gaze
raptly at him. Telling herself she was glad that Fiona liked
him, she had nonetheless to relax fists that had somehow
clenched so hard in her lap as to leave fingernail marks in
her palms.

It became clear that Olivia intended to make the evening
last as long as possible, but Fiona was soon yawning behind
her hand.

The tables in the lower hall had been cleared and dis-
mantled, and only the jug of claret remained on the high
table when Kit said, "Perhaps you should seek your bed,
Mistress Carmichael, before you fall asleep before our
eyes."

"Yes, do go up, my dear," Olivia said. "Sir Christopher is
right. I can see that he is a man who knows how to look after
his own."

Anne blinked, finding it suddenly hard to maintain her
serene expression. Apparently, Olivia had decided to shift
her support from Eustace to his nephew, and she wondered
what Eustace would think of that. Indeed, she wondered
what she thought of it herself. Surely, it was a good thing,
because Sir Christopher would certainly make an excellent
husband, so it was vexing that just that thought alone was
enough to make her want to cry.

She arose from the table when Fiona and Olivia did, but
to her surprise, Sir Christopher said, "I wonder if I might
have a word with you, Lady Anne."

Olivia looked from one to the other. "It is late, sir, and

Fiona and I long for our beds. I thought you understood that we mean to retire."

"I won't keep either of you, madam. I just want a word with her ladyship."

"The young women in this household understand that they are not to have private words with young men," Olivia said sternly. "Anne will go upstairs with us. If you want to speak with her, you may see her in the morning when we break our fast. Until then, good night, sir. Come along, Anne."

Obeying, Anne glanced over her shoulder. Encountering a teasing grin, she knew as surely as if he had said so that he was thinking again of their first meeting.

His attempt to steal a private moment with Anne thus foiled, Kit sat comfortably in front of the fire, enjoying the solitude of the empty hall until he heard sounds heralding the return of the men from the alehouse. Deciding it would be less than helpful to confront his uncle when Eustace had undoubtedly (from the sound of it) imbibed more ale than was good for him, he got up and left before the revelers entered the chamber.

He had not found Willie or anyone who had seen the lad. It occurred to him that until supper, Anne had been his only friend, although he doubted she believed that after what she had done to him. Lady Carmichael seemed disposed to like him, but he had seen enough of her to realize she was fickle at best, so he could not count on her. He would doubtless be safer in his bedchamber, but he would not be completely safe until he could reclaim Hawks Rig and man it with his own people.

Taking what he hoped was the right stairway, he went upstairs and along the first gallery he came to until he found the second stairway at the end. On the next level, he easily found the door he sought.

He opened it and stepped into the darkened room.

Someone had shut the window and kindled a fire in the fireplace, clearly having expected him to return sooner, since it had burned to embers. Using the orange-gold glow to light his way, he crossed to the window, pushed aside the curtain, and opened the shutters, drawing a welcome breath of the cold night air.

"Faith, but you're as bad as your horrid uncle!"

Turning sharply to find himself face-to-face with an angry Anne Ellyson sitting bolt upright in her night shift and apparently nothing else, he snapped, "What the devil are you doing in my bed and where are your clothes?"

Unable to sleep, Anne had been staring at the canopy overhead, thinking she probably owed a debt of gratitude to Olivia for sparing her "just a word" with Kit Chisholm, when she heard him come in. At first, she thought Peg must have forgotten something and, fearing to wake her, had entered without her usual double rap to announce herself. Anne nearly spoke before she realized that the footsteps of the person rapidly crossing the room were much heavier than Peg's.

Sitting up and peeping between the bed curtains, she watched the tall, shadowy figure stride across the room and open the shutters before it dawned on her that it was Sir Christopher.

Shocked and furious to think that he would enter her room, she had shoved the bed curtains aside and told him exactly what she thought of such behavior.

When he whirled to face her, demanding to know what she was doing in *his* bedchamber, she realized what must have happened and saw the same realization dawn in his expression.

"Faith, I've come to the wrong room, haven't I?" he said.

"Aye, sir, you have," she said, striving to recover her calm and failing completely. He was in her room with her and far too close for comfort, and she was sure, despite his teasing look earlier, that he must still be angry with her for pushing him into the brook. "There are separate stairs leading to the east and west wings of the house," she explained. "The rooms and galleries are much the same on both sides, and in the guest bedchambers the furnishings generally sit in the same positions with respect to the fireplace. If your fireplace is in the same—"

"Put a robe on, lass," he said, his tone still harsh.

"You need not bite my nose off," she snapped. "You are in *my* room, after all, and you must leave at once, so it does not matter if I put on my robe or not."

"It matters," he said.

"Now, see here—"

"No, you listen to me for once," he said. "I wanted to speak to you below, but your aunt prevented that. Still, until this moment I have not been able to find two minutes to speak privately with you, except when I got doused for my efforts, and I do not want to have this conversation before an audience."

"There can be no conversation," she said. "I know I owe you an apology, and I do apologize, so if that is what you came here seeking, you have it. Now, go."

His gaze fell upon her old robe draped across a nearby stool, and he snatched it up, flinging it at her. "Put that on, or I won't hold myself responsible for my actions. I've warned you before, my manners are not up to their old standard."

"Because of being with sailors so long," she said acidly. "Yes, you told me." But when he continued to look grimly at her, she sighed and put on the robe, saying, "Very well, but I cannot imagine what you think you must say to me."

"First, I am not angry with you. If I were, you'd have had no doubt of it, because my temper is the sort that flames high and loud, and burns quickly."

"You were angry when I left you sitting in the water."

To her surprise, he grinned but turned toward the fireplace as he said, "I was, and you should consider yourself lucky that I couldn't reach out and grab you then, because you'd have found yourself sitting beside me. Still, I know I deserved your anger, lass. I behaved badly, and I know what I'd do to any man who treated a woman the way I treated you on that bridge, so I have nothing to say about that aside from offering you *my* apology."

Anne could not remember any man other than a servant apologizing to her before. The experience was unique and surprisingly pleasant. Moreover, it instantly put an end to the nagging distress she had felt since running from the bridge.

He knelt beside the fireplace, took a log from the nearby basket and put it on, then began to blow on the hot embers to encourage their appetite.

She said, "If you are not angry, then what have we to discuss?"

Flames leaped in the fireplace, and as he stood and turned, they cast a flickering glow behind him that outlined his tall figure, making him look larger than life. Anne realized that she felt no less vulnerable with her robe on than she had felt without it. He was too large, too near, and entirely too masculine. Moreover, she had already learned that his behavior was unpredictable.

She started to get out of the bed, thinking that she might feel more able to cope with him while standing.

In a strained voice, he said, "Stay where you are."

"Now, really, sir, I suppose I may do as I please in my own chamber. Pray tell me what you wish to discuss."

"At least stay where you are, lass. I am truly no saint, nor am I accustomed to resisting temptation when it flaunts itself at me."

"But you must not *let* yourself be tempted! You are betrothed to my cousin."

"That is exactly what I want to discuss," he said. "I am not persuaded that I did the right thing today by interfering in her wedding. The more I see of young Fiona, the more I think that someone like Eustace is just what she needs. He is older, clearly admires her, and would be bound to treat her kindly. Faith, but he must feel like her father."

"You can know nothing about your uncle if you think his behavior toward any female is the tiniest bit fatherly," Anne said tartly.

"I know that is what you have told me, and I know it is what you believe of him, but although he has not seen fit yet to acknowledge me, I have seen nothing in his actions to indicate a predatory attitude toward your cousin. And she—"

"You have scarcely seen him at all," she pointed out. "He left with Toby an hour after you arrived, and they have not yet returned."

"Oh, they've returned," he said. "I heard them coming in and left the hall in a hurry, which is most likely why I took the wrong stairway. They sounded as if they had been drinking heavily, and they had others with them. It sounded like a party."

Anne grimaced. "Then they will be carousing until all hours," she said. "I just hope your uncle does not come wandering up here. He's done that before, too."

"Has he? He'd better not try it whilst I am here."

A bubble of laughter gurgled out before she could stop it. "I wish I may see that," she said. "Do you mean to say that if you were to hear him at Fiona's door, you'd storm out of here to tell him he has no business to be there."

"From what you have told me, he is as likely to be at this door as Fiona's," he said, but he was smiling at the picture she had painted for him.

"I see nothing amusing in the thought of Sir Eustace at my door," she said, trying to sound stern but failing. "Faith, but I would like to see his face," she admitted, "even at the risk of my own ruin."

Kit sobered. "That mustn't happen," he said, stepping forward and catching her by the shoulders.

Anne's breath caught in her throat. She could no more have protested than she could have flown. Instead, she looked up at him, wondering if he would dare to kiss her again. Every cell in her body cried out for him to do so, stirring impulses she scarcely recognized as her own.

He seemed to have stopped breathing, too, for he said no more but stood looking down at her, his hands still gripping her shoulders.

She wanted to touch his face, but she kept her hands at her sides, knowing that if she so much as reached up to touch one of the hands on her shoulders, she would be asking for trouble.

His right hand moved to her cheek, as if he were reading her thoughts and echoing them with his actions. His fingertips were rough as he drew two of them down her left cheek to the corner of her mouth and then across her lower lip. The impulse to kiss his fingers nearly overwhelmed her. Her nipples tingled and other parts of her body did as well. Sensations she had never felt before coursed through her, and when he fisted his hand and rubbed the backs of his knuckles across her chin and up to her cheek again, her lips parted invitingly.

His right hand slid to the back of her neck, and with a near growl from deep in his throat, he pulled her toward him, and his mouth came down hard on hers.

Anne leaned into him, all resistance melting at the first touch of his lips on hers. With a moan of pleasure, she pushed proprieties aside and kissed him back.

His hands moved over her body, exploring her, but she scarcely paid them heed, because his kisses continued and became more passionate. His tongue traced her lower lip and then thrust possessively inside her mouth, and as he pressed her tightly against him, she felt his lower body stir against hers, sending a flood of new sensations through her.

His right hand moved to cup one breast, but as it did, he paused and raised his head. She felt his body stiffen.

"What?" she murmured.

"Hush, listen," he whispered.

She heard then what he had heard, a footstep just outside her door.

"Fergus, what are ye doing?" Catriona exclaimed. "How did *he* get there?"

Giving her a stern look, Fergus said, "I canna allow me

lass tae put herself in jeopardy, say what ye will. I did nowt tae stop Sir Christopher afore now, thinking she'd be outraged and send him away, but he's confusing her now wi' his stroking and kissing. I ken what *she* wants, though, and that be for him tae marry Mistress Fiona. And dinna ye look so fierce, lass. I ken fine who must ha' steered him tae the wrong stairway. Ye're a fine one tae scold me for interfering."

"I did no such thing, but ye brought that mincing—!"

"Who's been interfering?" Maggie Malloch demanded from behind them. "Ye both ken the rules, and so far we ha' been gey careful."

"But now Fergus has interfered, and I do not know why," Catriona complained. "He must fix matters quickly, before he brings all to ruin."

"Leave your mortals tae deal wi' the new difficulty," Maggie ordered. "What happens will happen."

Catriona gave her a look that told her clearly she wanted to say more, perhaps even to suggest that Maggie was treading a thin line when she scolded others for interference, but when Maggie met the look with a straight one of her own, Catriona looked away.

Swiftly and without a word, just as Anne heard the click of the latch, Kit left her side and leaped behind the door. Just as swiftly, she moved to the fireplace and knelt, grabbing the poker as if to stir the fire.

As the door opened, she turned her head and stood up sharply, stiff with shock and rising fury, as Malcolm Vole stepped into the room.

Outrage that he would walk in without permission vanquished any feeling of guilt she might have felt as she faced him, leaving only fury.

"How dare you enter my bedchamber!"

"I beg your pardon, my lady, but I thought I heard voices in here."

"Even were that so, you have no right to enter my room, Malcolm, so be sure that Lady Carmichael will hear of this as soon as I see her in the morning. I do not know what you thought you could accomplish, even had you chanced to overhear me speaking to my maid, but as you see she is not here. Now, begone before I set up a screaming fit that will bring the house down around your ears."

As she spoke, she stepped toward him, glaring at him, determined to keep his full attention on her lest he look behind the door and see Kit standing there.

Malcolm wrung his hands, and said, "Indeed, my lady, I had no intention of disturbing you, which is why I did not rap or call out your name. Sir Toby brought a number of questionable persons home with him. I tried to tell him they were being too noisy, but he refused to listen, and when I found two men in her ladyship's bower, I feared others might have penetrated further into the house."

"Faith, how many did he bring home?"

"I don't know, for when I asked him, he told me to mind my place. Very high in the instep is Sir Toby when his ire is aroused."

"Malcolm, you know you have no authority over him. He is right to snub you when you overstep."

"I do not answer to you, however," he said.

"You are impertinent," Anne said, looking him in the eye and scarcely realizing that the poker in her hand twitched menacingly with each word. "You are not to address me in such a way unless you want me to relate the details of your disrespect to my aunt. And do not think for one moment that I cannot persuade her of your insolence."

"I beg your pardon," he said swiftly. "But amongst those whom Sir Toby has brought home is one friend of his that he insists must have a bedchamber because the man means to stay. Sir Toby would not say how long, but at least this one appears to be a cut above most of the others. Milo, Lord Berridge, he says his name is, although I know naught of him or his family. But that is not the worst of it."

"What, then?" Anne said, feeling a smidgen of sympathy for him at last.

"A jester, my lady."

"A jester?"

"Aye, or a minstrel, for he had a lute in hand, but mostly he narrates dreadful tales. I do not find them amusing, nor will her ladyship, but those ape-shot men laughed loud and long at them. Sir Toby says the jester must stay too. However, Sir Eustace said Sir Toby won him at dice and that he—Sir Eustace, that is—means to win him back before he returns to Hawks Rig. 'Twould amuse him, he said."

"Sir Eustace is planning to return soon, then?" Anne said, knowing that Kit would want the information as much as she did.

"I believe he intends to go tomorrow afternoon or early Sunday, my lady."

"I see now that you had cause to be concerned for my safety and for that of Mistress Fiona and Lady Carmichael, Malcolm, but henceforth you must knock before you enter any lady's room. You may go now."

With a bow but without comment, he did so, and Anne

drew a long breath and let it out slowly as the door shut behind him.

"There, ye see," Maggie said. "Lady Anne ha' dealt easily wi' him."

Fergus gave her a sour look from under his thin brows. "She'll be that sorry now if Catriona's lad focuses his attention on her instead o' the lass she means him tae marry. Just ye watch, Maggie. Ye're the one wha' interfered! Ye be siding wi' Catriona, and she doesna care a whit if my Lady Anne be happy or no."

"That's not so," Catriona snapped indignantly. "I'll have you know—"

"Whisst, the pair o' ye," Maggie said. "I want tae see what happens, but ye're tae come tae me parlor as soon as they be asleep, for I've summat tae tell ye, and 'tis plain now that I must tell ye both, but I canna do it whilst ye're busy."

As soon as Malcolm left, Kit put an ear to the door, and Anne said nothing until he straightened and turned to face her.

"Lord, what a little termagant you are," he said, chuckling. "You must have ruled your father's household with an iron rod. I almost felt sorry for the fellow."

"Are you sure he is gone?" she asked.

"I am," he said, "but that was too close. You should not take such chances."

"*I* should not?"

"Well, I did tell you to stay in your bed and to put on your robe, did I not?"

"You did," she admitted, realizing suddenly what they had done. "We are both at fault, sir, but I am *not* the one who is betrothed to another." Even as she said those words, she realized they did not excuse her. "Faith, though, I *am* her cousin."

One moment she felt hideously guilty, knowing he was bound to marry Fiona, but the next moment, her guilt vanished, and she felt calm again. It was as if a curtain had fallen inside her mind, making it impossible to dwell on her feelings. Nevertheless, she fought for the strength to do what she knew was right.

"Lass—"

"No, Sir Christopher—"

"I wish you would call me Kit," he complained. "I dislike hearing formality in every breath you take."

"Pray, sir, do not tempt me further. We cannot allow this to happen again. Between us, we stopped Fiona's wedding because we knew it was wrong. But consequences do follow that action, and for a few moments I foolishly allowed myself to forget what they are."

"The present situation is a farce," he said, his tone sharp again.

Doggedly, she went on. "You are betrothed to her, legally, and therefore you must marry her, for I am sure that is the right and proper thing to do. Indeed, had you failed to speak up during the ceremony as you did and allowed her to marry your uncle before you came forward to claim your estates and titles, her marriage to him surely would have been annulled. Betrothals are often deemed more binding than weddings, are they not?"

"They are no less so, certainly," he said with a sigh. "Many of the same rules apply to both, I believe. I think there are also degrees of strength in betrothals, however, depending on what the actual vows are and whether the parties are of age, nearly of age, or are still children. Nevertheless, I do see your point, lass, and I'll admit that I did not think either. I'll go now, and I will leave when Eustace does."

"So you will not teach me to shoot a gun, after all," she said, her disappointment evident although she had not meant to express it aloud.

He grinned. "I'll gladly teach you, if only so you can defend yourself against such men as my lecherous uncle and his equally dangerous nephew. But perhaps you should decide first if you mean to avoid me or let yourself be seen with me."

She knew what she ought to do, but the opportunity to have him teach her to shoot was too tempting. At least, she hoped it was just the opportunity to shoot. "Surely, if my maid accompanies me—"

"I'll teach her, too," he said. "We'll have a lesson after breakfast if you like, but I must leave when Eustace does. This situation is fraught with peril, and although I mean to search every cranny of the law to see what may be done about it, I agree that until I know where I stand, it will be best for us to keep apart."

"But you cannot mean to overset your betrothal to Fiona," Anne exclaimed. "Only a scoundrel could do such a thing! If you cry off, everyone will assume she must have done something dreadful. She would be ruined!"

"It cannot be as bad as that," he said, eyeing her with irritation.

"It would be, and you know it. Oh, I wish it were not, but people always blame the woman when things go wrong before a wedding."

"She is an heiress," he said. "She will draw suitors like flies to a honey pot."

"I will not be a party to that," she said, anger stirring again. "You do not realize how fragile she is. This business today has upset her dreadfully, despite not wanting to marry Eustace. To have another betrothal set aside so soon afterward, or ever—particularly since your uncle means to fight for her—" She broke off as a worse thought occurred to her. "Merciful heaven, don't you see what will happen if you discard her? That horrid man will demand that she honor her betrothal to him, and my aunt will make her marry him, if only to avoid more scandal!"

"No, she won't," he said. "You forget what Parson Allardice said about the degrees of consanguinity. Since I was betrothed to her, my uncle cannot marry her."

Anne shook her head. "You cannot have it both ways, sir. If your betrothal was legal, it stands, and you must marry her. If it was not legal or your being declared dead rendered it moot, then it won't prevent his marrying her. In any event, you heard his response to Parson Allardice. He can get a special license."

"They are not so easy to get, and they are ruinously expensive," he said.

"Your uncle did not see any obstacle. Perhaps you do not realize how many powerful friends he has, on both sides of the line."

Kit frowned. "I see that we should not discuss this further tonight," he said. "If you can tell me how to get back to my bedchamber without encountering more members of the household, I'll go now."

"Use the service stairs at the left end of the gallery, and go up one flight," she said. "There is a corridor there that connects the two sides of the house. You'll find another service stair at the end that leads to the gallery where your room is. Only the servants use that route, and most of them have gone to bed by now."

"Not all of them, however. I'd as lief not run into your aunt's steward again. What a pompous fellow he is, to be sure."

"Oh, yes," Anne agreed. "He behaves as if he owns the house, and my aunt does little to curb him. I did seem to make an impression tonight, though."

He grinned again. "You are too small to take such a high hand, my lass. Take care that you do not attempt it again with the wrong man."

Certain that he meant himself, she raised her chin and said, "It is not I who takes the high hand, Sir Christopher. You would do well to mind your manners."

He chuckled again and stepped close to her—too close. Looking down into her eyes, he said, "If you are going to insist that I mind all the rules, lass, I'm going to claim that forfeit I demanded earlier before I go."

"You already claimed it," she reminded him.

"Did I?" He leaned closer, his face only inches from hers. "Art sure, lassie?"

"Don't you remember?" she retorted, but her voice was weak.

He put a hand to the back of her head and touched his lips lightly to hers. "Ah, yes," he said as he released her and straightened, "now I remember." And with that, he turned about and left the room, shutting the door quietly behind him.

Anne stood for several moments, staring at the door, while thoughts and emotions tumbled over one another and she tried to decide what she felt. Her body ached for him to return, but she reminded herself firmly that despite any feelings she might have for him, it was her duty to see that Fiona married him.

It was not, she told herself firmly, that she wanted to marry him herself. She reminded herself that marriage to such an unpredictable man—and one who clearly thought rules were for others and never for himself—would be most uncomfortable. She believed in rules, and in obedience, too—at least, when it was sensible—but she also had her opinions, and he, like most men, never seemed to listen to them.

Like most men, he went his own road and expected her to obey him. When she had done no more than remind Malcolm of his place, Kit had called her a termagant. Fiona would make him a much more satisfactory wife, because Fiona would agree with everything he said and would obey his every command.

Having thereby settled her mind, she went back to bed cloaked in depression, and after an hour or two spent thinking about everything that had happened since she had met him, she managed at last to fall into a restless sleep.

Chapter 12

Now then," Maggie said, flicking a finger at the parlor fire-place, where a cheerful fire instantly sprang to life, "the three o' us ha' tae talk."

"What's amiss?" Catriona asked, making herself comfortable in a chair by the hearth.

Producing matching chairs for Fergus and herself with another flick of her finger, Maggie said, "I told ye afore that all plans develop a hitch or two."

"Aye," Fergus said, "but we did like ye said, and I'll admit things look tae be marching more smoothly now."

Catriona frowned but did not argue the point. Instead, she said, "I think Maggie means plans other than just what happened tonight, Fergus."

"I do," Maggie said, grimacing. "Ye'll both fly into a pelter when I tell ye, but it willna aid matters, so if ye dinna want tae stir me wrath, ye'll maintain your civility until we ha' talked it through."

Catriona looked alarmed. "Has something more happened to Claud?"

He could see them and hear them clearly. It was as if he had abruptly shifted from gray space to a chair of his own near theirs. He could almost feel the heat of Maggie's fire, could almost reach out and touch Catriona— almost, but not quite.

Maggie glanced at Fergus, who had nearly faded to empty air. "Show yourself properly, lad," she said, but her tone was oddly gentle as she said it.

Fergus obeyed her, turning red, as he said, "I forget about that when I get scared. Moreover, I can sense Jonah's presence the way ye sense Claud's, and he seems tae be near us all the time now."

He looked around, seeking that other, evil presence, but saw nothing amiss.

"Ye're just afraid," Maggie said. "D'ye no think I'd ken if he were so near?"

Fergus shrugged, clearly not convinced.

"Still, it's Jonah you want to discuss," Catriona said. "What's he done now?"

"Seems he added a wee trap tae his spell," Maggie admitted.

"Of course he did," Catriona said. "He always does."

"Aye, but we didna pay that factor enough heed." Drawing breath, she said, "There be only one way tae free Claud from his mortal."

The other two looked at her expectantly. Neither asked the obvious question.

He held his breath, watching Maggie.

"I ha' tae kill the mortal," she said.

Fergus vanished.

The dense gray cloud swirled around him, and the entire parlor disappeared.

Despite Anne's trouble falling asleep the previous night, she awoke at her usual time when Peg Elliot entered the room. As memory stirred of what the morning promised, all lingering sleepiness disappeared.

"Sakes, mistress," Peg said as she closed the shutters with a snap, "what demon possessed ye tae open this window? Last night were gey chilly."

"I was not cold," Anne said, remembering who opened the window. "I'll wear the russet gown with the lace trim," she added quickly, so Peg would not realize she had not answered her question. "Is Mistress Fiona awake?"

"Nay, not her. The only one I ken tae be up and about be Sir Christopher, and if any o' the other men ha' wakened, I'll be astonished, for they were up nearly till dawn, making such a din that I'm surprised they didna wake the whole house."

"Mercy."

"Aye, and that Malcolm tried tae shush them, too, he said, but Sir Toby sent him off wi' a kick tae his backside that nearly overset him, the foolish man."

"Sir Toby?"

"Aye, and when Malcolm told me, I said he should ha' had more sense than tae scold Sir Toby, but he said 'tis Toby who should walk soft, 'cause he heard Lady Carmichael say that if she could choose a husband, she'd choose Malcolm."

Anne gasped, not even trying to hide her mirth. "Oh, Peg,

she did say some such thing only the other day, for I heard her, but even a fool like Malcolm could never have believed that she meant it."

"Well, he did, but I think he knows even so that he cannot allow himself tae be insolent tae Sir Toby or his friends. He's worried about that fox, though."

"The fox?"

"Aye, for it frightened one o' the maids nearly witless by running out from under her cot just as she were walking into her room last night, and now the other lasses say the men must get it out o' the house."

They continued to chat as Anne finished dressing, and then she went down to the hall. Finding Kit ahead of her, she felt her body hum in response to his presence but greeted him calmly before she turned to tell a servant what she wanted.

"Just cold beef and bread," she said, taking her place on her usual stool. "And if there is apple juice in that jug, I'll have a mug of that, too."

Although she and Kit were alone at the high table, a number of persons were breaking their fast in the lower hall. Two lads attended them all, but one or the other hovered constantly near Anne and Kit, so their conversation was perforce desultory.

After a polite reply to his equally polite hope that she had slept well, and a few observations about the weather, she said with a smile, "You may recall that I told you . . . um, once before, that a pack of hounds chased a fox into this house."

"I remember," he said, shooting her the twinkling look she always received when something she said reminded him of their first meeting. "Do you mean to tell me the poor beast is still somewhere inside?" he added.

"It is, because my woman, Peg, said it frightened one of the maidservants just this morning," Anne said. "It dashed right out from under her bed."

He chuckled, saying. "I'd call that an omen if it had happened to me."

"What sort of omen?"

"A good one, I hope. You see, when I was in the Highlands, there was a chap riding about, trying to right certain wrongs. They called him *Sionnach Dubh*, which in Gaelic means 'the Black Fox.' "

"But who is he?" she asked.

"Oh, some fellow who believes ordinary folks sometimes need a strong arm to help them. Inverness was suffering under the rule of a bad sheriff."

"I thought you said your cousin's father was the sheriff."

"He is now, but one of Cardinal Beaton's toadies held the post then. He and his son, who was worse, wreaked havoc amongst the common folk there, and no one seemed willing or able to do anything about it."

"I am surprised that one of the more powerful Highland chiefs did not take a hand," Anne said.

"Most of them had already come south to support Jamie in his attempt to keep Henry on his own side of the line. The King of Scots and I have that much in common," he added with another twinkle. "We're both beset by wicked uncles."

"Tell me more about this . . . this Black Fox," she said, intrigued.

He shrugged. "There's not much more to tell. He made a great figure of himself in a long black cloak and a hood that covered his face, with eyeholes cut so he could see. He carried a sword and pistols, and made great play out of waving them about. Still, he bested the wicked sheriff and his son, so Inverness is calm again now, and I warrant we'll hear no more from *Sionnach Dubh.*"

"But he sounds wonderful," she said.

"Folks up there liked him. Are you ready for your lesson?"

"Yes, please," she said, instantly pushing back her stool and getting up.

He stood as well, and picked up a satchel that lay near his feet, saying as he straightened, "Where is your woman?"

"I don't need her," Anne said glibly, having decided that she did not want to hear Peg's opinion of the shooting lesson or of Kit Chisholm. "Any number of stable lads and other servants will be wandering about, after all."

"Aye, but you should have a woman with you, lass. It will look better so."

She eyed him speculatively, but his jaw was set. "Very well," she said, and asked one of the lads to tell Peg to meet her in the stableyard.

They walked outside together, but when they found the stableyard teeming with servants and men-at-arms, Kit spoke briefly with one of the latter while Anne went to wait for Peg at the door near the kitchen.

When the two women joined Kit, he said, "The men have an area outside the gates where they practice their marksmanship with longbows and pistols. I suggest we walk out there, so you don't shoot anything you ought not to shoot."

Peg shook her head at her mistress. "I dinna ken what ye'll think of next. A woman shooting a pistol! Think what a scandal it would be did ye shoot anyone."

"She won't shoot anyone," Kit said confidently. "She

does not have a pistol of her own, for one thing, and even if she did, it's harder than you might think to hit anything with one shot, and although I've heard of pistols that can discharge more than once before reloading, I've never seen one. I prefer to defend myself with either a sword or a longbow."

"I want to learn to shoot," Anne said. "One never knows when knowledge of any sort may prove useful."

"That's true enough," he said, waving to the man he had spoken to earlier. "He will show us where their practice area lies."

They walked outside the wall and a short way downhill through woodland to a clearing where archery butts stood at increasing distances. Their guide indicated a man-high pile of river sand that stood some way to the left of the butts.

"Ye can put anything ye like in front o' that sand for a target, sir."

Kit nodded. "The sand pile itself will do well enough," he said. "If she can hit that from ten feet, I'll be astounded."

The man looked surprised. "She?"

"Aye, Lady Anne wants to learn how to shoot."

A smile split the man's face, and Kit grinned back at him.

"Do you two find such amusement in that?" Anne asked evenly.

The man-at-arms stopped smiling, but Kit did not. "Don't fly into a temper, Anne-lass. You'll want your aim to be steady. In any event, I was not laughing at you. I just don't want you to be disappointed when you don't hit anything. Even men skilled in the art usually hit their targets only when they're on top of them. Pistols, to my mind, are more useful as weapons to throw than weapons to shoot."

"Well, I must have a target I can see," she said. "What is

the use of shooting at a pile of sand? Even if I hit it, I won't know I did. Haven't you a handkerchief or something that you could put in the middle of it?"

"Aye, but only one of fine cambric," he said.

"Well, if you're so sure that I can't hit it . . ."

Kit sighed. "Very well, but I should think you'd see a puff of sand, at least." He handed his kerchief to the man-at-arms and gestured toward the pile. As the man moved to set the white square in place, Kit said, "Now, watch me, and I'll show you how to load a pistol. The first part is the same as for a matchlock or even a cannon. Hand me that powder flask, if you will, lass."

When their hands touched, guilt stirred at the delight she felt in being so close to him, so she focused her attention firmly on his actions.

Opening the flask with his teeth, he poured a bit of its contents into the barrel of the pistol. "Now we'll put this paper wad in and use the rod to tamp it down . . . so. Next, the ball—that leather sack beside the second wee flask."

She took a lead ball from the sack and handed it to him, watching as he used the rod to ram it in. "Now we'll wind the wheel," he said, doing so with a small spanner that fit over the tiny axle. Sprinkling more powder into the pan atop the wheel and alongside the barrel vent, he closed the pan cover.

"That looks simple enough," Anne said, hoping she could remember it all.

"Open that other flask and take out a piece of pyrites. That's our flint." He showed her where to put it, how the cock worked, and then let her tighten the pin.

Carefully following his instructions, she said, "Now what?"

"The wheel has tiny teeth," he explained. "When you pull the trigger, the wheel turns, striking the flint and creating a shower of sparks to ignite the powder and discharge the ball."

"Faith, does one have to do all that each time before one shoots?" she asked.

"Aye, but the closed pan on the wheel-lock means you can load it and put it in a saddle holster, so it's ready to shoot when you need it even when it rains. Just don't need it twice, because the only good you'll get then is if you throw it at your enemy. Now," he added, handing it to her, "Use both hands to hold it steady, and when you're ready, just pull the trigger."

Anne held the pistol in front of her, hefting it to feel its balance, then looked at the handkerchief on the sand pile, drew a breath, and fired.

The explosion from the gun startled her, and she had all she could do to keep it from flying out of her hands. Beside her, Peg let out a screech, echoed by a cry of astonishment from the man-at-arms.

The handkerchief had jumped and folded in upon itself.

"I hit it!" Anne exclaimed gleefully.

"My best handkerchief," Kit wailed.

Fergus said, "I kent fine the lass could do it."

"There you are!" Catriona exclaimed. "We thought you had abandoned us."

"Nay, I were just scared is all," Fergus said. "I wouldna abandon me lass. Recall that we Ellyllon can make ourselves invisible tae other members o' the Clan, just as we can make ourselves visible though not audible tae mortals."

Catriona frowned. "I did not realize you could do either.

I thought you just accidentally faded away when you were frightened. And in any event, if you guided that ball for her, I'll have something to say—"

"Sakes, I never thought o' doing that!"

"I did it," Maggie muttered. "Those men annoyed me, acting as if a female couldna shoot straight. They needed a wee lesson."

Catriona burst into a peal of laughter. "And you told us to be sure to follow the rules! Oh, mercy, just look at his face!"

Kit stared at Anne in awe. Not for a moment had he imagined that she would hit the kerchief. He had never known even an experienced man-at-arms to hit anything when firing a new pistol for the first time.

She looked as astonished as he was.

"Do you want to try again?" he asked.

"No, sir, not today," she said. Then, endearing herself to him yet again, she added, "I prefer to remember that I hit something, and I am sure I could not do so twice. I'd like to reload it by myself, however, to be sure I remember how. May I?"

"Aye, sure, lass," he said, looking again at the handkerchief. "Let the barrel cool for a few moments, though, so you don't burn yourself."

"Mistress," Peg said, "I do not think you should be doing this. Only think what people will say when they learn that Lady Anne Ellyson goes about firing pistols at handkerchiefs."

"Let them say what they like," Anne said. "I cannot be the first lady to shoot."

"Certainly not, mistress," Kit said. "Scott of Buccleuch's

mother shot at Henry's men when they burned Branxholme some years ago."

"That fire destroyed Branxholme, did it not?"

"Aye, and Buccleuch's been rebuilding since. The place is splendid again, but his marriage has suffered."

"My aunt said he means to set aside his present wife and marry another."

Peg sniffed. "Marriages are not meant to be set aside so lightly. I'm sure only men like that awful King Henry even consider such dreadful things."

Kit smiled. "Only the most powerful—that is, the wealthiest—can afford to divorce their wives. One must pay extraordinary fees to persuade the Pope to allow it."

"I've heard that Buccleuch can succeed by applying to Cardinal Beaton," Anne said. "Could that be so?"

"Aye, for the cardinal is the Lateran Legate, which means Beaton acts as the Pope in Scotland. If he supports Buccleuch, that marriage is as good as over."

Anne said thoughtfully, "The woman Buccleuch wants is called Janet Beaton. Do you think she can be related to the cardinal?"

"That would explain Buccleuch's haste to marry her," he said. "A connection to the cardinal would increase his power substantially, and I wager Beaton believes alliance with Buccleuch will greatly increase his own power in the Borders."

As they talked, Anne had been reloading his pistol. She held it out now for his inspection.

Examining it, he said, "Aye, that's it. Take care not to wind it too tightly, and remember that pistols are notoriously undependable."

"Still, I think I will purchase one if you can tell me how

to go about doing that," she said. "With Henry's men in the area, and the chance of invasion growing stronger by the day, I'd like to have one by me if I need it."

He nodded. "Before I saw you shoot, I'd have advised strongly against it," he admitted, "but you possess a natural talent. I'll find one for you myself if you like."

To his delight, she favored him with a wide smile as she said, "Thank you, sir. If you get one for me, I know it will be exactly what I require."

He had not seen her smile so before, and he was not prepared for the warmth that surged through him when she did. She had attracted him powerfully from their first meeting, but she was beginning to affect him in ways he had never experienced before, and he was not sure what to think—or what to do about it.

Having expected him to declare flatly that no woman should have a pistol, Anne was amazed to receive his support instead. Really, she thought, the man was an oddity. Just when he had exasperated her by seeming never to listen, he could do something like this that showed understanding beyond what anyone could expect.

Feeling perfectly in charity with the entire world as a result, she agreed when Peg suggested that she should change her dress before dinner, and the three of them returned to the house by way of the garden door.

Since she had not seen Fiona all day, Anne decided to visit her as soon as she exchanged the russet gown for one of her favorite mossy green. Peg would not let her go until she had brushed her hair and arranged it in plaits beneath a soft French hood that matched the gown, but at last, she was ready and hurried to her cousin's room to find Fiona preparing to descend to the hall for the day's main meal.

Molly was fussing over her near one of the windows, twitching Fiona's pink skirts into place over a wide French farthingale. Fiona stood patiently enough, however, apparently having recovered her usual amiable disposition at last.

"You have not worn that dress in months," Anne exclaimed as she entered. "I'd forgotten how well it becomes you."

Fiona smiled and said cheerfully, "Now that I no longer have to marry Eustace Chisholm, there can be no reason for me to wear blue all the time. I look forward to recalling any number of my dresses to your memory." Lifting her lace-trimmed skirt, she showed off matching pink silk slippers.

"You are very grand, love," Anne said, laughing. "I believe you mean to flirt with Sir Christopher."

"He is exceedingly large, is he not?" Fiona said.

"He is, but he is also kind," Anne said. She nearly told Fiona about her shooting lesson, but it occurred to her that her gentle cousin would most likely think it an odd pastime to have enjoyed, and she did not want to spoil her own memories, so she kept her counsel, saying instead, "Are you ready to go downstairs? I feared you would insist on taking your meals in this room for at least the rest of the week."

"Oh, no, for Mother would never allow it," Fiona said. "Moreover, Uncle Toby said he has hired a most amusing jester who can play the lute and sing, and I want to hear him. Uncle Toby says he is an excellent minstrel and very funny, too."

"Well, do not grow too fond of him," Anne said. "I doubt that your mother will be as pleased with him as Toby is.

Moreover, I heard from Peg that Eustace said he means to take the jester back to Hawks Rig with him."

"Oh, that would be too bad of him," Fiona exclaimed.

"Mayhap you should hear the man sing before you decide that we would miss him," Anne said with a grin.

Fiona chuckled, and they went downstairs together, entering the hall to find Toby and Eustace chatting with a third man. The latter was slightly older than the other two but dressed as grandly as they were.

"There you are," Toby exclaimed jovially as Anne and Fiona entered. "Pray, allow me to introduce to you my good friend Milo, Lord Berridge of Midlothian. My lord, this is Lady Anne Ellyson and Mistress Carmichael."

The older gentleman made a profound leg, saying in a deep, rather harsh voice, "I am charmed, ladies. Such a privilege to be a guest in this splendid house."

"You are most welcome, sir," Fiona said politely.

Berridge was a stocky man, but he dressed well and bore an air of distinction wholly lacking in his host or in Eustace.

He smiled at Fiona, adding, "It surprises me that two such young ladies would come downstairs before Lady Carmichael has made her appearance."

"No matter, no matter," Toby said, "for here is Olivia now. Olivia, my dear, I decided that it is past time for you to be setting aside your megrims and your blacks, and to that end I have brought you a guest and a present, for all that Eustace here thinks he will take the latter away with him when he returns to Hawks Rig."

"Whatever are you talking about, uncle?" Olivia asked in a faint voice as she made her way to her chair at the high table.

"I've brought you something that will vastly amuse you,"

he said confidently. "Here now, Mad Jake, show yourself, you rascal!"

At his command, a flurry of red and gold erupted from the doorway to the central stairs. Spinning and whirling, the figure came, turning cartwheels and doing flips the length of the hall.

Other members of the household who had taken their places at the trestle tables burst into applause as the figure bounced upright before Olivia and then swept her a bow so swift and deep that he seemed in danger of banging his nose on the floor, if not toppling right over into a somersault.

When he straightened, Anne saw that he was a well-favored young man of no great height, but slender and wiry. He wore hugely puffed red hose, slashed with yellow, and a matching, trim-fitting doublet. On his head, he wore a funny little cap with points and bells round the rim, while more bells tinkled on the long pointed tips of his shoes. His grin was infectious, and his blue eyes twinkled merrily.

"Tell us a tale, lad," Toby commanded.

"Aye, well, shall I tell ye about the two times I met King Henry, then?"

"Have you really met him?" Fiona asked, visibly awed.

"Och, aye, me lady, and he'll be the fattest man I ha' ever seen. Makes Sir Toby here seem nobbut a thin shadow by comparison."

"But how did you meet him?" Olivia asked.

"Now, that were the easy part," the jester said, "for his men did capture me and carry me tae his presence bound up in a prodigious big sack. Dumped me right out on the floor in front o' his great throne. And Henry were fierce, too. He did say that if I ever set foot on English soil again, he'd cut off me head."

"Then you must never go back," Fiona said earnestly.

"Ye didna listen, lass," he said drolly. "I already said I ha' been there twice."

"Then why did he not cut off your head?"

"Well, like I told ye, he said I were no tae set foot on English soil, and when they carried me in tae see him, I swore tae him I'd no done that at all."

"But how could that be?" Fiona demanded.

In answer, the jester pulled off one boot and turned it upside down. A pile of dirt fell onto the floor. "Like that," he said. "Ye see, wherever I go, I always keeps me both feet planted in good Scottish soil."

A burst of laughter greeted Kit as he entered the hall, but he had heard the tale before and anticipated the last line. He also recognized the storyteller's voice, so he was able to conceal his shock at seeing Willie Armstrong playing the fool.

Lady Carmichael caught his eye and said, "Welcome, Sir Christopher. You must hear the amusing story my uncle's new jester has told us."

"Och now, me lady, I never repeats me stories," Willie said, winking at Kit.

"Pray, let me introduce Kit to our newest guest, Olivia," Sir Toby said, turning slightly to reveal another man who had hitherto been concealed by his bulk. "Allow me to make you known to Lord Berridge, lad," he said in his jovial way.

As the other man turned toward him, Kit nearly let his jaw drop.

"How do you do?" Tam said affably in accents far different from the Border brogue Kit was accustomed to hear from him. "You must be young Chisholm."

Collecting his scattered wits, Kit returned the older man's bow, murmuring politely, "I am indeed he, your lordship. Have we met before?"

"Nay, lad, but your uncle Eustace has been telling me all about you."

"Has he?" This was a new turn-up, Kit thought, shifting his gaze to Eustace.

"Aye, he tells me you've been missing so long he had you declared officially dead. Said it were a fair shock to him to see you turn up alive after all."

Kit turned to Eustace. "Forgive my astonishment, sir, but I thought you had refused to accept me as Kit Chisholm and intended to contest my claim."

"I do intend to contest your claim to the fair Fiona, lad, for I'd be a fool if I did not," Eustace said in a much friendlier tone than any Kit had heard from him since arriving at Mute Hill. "As to Hawks Rig, I'll make no promises until I've had a chance to examine the law as it pertains to such things," Eustace added. "We are not yet sure, after all, that someone who is officially dead can be made to live again—officially, that is. However, I've come to realize that you must be who you say you are, and as such, I shall welcome you at Hawks Rig."

"Thank you," Kit said dryly. "You are very generous, sir."

Anne heard the odd note in Kit's voice when he greeted Berridge, and the irony in it when he responded to Eustace, and if she did not understand the former, she could easily understand the latter. She only wondered at his calm, knowing he must be seething at what was no more than an invitation to stay at his own house.

Olivia said to no one in particular, "Do you know, I believe I have just hit upon the answer to all this."

"Have you, my dear?" Toby said with his usual grin.

"Oh, I know I generally leave it to you men to decide what we should do; however, I believe this time that my notion is the perfect solution to everything."

"Let us sit down before you tell us about it," Toby said. "I'm too large a man to stand longer than I must. Take your seats, gentlemen, so the lads can begin serving, and you there, Mad Jake, bring out your lute and play us a tune. Not too loudly, mind. We want to hear ourselves talk."

The jester did a back flip and ran to the rear of the room, reappearing a moment later, lute in hand. Looking about, he found a three-legged stool that he drew near the fireplace, where he sat down and began to strum.

"Now, lass, explain this brilliant notion of yours to us," Toby invited. "I'm sure we are all eager to hear it."

"You mock me, sir, but you will soon agree that it is the very thing. You will recall that Buccleuch and his lady were here yesterday for the wedding."

"Aye, as who could forget," Toby said. "His lady dragged herself around all afternoon as if it were her wedding that we'd called off instead of poor Fiona's."

"Well, Janet is upset, of course," Olivia said. "I know you must all have heard the rumors that her marriage to Buccleuch is about to end."

"Aye, for he's tired o' the lass and none too particular about who knows it."

"Janet said she came because she wanted to see Fiona married, but on their return to Branxholme, she will go home to her family at Ferniehirst," Olivia said.

"Mercy," Fiona breathed. "How awful for her!"

"Is there to be a divorce, then?" Eustace asked.

"It is as good as done, Janet told me, because Beaton is coming to the Borders soon to confer with Buccleuch, and he is bound to support both the divorce and Buccleuch's new wife, who is his own cousin, after all."

"Buccleuch's cousin?"

"No, Beaton's, and that is what stirred this notion in my head."

"Tell us," Toby commanded, gesturing to Malcolm to carve him a more generous slice of the great roast of beef.

"As you know," Olivia said, "Sir Eustace insists that his betrothal to my daughter must take precedence over the earlier one with Sir Christopher, because Sir Christopher is legally dead and did not take a part in that earlier one."

"Not to mention," Eustace interjected, "that I spoke my own vows."

"With respect, sir," Olivia said, "that can make no difference, because your nephew had an excellent proxy in his father." To the table at large, she said, "I am persuaded that both betrothals are perfectly legal. After all, our own High King of Scots married in France without setting a foot there."

"But where does this brilliant notion of yours enter into it?" Toby asked.

"Why, with Cardinal Beaton, of course. If he is coming here to confer with Buccleuch and put an end to his marriage—"

"More likely, he's coming to see how strong our defenses are before he lets Jamie come within a hundred miles of the line," Eustace said.

"Even so, he will be talking with Buccleuch at Branxholme, which is less than two hours from here on horseback.

I mean to invite him to Mute Hill, and I warrant he will come. Then he can decide which of you Fiona must marry. Indeed, I shall be surprised if I cannot persuade him to perform the ceremony himself."

Glancing at Kit, Anne thought he looked pale.

Lord Berridge said mildly, "What an exciting household this promises to be. Do you know how soon Beaton expects to be in the Borders, my lady?"

"Janet thought he would be at Branxholme within the next sennight," Olivia said, smiling. "If you are still here, sir, I hope you will attend the wedding."

"Indeed, I will. Dear me, I am sure it must be the first wedding to which I have ever been invited where no one knows who will act the part of the groom!"

Chapter 13

Fergus had disappeared again.

"I cannot find him anywhere," Catriona said to Maggie, when the two met again in the latter's parlor. "He's simply vanished. I think he's terrified of Jonah."

"Aye, and I canna blame the lad," Maggie said. "Jonah's gey wicked."

It had happened again! One moment gray mist, the next the cozy parlor and lovely Catriona only inches away, her soft breasts peeping ever so invitingly from her low-cut green, gauzy gown—so close, but maddeningly untouchable.

"What if Fergus really can sense Jonah's presence the way you can sense Claud's?" Catriona said. "What if Jonah is really near us all the time now? He can change his shape at will, after all. He could be anyone, or anything, for that matter."

"Fergus is just afraid," Maggie said. "I dinna doubt that Jonah be watching, but we canna worry about him until we find Claud."

"I am watching." He tried to say the words aloud, but
no sound issued forth. They could neither hear nor see
him, and even Maggie seemed unable to sense how
near he was, although he was strongly aware of a
third, unseen person with them in the room. Clearly,
Jonah—or someone else—was enjoying this dreadful
game.

"Fergus said you talked with his lass," Catriona said.

"Aye, and what of it?"

"I just wondered if you talked with Kit Chisholm, too,
that's all."

"I havena talked wi' him yet, but I did peek into his
thoughts the day the lass pushed him into the brook," Maggie said. "He's a good man, so dinna vex me by complain-
ing, Catriona, for I havena told ye all o' Jonah's wickedness
yet."

"There's more?"

"Aye, but when Fergus vanished after I mentioned it the
first time . . ." She paused, then added bluntly, "I didna want
tae frighten ye away, too."

"I won't go anywhere," Catriona said. "I mean to see this
through, but you cannot kill a mortal, Maggie, whatever else
we do. You'd be banished forever."

"I ken that, lass, but I'll no let that Jonah leave my Claud
stuck tae any mortal till they both die. The thing is," she
added reluctantly, "Jonah said if I kill the wrong one, then
his spell will allow the Host tae take our Claud."

*A scream of terror filled his mind, and the gray mist
rose to enclose him.*

Catriona clapped a hand to her breast. "No! Oh, what are we to do?"

"We'll do what we must," Maggie said grimly. "And that Fergus will, too."

"I'm here," a small voice said. "I'm afeared tae let Jonah Bonewits see me wi' ye, but I'll do what I must tae protect my lass."

"Good lad," Maggie said, suppressing the urge to make him show himself so she could vent her true feelings by shaking the wee eavesdropper till his ears flew off.

The afternoon and evening passed pleasantly, thanks to the skills of Toby's jester. However, Anne noted with disappointment and mild exasperation that Fiona was more taken with the jester's music and stories than she was by Sir Christopher. She was polite and responsive to any comment he addressed to her, but the lively jester was a fascinating novelty.

Kit tried more than once to introduce the problem of the betrothal, clearly wanting to understand his uncle's puzzling position in the matter, but none of the others seemed interested in discussing it. Apparently, Eustace and Toby had decided to let Olivia have her way and leave everything to the cardinal.

Eustace seemed unconcerned about Beaton choosing Fiona's bridegroom. When he left Sunday morning after Parson Allardice celebrated mass in the chapel, Anne thought he seemed unnaturally cheerful, as if he were certain Beaton would select him. She tried to assure herself that his good humor might stem from nothing more than winning the new jester from Toby, as he had said he would, but it was far easier to suspect him of further nefarious plotting. She did not trust Eustace an inch.

Toby was not cast down by losing the jester, having decided the household at Hawks Rig would have more need of entertainment than the one at Mute Hill.

"That fellow's too energetic by half," he explained when Fiona asked why he had let Eustace take Mad Jake away with him. "All that flipping and jumping around, and when he pulled a coin out of a maidservant's ear whilst she was pouring my ale . . . Well, I just thought that was enough, that's all."

"But I thought he was funny, Uncle Toby, and he played his lute very well, too," Fiona said. "Moreover, he sings songs I like, and he teaches me new ones, which our other minstrels never did."

"Well, if I'd realized you were taken with the chap, I'd have kept him, my dear," Toby said, fondly patting her hand.

They were in Olivia's bower, having retired there after their chief guest's departure. Kit was also preparing to leave. He, too, intended to ride to Hawks Rig, as everyone knew, but Eustace had not invited him to ride with his party.

"Pray do not concern yourself over the jester, uncle," Olivia said as she drew her tambour frame nearer. "I would remind you that despite our recent company and the plans that continue for Fiona's wedding, this is still a house of mourning. Anne, pray draw that curtain a little more so the sunlight does not strike my face. I should think you would have noticed that it is practically blinding me."

"Yes, Aunt Olivia," Anne said, hurrying to obey. From the window, she had a view of the garden, and to her surprise, she saw Kit walking there with Lord Berridge. They were too far away for her to read the expressions on their faces, but she could tell by the way Kit moved that he was speaking forcefully, and she wondered what his lordship had said to annoy him.

Kit had waited only long enough to be sure no one was near enough to overhear them before he said grimly, "What the devil do you and Willie think you are doing, Tam? Someone is bound to know you cannot be Berridge of Midlothian."

"How would they?" Tam asked reasonably. "As far as I know, nae one uses such a title."

"Beaton, for one, will certainly know it's false, don't you think?"

"I canna imagine why he would. There be any number o' titles hanging about, and some folks just style themselves as they please. Think o' Beaton himself. First, he were plain Davy Beaton, then Father Davy when he decided he had tae be a priest, and now his eminence. I'm doing nowt but playing a wee charade."

"A most dangerous charade."

"Nay, lad. Tae my mind, there be nobles aplenty who never mention their minor titles. Who could remember them all, anyway? Sons take minor titles, too, sithee? Ha' ye never been introduced tae some young sprig, styling himself Lord This or That wi' a title that belongs tae his father?"

Kit nodded. "That's a point, but though you seem able to affect the accents, how do you intend to play the part of a lord when you've never done it before?"

Tam chuckled. "Playing the part is easy. I had plenty of time tae study an excellent example of lordly behavior whilst we were aboard the *Marion Ogilvy*."

"Not the captain, surely, for I can tell you—"

"Nay, lad. A gentleman, in his own way, the captain were, but obsequious to them he considered his betters. Knowing it would take someone more arrogant tae impress Toby and Eustace, I took that bastard Gibson for my model."

Kit suppressed an urge to laugh. "Our villainous first mate!"

"Aye, for a more pompous sort I never hope tae meet. Pretending tae be Gibson wi' a royal accent seemed just the course tae take wi' Toby and your uncle. That lass, though, she'll be another concern. I'll ha' tae watch m'self wi' her."

Kit did not have to ask which lass he meant. Fiona would not suspect a thing, but Anne was far more perceptive. He shook his head. "I do not know what you or Willie were thinking to get up these masquerades."

"We're guarding your back, lad. Willie winkled an invitation tae Hawks Rig out o' that uncle o' yours, did he not?"

"Eustace won him, dicing," Kit reminded him.

"Aye, as Toby did," Tam said. "Sithee, what they didna tell ye is that them dice they cast was Willie's. Sly as a hill fox, that lad is, to fool your foumart uncle."

"Aye, he is, though since Eustace is about all that's left of my family, I suppose I should object to your calling him a weasel."

"No gentleman steals from his kin."

Kit agreed, so he changed the subject, saying mildly, "So then, you mean to impose on her ladyship's hospitality, whilst Willie takes up residence at Hawks Rig. Is that your grand plan?"

"Aye, although we came by the notion separately. I began hearing tales o' your uncle's doings as soon as I left Dunsithe, and knew straightaway that ye'd welcome information if I could find a way to slip into the enemy's camp."

"But as Lord Berridge?"

"A more likely role for me than playing the jester," Tam said with a rueful smile. "I dinna deny that if I had tae deal daily with a man o' your uncle's stamp, I'd soon be sped, for he's as sharp as he can stare. But Toby Bell be nobbut a fat fool, so once I saw that Willie had hit on the very way to keep close to Eustace—"

"I was astonished to see him, I can tell you."

Tam chuckled. "I believe ye, for I were, too. I found him in possession of the alehouse when I wandered in. Still, I dinna think Eustace would have thought tae take him tae Hawks Rig had Willie no managed tae slip the notion into Toby's head at the start that the pair o' them should cast dice for possession o' him."

"Faith, is that how he did it?"

"Aye, *and* fixed it so Toby won, which just made Eustace want Willie more. Your uncle is a covetous man, lad."

"He is that," Kit agreed. "I don't like any of this. The more I see of him, the less I understand. First, he refused to recognize me. Yesterday, he said he looks forward to welcoming me at Hawks Rig, but when I suggested riding with him this morning, he said he had business to attend on the way and would look for me late this afternoon or evening, or even tomorrow, that I had no cause to hurry."

"Your stopping his marriage dismayed the man," Tam said. "I'd say he showed his true nature then. He doesna want ye here, and 'tis me own belief he did think ye were dead. 'Tis almost as if he had cause tae believe it."

"He was certainly not happy to see me," Kit agreed.

"Aye, well, he's settled in comfortably at Hawks Rig, especially as he's turned out your people and replaced them wi' his own. He meant tae install Mistress Fiona there—aye, *and* her inheritance—so he canna be happy that ye upset all his plans. Whether or no he were dangerous afore, he will be now."

"Her ladyship invited us both to visit as often as we like," Kit said. "I had not intended to spend much time at Mute Hill before his eminence's arrival—"

"*If* he arrives," Tam interjected. "It's occurred tae me that he can answer her ladyship's question easily enough in a letter."

"Aye," Kit said. "Then what? Does she simply send word to Hawks Rig, commanding the chosen bridegroom to present himself forthwith?"

Tam shrugged, and Kit was no wiser an hour later when he took his leave of Lady Carmichael.

She fluttered her lashes at him as she bade him farewell, repeating her invitation to ride over as often as he liked until they learned what Beaton's decision would be. "For I am certain, sir, that his eminence will agree that yours is the betrothal our dearest Fiona must honor," she said. "It came first, after all, and thus must take precedence. You will see, for I know I am right."

"We shall all see, madam," he said, glancing at Anne.

She had been quiet at the noon meal and paid him little heed now except to nod when he included her in his farewells. Doubtless she'd be glad to see the back of him, he thought. He had not behaved well toward her, and that was plain fact. She had a knack for bringing out the worst in him, and he could not understand it. He wanted her, of all people, to think well of him, but even during their shooting lesson, with her maid present, it had taken every ounce of strength he had to keep his hands off her. He could not deny that she intrigued him far more than her cousin did, and under ordinary circumstances, he would have enjoyed a light flirtation with her that might well have led to something more, but she was right to keep him at arm's length until they sorted out the betrothal nonsense, if they could sort it out. In any event, he was a villain to tease her. He just could not seem to help it.

He shook hands with Toby and with the false Berridge, and as he left the room, he heard the latter cheerfully accept Toby's invitation to play Cent at the extravagant sum of sixpence a game.

Wondering how Tam expected to pay his debt if he lost, Kit mentally shook his head at the older man. He had said he had friends who helped him learn what was going on at Hawks Rig. Apparently, he also had friends with sufficient resources to lend him the fine clothing he wore, so perhaps their generosity would extend itself to financing his losses as Lord Berridge.

On the other hand, neither Kit nor Willie had ever learned why Tam had been sentenced to the *Marion Ogilvy*. The older man had had kept his counsel with regard to the details of his previous life.

In the stableyard, Kit found his horse saddled and waiting, so he mounted and rode outside the gates, feeling strangely bereft and hesitant about the course he had set for himself. He had grown accustomed to having companions when he rode, and he missed them. Riding to attend the wedding, he had had Willie with him and had been able to discuss his dilemma and what he might do about it. Now, however, even had Willie been with him, Kit knew he would have felt at least a little uneasy discussing his continuing suspicions of and profound dislike for his uncle. Eustace was, after all, family, while Willie, however close a friend, was not.

He thought of Anne again then, and smiled. She had probably seen more of Eustace in past months than he ever had, and since she was clearly intelligent and sensible, she might well have provided some helpful insights into his character. It was a pity that he had not found an opportunity to discuss him further with her.

Now, however, he was alone, and the fact that Eustace had not wanted him to ride with his party was unsettling. Equally unsettling was the cold shoulder he had received from other members of the Chisholm family, although, to be sure, very few that he knew or even recognized had attended the wedding.

It occurred to him then that the other Chisholms scarcely knew him. His father had not been one who gathered family around him even on festive occasions, and he had not done so at all after Kit's mother died when Kit was fifteen. Three years later, the old laird had sent him to the Highlands. And in truth, Kit admitted, he had done little himself to cultivate the acquaintance of his Border kinsmen.

That he would one day be Laird of Ashkirk and Torness had been but a fact of knowledge, nothing more. His father had shown small interest in training him to take his place, leaving him to learn about the power of his position and the proper way to wield it from his Highland relatives, particularly from Lord Chisholm of Dundreggan. The irony of that was that Chisholm had done nothing to train the son who would succeed *him*. Kit smiled. That was something he and Alex had in common, but their reasons were very different. Chisholm, with two other, far more redoubtable sons, had never expected Alex, the youngest, to become his heir. But the murders of those two elder sons had altered many lives.

Now, however, the sun was shining, birds sang, and a light breeze stirred the golden grass on the hillsides. The track was clearly marked, and Kit's mood improved considerably as he rode into the steep hills beyond Ewes village. He was eager to see Hawks Rig again after his long absence, and the closer he drew, the more eager he became, but the wariness he felt grew by equal measures.

He thought it was odd that Eustace hadn't made more of a push to be sure he was dead. Had he simply inquired at Torness, Kit's steward would have warned him that Kit had only disappeared and that it was by no means certain he had died. But Eustace had assumed that Kit was dead and had taken control. Certainly, Kit could not trust him. Nor could he trust Cardinal Beaton, who seemed constantly to hover at the edges of his life, because Eustace was entirely too confident of Beaton.

Kit was not looking forward to the cardinal's arrival in any case. He was as certain as he could be now that he did not want to marry Fiona Carmichael, but if Beaton declared that he must, he would have little choice. That Beaton might be in league with Eustace complicated things, but he could not imagine what Beaton might gain by standing with Eustace against him.

Despite his unhappy fifteen months Kit had spent as a prisoner aboard the cardinal's ship, he knew of no particular reason that Beaton should even be aware of his existence, since the Sheriff of Inverness had instigated that particular arrangement. Even as the thought crossed his mind, he recalled that the sheriff had been eager to please Beaton, but since Kit could think of no reason that imprisoning him should do any such thing, that point seemed to lead nowhere.

Anne clearly had said nothing to Lady Carmichael about his time as a shipboard prisoner, because if she had, he was certain her ladyship would not have treated him so kindly, nor would she be so eager to effect his marriage to her daughter now if she knew he had once faced life servitude for murder.

That it might aid his case to tell her himself also occurred to him, but that seemed a scurvy thing to do. Moreover, the embarrassment to himself and everyone involved was too great a price to pay, and too, he had the unhappy feeling that his would-be future mother-in-law would not care a whisker for the charges if she could just marry her daughter to the Laird of Ashkirk.

Afternoon lengthened to dusk before Hawks Rig hove into sight on the high, rocky ridge from whence it drew its name. Beyond, to the north the castle looked down on the swiftly flowing Teviot. Here to the southeast, it overlooked the steep hills serving as the watershed for Ewesdale. The landscape was thus more rugged but familiar, and a short while later, he came to the steep track leading to the ridge.

The light had faded nearly to darkness; however, despite his long absence, he knew the track was unlikely to have changed, and although it wound among huge boulders, over and between running streams that fed Ewes Water, and alongside treacherous slides of scree, he remembered it well.

The castle had been visible from below, but once he started up the track, he soon lost sight of it. Not only was the light disappearing but rocky ledges jutted from the hillside above to obscure his view, and thickets of trees, now nearly denuded of leaves, made tall screens near the larger streams. Apart from the trees and a few patches of dry grass, the hillside was stark, barren, and lonely, making Kit feel as if he were the only human for miles, so when the shot rang out, it startled both him and his horse and thus nearly unseated him.

"Sakes," Catriona exclaimed, flitting to a nearby boulder as echoes of the gunshot reverberated across the hill, "why does the great noddy not jump down and hide? He'll be killed, and then where shall I be?"

Fergus was nowhere to be seen, but his voice followed her as he said, "I dinna want that any more than ye do, Catriona. 'Twould sorely disappoint me if he's no at hand tae marry the lovely Fiona, but there now, he's off his pony and behind one o' them boulders. Did ye see where yon shot came from?"

"Above him on the hill," she said as a second shot echoed over the hillside. "If we do not interfere, he may die! Oh, Fergus, what shall we do?"

"Nowt," Fergus said, pointing. "Look yonder."

"Where?" she demanded, reminding him that she could not see him.

A single hand appeared in the air, pointing. "There," he said.

Flinging himself from his saddle, Kit grabbed his own pistol from its holster. He had also brought his longbow and sword, both of which he had carried with him from the Highlands, but since he was below the would-be assassin and unable to see him, he was at a distinct disadvantage for any bowshot he might attempt. And swordplay on such terrain would be foolhardy.

The pistol was a weapon for closer quarters, and the boulders would provide cover for him to make his way nearer whenever the shooter was distracted. The other weapon had sounded like a matchlock, which took time and care to reload.

As he moved cautiously from one boulder to the next, he heard shouting above him on the hill, then sounds of struggle and two more shots.

A short silence fell, followed by a familiar voice yelling, "Laird, ye can show yourself now. We ha' the villain well in hand!"

Kit looked around the boulder and, even in the fading, dusky light, recognized Blind Sammy Crosier waving from a short distance up the hill. Leaving his horse where it stood, Kit scrambled up to meet him.

"What are you doing here, and who the devil was shooting at me?" he asked when he was near enough to make himself heard without shouting.

"I dinna ken the lout," Sammy said, "but he's yonder wi' me lads."

Following him, Kit found the others zealously tying up a man he had never seen before. "Who are you?" he demanded, standing over him with his hands on his hips. "Why did you shoot at me?"

The man, as rough looking as the reivers, gazed back at him sullenly.

"Likely he'll be following your uncle's orders," Sammy said.

Kit frowned. "Why do you say so?"

"Because we watched him make his way tae this ambush

o' his," Sammy said. "He came down the hill, laird, from Hawks Rig."

"Then why the devil did you not stop him before he fired at me?"

"We were behind him," Sammy said. "We couldna shoot, especially in this poor light, because dodging in and out amongst them rocks as he did, he were never in sight long enough tae take aim. If we'd shouted, he might ha' got away. Would ye ha' believed us if we'd told ye a man ye couldna see were trying tae murder ye?"

"I don't know," Kit said honestly, "but your way, I might have been dead."

Sammy smiled, revealing broken, yellowing teeth. "Aye, I'll grant ye that. Ye're a good man, laird, and I'll own that had he waited till ye were closer, we'd likely ha' shouted. As tae what we be doing here, if ye'll come awa' over where the lout canna hear us, I'll tell ye."

Kit followed him to the bank of one of the little, trickling streams, where Sammy muttered, "It were our Willie, sir. He said ye'd be coming home today, and we should keep near the track and watch for ye. Did we see anything out o' the ordinary, we was tae take steps, he said. Seemed tae me that a chap slithering down the hill wi' a great matchlock gun under his arm counted as out o' the ordinary."

"I'd agree with that," Kit said dryly.

"What'll we do wi' him?"

"Keep him," Kit said. "I don't want him; and, from the look of him, he'll deny having anything to do with my uncle. And my uncle will certainly deny him."

"Aye, but we've ways and all tae make him sing like a wee bird, if ye like. He'd ha' killed ye wi'out a blink, I'm thinking."

"Just keep him out of my way," Kit said. "And if you've a pair of stout lads you can set to watch him, and your own horses nearby, I'd be grateful if you and the others would ride the rest of the way with me. 'Twould give me a proper tail when I reach Hawks Rig, and one I think I can trust." He gave Sammy a direct look.

"Aye, ye can trust us, sir. We're Willie's lads, like always, and he did say we should look after ye now that ye're one of us, and all."

Kit frowned again. "Willie's lads? I know that he rides with you, but—"

"Aye, that's all I meant, sir. We stick together, sithee, one and all. 'Tis the reivers' way, ye ken."

Kit nodded. He had heard of the reivers' way. Generally, each band came from a single clan or an alliance of clans, and where one member went, they all went. When one member lied, they all lied together, and swore they were elsewhere if anyone accused a single member or all of them of lifting a herd.

Still, the way Sammy had referred to Willie was unusual. Gently, Kit said, "Who is Willie's father?"

"His da?" Sammy grinned. "Aye, well, that would be Ill Will Armstrong."

"So Willie is Mangerton's cousin," Kit said thoughtfully, referring to the prickly, powerful laird who had long created uproar in fractious Liddesdale.

"Aye, he is, and cousin tae Black Jock o' vivid memory," Sammy said.

Black Jock, as everyone in the Borders knew, was Johnny Armstrong, a notorious reiver hanged by the King more than a decade before. Ill Will Armstrong had hanged with him, and the event had poisoned the relationship between the western Scottish Borders and the Scottish Crown, and was a primary reason that Jamie could not trust his Border lords to support him against Henry now. Willie came by his reiving naturally.

Sammy told two of his men to look after the gunman and sent a third to collect Kit's horse. Then he led the way to where he and his men had left their mounts. From where they stood, Kit noted, they could not even see light from Hawks Rig, let alone the shadowy bulk of the castle. Nevertheless, anyone watching the track from atop its wall must have seen his approach before he started up the track and must certainly have heard the gunshots.

He heard no sound of anyone riding down from above.

Sammy easily followed his train of thought, for he said, "That uncle o' yours takes small interest in his own safety, I'm thinking, since he doesna seem tae care that some'un be shooting on Chisholm property."

"How did you get up here without the men on the wall seeing you?"

"Slipped up in the dark last night, we did, then hid amongst the rocks when Eustace and his lot rode up the hill at noon today. Nae one saw us."

"But how did Willie get word to you in time? He must have done so before he and Eustace left Mute Hill House."

"Aye, now that would be telling," Sammy said, grinning.

Kit realized they must have made their plan before Willie adopted his role as jester. The only information the reivers would have needed after that was the exact day or days that Eustace and Kit would arrive at Hawks Rig.

He asked no more questions, keeping his mind on the hillside ahead, lest there be more surprises. There were none, but when he and his escort approached the tall torch-lit gates to the castle, they found them closed.

"Happen they won't let ye in, laird," Sammy said.

That had already occurred to Kit, particularly in light of the dubious company with him. Nevertheless, it had also occurred to him that Eustace had no good reason to deny him and several excellent ones for letting him enter.

"If I can judge by his behavior at Mute Hill House, he will not challenge me openly whilst he still thinks he has a chance of winning at least a portion of what he seeks legally," Kit said. "I am the rightful laird, after all. He must know that I can call upon allies to support me unless he has somehow won them all to his side."

"He won't have done that, sir. Ye could easily raise a thousand Chisholms in a day, I'm thinking, and our lads from Liddesdale as well. Most folks hereabouts dinna approve o' what Eustace ha' done wi' your father's people, just turning them out o' their homes without so much as a day's warning, the way he did."

Kit nodded and then urged his horse near enough to the gate so the torches would light his features. "Open for the master of this house," he shouted. "I am Sir Christopher Chisholm, Laird of Ashkirk and Torness."

Without hesitation, a sentry relayed his command and the gates swung wide.

Wondering if he were riding into a greater ambush than the one he had just avoided, Kit gestured to the others to follow and rode into the courtyard.

To his surprise, Eustace strode from the main entrance to meet them. If he was not smiling, neither did he look displeased, but only when Willie Armstrong appeared behind him in the motley guise of Mad Jake and nodded reassuringly did Kit relax. At least Eustace did not mean to order him murdered on the spot.

"You must be glad to see Hawks Rig again, nephew," Eustace said affably as Kit dismounted. "As you will soon see, I've kept it in good repair for you."

"Thank you, sir," Kit said, politely gripping his outstretched hand and wondering if he ought to mention the incident below.

"My lads shouted some time ago that you were on your way up the hill," Eustace said. "They did not mention your entourage, so I expected your arrival sooner than this. Doubtless these others with you, being unacquainted with the track, slowed you considerably."

"It was a gunman that slowed us," Kit said bluntly. "Someone fired on me below. Surely, your men must have heard the shots."

Eustace looked shocked. "Had they heard shooting, you may be sure they would have told me, and I'd have sent an army to meet you. Where is the villain?"

"I don't know," Kit said truthfully. "It was nearly dark, you see."

"Damnation," Eustace said. "The man responsible ought to hang."

"I am not opposed to that," Kit said, avoiding Sammy's bland gaze.

Chapter 14

Although Anne could easily see for herself that the sun still shone and the birds in the garden still sang, the day seemed to have grown gray and dismal after Kit's departure. But although her enthusiasm for his match with Fiona had waned, she exerted herself to persuade her cousin that he would make an excellent husband.

"He's certainly younger than Eustace," Fiona said as they walked in the garden, enjoying the peacefulness after so many guests and uproar. "At least Mother is not talking me to death and I need not try on more dresses or do anything else for the wedding until she receives a reply from his eminence."

"She sent her message to him at Branxholme yesterday, but we do not know if he has arrived there yet," Anne said. "He may not do so for another sennight."

"One of the maidservants whose cousin came here with the party from Branxholme told Molly that Lady Scott's things were all packed before they left, so I warrant she has already moved back with her parents at Ferniehirst," Fiona said.

"Do you not think Sir Christopher is much handsomer than Eustace?"

Fiona shrugged. "Anyone would be," she said. "The jester is better looking than either of them. However, at least Sir Christopher talks to me as if I were a person, which Sir Eustace never does. I'll have no choice anyway, Anne, so what I think about either of them does not signify in the least."

Having no wish to agitate her, Anne dropped the subject.

Olivia, too, seemed disinclined now to support either gentleman's suit, and after nearly a sennight of inactivity, Anne told Fiona on Saturday morning that she had decided to ride to Ellyson Towers again if only to break the monotony.

"You never used to be bored here, Anne. Have you come to dislike us?"

"No, of course I have not, love. I just need exercise. Why do you not come with me? We'll take an escort of men to protect us, ride to the Towers for dinner, and be back long before supper."

"I do not think Mother will permit it," Fiona said, but it was clear that the notion of an outing appealed to her. In the event, however, her assessment of Olivia's reaction proved correct. She would not hear of such an outing.

"I cannot think what gets into you, Anne, that you must always be tempting fate as you do," she scolded. "But I will not permit you to lead Fiona into danger. One of the lads told me only an hour ago that Henry's troops crossed the line near Larriston Fells yesterday and burned a whole village to the ground."

"We would take an armed escort, Aunt Olivia," Anne said. "Larriston Fells is miles from here."

"Only fifteen miles, which is not nearly enough," Olivia retorted. "You are not to take Fiona outside our wall, so let that be an end to it."

As they left the chamber, Fiona said, "I told you she would not let me go."

"Well, I still mean to, just as soon as I collect my cloak and gloves," Anne said. "I simply must have some exercise."

"But the danger! Really, Anne, you should not."

"I'll take some men with me, love. I'm sure I shan't need them, but I know they'll make your mother feel easier about my going."

"Are you going to tell her?" Fiona asked.

"I don't think so. You may certainly do so if she asks you."

"I won't, but I am glad you mean to take an escort," Fiona said.

Anne did not want to burden herself with one, but she likewise had no wish to cross swords with an angry Kit Chisholm, and she was certain he had meant every word he said to her on the subject. She would take the escort.

However, when she made her wishes known to the stablemaster a short time later, she discovered that Olivia had already sent him explicit orders.

He said bluntly, "I canna send any o' my lads wi' ye, m'lady. I ken ye may still be determined tae go, but the mistress said ye're no tae endanger anyone else."

Anne hesitated. Henry of England's armies had been threatening the area for so long that it was hard to believe they threatened more danger one day than any other. Still, the unexpected could happen, as her last expedition had proved.

On that thought, Kit's image leaped to mind. Deciding she would be wiser not to annoy him just when he seemed on the brink of doing as she had asked by marrying Fiona, she submitted gracefully and returned to the house.

Being stuck at Mute Hill irritated her, but she and Fiona rejoined Olivia in her bower, and when Malcolm entered shortly before noon to announce the arrival of Eustace, his nephew, and his new jester, Anne was glad she had decided to stay.

"What a pleasant surprise," Olivia declared as the gentlemen made their bows. "We mean to dine soon, so if you want to wash the dirt of your journey away whilst Malcolm warns the kitchen and sets extra places, you may do so at once."

Anne was not pleased to see Eustace but felt a rush of pleasure at seeing Kit.

Fiona said shyly, "You are all most welcome. We were feeling rather moped, particularly Anne, but I know Mad Jake will make us laugh, won't you, Jake?"

Kit had caught Anne's gaze the moment Malcolm showed them into the room, and he raised his eyebrows now, saying, "Moped, Lady Anne? But the weather has vastly improved. I should think these sunny days would please you."

"They are beautiful," she agreed, wishing he would not look at her so intently.

"She was going to ride to Ellyson Towers," Fiona said, ignoring Anne's quick headshake. "But Mother would not let me go with her, nor would she let her take any of our men along, so Anne decided to stay home."

Kit looked directly into Anne's eyes as he said, "How wise of her. I am sure that Lady Carmichael was wise, too. We heard rumors—"

"Yes," Anne interjected, having no wish to hear more about English Harry. "We heard the rumors, too, sir. But you must be wondering if we have had news from Branxholme. I do not think my aunt has heard from his eminence yet."

Kit's wry smile told her he did not relish the abrupt diversion but understood her reason for it. Then his expression warmed, and it was as if he had touched her.

"I've had no word yet, but I expect Cardinal Beaton will reply soon," Olivia said, recalling them to the moment. Turning to Eustace, she added, "Do you mean to extend us the pleasure of your company overnight, sir?"

"Indeed I do, madam." He shot an ardent look at Fiona, adding, "Doubtless, you are flattered to have two such devoted suitors, puss, but pleased as I am to be here, I own that my coming was but an impulse. I had formed the notion of sending a lad to discover if you had heard yet from Beaton, and when Jake offered to carry the message, because he wanted to visit kinsmen in the area, Kit decided to ride with him for the exercise." With a teasing laugh, he added, "I could scarcely let my competitor ride over without coming myself."

Fiona gazed blankly at him, so Anne said hastily, "We were saying only this morning how quiet the house has seemed since everyone left."

"Won't you play us a tune, Jake?" Fiona said, smiling kindly at the jester.

"He can entertain us whilst we eat our dinner," Olivia said. "I am persuaded that the gentlemen would like time to tidy themselves first."

They did so, and when everyone gathered again at the high table, their number had grown to include Toby and

Lord Berridge, both of whom expressed pleasure at seeing the visitors.

Laughing, Toby said, "Couldn't stay away longer than a sennight, eh? Well, I don't mind admitting I missed Mad Jake's tales and tunes. Play us one now, lad."

"Aye, sir, gladly." Jake pulled his stool near the fireplace and took his lute in hand. Its light notes accompanied their conversation while they ate their meal.

Although the entire household had gathered, as usual, for the main meal of the day, the servants and men-at-arms ate quickly, and with the privacy screen in place, those at the high table could converse without being watched or overheard by anyone other than the servants who waited on them.

Olivia soon turned to the matter on everyone's mind. "I have been thinking about what you said, Sir Eustace," she began, smiling at that gentleman.

"Which comment in particular, my lady?" he asked.

"About Fiona's having two suitors," she said. "I do realize we have not yet received a decision from his eminence, but it has become clear to me which way he must decide, and I believe it is always best to avoid furthering false hope. We have come to be friends, sir, and I should like us to remain so, but I am afraid that if you continue to believe Cardinal Beaton will decide in your favor, you will be disappointed, because your nephew's claim must supersede yours."

Clearly unperturbed, he returned her smile, saying, "I refuse to give up hope until the decision is made. That is not my way, and I believe you are mistaken."

"When things are wrong, sir, they must be set right," Olivia said. "And so I shall tell his eminence. Indeed, I did tell him as much in the letter I sent him. I am sorry if that distresses you, but as I said, I do not want to foster false hope."

"It is not false, madam, and thus you do not cast me down. This is excellent beef. You must hope that the local reivers never learn how good it is."

Jake missed a note but quickly recovered.

Never one to let a serious conversation last long, Toby made a joke about the reivers, and when Berridge aided his efforts to promote conversation of a more cheerful nature, the banter among the three older men grew so cheerful that Olivia soon bestirred herself to call them to order.

"That jest was not suitable for my ears, uncle, let alone for such innocent ears as Fiona's," she warned. "Pray, recall that I am in mourning, and reserve such humor for the other gentlemen."

Toby rolled his eyes. "Have done with your mourning, lass! Had Stephen been here, he would never have allowed it to go on so long, particularly not once he saw that you'd so far forgot your grief for him as to topple head over ears—"

"That will do," Olivia interjected coldly.

Caught up short for once, Toby looked ruefully at Kit but said only, "Just so, not a conversation for this company. I say, Eustace, you will be astounded to know that that damned fox is still in the house. Yesterday, Cook nearly caught him on her chopping block, devouring a whole chicken she'd meant for our supper."

Olivia excused herself a few minutes later, commanding Fiona and Anne to accompany her to her bower. "We will leave the gentlemen to their claret and their silly, sordid stories," she said.

"May we invite Jake to come and play for us, madam?" Fiona asked.

"I suppose he can as easily strum his lute in there as in here," Olivia said, signing to the jester to accompany them. "You must work on your stitchery though, Fiona. Lazy girls are in small demand as wives."

Fiona nodded submissively, and the three retired to her ladyship's bower. However, when Jake began to sing an amusing song, Olivia stopped him.

"That may be what you are accustomed to sing at Hawks Rig," she said austerely, "but it will not do for Mute Hill House. You will respect my wishes by playing more somber tunes appropriate to our state of mourning."

"Oh, Mother, really," Fiona protested.

"That will be enough, Fiona. Find your work and get to it."

Fiona sighed but obeyed, casting an apologetic look at the jester, who only grinned impudently at her.

"Aunt Olivia," Anne said quietly, "it is doubtless not my place to mention this, but do you not fear that if you so frequently recall everyone's attention to your mourning, some people—unkind ones, at least—might begin to wonder why you are so strongly set on Fiona's marrying at such a time?"

Olivia looked astonished. "How can you suggest such a thing? You, of all people, ought to understand my position, Anne. We are Borderers, and mourning is a continual state here for most people. If we suspended all other aspects of our lives whilst we mourned, most families would live forever in such suspension. You certainly have not stopped all your usual activities to wallow in grief. Indeed, if you have felt any grief at the loss of your family, I have seen no sign of it."

The music stopped, but Anne scarcely noticed. The attack had come so swiftly and unexpectedly that it was all she could do to hold her tongue, but long training in minding her composure stood her in good stead now.

The sadness that had followed her brother's death had become an ache that had settled in her soul after her mother's. That ache settled deeper with the deaths of each of her little sisters and the subsequent loss of her father. But the upheaval that followed her father's death had made it impossible for her to wear her grief on her sleeve as Olivia constantly did, even had she been prone to behave in such a way. She knew she could not have conducted herself so, had she wanted to, but to be attacked for not grieving sufficiently when Olivia had not cared enough about her grief before even to acknowledge its existence, was too much.

It never seemed to occur to Olivia that although she had lost her husband, her brother, and (if Toby were to be believed) her lover over a period of two years, Anne had lost the last four members of her immediate family in as many weeks.

Jake's strumming soothed her, so she was able to draw a deep breath and let it out again, and to realize she could accomplish nothing by ripping up at Olivia.

"I expect I should not have said that, Anne," Olivia said abruptly. "We both have a duty to mourn your father, but I had little love for him, so I should not scold you for your lack of feeling. Armadale was a cold person who never understood anyone's wishes and emotions but his own. Your mother was kinder, however, and I expect you miss her."

"I loved her very much, and I had great respect for my father as well," Anne said. "I miss them both." Hearing a quaver in her voice, she took another breath and let it out before she turned to Fiona and said, "Have you enough light there, love? Mayhap you could see better if you moved your stool nearer the window."

Suddenly the room seemed too close and too warm. When Olivia said she hoped the gentlemen would not linger long over their claret and their regrettable stories, Anne excused herself, saying she had developed a dreadful headache.

Kit had likewise excused himself, having borne a surfeit of Eustace's baffling behavior over the past sennight and finding little refreshment in the raucous company of Toby Bell, who received far too much encouragement from the false Lord Berridge. The only light moment had come when Toby announced that he thought Berridge was making headway in his pursuit of Lady Carmichael.

Nearby, the steward had picked up the tray of carving knives and was directing a minion to remove the remains of the roast Eustace had praised, but at this, he turned a startled look toward Toby and dropped the tray with a clatter.

"Damnation, Malcolm!" Toby bellowed. "If one o' them knives is scratched, ye'll answer to me. Get out now, and take the others with ye."

"I believe you upset him," Eustace said when Malcolm had stalked out with his nose in the air. "He fancies himself in love with your niece, you know."

"What, with Olivia? The man's mad. Ye should see how his lordship twists her ladyship round his finger, though," he added, swilling claret and wiping his mouth with the back of his hand. "He bows, scrapes, and says he can see where Fiona inherited her beauty. He's already got farther with Olivia than any o' the others I've introduced to her these past months, and I hope he may go all the way." Grinning at the supposed Berridge, he said, "Mark me, but this place needs a strong man to run it. Anyone can see that."

"Aye, it does," Eustace agreed, "and I'm surprised that you don't do more to call the tune here."

"I've better things to do with my time," Toby replied with a shrug. "Besides, the lass don't listen to me. She needs a man who'll keep a firm hand on the rein."

When it looked as if the conversation would go on for some time, Kit excused himself and, not wanting to join the ladies lest Lady Carmichael urge him to charm her daughter, he decided to walk to his bedchamber and back in the hope that she would soon dismiss Willie so they could talk. Kit's room was the same as before, and from the gallery it faced, he could see the garden. When he saw a forlorn figure cross the plank bridge from the stableyard and disappear behind the tallest hedge, he turned on his heel and headed back to the stairs.

Hurrying down, he strode outside and toward the arched stone bridge at the other end of the garden. The afternoon sun was shining, but the air was crisp and cold. He hoped she had worn something warm, but his impression from the brief look he had had was that she wore only the thin silk dress she had worn to dinner.

It was a most becoming dress and became her slender but pleasingly curvaceous figure well. He liked her even features, speaking eyes, and soft auburn curls, but compared to her extraordinarily beautiful cousin, Anne's beauty was less obvious. Her expression contained warmth that was missing from Fiona's, however, and her eyes held an expression of intelligence and wry humor that appealed to him much more than Fiona's vague, disinterested gaze ever could.

Although he had told Eustace he wanted to ride with the jester merely for the exercise, and had certainly hoped to talk with Willie, the real lodestone that had drawn him back to Mute Hill House was the same one calling urgently to him now.

Crossing the bridge, he made for the hedge garden, but when he arrived, he did not see her at first. Only when he heard what sounded like a sob did he realize she stood behind a tree at the far side of the hedged area, leaning against its far side with her back to him. The gray silk of her dress nearly matched the tree bark, so without the slight noise to guide him, he might have passed her by.

Making no effort to muffle his footsteps on the pebbled path, he strode toward her, expecting her to hear the crunching sounds he made and step out to greet him. But she remained perfectly still.

"Lady Anne?" He spoke quietly, believing she must be deep in her own thoughts, and not wanting to startle her.

He saw her stiffen, but when she turned and moved out from behind the tree, he strode quickly to her and caught her by the shoulders to look into her eyes.

"What's amiss, lass?"

"I . . . I'm sorry you saw me," she muttered, looking down at the ground. "I hoped you would walk on without stopping."

Gently, he put a hand under her chin, making her look up. "If you haven't been crying," he said, "you're as near as makes no difference. Who has upset you?"

"N-no one," she said. "I don't c-cry."

He moved the hand back to her shoulder and pulled her close, at this thoughtful gesture she buried her face against his chest and burst into tears.

When his arms tightened around her, Anne wondered at herself, but she could not stop crying. Greater sobs wracked her body than any she could remember even in childhood, and only his strong arms kept her upright.

He did not speak. He just held her, wrapped securely in his arms, until the storm passed.

At last, the paroxysms eased and she was able to draw breath without sobbing, but she remained where she was, feeling safe, until her heart eased its pounding. However, when he pulled a handkerchief from somewhere and pushed it into her hand, she kept her face pressed against his chest, because she was uncertain how to extricate herself gracefully from a place she had no business being.

It grew hard to breathe again, but once she had blown her nose, that difficulty had nothing to do with her tears. Guilt overwhelmed her, and with it came a flood of sorrow.

"You haven't been meeting Eustace on the stairs again, I trust."

The absurd suggestion nearly made her smile, but although she could not quite manage that, she felt instantly steadier and able at last to collect her wits.

"You must know I did not," she said, raising her head at last and looking up at him. "Have you not been sitting with him ever since we left the table?"

"I grew bored with their conversation, so I came out to get some fresh air."

"And walked into a rain cloud instead," she said ruefully. "What you must think of me, flinging myself at you like that!"

"What I think is that something upset you, and I want to know what it is."

"It's nothing, really."

"You cannot cry all over my fine doublet and then say it is nothing," he said. "I haven't known you long, lass, but I do know you would never burst into tears like that for no reason."

"We should not be here alone, and certainly not like this," she said, feeling a sudden sense of urgency and starting to step back.

He held her a moment longer, then released her, letting his hands drop to his sides. But he continued to stand where he was, blocking her way.

"We can walk back inside if you like," he said, "just as soon as you tell me what or who has upset you."

"You are the most exasperating man," she muttered.

"You are not the first person to tell me that, but we are not leaving here until you explain that little rainstorm. So, tell me."

"It is nothing that important," she insisted. "I am merely feeling a trifle abused, but you should not encourage me. Indeed, you are the one who told me not long ago that my aunt should scold me fiercely for my sins."

"She certainly didn't scold you today for something you did ten days ago, however. What new sins have you committed?"

"None," she said. "I even stayed home today rather than ride to the Towers without an escort, as Fiona was so quick to tell you."

"Yes, she did, didn't she, so it is a good thing you made such a sensible decision." His eyes narrowed, and he said more sternly, "You will not divert me from my purpose so easily, lass. Why did her ladyship scold you?"

"She didn't, not really." Reading equal amounts of sympathy and irritation in his expression, she said, "Now you are making me feel stupid for making such a fuss about . . . about nothing at all."

"I don't believe it was nothing."

The emotions that Olivia reawakened and that his initial sympathy had unleashed stirred again, and another tear trickled down her cheek. Annoyed with herself, she brushed it away with the back of her hand.

If the gesture renewed his sympathy, he did not show it, saying only, "I should perhaps warn you that at the best of times my temper is unpredictable and my patience short."

"Oh, very well, but it will serve you right if I start raining all over you again just because you are making me talk about it."

"Anne."

The warning was clear now, and although she could not imagine why her refusal to burden him with her woes should irritate him, she did not want to make him angry with her. Also, his sharp tone had banished any lingering impulse to cry.

"I managed to provoke Olivia," she said with a sigh.

His lips twitched. "I can't think how."

"She stopped Jake when he began to sing, telling him the merry song he chose did not suit her state of mourning. Fiona was enjoying it, and she needs to laugh again, so although I know it is not my place to rebuke Olivia, I asked her if some people might not think it wrong to urge a wedding whilst she is in mourning."

His eyes began to twinkle, but he said, "As I recall life in the Borders, folks don't stop the business of life overlong to grieve. Death is too much with us here."

"That is what she said," Anne admitted. "Then she said I

would understand her grief, except that if I felt any myself, she had not seen any sign of it."

"Blinded, no doubt, by her own constant tears for herself," he said dryly.

She nodded. "My aunt rarely spares a thought for anyone else unless it's Fiona, and even then I'm not so sure it is Fiona she thinks of. She just wants—"

She hesitated, knowing she ought not to speak the thought aloud.

"She just wants the connection to the Chisholm wealth and power," he said.

"You see that, too," she said. "It is not unusual, I suppose. Doubtless, if my uncle Stephen were alive, he would be doing his best to see Fiona well married, too. It is her parents' duty, after all, and not something we should condemn in Olivia."

"It is completely normal," he agreed, "but this wedding business is something else we need to talk about."

"Oh, but there is nothing to discuss," she said. "I know that your uncle believes his suit must prevail, but I don't imagine Aunt Olivia can be wrong about the decision Cardinal Beaton will make. Clearly, the first betrothal must stand, since the second was based on a falsehood."

"Do you really *want* me to marry your cousin?"

It was an awful question to ask her, and the very last one she wanted to answer, but she forced herself to say quickly, "Yes, of course, because you must, since her only alternative is to marry your horrid uncle. I'd have to be the greatest villain living to condemn her to that. So would you!"

"Are you going to give me back my handkerchief?"

"Don't be silly. I'll see that it's washed first. May I go in now?"

"I'll walk with you."

Although she knew she ought to refuse lest someone see them together and tell her aunt, she did not. As they were crossing the plank bridge, she said, "I'm sorry to have treated you to such a display, sir. I don't know what came over me."

"You lost your entire family within the past year, lass," he said gently, "and I'll wager you've had little or no time to grieve properly. As I understand it, whilst you were still recovering from the shock of your brother's death, you had to help nurse your mother and little sisters, and when they died, you nursed your father. Directly after his death, you came here to Mute Hill House, where you have done your best to serve your aunt and look after your cousin. When have you taken time even to think about yourself and all that you have lost?"

"I was not raised to believe that thinking about myself should be a priority."

"Not a priority, perhaps, but neither should you neglect your own needs to the point of making yourself ill."

"Is that what you think I've done?"

"Not yet, but you had made a good start before your aunt stirred the coals."

She thought about that. His blunt description of her past year had awakened the aching grief again, but she felt no further urge to cry. Talking with him about her feelings had provided a solace she had not expected.

"You are very kind," she said. "You will make Fiona an excellent husband."

His expression turned grim. "I doubt that."

Attempting to striker a lighter note, she said, "You did

say, did you not, that your temper is unpredictable and your patience short?"

"Those are scarcely qualities that will recommend me to your cousin."

"No, but only think how fortunate it is for you that she is meek and biddable. She will not try your temper or your patience, so it will be an excellent match."

"You don't know what tries my patience," he retorted. "Look at me."

He had stopped where the shrubbery still screened them from the stableyard, and when she looked up, he searched her face carefully.

"Have I got a smudge on my cheek?" she asked.

"No, but a blind man could see that you've been crying. Why the devil did you not think to wear a cloak out here? One with a nice, large, concealing hood. I have one of those myself. Perhaps I should give it to you."

"I didn't think at all," she said. "I just wanted to get out of the room. Besides, I don't feel the cold easily, so I wouldn't have thought to fetch a cloak, anyway."

"Well, walk briskly then, and we'll go in at the kitchen door. You can slip up the stairs there, whilst I'll go round to the main entrance. With luck, no one will question either of us."

Accordingly, he left her at the postern door, and she hurried up to her bedchamber without meeting anyone. Opening her door, she slipped quickly inside, only to stop short as she began to shut the door.

Fiona and the jester sat side by side on her window bench.

Chapter 15

"Hello, Anne," Fiona said. "Where have you been?"

Shutting the door firmly, Anne turned back to the pair on the window bench. Controlling her voice with difficulty, she said, "What is Jake doing here, Fiona?"

Fiona's eyes widened. "H-he is teaching me to play the lute."

"But why in my bedchamber? Surely, you must realize how unseemly it is for the pair of you to be alone in here."

"Mama said she was going to take her nap," Fiona explained. "I knew he should not be in *my* bedchamber, although I cannot think why, when Molly is most likely in there, tidying things, and would make an excellent chaperone."

"*Definitely* not in your bedchamber," Anne said, striving for patience.

"Well, yes, I could see that, but I did not think you would mind if we came in here to wait for you, and Mother will not object, because he is not in my room."

"She would certainly object just as strenuously to his being in mine," Anne said, her voice sharpening despite her resolve.

"But you were not here," Fiona said, as if that made it all right.

With a sigh, Anne said, "I see that we need to discuss this at length, but we need not do so until Jake leaves, which he is going to do right now. And if you would keep my good opinion," she added with a stern look at the jester, whose head was down but whose shoulders shook suspiciously, as if he were suppressing laughter, "you will say nothing about this to anyone, and you will show the good sense in future to have more care for Mistress Carmichael's reputation."

"Yes, my lady," he murmured, taking his lute from Fiona as he arose but keeping his head down and moving hastily toward the door. As he neared Anne, he shot a swift look at her from under his eyebrows, frowned, and lowered his gaze.

"Try not to meet half the household as you leave the gallery," she added frostily as she stepped aside to let him open the door.

Nodding, he slipped out and shut it, leaving her alone with Fiona.

Wondering what on earth she could say that would neither frighten her cousin nor anger her, Anne thanked the fates that Lady Armadale had explained to her certain things that married people did and why it was unwise to encourage attentions from anyone other than one's husband or betrothed. Her ladyship had not had to deal with Fiona, however, or anyone else who jumped at the least sound and worried about what others might think about everything she said or did.

Fiona did not look at Anne but stared at her own hands clenched in her lap.

Moving to sit beside her on the bench, Anne said gently,

"Whatever possessed you, love, to steal away up here with the jester?"

Tears welled in Fiona's eyes as she looked up, saying, "He is kind to me, Anne, and he sings pretty songs. He said he would teach me to play the lute, and I want to learn. Why can't I ever do what *I* want?"

"It must seem hard sometimes," Anne agreed sympathetically.

"You look dreadful," Fiona said, looking closely at her for the first time since her entrance had startled them. "You look as if you'd been crying, but you never do, so you must still have that awful headache. Do you want to go to bed?"

"No, and never mind about me," Anne said. "I want to know why you and the jester came in here."

"Well, we couldn't sit in the hall, because it's too noisy there, what with Sir Eustace's men—or Sir Christopher's, as I suppose they must be now—plus our own. Besides, Mother does not like me to linger there. Still, it did not feel right to stay in her bower without her either, particularly after she suggested rather firmly that I take a nap, too. I was sure she would not want me to stay there with Jake. I wasn't sure what to do, so we came up to your bedchamber to seek your advice, and when you weren't here, I said we should just wait for you."

"And the jester saw nothing wrong with that?"

"Well, he could hardly refuse after I'd said I wanted to," Fiona said reasonably. "He is only a servant, after all."

"He is not our servant, however," Anne pointed out. "Did you not stop to think what Eustace or Sir Christopher might say about this?"

Paling, Fiona exclaimed, "Faith, you won't tell them!"

"No, of course I won't, but can you imagine what they

would do to the jester if they even suspected he had been alone with you like that?"

"What?"

"I don't know exactly," Anne said honestly, "but I would not be surprised if Eustace ordered the poor lad flogged."

"Then we mustn't tell him. I won't do it again, Anne, I swear. Just don't tell anyone. Mercy, if I were to cause anything like that . . ." She fell silent, and Anne watched in fascination to see if the tears that threatened to spill over and down her cheeks would do so. It seemed utterly unfair that Fiona and Olivia could both cry at the slightest thing and never suffer from swollen eyes or similar signs of weeping, while other people looked so awful that their relatives thought they had fallen ill.

Having come to the conclusion that it would be useless to try to make Fiona understand, and hoping she was frightened enough for the jester's safety to avoid being alone with him again, Anne was about to suggest tactfully that her cousin go to her own bedchamber to rest when Fiona said abruptly, "He told me something dreadful, Anne."

"Mad Jake?"

"He said someone tried to kill Sir Christopher. And he wasn't jesting, either, because I asked him if he was."

Aware of a sudden chill, Anne said sharply, "Did he say how it happened?"

"Someone shot at him on his way home. Jake said he was riding up to Hawks Rig, and the track he was on doesn't go anywhere else. Jake thinks the person who shot at him knew it was Sir Christopher, but why should anyone try to kill him?"

"I don't know," Anne said, not thinking it wise or appropriate to declare her certainty that Eustace would like nothing better than for his nephew to be officially dead again, as long as Eustace could provide a strong alibi for himself.

"What if I have to marry him," Fiona demanded, "and someone tries to shoot him then? What if they accidentally shoot me instead?"

"Don't borrow trouble, love. No one is likely to shoot at you."

"Well, I don't want to be a widow either," Fiona said flatly.

Changing the subject, Anne soon persuaded her to go to her own chamber and rest, whereupon she was able at last to fetch her looking glass and try to repair the ravages of her weeping.

Cold water and a few hours of peace did much to restore both her complexion and her spirits, and she was able to descend to the hall for supper with her normal composure reestablished.

Believing the men would linger at the high table until all hours, as usual, she doubted that she would find any opportunity to ask Kit about the shooting incident. However, if that was their plan, Olivia foiled it by saying as the ladies rose from the table, "Pray, join us soon, gentlemen. I would enjoy more of your company before Sir Eustace and Sir Christopher depart tomorrow. I know Toby has challenged Sir Eustace to a game of chess, so mayhap we can make a games night of it."

Fiona looked startled. "I do not know how to play chess!"

"You do enjoy playing Fox and Geese, however," Olivia said, "and I believe Sir Christopher will gladly indulge you in a game or two, will you not, sir?"

"Indeed, I will," that gentleman responded, "but only if Lady Anne or someone else who has played the game more recently than I have agrees to act as my tutor, so Mistress Carmichael does not turn me into a pauper."

Fiona giggled. "We do not make wagers over Fox and Geese, sir."

"Be a more interesting game if you did," Toby declared. "Children's stuff! If you want a simple war game, try draughts."

"We have boards, men, and cards for any number of games," Olivia said pacifically. "You gentlemen may choose what you like when you join us."

"Berridge," Toby said to that gentleman, "what will you choose?"

"I like poque," his lordship said, "because nearly any number can play."

"Aye, poque's good," Eustace agreed. "We can play a few hands after I beat Toby at chess."

"Now that's a wagering game, poque is," Fiona said wisely.

"Aye, puss, so it is," Eustace agreed before turning back to his lordship to say, "If Kit's going to be stuck playing children's games, Berridge, you'd best have a few hands of Cent with Olivia, so she don't grow bored, waiting."

"It will be my pleasure," Berridge said, bowing to Olivia, who smiled and said she would be delighted.

Accompanying her to her bower, Anne and Fiona discovered that she had already caused numerous games to be laid out on the largest table, and Fiona went at once to get the board for Fox and Geese.

"We'll play on that round table near the fire, Anne," she said. "It has room for all three of us, so you can be comfortable whilst you help Sir Christopher. Perhaps you should count the geese to be sure that all thirteen are here."

Obediently, Anne tipped the polished wooden game figures out of their box. The geese were white with yellow beaks and feet, and black eyes. The little fox was bright red with black eyes and boasted a white tip to its tail. Picking it up, she said, "Has anyone seen our fox since it tried to eat Cook's chicken?"

Olivia grimaced. "Do not mention that beast to me. Moira found evidence of its presence in my bedchamber this afternoon. Do not ask me what sort of evidence, I beg of you, for I do not want to discuss it. I have told Malcolm that he simply must find the creature and get rid of it. I do not care how he does it."

"He mustn't hurt it," Fiona exclaimed. "It is not the fox's fault it is trapped in the house. Mayhap if we left the doors open for a day, it would run out again."

"Or other beasts would run in," her mother said tartly. "We'd certainly have every one of my uncle's dogs inside if we were so rash as to leave doors open. Do be sensible, Fiona. You will soon be managing a household of your own after all."

Deflated by the suggestion, Fiona idly fingered the little geese until Anne suggested that perhaps they should play a game while they waited for the men. "Because I'm not sure that I remember all the rules," she said. "I don't want to make a fool of myself when Sir Christopher asks questions."

Fiona agreed to the game, and Anne discovered that she easily remembered how to play, but she also discovered when the gentlemen joined them a quarter of an hour later that Kit had no need whatsoever of her sage advice.

"You know this game better than I do," she said accusingly when he had easily "killed" all of Fiona's geese for the second time.

"I confess," he said, eyes twinkling. "My Highland cousins and I often played this game. And," he added, grinning at Fiona, "we made wagers on the outcome when we did. But in my own defense, let me add that it has been years since we played. I'm glad to see you looking so much more rested, Lady Anne."

Anne shot him a dagger look, but he met it with a provocative smile.

"Oh, yes, she does look better, does she not?" Fiona said. "I thought perhaps she had fallen ill when I saw her this afternoon. She looked dreadful."

Deciding to serve Kit with some of his own sauce, Anne said, "I'm told that someone shot at you last week, sir. That must have been terrifying."

"Now, I wonder what little bird can have told you that," he said.

Fiona opened her mouth, but when Anne gave her a stern look, she shut it again, turning fiery red.

"Is it true?" Anne asked.

"Aye, it is," he said. "I doubt it's anything to worry about, though. I've a notion it was an impulsive act, because aside from that incident, my homecoming was unexpectedly pleasant. Uncle Eustace has proved a most generous host."

"Host?"

"Oh, aye, he persists in behaving as though he owns Hawks Rig, but since I am still legally dead, I suppose that by law perhaps he does."

"He sounds as horrid as ever," Anne said, lowering her voice and glancing at the other table to be sure no one there was paying heed to them. "You should do something to straighten that business out," she added firmly.

"I will," he said, "but I thought I'd wait and see just how my being officially dead affects other matters first."

She had neither the need nor the inclination to ask him to explain that statement, knowing he hoped the odd situation would spare him the necessity of marrying Fiona, so she asked instead if Fiona wanted to play another game.

"You play him, Anne. You will enjoy it much more than sitting and watching us play."

"Aye, give me a game, my lady. I'll let you be the fox if you like."

"No, thank you," she said. "If I am to make the choice, I'd prefer the geese."

He gave her another teasing look, and she soon saw that he paid little heed to his moves. Nevertheless, she concentrated carefully on hers.

The trick was to use one's geese to crowd the fox into a corner of the board until it could no longer move, but one could only do that if one did not lose too many geese. The fox "killed" a goose by jumping over it and could kill several in one turn with a series of hops if the gooseherd was not careful.

"You *let* me take that fellow," he said a few minutes later.

"Yes, I want to put this goose where the fox was," she said, doing so.

He frowned and began to play more carefully.

"You two don't need me," Fiona said with a chuckle. "Mother and Lord Berridge are playing cards with the others now, so I am going to watch them for a while and listen to Jake sing and play his lute."

Anne scarcely heeded her, so engrossed had she become in her strategy, but a moment later, Kit said, "Who told you about the shooting?"

Startled, she met his gaze and said, "Jake told Fiona. I'm sorry I brought it up, though. I should not have done so. I was just annoyed that you had mentioned how much better I looked."

"But I was glad to see you looking more yourself again."

"Thank you, but you ought not to mention such things to Fiona. She doesn't understand the meaning of discretion but just blurts out whatever comes into her head. I should not have mentioned the shooting for the same reason. It upset her, and I had no intention of doing that, but how dreadful to be fired upon."

His gaze met hers again, and the intensity of it made her realize she ought to look away, but she could not do so. Gently, he said, "It would have been more dreadful to be shot or killed, I assure you."

"Yes, of course, but do you think your uncle did it?"

"He did not do the actual shooting, because we caught the man who did, but he will not talk, so we cannot be sure Eustace put him up to it."

"But who else might have done so?"

"Ah, you see the business as I do. Moreover, I suspect that quite a few items are missing from Hawks Rig. Some rather valuable things amongst them."

"So he's stolen from you, too," Anne said grimly. "How vexatious!"

"Yes, you might well say so. However, I'm at a stand, because in truth, I don't remember exactly what was there when I left, and my father might have sold any number of the things I do recall without telling me. I don't think he did, but I cannot prove it one way or the other unless I can find a dated inventory."

"I would say that the sooner Eustace Chisholm goes back

to wherever he came from, the better it will be for you, and for Fiona, too."

"I do wish you would not keep flinging Fiona at me," he said. "Moreover, if you mean to immobilize my poor fox in that tiny corner you've left for him, I wish you'd get it over with. I should have known you'd be skilled at this game."

"Well, yes, I think you might. I told you that I'd had little sisters. My brother was a good player, too. Moreover, my father taught us when we were small that the fox must always lose if the player with the geese plays them correctly."

He shook his head at her, but he was smiling. "Shall we play again, mistress, or would you prefer to join the others?"

She had seen Olivia looking their way more than once, and much as she would have liked to continue playing, she knew her duty. "We should join the others," she said. "Poor Fiona must be dreadfully bored. Look at her. She is nearly asleep on that stool."

"Either that, or she is entranced by the lad's music," he said with a chuckle. "Since his skill is scarcely great enough to cause anyone to go into a trance, I'd agree that she's bored."

"Have you come to join our game?" Berridge asked as they approached the other table. "I warn you, her ladyship is beating us all. If I have a pair, she has a triplet. If I have a triplet, she has a quartet. And she scoops the aces at every hand. At the rate she's cleaning my pockets, I shall be under arrest for debt by morning."

"You exaggerate, sir," Olivia said, but she looked much more cheerful than usual. "Fiona, would you like to take my place? I should stop whilst I'm winning lest they see how easily my luck can change."

Fiona opened her eyes and straightened on her stool,

looking like a startled fawn. "I . . . I do not know how to play poque," she said.

"These gentlemen will be happy to teach you," Olivia said. "You must show an interest in the things men enjoy, you know, so you will know how to entertain them when your husband's friends visit Hawks Rig."

The statement produced a pregnant silence, since her careful phrasing made it clear that she believed even the ownership of the Chisholm estates remained in doubt. Anne shot a look at Kit, saw that he was amused, and decided he had every right to be. Whatever the standing of the betrothal, no magistrate would refuse to void the official declaration of his death. Even Eustace could not be so foolish as to think he would retain control of Hawks Rig.

Berridge said, "I for one am content to stop playing this wicked game. My luck is out, and I warrant that will not change even if her ladyship departs the lists. If you are not going to join our table, Sir Christopher, perhaps you might take a turn about the hall with me. I believe we have kinsmen in common."

"Do we, sir? I'd be happy to explore our family trees together, but only if our hostess will be kind enough to excuse us."

"Lord, yes, she'll excuse you," Toby said with a laugh. "Wants to count her winnings, don't she? Moreover, it's past time our Fiona went to bed. She'll soon fall asleep and topple right off that stool of hers."

Olivia frowned at Fiona but said, "Perhaps you had better take her upstairs, Anne. She has scarcely moved this past hour. Go with your cousin, Fiona."

Kit caught Anne's eye, and his expression told her that he was either annoyed with her or annoyed that Olivia was sending her away. She was irked about that herself. It was not so much having her activity directed, for she was used to that, but she did not want to leave. She had enjoyed the evening, although she could not congratulate herself on the success of Fox and Geese as an opportunity for Kit to get to know Fiona better, since she had played with him longer than Fiona had and neither one had spared her a thought after she had left them.

As she and Fiona went upstairs together, she wondered why her cousin could not seem to see what an excellent man he was, how superior to his uncle in every way. To be fair, she did know that Fiona saw Kit's superiority. The problem was that Fiona was not taken with either man, and unlike most girls her age, she displayed little interest in marriage. Whether it was the result of her mother's constant scheming to unite her with power and wealth, or simply something lacking in the girl, the desire to wed seemed never to have stirred in her.

As they entered Fiona's chamber, Anne said bluntly, "Do you never want to marry, Fiona, or do you simply not like Sir Christopher any better than his uncle?"

"He is very kind," Fiona said, "but he is rather old, too, is he not? At least eight or nine and twenty. If I were able to choose my husband, I should choose someone closer to my own age, would not you, Anne?"

Since she did not think Kit old at all, Anne wondered if Fiona had forgotten she was by only two years the younger cousin, but she did not ask. Kit, after all, had expressed the same yearning to choose his own spouse. She wished Cardinal Beaton would send his reply soon, so they could all be done with wondering.

Olivia was supremely confident that the matter would

end happily for her daughter. But since Olivia was interested only in the Chisholm power and wealth, and since her words indicated that she was still uncertain which man would retain control of both, Anne could only believe she expected Fiona to marry the winner, regardless of what his eminence decided.

Eustace seemed supremely confident. He flirted just as blatantly as ever with Fiona, but he likewise flirted with Olivia. And while the latter might say what she chose about having sworn off men, Anne had watched her flutter her lashes and smile at every gentleman in the house save Sir Toby.

"Sakes, d'ye hear what that lass be thinking?" Maggie demanded of her two companions. "Why ha' we taken nae notice o' that afore?"

"Notice o' what?" the still-invisible Fergus demanded. "Ye shouldna peer into me lass's mind like that."

"Whisst now, let me think," Maggie snapped. "'Tis true, she does do that."

"Who does what?" Catriona asked. "You are making my head spin, Maggie. I don't know what she is thinking. Indeed, I can rarely tell what Kit is thinking."

"Then I'll tell ye," Maggie said. "She were thinking how Olivia, the black-draped widow wi' her megrims and fusses, has only tae look at a man tae flirt wi' him. I'd no be surprised but one touch o' a man's finger would stir her tae forget things as easily as any member o' the Forgetful People."

"Here now," Fergus protested. "There be nae need tae cast stones, Maggie Malloch. I havena forgotten anything o' importance in centuries."

"Only how tae keep yourself visible tae us," she retorted.

Turning to Catriona, she said, "Ye see where me thoughts be taking me, for when ye wiggle one o' your wee fingers at our Claud . . ." She paused expectantly.

"Aye, that's right, his mind turns instantly to lust," Catriona said, her eyes widening. "Oh, Maggie, do you think it's possible we've found him at last?"

"But ye canna just murder the widow and hope her death frees your Claud," Fergus said, showing himself at last. "Ye ken what'll happen if ye're wrong!"

"Aye, now there's the rub," Maggie said with a sigh.

"Aye, sure," Catriona agreed. "Recall that if you kill the wrong one, Jonah's spell will allow the Evil Host to claim Claud for all time, and quite likely yourself and anyone else who touches upon that spell, right along with him."

"What?" shrieked Fergus. "Ye never told me we could go, too!"

"Pish tush," Maggie said. "There be nae reason tae think—"

"And ye call me the forgetful one!" Fergus snapped, still in high dudgeon. "Did ye chance tae think that if ye kill any mortal, the High Circle will most likely blame all three o' us for it? If we're banished, we'll all be fair game for the Host!"

"Ye leave that tae me," Maggie said. "I can manage the Circle. Nobbut I'll agree this would all be much easier if I could just snap me fingers and the right mortal would just perish on the spot without anyone else being the wiser!"

Kit and Eustace returned to Hawks Rig the next day, taking the jester with them, but when the anticipated message from Branxholme arrived late Tuesday morning, Olivia sent a rider at once to Hawks Rig to request their return.

"His eminence is coming here on Thursday," she informed Anne and Fiona when she had read the message, "and Buccleuch will come with him. That gives us less than two full days to prepare, and I imagine they will bring a large party, because the cardinal enjoys puffing off his importance. Find Malcolm, and send him to me. We must be sure they find nothing amiss at Mute Hill House."

Anne had been only fourteen when James, King of Scots, had stayed at Ellyson Towers during his second visit to the Borders, but she recalled the bustle and uproar that preceded his visit. Her mother had remained calm, however, saying that the King was a young man like any other, and would doubtless enjoy his stay very much. And so it had proved.

Since she could not imagine that Cardinal Beaton would be any more difficult to please than the King of Scots, she set about with her usual calm doing all she could to help prepare for the visit. Since Olivia sincerely believed that his eminence must be looking forward to visiting such a fine place as Mute Hill House, she was content to let Anne and Malcolm carry the burden, offering occasional casual suggestions that sent servants scurrying. Fiona helped, too, although she seemed to be looking forward to the return of the jester more than to the return of her suitors or to meeting the powerful cardinal and learning of his decision.

The party from Hawks Rig returned Wednesday evening in time for supper, and to Toby and Fiona's delight, Mad Jake accompanied them.

By the time the cardinal's party rode into the yard the following afternoon, all was in order, and although Anne was astonished at the number of visitors, she knew that everyone could be comfortably accommodated.

Malcolm had been nearly civil to her throughout the bustle, clearly grateful for several of her suggestions, particularly after she mentioned that she had gleaned her knowledge through watching her mother prepare for a royal visit.

"We have never received his grace at Mute Hill House," Malcolm admitted. "I'm told, though, that 'tis the cardinal who is the most powerful man in Scotland."

"I think perhaps his grace would disagree," Anne said with a smile, "but doubtless his eminence believes as you do."

When the party from Branxholme entered the house, she saw at once that Cardinal David Beaton knew his worth. Dressed in red from head to toe, he led the way, looking as magnificent as he might have for an appearance at court. The trumpets were missing, but Malcolm's stentorian announcement of his entrance surely rivaled that of any court chamberlain.

Buccleuch walked a few steps behind Beaton, followed by a colorful retinue, including several ladies. Lady Scott was not one of them, however, so it seemed that the rumormongers were right and she had returned to her parents' home.

Olivia swept a deep curtsy as Beaton approached her, and kissed his ring when he held out his hand. Rising gracefully, she included Buccleuch in her smiling gaze as she welcomed them to Mute Hill House.

"We are honored, your eminence. For you to come here . . ." She paused, fluttering her lashes. "Indeed, sir, I am rendered speechless."

He smiled, and Anne saw that he possessed great charm as well as an aura of great power. "I hope we do not inconvenience you, Lady Carmichael, but we shall not stay long. I am on a pilgrimage, as it were, visiting great lords here in the Borders, gathering their support to insure that we remain strong enough to keep the English out of Scotland. From here, I travel to Maxwell at Caerlaverock, so you see, Mute Hill provides a comfortable place along the way to spend a night. Allow me to present some of my companions. I'm told that you already know Buccleuch."

"Indeed, yes," Olivia said, turning to that gentleman. "Welcome, sir."

Beaton went on to introduce other gentlemen in his train before he said casually, "I do not believe you know my cousin, Janet Beaton, but I trust she will find a good friend in you, madam."

"Oh, yes, of course. Welcome, Mistress Beaton," Olivia said, staring at the handsomely fair young woman Beaton drew forth.

If Olivia looked amazed, Anne could not blame her. Buccleuch's marriage was not officially ended yet, and yet here he was, traveling in company with the woman who was apparently to be his next wife and expecting his hostess to welcome her—as indeed she must since the woman was Davy Beaton's cousin.

Chapter 16

It soon became evident to everyone at Mute Hill House that the cardinal had a particular reason for including his cousin in his entourage, and Anne and Fiona learned what it was when Olivia commanded them to attend her in her bedchamber after they had finished dressing for supper.

"As you heard, his eminence desires to please his grace's Border lords," she said. "Eustace . . . that is, Sir Eustace tells me Buccleuch can raise thousands of men in just a few days' time, so neither the King nor his eminence wants to put him out of temper just now when the royal need is so great."

Anne and Fiona both nodded.

Buccleuch's temper was said to rival that of the late Earl of Armadale, even to exceed it, and since he followed his own law, as nearly all powerful Border lords did, ruling as absolute monarch of his own domain, it did not matter a whit to him who claimed to be his king or the master of his kirk. Most Borderers were fickle about such matters, because they could see no reason to bend a knee to the Pope far away in Rome or the King miles away at Stirling.

"The cardinal desires us to treat his cousin with extraordinary courtesy," Olivia continued. "He means to expedite Buccleuch's divorce from Janet Kerr and open the way for him to marry Janet Beaton as soon as possible, but he fears some people might disapprove and loudly voice that disapproval. Therefore, he hopes to forestall such a reaction by showing at once that the finest people receive her."

"But how can he show that?" Fiona asked. "I like Janet Kerr. I do not think Buccleuch should set her aside so easily. Surely, many others will agree with me."

"Whether they do or not, you must not speak so critically of any guest in our home," Olivia said severely. "You are about to bestow a signal honor upon Janet Beaton, my dear, so do not let me hear such hasty words from you again."

"No, madam. I apologize."

Anne said, "But what honor could Fiona bestow, Aunt Olivia?"

"It concerns you, too, Anne dear, for when his eminence suggested that perhaps Janet Beaton might serve as an attendant in Fiona's wedding, you may be sure that I instantly said she must serve as her chief attendant. I know you will not mind giving up that position in such an excellent cause."

"But I do not even know her," Fiona protested. "Will not our friends stare to see her in Anne's place?"

"All that matters is that it will please Buccleuch, whom we have no wish or cause to displease," Olivia said with a stern look.

"I don't even know whom I'm going to marry," Fiona said with a sigh. "I suppose I should not quibble about my chief attendant being a total stranger."

"Exactly so," her mother said. "However, you will know your bridegroom by the time you go to bed tonight, for his eminence has said we will discuss that matter directly after supper."

His eminence having requested that the discussion take place in the hall, which was of a more convenient size to contain his retinue than Olivia's bower, everyone at the high table remained seated while Malcolm hustled his minions through their postprandial duties, leaving trestles up to accommodate those of the cardinal's people for whom the high table lacked seating.

Beaton occupied the central place there. When the household servants and others who were not expected to remain, or chose not to, had departed, he said in a voice that easily carried to the back of the hall, "I had intended to hear from each person concerned in this difficulty before making my decision. However, I've come to see that the road I must follow is plain."

A murmur of comment filled the chamber, and as Beaton waited pointedly for it to cease, Anne glanced at Kit, who was intently watching the cardinal. Beside her, Fiona stared into space as if the proceedings had nothing to do with her.

Eustace still looked supremely confident, as did Olivia.

Two places away from Anne, Berridge pared his nails with a knife someone had left on the table. He kept his hands below the tabletop, but she could easily see what he was doing. He glanced her way and winked.

Nearly startled into a laugh, she looked quickly down at her own lap.

Other than a brief shuffling of feet, the chamber fell silent again.

Beaton said, "I warrant everyone in this room knows the quandary we face. Sir Christopher Chisholm, son of the late

Laird of Ashkirk and Torness, after disappearing for more than a year and being presumed dead, was officially declared so after his father's unfortunate demise. Before his disappearance, Sir Christopher was betrothed to Mistress Fiona Carmichael, and as I understand the matter, those betrothal vows were exchanged by proxy. Is that not so, madam?"

Clearly taken aback when he turned abruptly to ask the question, Olivia recovered quickly. "Yes," she said. "His father stood proxy for him."

Beaton nodded. "Then the answer is plain. Despite the official declaration of his death, the original betrothal must stand, because the second one is rendered null and void by the obviously false declaration on which it was based. Mistress Fiona must marry Sir Christopher, whose lands and titles will certainly be restored to him, since he is undeniably the rightful heir and the true Laird of Ashkirk and Torness."

A gasp sounded from somewhere to Anne's right, but she could not at first discern the source. Then Eustace leaned forward as if to see the cardinal more clearly, and the plain, raw fury he displayed gave him away.

For a moment, she thought he would protest aloud, but he did not, and she decided he must at least possess his fair share of common sense. To argue with the man who spoke as the Pope in Scotland would be folly, if not madness.

Olivia, evidently oblivious to anything but the Cardinal's words, said with a smile, "We would be honored, your eminence, if you would condescend to perform the wedding ceremony."

"That will be my pleasure, madam," Beaton said, as if they had not already discussed the matter and decided upon such details as Fiona's chief attendant.

Olivia said, "Fiona, surely you must have something to say, my dear."

Fiona looked as if her thoughts were miles away and the decision just announced had nothing whatsoever to do with her, and she continued to gaze into the distance until Anne pinched her.

Starting, Fiona looked at her indignantly and said, "What?"

Anne flicked a pointed glance toward Olivia and Beaton.

Still visibly confused, Fiona looked hesitantly in that direction.

Sir Toby said with a laugh, "Wake up, child. Your future has just been decided for ye, and your fond mother would like ye to thank his eminence."

Confusion turned instantly to dismay as she fixed her attention upon her mother, saying, "I-I'm sorry, madam. I fear I was not . . . That is, I—"

To everyone's surprise, Beaton came to her rescue, saying with his charming smile, "One cannot doubt that this misunderstanding has been a great trial to you, mistress. I warrant you must be relieved to have it resolved at last."

"R-resolved? Oh, of course," she stammered. "Thank you, your eminence."

Kit nearly rolled his eyes. As if it were not infuriating enough to have his future decided for him so abruptly and without the slightest query as to his wishes or beliefs, to have his intended wife behave like the simpleton he thought her did not help. Or had the lass simply never been allowed to think for herself?

Lady Carmichael leaned close to Beaton, nodding as he murmured to her, but she caught Kit's gaze and beamed fondly at him. That she would welcome him as her son-in-law could not have been clearer. He gritted his teeth.

He saw then that Lady Anne was also watching him and strove to keep his countenance from revealing his anger even to her. Revealing that anger to anyone would do him no good if the law decreed that the earlier betrothal must stand. He could scarcely rail against the law when it stood against him and then demand its support to regain his title and estates. His frustration was nearly overwhelming, however, and Anne was perceptive. He feared she could easily discern all he felt.

Just catching her eye and seeing her concern stirred tension in his loins even as it encouraged him to control his temper. Fiona was the loveliest girl he had ever clapped eyes on, but she did not hold a candle to her cousin when it came to feminine allure. All Anne Ellyson had to do was look at him. Indeed, even that was unnecessary. If she walked away, the desire to follow her was overwhelming.

When Tam caught his eye just then and winked, Kit's jaw tightened. That one of his best friends found amusement in the lamentable business was infuriating, too. Willie, on the other hand, doubtless counting himself amongst the servants, had left the hall when they did. Kit only wished he might have joined them.

Beaton cleared his throat and the hall fell silent again.

"I have been conferring with her ladyship," he said, "and we have decided the ceremony will take place tomorrow morning at ten o'clock. Although we must not linger longer at Mute Hill, and therefore Mistress Carmichael may find herself with fewer guests than she hoped," he added, smiling at Fiona, who gazed blankly back at him, "we will do our best to make the occasion a memorable one for her."

Kit wished he could see his uncle's face, but they sat at opposite ends of the table on the same side, and he could see only Eustace's clenched hands on the table. Clearly, from the way they kept tightening, he was angry, too.

The only satisfaction as far as Kit was concerned was Beaton's assurance that the titles and estates would be restored to him, but he doubted Eustace would submit tamely to that decision or any other. More likely, he would continue to cause trouble any way he could even after the wedding.

It occurred to him then to wonder how his eminence thought a man who was still officially dead could legally marry, but apparently that was a minor detail to everyone but Kit himself. Perhaps, he decided, the Pope in Scotland believed he also called the tune in secular law. In any event, Kit doubted that any mere magistrate would dare to oppose Davy Beaton.

Anne wished she were privy to Kit's thoughts. He looked much as his uncle did, as if he were ripe for murder.

Fiona whispered, "Can we go now, Anne?"

"I think your mother will object if we ask to leave before his eminence does," Anne said tactfully, knowing the threat of Olivia's displeasure was usually sufficient to stifle any desire Fiona expressed to run counter to her wishes.

To her surprise, however, Fiona said, "But I want to go upstairs. I have the most awful headache. It's just pounding behind my eyes, Anne. Please!"

"Very well, I'll speak to her," Anne said, pushing back her stool to stand.

To her surprise, Berridge stood and moved to assist her. "Are you ill, Lady Anne?" he asked quietly as he put a firm hand under her elbow.

"No, my lord, but my cousin is suffering from a bad headache," she said, surprised by his concern. "She desires to retire to her chamber, so I mean to ask my aunt and his eminence to excuse her."

"An excellent notion," he said. "You will go upstairs with her, of course."

"Yes, my lord, certainly."

"What is it, Anne?" Olivia asked sharply.

Curtsying, Anne said, "Forgive me, madam, but Fiona has developed a headache and I believe she should retire before it worsens."

Olivia frowned, but Beaton said, "By all means, Lady Anne, take her up to her bedchamber and see that she is made comfortable. A lass needs rest to look her best, you know. She must not have dark circles under her eyes on her wedding day."

"Thank you, your eminence," Fiona said, standing to make her own curtsy.

He nodded, and Anne hustled Fiona out of the hall and up the stairs.

When they entered Fiona's bedchamber to find Molly busily tidying the room, Fiona breathed a sigh and said, "You need not stay, Anne, if you'd liefer return to the hall. Molly will look after me."

"Don't be absurd," Anne said. "Now that you have so kindly provided me with an excuse to leave, I certainly do not intend to waste it by returning. But you do not really have a headache, do you?"

Reddening, Fiona nibbled her lower lip. "Don't be angry."

"Of course, I am not angry, love, but how daring of you!"

"I don't want to marry him, Anne."

"I don't suppose you do," Anne said sympathetically, "although I cannot imagine why you don't want him. He is a wonderful man."

"I am sure he is, but I don't want either of them."

"Betrothals are not easily broken," Anne warned her. "And most girls have no choice. You must obey your mother or stand up to her, Fiona. You know that."

Fiona raised her chin.

Anne saw Molly's eyes widen and felt her own mouth drop open. Her gentle, biddable cousin looked as stubborn at that moment as Anne herself had ever felt.

"Fiona?"

"I won't do it," Fiona said, stamping one little foot. "I shall enter a nunnery, and the sisters will just have to take me with or without my fortune. You do not think they really would turn me away, do you, Anne?"

No, Anne did not believe any self-respecting nunnery would turn away an heiress of Fiona's worth. More than likely, they would believe that in the long run, particularly if she took her vows, they would win complete control of her fortune.

"But think of the scandal, love! You would not like that."

"I shouldn't like it at all, but if I am in a nunnery, I shan't have to bear it."

Anne frowned. "Fiona, you are babbling absurdities. You know you will never have the nerve to defy your mother, let alone Cardinal Beaton, in such an outrageous way. Do you think he will allow you to enter a nunnery or that any abbess, no matter how greedy or stout-hearted, will dare defy him?"

Fiona shrugged. "Why would he want to stop me? 'Tis the Kirk—*his* Kirk—that will claim my inheritance. Would he not rather keep it than see it go into the Chisholm coffers?"

Her logic was unassailable, but Anne had a suspicion that Davy Beaton, having decreed what was to happen, would not be so understanding of Fiona's defiance, no matter how he or his Kirk might profit from it. One needed no great power of discernment to see that he was a man wholly accustomed to being obeyed and one, moreover, who would not let defiance of his decisions pass lightly.

"You need not look as though I were contemplating suicide," Fiona said with a smile. "I warrant it will all come right in the end, but I've never been allowed to express my wishes in any of this, and I want them all to know I loathe being pushed like this to marry. First it was Sir Eustace, and now it is his nephew, and although I am sure Sir Christopher is all that is kind, I do not know him, and even in his kindness, he has scarcely spoken more than two words to me in all the time he has been here. I want a husband who will value me and love me, Anne, at least enough to speak to me without treating me as if I were an infant or an idiot."

That declaration struck a respondent chord in Anne. Did she not want the same thing in her husband, despite the rarity of such men? She certainly knew, if others did not, that Fiona had opinions of her own. The younger girl did not often dare to voice them, however, and this fierce rebellion seemed out of character for her. Clearly, this matter was of vital importance to her.

Gently, Anne said, "Even if you mean everything you say, love, I cannot imagine how you can succeed in escaping Mute Hill House and traveling to a nunnery, nor do I think the nuns are allowed to accept young women without their mothers' permission or that of a legal guardian. They would just send you back."

"I don't care," Fiona declared. "At least I will have shown them all that I am not a toy they can simply present to someone, to fondle or destroy as he pleases."

"But how will you manage it?" Anne asked, appalled by the image her cousin had presented.

Fiona smiled. "I have a plan."

If anything could have surprised Anne more than her cousin's defiance, it was this. Having only come to know her during the past several months at Mute Hill House, she could not say that Fiona had never before devised a plan of her own, but she certainly had shown no ability to do so while Anne had lived with her. Fiona had simply followed where others, particularly her mother, had led her.

"But how do you imagine your plan could succeed?" Anne asked. "Your mother need only learn where you have gone to bring you back again, and in disgrace, Fiona. Do not forget that. You would face severe punishment."

"She won't be able to follow straightaway," Fiona said.

"Faith, why ever not?"

"Because she will not know where I have gone," Fiona said. "I don't mean to tell anyone, not even you, Anne."

"But there are very few nunneries hereabouts," Anne pointed out. "Indeed, I do not know of any nearer than Melrose. And how will you get away? You cannot simply go to the main gate and order the men to open it. They won't do it, and even if by some miracle, someone did let you ride out, you would have to take an escort, and the escort would see exactly where you went."

"Well, they won't, because I won't take one. I'll go dur-

ing the wedding, when everyone is distracted by the ceremony on the church porch."

"But—"

"No, let me finish," Fiona begged. "I know you must
think me mad, and had Mother not decided to ask Janet
Beaton to serve as my chief attendant, no plan could have
succeeded. But she did, and when she did, I began to think
and scheme as I never have before. My plan is simple,
though. You will just take my place."

Anne stared at her in disbelief. "I told you that was a
crazy plan when you suggested it the first time. You *must* be
mad, Fiona."

"Perhaps I am," Fiona agreed. "I certainly would be if I
let them force me into this marriage without making the
least push to defend myself."

"But why now, when you have never made such a push
before?"

"Perhaps because I have never cared so much before,"
Fiona said softly.

Something in her expression gave Anne to understand at
last that her cousin was determined to go through with her
plan, however mad it was. But there was at least one hitch.
"Much as I'd like to help, I cannot take your place, Fiona,"
she said reluctantly. "Everyone would know me at a glance.
You know they would."

"Not if you wear the veil," Fiona said. "You will recall
that, last time, until just at the last moment, my mother insisted I wear one. This time I'll insist upon it. I shall tell her
I don't want to have to pretend to enjoy seeing everyone
stare at me."

"But even if I wore the veil, I'd have to take it off at some
point."

"Not until the very end of the ceremony, at the presentation," Fiona assured her. "That is what Mother told me last time, and by then it won't matter."

"To you, perhaps," Anne said grimly. "Why, we'd be married then, Fiona! Just what do you suppose they would do to me for such a deception, especially if I were so daft as to wait until the presentation before revealing myself?"

"Nothing very much, I'm sure," was the airy response. "His eminence can simply annul the marriage, and I do not suppose for a moment that Sir Christopher would allow anyone to harm you merely for helping me. Not if he is as kind as you say he is, and I should think you must know him better than I do. He has certainly talked with you more, and has even walked with you at least twice in the garden."

Briefly, Anne wondered if Fiona were jealous or suspected that she harbored deep feelings for Kit. She could scarcely deny them if asked, because she could imagine no finer husband for herself and had been wishing from the moment she realized Fiona did not want him that he were free to ask her instead. Indeed, she had no doubt that her primary reason for doubting Fiona's sanity was her own belief that anyone must be mad not to want Kit. He had only to look at her to make her whole body sing. She knew he liked her, perhaps even harbored similar, deep feelings for her, but likewise she knew what he would think of such a deception and how he would view the resulting scandal. For her own sake, she had to dissuade Fiona.

"Really, Fiona, such a plan is doomed to fail, and it is quite unnecessary," she said. "You need only tell them that you do not *want* to marry him. Scottish law protects women from being forced into unwanted marriages. You know it does."

"Not in this instance, because I asked Mother about that only yesterday, and I should warn you that she is vexed with you for telling me it was all I need do. She explained that if one party to a betrothal is not of age, like me, the betrothal is utterly binding on both parties. Even so, I believe Cardinal Beaton can overset any betrothal if I can just make him want to, so I mean to give him good cause even if they catch me before I get well away. If he refuses to annul it, then I shall tell him I want to enter a nunnery, and you will see then how quickly he will help a great heiress who wants to dedicate herself and her wealth to the Holy Kirk."

"But why do you not go to him and tell him that now?"

"Because I want to avoid the fratching if I can, Anne. Surely, you understand that. Only think how they will all carp at me and scold. I couldn't bear it!"

Anne could easily imagine it. At this point, she would not put it past Olivia to take a switch to her beautiful daughter to force her to marry the Chisholm power and wealth. And if Olivia did such a thing, Beaton certainly would not stop her.

"I simply cannot do it, Fiona," she said at last. "You must realize that it is too much to ask of anyone. Think of the scandal it would cause."

"If you won't do it, then Molly must," Fiona said flatly.

Molly turned white. "Nay, mistress! I'd be a-quaking in me shoes, knowing your mam would ha' me flogged, sure as anything."

"You must, Molly. Go away, Anne," Fiona added. "If you will not do this tiny thing for me, I don't want to talk to you anymore."

"It is *not* a tiny thing," Anne said. Nevertheless, deciding she would accomplish nothing by staying, and hoping Molly might still succeed in talking Fiona out of her foolish plan, Anne went to her own room.

Thinking furiously and paying no heed to anything beyond her own tangled thoughts, she was passing the service stair when a sudden hiss made her jump.

Stopping, she looked around, half expecting to see the ubiquitous fox, although the noise was certainly unlike any she had ever heard from one. At first, in the shadowy stairway, she saw nothing, but then a movement from the darkest shadow shifted into the shape of a man, and she recognized the jester.

"Mercy, Jake, what are you doing in this part of the house?" she demanded. "Did I not order you to stay away from here?"

"Aye, my lady, so ye did," the jester said, nodding. "But—"

"If you have thoughts of giving Mistress Fiona another lesson on the lute—"

"Nay, mistress," the lad said hastily. "'Tis yourself I were waiting for."

"Me! But why?"

"Because 'tis my belief ye'd no like anything bad tae happen tae Kit— that is, tae Sir Christopher," the jester said evenly.

Alarmed, she exclaimed, "I don't want anything bad to happen to anyone!"

"Aye, but I'm telling ye summat may happen tae Sir Christopher. I ken fine ye heard wha' happened when he returned tae Hawks Rig."

"Yes, I did. You told my cousin, and she told me."

"Aye, 'tis so, and me ears be still burning from wha' Sir Christopher said tae me about me loose tongue and what he'd do did I wag it again about his affairs, but I'm thinking I'd rather have him skelp me good than find m'self watching his burial because I held me tongue."

"His burial!" Anne's stomach lurched as a shiver shot up her spine. Clapping a hand to her midsection and ignoring the shiver, she forced herself to concentrate. "What makes you imagine such a horrible thing?" she demanded.

"Sir Eustace, that's what," the jester said. "He'll be planning tae kill him, or I dinna ken the man. It were bad enough afore the cardinal made his decision, sithee, but Eustace could play the part o' the good uncle whilst he thought he'd win free in the end. Mayhap ye didna see his smirk when his eminence said he'd decided. Or how that smirk turned tae fury when he said the first betrothal must stand."

"I did see how angry he looked," Anne said. "But I did not see you."

"Nay, for I were up in the minstrels' gallery. There be a place where a man can hunker down there and see all that goes on in the hall without being remarked himself. I ha' found it useful even afore today."

"Mercy, do you spy on us?"

"I've done nowt tae concern ye, m'lady," he said earnestly. "I ha' me own reasons for taking interest here— aye, and at Hawks Rig, too."

"What possible reason could you have?" she said indignantly. "For a jester to spy upon the household where he entertains is despicable."

"Aye, if I were nobbut an ordinary jester," he said with an impish grin.

"Are you not then?"

"Oh, I'm a canny jester right enough, but I'm also Kit

Chisholm's good friend, and there be nowt I can think of that I wouldna do for the man."

"Did you know him in the Highlands then?"

"Nay, I'm Border born and bred, same as yourself." He hesitated, then added in a rush, "He said he'd told ye about the ship, mistress."

"He did not tell me much," Anne said, remembering how he had flung the words at her in the yard as he was leaving, the night they met. "Only that he'd been on a prison ship, condemned to it for life."

"Aye, for murder."

"Murder!"

"Aye, and 'twas the cardinal's ship," he went on, oblivious to her dismay as she remembered only a short while before thinking that Kit had looked ripe for murder. "I were on that ship, too, sithee," he added.

"Tell me about this murder," Anne said.

"Nay, ye'll ha' tae ask him. I can tell ye he were falsely accused, but even were me tongue as loose as he said, we've nae time for long tales. Still, I wanted tae warn ye about Eustace, because Kit's in no frame o' mind now tae hear me. I'm thinking I'll ha' better luck finding him some help on me own."

"If you mean me, I cannot imagine what you expect me to do."

"Just tae keep your eyes open," he said. "He has other friends not too far from here, at Dunsithe Castle. I'll ride there tomorrow and tell them what's happened. And I've friends o' me own hereabouts, too, who will help us."

"Why do you care so much about him?" Anne asked curiously.

"He's me friend," he said simply. "Even went a-reiving

wi' us. It were me pony Kit rode the night he brought ye home, m'lady."

"Yours? But that man's name was—"

"Willie," he said, bowing deeply. "I'm Mad Jake here, sithee, but the reivers do call me Willie."

"Well, I'm afraid your having been prisoners or reivers together does little to increase my trust in you or in your judgment on this matter," Anne said.

"It should," Willie said earnestly. "Nowt bonds men more than sharing such experiences. Moreover, Kit likely saved me life at least once."

"How?"

He reddened. "Our first mate ordered me flogged for nae good reason, and Kit stopped it. Said the flogging would kill me, that he'd take it instead."

She gasped. "What happened?"

"As ye've seen, me lady, we're both here," he said. "D'ye want details, ye'll ha' tae get them from Kit. I just wanted tae tell someone afore I leave what I suspect about Eustace. I doubt ye can prevent his mischief, seeing who he counts as his friends, but I'll feel better knowing someone here kens what I do."

"But you only *suspect* he plans murder," Anne said, hoping desperately that that was all. The chill along her spine turned to icicles when he shook his head.

"It's no just a suspicion," he said. "That man's got a plan, and only one plan I can think of would do him any good. If Kit marries your cousin, Eustace loses her unless Kit dies and Eustace persuades his eminence tae put aside the consanguinity laws. He were angry at table, but a short while ago, he were all smiles again. That isna natural for the man at the best of times. I ken fine, he be plotting mischief."

Anne had to agree. "Is your true name Jake or Willie?" she asked.

He hesitated, then said with a wry grin, "Me name's Willie Armstrong."

"A good Border name," she said, smiling. "Kit is lucky to have a friend like you to watch his back."

"Aye, that he is, because the one thing I've learned since we returned is that nowt is what it seems tae be, especially betwixt Eustace and the cardinal."

"But what else—?"

At a sound below them on the stairs, he stiffened, and before Anne could finish her sentence, he slipped silently away up the stairs.

She wasted no time following but hurried back to Fiona's room and entered without ceremony, saying, "You can stop badgering poor Molly, Fiona. I'll do it."

Chapter 17

As it happened, their deception proved remarkably easy to carry out, and Fiona's unexpected capacity for prevarication astonished her cousin.

Shortly after Anne returned to the house, when Olivia entered Fiona's room to tell her she had invited the women to help her dress in the morning as they had before, Fiona agreed with a sigh, and Anne was able to indulge briefly in a hope that the terrifying plan had failed before it had begun. But when Olivia had gone away again, Fiona said, "That's all right, then. We'll have them in, so they will all see me dress, and then no one will suspect afterward that anything is amiss."

"But how—?"

"You'll see. It will be easy. In the morning, we'll tell everyone you have fallen ill and cannot attend me. Mother will not care about your absence, because she wants only to impress Buccleuch and the cardinal with her kindness toward Janet Beaton. But if anyone tries to visit you, your Peg must keep them away."

Anne sighed.

"What?"

"Nothing, except that I have never known you to be so decisive before. Pray, explain the rest of this plan of yours."

"It is simple, Anne. I shall let them dress me, and then I shall tell them I want a few minutes alone before I go downstairs. You will be waiting, and Molly and I will help you change into my wedding dress and veil."

"Fiona, it will never work. What shall I do when someone speaks to me?"

"No one spoke to me when the procession gathered last time, but if anyone does, just murmur as if you are angry or unhappy or just shy. It is what I would do."

Anne frowned, but she suspected that her cousin was right. The bride was no more in this marriage game than the fox was in its game against geese determined to force it to a corner where they could control it.

Olivia had expressed no surprise at finding her daughter up and had not mentioned her supposed headache.

The next morning went exactly as Fiona had predicted, and only Anne retained doubts about the plan's likelihood for success. How, she wondered, as she stood quietly beside Sir Toby waiting for the procession to begin, could she have let herself agree to such a masquerade even if Willie Armstrong was right and Kit's life was in danger? She could not deny wanting to marry Kit, but in the ordinary way, not like this. Never before had she so much as considered such rash, scandalous behavior. On the contrary, she had carefully avoided upsetting anyone.

She had always disliked noisy scenes. Her brother having inherited the earl's fiery, unpredictable temper, loud arguments had been frequent at the Towers. She had hated them, yet her present actions were sure to incite just such angry chaos.

When such scenes had erupted at home, she had nearly always sought the sanctuary of her mother's chamber and placid nature, but there was no sanctuary now. Trying to ignore sudden tears stinging her eyes, she realized belatedly that to think of Lady Armadale now was dangerous. What she would think of this mad start did not bear consideration.

Beneath the concealing veil, she winced as the unexpected, warring emotions struggled to surface. She realized that she missed her mother more desperately than ever, both to seek her advice and because a girl's mother should be at her wedding, even a sham wedding like this one. On the other hand, and for the first time since Lady Armadale's death, Anne could be glad that that tragic event would spare her the indignity of watching her daughter create a scandal of the highest order.

Even so, and although Anne knew she ought to be riddled with guilt for the deception in which she was playing the leading role, of the emotions whirling through her as she waited, guilt remained remarkably absent. Certain that it had simply not struck yet, that when it did, it would flatten her, she told herself she was doing all she could to protect Kit from his uncle's evil plotting, but it was still hard to believe that Eustace might really kill him.

Indeed, aside from missing her mother and a certain awe-inspiring sense of the magnitude of her deception, she felt only the fear of discovery and a strange pulsating excitement that settled deep within her.

Whenever her thoughts began to drift to what would happen when she had to lift her veil and reveal what she had done, her imagination failed and those drifting thoughts turned without conscious direction to other matters.

Toby touched her elbow, and she realized that the musicians had begun playing and that Janet Beaton and the little girls strewing flowers had walked on ahead. Janet had nearly reached the arched stone bridge.

Remembering when Fiona and Toby had barely made it across side-by-side, and remembering too, the day that she had pushed Kit into the brook, Anne smiled under her veil and rested her hand on the plump forearm Toby extended to her.

Standing on the porch with Beaton and the supposed Lord Berridge, who had cheerfully offered to serve as his best man, Kit remained silent, listening to two musicians strum lutes while a third played the pipe. He was surprised that Willie was not with them, but decided the lad must have annoyed someone and been banished to the kitchen or elsewhere for his impudence.

As he watched his bride cross the bridge with Sir Toby's arm around her to keep them from tumbling into the brook, he saw that this time she was veiled, doubtless to protect her sorely tried sensibilities. Her chief attendant was different, too, but much as he would have liked to see Anne, he was glad she would not be standing beside her cousin throughout this wedding. He doubted Fiona would agree, though. She depended a great deal on Anne and would doubtless miss her support.

Despite his opposition to the union, he could feel sympathy for Fiona. It had to be hard to repeat the long walk through the garden before a new audience, and she might well fear that someone would speak up to stop this wedding, too. He rather hoped for such a miracle, himself, to end the farce. His anger after Beaton's announcement had burned quickly. Stuffing the pair of them into marriage together still seemed mad, but he had not been given any chance to talk with her since the cardinal's decision, let alone to persuade her to cry off, and now he felt only the resignation of knowing he was helpless against the laws of both Kirk and Crown.

Even had he managed to talk to her, Beaton was the most powerful man in Scotland and could easily undermine his attempt to recover his titles and estates. That factor more than any was the reason he stood meekly now awaiting his fate.

At least the cardinal seemed unaware of his imprisonment aboard the *Marion Ogilvy,* for surely he would have mentioned it by now had he known. However, should someone bring it to his attention, even now, the resulting scene would be both awkward and humiliating, because Kit had no proof of his exoneration except his own word and that of Tam and Willie. Neither was of sufficient stature to impress anyone, and the others who knew of his innocence were all elsewhere.

The likely reaction if Tam and Willie were to speak for him after having perpetrated their separate, unholy deceptions at Mute Hill House would be flat disbelief. Imagining that scene nearly made him smile.

It would be much better if his eminence were truly unaware and remained so.

The bridal party neared the chapel porch, and he saw Eustace near the path, watching. With him were two Chisholm cousins who still had not deigned to acknowledge Kit's presence in their midst, clearly counting themselves Eustace's allies. Kit had thought he understood their position before, but since the cardinal had decided in his favor and assured everyone that he was certain to regain his rank and holdings, he did not understand them now. Unless, he reminded himself, Willie was right, and Eustace expected him to die soon. The thought jarred, but he rejected it, unable to imagine how Eustace could think he might win by killing him now.

The music stopped, and as his bride stepped onto the porch and took her place beside him, Kit turned to face the altar and the cardinal.

Sir Toby remained at the foot of the steps, poised to give the bride away.

Beaton raised both hands, and the huge crowd fell silent.

"Dearly beloved, we are gathered together here in the sight of God, and in the face of this company . . ."

Anne felt as if she had somehow been trapped in a dream that was repeating itself without getting the details right. The cardinal's voice was the wrong voice, and her own role was certainly wrong. Her breath came in shallow gasps until Beaton reached the first crucial point, and then she could not seem to breathe at all.

"If any man knows cause or can show just impediment why these two persons should not be joined together in holy matrimony, let him speak now or forever after hold his peace."

Her heart thudded, and the assembly apparently held its collective breath just as she held hers. So silent did it become that she did not hear even a bird's chirp, so that only the distant murmur of the brook served as evidence that her hearing had not failed. She half expected Eustace Chisholm to shout out that the marriage was a sham, or even for Fiona herself to step up, announce that she had changed her mind, and please could she marry Kit after all?

No one spoke, and at last, the cardinal looked away from the gathering and directly at the bridal pair. In her relief, Anne dared to release the breath she had been holding, but worse was to come.

Speaking directly to them, Beaton said solemnly, "I require and charge ye both, as ye will answer at the dreadful day of judgment when the secrets of all hearts shall be disclosed, that if either of ye knows any impediment why ye may not be lawfully joined together in matrimony, ye do now confess it. For I assure ye, if any persons be joined together otherwise than as God's word doth allow, their marriage is not lawful."

She had been frightened enough just knowing that soon she would have to answer to Kit for her deception. Suddenly realizing that she would have to answer to God was far worse. Anne opened her mouth to blurt out a confession, but no words came. It was as if an unseen hand had clapped over her mouth.

"Catriona, ye canna do that!" Fergus shrieked. "Ye've nowt tae do wi' her! Anyhow, how did ye do it? I thought we, none o' us, had any power in a kirk."

"We are not in the kirk, Fergus, but only on its porch," Catriona retorted. "Moreover, whilst she may be your lass to guard, she is exactly where she wants to be, doing exactly what she wants to do, whilst you seem still to be stuck on forcing her to hold by her earlier intention. This way, she fulfills my task, too, because she will make Kit Chisholm happier than her cousin would, so pray, use some of that talent you Ellyllon have for forgetting, and forget your foolish notion of marrying him to Lady Anne's cousin. That is not going to happen now, nor should it."

"It wasna *my* notion but *yours*," he reminded her angrily.

"I changed my mind, and so did she, although apparently you failed to notice."

"Where's Maggie?" he demanded.

"You go and find her if you like," Catriona recommended. "But do not get in my way again, or I will make you sorry."

Flinging his hands in the air, Fergus vanished.

Beaton scarcely paused for breath before he went on, "Who giveth this woman to be married to this man?"

Behind them, solemnly, Toby said, "I do."

Beaton acknowledged him with a nod before saying, "Christopher, if thou wilt have this woman to thy wedded wife, repeat after me . . ."

Still stunned by her inability to speak, Anne paid no heed to the cardinal's words or to Kit's until Kit turned toward her, took one limp hand in his much larger, much warmer one, and said in his familiar deep voice as he slipped a cool gold band onto her third finger, "With this ring I thee wed; with this gold and silver I thee serve; with my body I thee worship; and, with all my worldly chattel I thee honor."

She could barely see him through the blue lace veil, but she realized that her turn was coming. She could end it then, and if marriage to Fiona had been all that threatened Kit, she would have done her part to save him and Fiona as well. And if she had ruined any small possibility that might have existed of marrying him herself one day, she undoubtedly deserved the loss. Tears welled in her eyes at the thought, but at least the horrid veil kept anyone from seeing them.

The ring on her finger felt warm now, and she stroked it with a finger of her other hand. Wearing it felt right and good. The worst part of all would be giving it back to Kit in the face of his certain fury, especially since she knew now that she wanted more than anything in the world to be his wife. She had never known a man like him, had never felt so close to anyone before, or so well understood.

Beaton turned to her and said, "Fiona Anne, if thou wilt have this man to thy wedded husband, repeat after me . . ."

Instead of flinging back her veil and announcing her perfidy to the world, as she had intended, Anne heard her own voice repeat obediently, "I, Fiona Anne, take thee, Christopher, to my wedded husband, to have and to hold, for fairer for fouler, for better for worse, for richer for poorer, in sickness and in health, and I vow to be meek and obedient in bed and at board until death us depart. From this time forward, and if Holy Kirk it will ordain, thereto I plight thee my troth."

"For as much as Christopher and Fiona Anne have consented together in holy wedlock before God and this company," Beaton said, "I pronounce that they are man and wife. Those whom God hath joined together let no man put asunder." Quietly then, he said to them, "You may turn and face the company before we go inside to celebrate the nuptial mass."

Anne put one shaking hand to the blue lace veil, then the other.

"Just this last bit now, and it will be over," Kit murmured gently beside her.

Knowing he meant only to be kind, to encourage Fiona, Anne nodded, and a tear spilled down her cheek.

Beaton said loudly to the crowd, "It is my great pleasure to present to you Sir Christopher and Lady Chisholm of Ashkirk and Torness."

The crowd began cheering.

Hesitating only long enough to use a fistful of the blue lace to brush the tear from her cheek, Anne flung back the veil.

The cheering stopped instantly. At Anne's left, Janet Beaton gasped. At her right, a heavy, ominous silence loomed and seemed to swirl darkly around her.

In the garden, pandemonium erupted, led by Olivia's shriek as she clapped a hand to her breast and collapsed into Eustace's arms. Toby looked stunned and Eustace speculative, although Olivia soon succeeded in claiming his full attention.

A large hand gripped Anne's upper right arm so tightly that she knew it would leave bruises, but she did not protest.

"Have you gone mad?" Kit demanded close to her ear.

"I expect so," she replied evenly.

"By heaven, what you deserve, my lass— What you and your cousin both deserve is a good skelping, and if I have anything to say—"

"Where is Fiona?" Olivia cried, recovering suddenly and jerking herself free from Eustace to confront Kit. "What have you done with my daughter?"

Still gripping Anne's arm, he said grimly, "What have *I* done with her?"

"As I recall, you were not as eager as one might expect to marry her, so doubtless you perpetrated this charade," Olivia retorted. "Where is she?"

"I haven't a notion," he said. "Why do you not ask your niece?"

Anne swallowed hard as every eye turned toward her. Stark silence fell again as the entire company awaited her response.

To her astonishment, the words came easily. "Fiona did not want to marry him," she told Olivia. "She said she would rather offer herself to a nunnery, and begged me to take her place, but I do not know where she is, for she would not tell me that. But I warrant, if she did go to a nunnery, she will not be hard to find."

"Oh, the poor dear," Janet Beaton said sympathetically.

"Do you know what you have done?" Cardinal Beaton demanded austerely.

An icy chill shot up Anne's spine at his tone, but she turned to face him. "I know I should not have agreed to take my cousin's place," she said. "At the time, however, it seemed to be the only way for her to make her position clear."

"All she had to do was announce her refusal to marry," Beaton said.

"I told her that," Anne said, "but she said my aunt had told her that when a girl who is under age is betrothed, that betrothal is utterly binding on both parties."

"That *is* the law, is it not?" Olivia snapped.

Beaton frowned, turning his stern gaze upon her. "Did you not tell me those vows were exchanged by proxy, madam, by adults?"

"Aye, they were," she said.

"Were they exchanged in the present tense or in the future tense?" he asked. "That is to say—"

"I know what it means," Olivia said, but now she was

frowning. "They were exchanged in the future tense, of course, promising for all time to come. It did not occur to me that they could be done otherwise."

Beaton nodded. "Then it is as I thought, and the vows were not unbreakable. A betrothal is mutually binding for all time only if the vows are exchanged in the present tense, as those of the marriage ceremony are. Since hers was a normal betrothal, your daughter could simply have declared her change of heart."

"But she has not changed anything," Olivia protested. "Moreover, I gave strict orders that no member of the household was to leave the grounds without permission, so she must still be inside. Malcolm shall go and find her and command her to present herself," she added, beckoning to the steward who stood nearby. "Go and fetch Mistress Fiona to me at once."

For once, Malcolm did not instantly obey her, looking uncertain instead. Then, still hesitant, he reached into his tunic and extracted a folded sheet of paper, which he silently handed to her.

"What is this?" she demanded.

"I do not know, your ladyship, as it is sealed, but I fear it is not at all what I was led to believe," he said. "Mistress Fiona's Molly asked me if I meant to attend the ceremony and when I said I did, she asked me to give that to you afterward. I assumed that Mistress Fiona had written some sort of thoughtful message that you would cherish long after she had gone away with her new husband, but I fear now that that cannot be the case."

Olivia had already broken the red wax seal on the message, and a hush fell again as she unfolded it and began to read.

"Merciful heaven," she exclaimed, "she has run away with the jester! She writes that they have declared themselves married and that the jester says such a marriage is legal. He has duped her!" Turning angrily to Anne, she said, "Did you know about this? Because, by heaven, if you did—"

"I did not," Anne said, dismayed anew by Fiona's apparent, newfound powers of deception. "As I told you, she said she would rather enter a nunnery than marry Sir Christopher, but I was certain the nuns would not take her without your permission, madam, and so I told her. She said nothing to me about the jester."

"But how came you to agree to this ridiculous charade?" Olivia asked.

"I suppose I felt sorry for her and believed she had no other way to make you see that she felt like an object to be given away—to be toyed with or destroyed, she said. If she has truly eloped with the jester, she fooled me completely. I would have wagered anything you like that she would never dare do such a thing."

As she said that, however, she remembered that her cousin had expressed a fondness for the jester almost from the moment of his arrival. She remembered, too, that the jester had said he was going to seek help for Kit from friends at Dunsithe Castle. If Fiona had lied, then certainly Mad Jake, or Willie, had lied as well, but perhaps that would not matter now that Fiona and Kit clearly would not marry.

Olivia was silent, and in that silence, Anne felt overwhelmed by Kit's looming presence beside her. He had not said another word, but she sensed his anger and did not look forward to the moment when he would break his silence.

"How do we unravel this coil?" Olivia asked at last, looking at the cardinal.

"Both marriages are legal, madam," he said grimly. "Your daughter's declaration, if supported by her jester, is as legal as he said it was, and although this young woman deserves to be flayed, the ceremony I performed is certainly legal. Except for one detail," he added thoughtfully. "The name was wrong, was it not?"

Olivia shot Anne a dagger look.

"I'm afraid not," Anne said quietly. "Fiona and I were both named Fiona Anne after our grandmother. I am called Anne only because my father preferred it."

"But surely you can annul this marriage and my daughter's as well," Olivia said to Beaton. "After all, the ceremony includes the words 'if Holy Kirk it does ordain,' and Anne is also underage."

"If your daughter and her jester have declared their marriage, I would be loath to interfere, particularly if she has run off with him. You may, of course, hail him before a magistrate if you do not mind the resulting scandal. As to this marriage, if Sir Christopher demands it, I suppose I shall have to annul it. If he does not, I cannot ... unless ..." He frowned thoughtfully, then added, "The lass's legal guardian can demand an annulment, if she has one."

"She does," Olivia said. "He is Thomas Ellyson, the new Earl of Armadale, and what is more, he strictly forbade her to marry without his permission."

Beaton looked around. "Where is he?"

"Alas, sir, he is not here, but I am certain he will demand an annulment."

"Well, he cannot demand it if he is not here, and if he

does not do so before the marriage is consummated, I shall be most reluctant to grant one."

"Then Sir Christopher must demand it," Olivia said, turning to him.

Throat-aching tension filled Anne as she waited for Kit to say the words. Without heeding what she was doing, she touched her ring again, rubbing it gently between her thumb and forefinger. The moments before he spoke seemed endless.

"I don't want an annulment," he said at last. "At least, not immediately. First, I have a few things to say to my wife whilst she is still my wife, and I won't be deprived of the opportunity to say them to her privately. I think, however, that we will dispense with the nuptial mass if that is acceptable to you, your eminence."

"It is," Beaton said with a stern look at Anne.

Toby, who had remained silent throughout these exchanges, said mildly now, "In that case, we should all adjourn to the hall. At least this time, whatever comes of it, we have had a proper wedding, so our meal will be a proper wedding feast."

Clearly relieved to have direction, most of the guests turned toward the house. Anne moved to follow them, but the large hand tightened on her arm, reminding her that she was still a prisoner.

"Not yet, my lass," Kit muttered for her ears alone. "You and I are going to have a talk that you will not enjoy, but we will not have it here or inside the house. That hedged garden where we spoke before will do, I think, but first we'll let the others move beyond earshot."

She swallowed hard and looked down at her hands, certain he would not spare her and knowing she deserved to hear every word. Considering his earlier description of what she deserved, she just hoped he would not *do* anything horrid.

"What the devil are *you* waiting for?"

Thinking he spoke to her, she jerked her head up, only to discover that although her chief attendant, Janet Beaton, had walked away with the others, Lord Berridge still stood beside Kit in the place he had occupied as best man.

Berridge gave her a searching look as if to judge her emotional state. When she met his gaze steadily, he nodded and said to Kit, "Don't murder her, lad. I'm persuaded she meant only to aid her cousin."

Kit did not respond, waiting with exaggerated patience until Berridge made a profound leg to Anne and strolled away toward the house.

"Please, sir," she said when she and Kit were alone, "I know you must be dreadfully vexed, and I'll willingly apologize, but—"

"Not another word if you value your skin," he snapped. "I do not want to create more entertainment for our wedding guests, so you will honor those vows you recited long enough to do as I bid you now. We will walk to the hedge garden, where you will continue to be silent and listen to what I say to you."

She had no energy left to argue even had she retained the will to do so. Whatever strength had sustained her through the ceremony and its aftermath had abandoned her the moment he spoke sharply to her.

If the few moments she had waited for him to demand an annulment had seemed long, the time it took to walk to the hedge garden seemed appallingly short. He continued to grip her arm, forcing her to hurry along beside him, while with her free hand, she strove to hold the heavy skirts of her wedding dress off the ground. Concern that she might trip passed through her mind only to vanish as he jerked her to a halt and pulled her to face him, grabbing both shoulders and giving her a shake as if he could not restrain his fury for another moment.

"What the devil were you thinking?" he demanded.

Although she opened her mouth to answer him, he gave her no time to do so, giving her another shake as he said, "Not only did you make me look a fool and risk your own good name to play a stupid, hoydenish prank but you helped your idiotic cousin run off with someone she scarcely knows."

"I think she knows him better than we thought," Anne said, striving to retain at least a semblance of her normal calm.

It was useless.

"You listen to me, my lass. I warned you that I was no man to trifle with or to defy, and the sooner you learn that I mean what I say, the better it will be for you. You don't know the first thing about your cousin's precious jester."

"But I—"

"Silence! Don't you see what a chance you took, what a scandal you have brewed? Folks will laugh about this damnable wedding for years. I believed you the most sensible of women, Anne, but had you purposely set out to destroy your reputation and make yourself a figure of fun, you could not have done a better job."

"But I didn't think about that. I—"

"You didn't think at all," he snapped.

She opened her mouth to refute that, but he forestalled her by going on without giving her a chance to speak, and shredding her character more thoroughly than anyone had ever done before or had cause to do. He did not raise his voice, but neither did he run out of things to say for so long that she began to fear that he must thoroughly dislike her.

Although she opened her mouth more than once to respond, she got no further, and the longer he went on, the more the pressure inside her built and the more she wanted to lash back, to tell him she had meant no harm, that she had wanted only to help Fiona and to protect him. But she said none of those things, although her silence now stemmed only from her guilt.

She did nod the two times he asked curtly if she was listening. But before long she stopped trying to respond or even to listen, letting his words spill over her in a battering flood. His anger remained palpable, but she could not blame him for it, so she simply endured the storm until at last he fell silent.

The silence lengthened then until she wondered if he were just trying to think of other, more dreadful things to say to her.

"Anne-lassie, the reasons you offered for your actions won't serve," he said then with surprising gentleness. "Despite all I have said to you, I don't believe you agreed to stand in for Fiona just so she could make some witless point in defiance of her mother's wishes, or even so she could run away with her damnable jester."

Anne's throat tightened, and although his furious scolding had not made her cry, her eyes welled again now and a tear spilled down her cheek.

"Ah, sweetheart, I'm a beast," he said, using his thumb to brush it away.

"No, you are not," she said, meeting his gaze at last. "You

said nothing I did not deserve to hear. It is just that my father sometimes called me Anne-lassie."

"Tell me the true reason you dared to do all this," he said, moving both hands back to her shoulders, but gently this time.

"He said Eustace would kill you if you married Fiona, that Eustace *wants* to kill you."

"Who said that?"

"Willie."

He stared at her. "You know who he is?"

"I know his name is Willie Armstrong. He told me so before he left."

His eyes narrowed. "Then you *did* know what they intended to do."

"No," she assured him hastily. "Only that he was worried about your safety. He said he was going to ride to Dunsithe to tell your friends you might need their help. He said nothing about Fiona, and she said nothing about him. I thought he had already gone. And Fiona was still in her room when I left the house. She knows her worth, too, so I cannot imagine that she eloped with a mere jester!"

Kit smiled, and she was relieved to see it. "He is an Armstrong," he said. "In fact, although I did not know it until recently, his father was one of their chieftains and cousin to Mangerton of Liddesdale, a close ally of the Carmichaels. Therefore, I doubt Sir Stephen would have forbidden the match, although your aunt may not like it. And while Armstrongs of any ilk take what they want when they want it, Willie would not take that lass against her will."

"I'm sure he did not," Anne said. "Mayhap Aunt Olivia will be so relieved to learn that he is no mere jester that she will not scold too fiercely," Anne said.

"I don't care if she does," he retorted. "Clearly, Willie and Fiona are even more to blame for this mess than you are, although—"

"Pray, sir, don't start again unless you truly want to turn me into a watering pot," she said. "I have apologized as abjectly as I know how and I was meek and silent whilst you scolded me, although I very much wanted to defend myself. You have made your point, though, so I expect you can go inside now and tell the cardinal that he can grant your annulment."

"May I, indeed?"

His grim tone caused her to look at him more searchingly. "It is what you want, is it not?"

"No, sweetheart, it is not. When you lifted your veil, I was shocked and my first inclination was to throttle you for your deception, but only because I feared what you might suffer as a result. If I've somehow made you believe that I'm disappointed or angry that I married you, you should know that I am not disappointed at all. On the contrary, I have *never* been so relieved as I was when I realized I had married you and *not* your simpleton cousin."

"She is not a simpleton!"

"Don't argue with your husband, madam. It is most unbecoming. Moreover, since I am still vexed with you, it is also foolhardy. I think you had better try to placate me instead."

"Indeed, sir, and how should I do that?"

"Like this," he said as he drew her close and kissed her.

Chapter 18

Anne responded instantly and willingly to Kit's kiss. Her body had reacted to his touch from the day they met, and now, knowing that she could give herself freely without feeling guilty about Fiona, she felt no reluctance at all.

His mouth claimed hers hungrily, and the fiery sensations that shot through her as she kissed him back warmed her soul as much as her body.

In that first moment, amidst myriad other emotions, that of relief stood uppermost, relief that he did not, after all, dislike her but shared many of her feelings. Even as her body reacted to the relief, however, melting against his and taking comfort as well as pleasure in his powerful embrace, passion overtook every other emotion, causing her body and mind to merge in a torrent of physical sensations unlike any she had ever known.

He kept one arm around her shoulders, holding her close, as his other hand moved caressingly over her body exploring its planes and curves in search of those secret places most sensitive to his touch. It moved from her shoulder down her arm to her sides and hip, then to the small of her back and slowly but inexorably back up her side to cup her breast. Every nerve ending stirred, tingling to be touched and stroked, and she began to caress him the same way, delighting in the soft texture of his velvet doublet and the hard muscles beneath it, as her imagination toyed with the secret wonders she had not yet seen.

As his thumb caressed the tip of her breast, his tongue thrust into her mouth.

Gasping, she thrust her own daringly back at it.

Suddenly, she felt well and truly married, certainly much more so than she had felt while standing by the altar on the chapel porch, hearing Beaton speak the words that bound them together. Her tongue dueled with his until a bubble of laughter rose in her throat that might have burst had there not been so many other, more overwhelming, less familiar emotions that easily trumped it.

With her body pressed hard against his, she easily recognized his desire as his lower body stirred against hers, and her yearning for him to possess her increased. Muscles tensed that she had not known before even existed.

Kit gripped her shoulders with both hands again, holding her tightly as he ended the kiss, straightened, and looked seriously down into her eyes.

"Well?" he said.

She detected a note of tension in his voice and wondered at it.

"Well, what?" she said softly. "Why did you stop?"

"Because if I hadn't, in a moment I'd have taken you right here on the path, and I thought perhaps I should find out first if you would object."

"Why should I?"

His eyes began to dance. "For one thing, I doubt we can

count on having much more time alone here before someone comes to see if I've murdered you."

A trill of laughter escaped her. "I doubt that Olivia would come, but oh, if she did, how she would shriek!"

"She would say such behavior shows no respect for her mourning," he said, grinning, "but more likely, she would send that officious steward of hers to find us."

Anne chuckled, easily able to imagine Malcolm's reaction.

"Look, lass," Kit said, "if you want me to request an annulment—"

"I did expect it," she admitted.

"Well, then, I shall tell Beat—"

"But I don't want one if you don't," she said quickly, feeling unexpected shyness at the knowledge that she was behaving badly again by putting her wishes forward in such a blunt way.

But Kit only grinned. "In that case," he said, putting his arm around her shoulders again, "let us instantly retire to my bedchamber."

She laughed again. "We cannot do that. We must attend the wedding feast."

"Why?"

"Well, just because," she said. "Everyone expects us, and it is what newly married people do."

"Do you *want* to go?"

Involuntarily, she shuddered. "It will be horrid," she said, "but we must go."

"On the contrary," he said. "If it will be horrid, we absolutely must not."

"But—"

"No, sweetheart," he said firmly, his eyes still dancing.

"You must cease this unnatural habit of arguing with your husband. I command you to accompany me to my bedchamber and let the folks in the hall enjoy our wedding feast without us. Just think of it as being ordered to bed without your dinner. I'll wager *that* has happened to you more than once in your life."

"Aye, it has," she agreed, "albeit not with the same consequences."

"So I should hope," he said, chuckling as he urged her on toward the plank bridge near the stableyard. "We'll use that handy kitchen door again, I think, and if we are so unfortunate as to meet anyone on the stairs, we'll just hope it's a servant who is willing to procure some food for us and deliver it upstairs."

They met no one on the first flight or afterward, because every servant was busy, if not working in the kitchen then carrying food to the hall or empty trays and platters back to the scullery. They went on past the gallery on which Anne's room and Fiona's were located to the floor that connected both sides of the house, and then down again to the gallery on which Kit's room and Eustace's faced.

When Kit opened his door with a flourish and Anne stepped inside, she felt suddenly shy again, for she had never entered a man's bedchamber other than that of her brother or father. Nothing about this one proclaimed its masculinity, however. The servant who had waited on him that morning had tidied it before leaving, the furniture and fireplace were in the same places as Anne's, so except for the dark red curtains in place of her blue ones, the room looked much as hers did.

Hearing the door shut and the lock snap into place, she

turned with a start to find him just behind her, hands behind his back, watching her.

"Art sure, Anne-lassie?" he said, his voice low and a little gruff.

"Aye, sir, if you are," she said calmly.

He needed no further encouragement but took her in his arms again and kissed her gently, then more passionately, before he scooped her into his arms and carried her toward the bed. Standing beside it, he murmured, "Do you know about being married, sweetheart? What married folk do when they share a bed?"

"Aye, sir, I have a good notion, for my mother explained much of it to me."

"A wise mother," he said. "Are you frightened?"

"Not with you," she said.

He kissed the tip of her nose. "I'm going to stir up the fire a bit, to take the chill off this room. You take off your shoes and anything else that you can manage by yourself. I'll help you with your laces and such."

"You sound quite knowledgeable, sir," she said, smiling as he sat her on the edge of his bed.

"Art jealous, lass?"

"Should I be?"

"Nay, I've lived like a monk for nearly two years."

"And before that?"

"Before that does not concern you."

"Does what I did concern you?"

He chuckled, dropping to one knee to deal with the fire and looking at her over his shoulder. "Have you so many secrets to hide from your husband, Annie?"

"I do not know that it should concern you," she said, putting her nose in the air. "If you do not tell me about your horrid past, then I need not admit mine."

He smiled as he reached for a log to throw atop the embers. "I'll know soon enough if you've got anything to hide, sweetheart. Whether you need to explain it or not can wait until then, but as amusing as this conversation might be, for a wife to keep secrets from her husband is unwise."

"What about the husband?" She watched him narrowly.

"Secrets on either side can damage a marriage, I should think," he said, standing and moving toward her as he added quietly, "although there may come a time when for reasons of defense or political necessity a man must keep his actions secret from all whom he may feel he cannot trust. And trust is not given lightly."

She nodded, understanding his point. But then, looking directly at him, she said, "And what of personal matters, or questions having to do with the character of the man? I should think such details provide the foundation of that trust."

His gaze grew wary. "I see where you are leading," he said. "Do you fear you cannot trust me, Anne?"

"No, sir, but I admit I'm curious, more so than I have been about anyone else. I feel as if I know you well, yet I have no good cause for that feeling other than my instincts. I trust them, and thus do I trust you. Still, I should like to—"

"—to know how I managed to get myself sentenced to a prison ship," he said, finishing the statement for her.

She nodded.

"Do you mind if I help you undress whilst I tell you?"

"No."

"Come here to me, then."

She obeyed, fixing her gaze on his face, trying to read him, and finding it as difficult as she always had. Although she believed she could trust him and had come to care so deeply for him that she believed she must love him, she could not tell what he was thinking when he looked at her as he did now, without expression.

"Turn around so I can reach the laces in the back," he said. "I could unlace you merely by putting my arms around you, but if I do that, this conversation will be too short to satisfy your thirst for knowledge."

"I want to watch your face."

"Then the quicker you turn and let me unlace you, the sooner you will be able to turn back," he said.

She did not argue, turning at once.

The touch of his fingers on her back distracted her for a moment, but his voice claimed her attention when he said, "Two of my Highland cousins were murdered, and I was accused of the crime."

"But you did not do it," she said.

"I did not. But when I disappeared, it was easy for certain enemies of my family to make the rest of Inverness-shire believe I had."

"Why did you disappear?"

"Before I knew about the murder, the sheriff's men ambushed me and captured me. I was given no trial. They simply trussed me up, hands and feet, and bore me off to the ship."

"But does a prison ship captain simply accept prisoners without seeing anything that proves they have been properly sentenced to his ship?"

"How wise you are, sweetheart. You put your finger instantly on a question I did not consider for weeks. When I told other crewmembers I was innocent and had been kidnapped, they just laughed. Apparently, every new man says much the same thing, so they did not believe it. However, by the time I'd resigned myself to my fate and made a few friends, I'd learned much more. The ship belonged to Beaton."

"Beaton!"

"Aye." He put his hands on her shoulders, easing the material from them.

When he moved her veil aside and she felt his warm lips on the bare skin of one shoulder, she turned toward him and put a hand to his cheek. "How did you win free?" she asked.

"I jumped ship at Glasgow and made for the Highlands," he said. "I found the cousin I told you about earlier and—"

"—and learned all about the legendary Black Fox," she said with a chuckle.

"Aye, I did that," he agreed, smiling. "But to get back to Beaton's ship—"

"What a villain that man must be!"

His smile faded. "Don't say that to anyone else, sweetheart, because even if it's true, we'd never prove it. For all I know to this day, the sheriff made a bargain with the cardinal's captain, and Beaton knows nothing about it. In any event, it's all over now, and I'm here with you," he added, smiling at her again.

"Willie told me you once offered to take a flogging for him," she said softly. "That was very courageous of you."

"It might have been the death of me if the first mate had had his way," Kit said, unpinning her veil and headdress and casting them aside. "As it happened, though, I've only a few scars from my shipboard experience and some bitter memories. I also made two very good friends."

"Two?"

"Aye," he said, grinning mischievously. "Willie is not the only one wandering around Mute Hill House under false pretenses."

Her eyes widened. "Berridge?"

"You are very quick."

"It was not much of a leap, sir. He is the only other stranger here if one does not count the wedding guests. Is he not really a lord then?"

"Devil if I know," Kit said. "He plays the part well enough, but on shipboard he was just another prisoner. He boarded shortly before I did but never talked much about himself, so I haven't a notion where he came from or what his antecedents are. The role of Berridge suits him, but so did the role of jester suit our Willie."

"I hope Fiona will be happy with him," Anne said with a sigh.

He pulled her close again, nuzzling her hair. "We can forget about them now," he said.

"She is still my cousin. He had better be good to her."

Kit claimed her lips again, silencing her, and when he stripped her clothes from her, shed his own, and took her to his bed, she soon forgot Fiona and Willie.

"What are ye staring at, Fergus Fishbait?" Maggie demanded curtly.

Fergus leaped into the air, fading as he did, but he quickly recovered himself and turned to face her. "I . . . I be looking after me lass, o' course."

"She doesna need ye now, and ye're intruding," Maggie said. "What if ye should forget and show yourself. Ye'd frighten the liver out o' the lass."

"I wouldna do that. It takes effort tae let a mortal see me, as ye should ken."

"Pish tush," she said. "Get ye hence wi' Catriona and keep a sharp eye out for trouble. I can feel Claud nearby, stronger than ever when I'm in this house, so I'm nearly sure he must be melded tae that fool Lady Carmichael."

"Nay, I'm telling ye, it be Eustace Chisholm," Fergus said stubbornly, "and also, ye should ken that Jonah be nearby, because *I* can feel *him*."

"Aye, well, we'll all keep a lookout for Jonah. As for this notion ye have about Eustace, I didna sense Claud nearly so much when I were wi' Catriona at Hawks Rig, but ye watch him if ye like. Just go, lad. They dinna need ye here."

Fergus went, and Maggie glided deep into the shadows where she could keep watch over the lovers without intruding on their privacy.

He was watching, too, for the mist had suddenly cleared and he had found himself in the room with them, but Maggie's words to Fergus strongly touched his conscience. Moreover, he too could feel Jonah's presence hovering at the edge of things, and he feared that his being there might have brought Jonah closer. Thus, he exerted himself, straining to leave, and the mists obediently descended.

Taking time to light a candle from the fire and set it on the bed-step table, Kit got gently into bed beside Anne, awed by her calm beauty. How, he wondered, had he ever thought Fiona beautiful when Anne was nearby? The soft springiness of her auburn curls fascinated him more than

Fiona's smooth blond tresses, and her intelligent serenity intrigued him far more than Fiona's bland disinterest.

He reached for her, and she moved to him willingly, her skin soft and warm to the touch and smooth to caress. "Lie still, sweetheart," he said. "I want to touch you and look at you by the candle's light."

She said not a word, making no protest when he pulled the coverlet back to gaze upon her naked beauty. Gently, he touched her right shoulder, cupping it in his palm and stroking down her upper arm until his hand lay tantalizingly near her breast. Reaching with his thumb, he stroked the nipple lightly, teasing it erect, watching her eyes as he did.

They were steady, watching him, but he heard her breath catch and knew he was arousing her natural passions as well as his own. Continuing to watch her eyes, he moved his hand lower, stroking her belly, then lower yet, brushing past the soft curls at the juncture of her thighs to the silken skin at the inside of her right one.

She stiffened a little, so he moved lower to her knee and then to her calf, pushing the covers out of his way and shifting his own position as he did.

Reaching for her right foot, he caressed the top of it, then held the foot in one hand, stroking its sole, glancing at her face again to see her eyes widen even more. Then, he moved to the left foot, stroking it first and then kissing her toes one by one, making her laugh and protest that he was tickling her. From there, he moved on to kiss her instep and calf. She was breathing faster now, but so was he. Forcing himself to think only of her and what she was feeling, he kissed one knee and then the other, lingering over them for a moment before moving to her thighs.

Using his hands more now, he stroked her as he kissed

silken skin, moving tantalizingly closer to the secret place. The temptation to possess her grew ever stronger, and he wanted nothing more than to use his lips and tongue to introduce her to the power of her own passionate nature, but he knew they both would enjoy the sensations more if he went slowly. So he slid upward, just brushing the fork of her legs again, to kiss her lower belly. Then, moving more slowly than ever, he kissed his way to her breasts, taking one nipple in his mouth and sucking gently, delighting in her moans of pleasure before repeating his efforts with the other one.

His hands stroked every curve of her that lay within his reach, exploring and delighting in what they found. Her body was perfection. She was beginning to writhe against him, so he slowed again and then moved a little away, murmuring, "Turn over, sweetheart."

"Why?"

"Because I want you to," he said.

She hesitated for a moment but then did as he asked.

He put both hands on her shoulders and stroked gently downward, saying softly as he did, "I want you to know my touch, to trust it and desire it. And I want to know every inch of you with my fingers, my lips, and my tongue."

She sighed lustily when his hands moved over the small of her back to her buttocks, cupping them. He let one of his fingers move between her legs then, and when she gasped, his body leaped in response.

Knowing his resolution would not hold out much longer, he lay down beside her, still stroking her as he turned her over and claimed her lips again. The inside of her mouth was velvety soft, and the way her tongue darted at his, playing with it and encouraging it, enchanted him. He moved his left hand more purposefully now, down over her stomach to the juncture of her legs, testing her readiness with two fingers before easing himself atop her. Then, stroking her, teasing her body until it strained beneath his, demanding satisfaction, he gently slid himself into her.

He heard another moan and knew he was hurting her at least a little, but he knew too that it couldn't be helped and would ease soon. Still, he waited, letting her body adjust itself to accommodate him. His desire was at its peak now, aching for relief, but he held himself in check until he could do so no longer. His body began to move faster of its own accord, then faster and faster, until it released him in a wave of pleasure greater than any he could remember feeling before.

She lay silent beneath him, and he knew he must feel heavy atop her, so he pushed himself up and gazed into her eyes, searching for her thoughts in them.

She gazed soberly back at him.

"Are you all right?"

"Yes, of course," she said. "Mother did not mention feet or the feelings that claim one at the height of things, but she did say that it would hurt the first time. I expected it to be worse than it was, but the other feelings I had were so much stronger than the pain. That was wonderful."

"It should not hurt at all in future," he said.

"How long does one wait between?" she asked.

He grinned at her. "When you look at me like that, sweetheart, I warrant we shan't have to wait any time at all. Would you like to do it again?"

"That depends," she said saucily. "Do I get to do the exploring this time?"

"Ah, lassie," he said, pulling her toward him, "explore as much as you like."

They slept at last, and Anne slid into the cavernous depths of exhaustion, sleeping so deeply that heavy pounding on the bedchamber door seemed only part of a vague dream until movement beside her in the bed startled her into waking. Her thoughts struggled before finding clarity, but then she remembered with welcome amazement that she was in bed with Kit and married to him.

He was already up. The fire had died, and the room was dark, but pale moonlight through the uncurtained windows was sufficient to let her see him snatch up his netherstocks and shirt. As she sat up in the bed, the pounding came again, and he turned toward the door to shout, "Who is it?"

"Beg pardon, Sir Christopher, but an important message ha' come for her ladyship—dire tidings, sir."

"Such a message can only have come from my guardian," Anne said, fully awake now. She had wondered why Thomas Ellyson had not arrived yet, and little though she had wanted him, she hoped nothing dreadful had happened to him.

The heavy knocking came again.

"Just a moment," Kit shouted, clearly irritated by the intrusion no matter what the reason was. Scrambling into netherstocks and shirt, he glanced over his shoulder, saying quietly, "Cover yourself, sweetheart, and do not forget that whatever the news is, you will not have to deal with it alone."

Instantly comforted, and realizing that the blanket she held to her breast with one hand was not high enough to accommodate modesty, Anne adjusted it and pressed back against the pillows, into the shadows.

Kit nodded his approval and turned to unlock the door.

"Now then," he said as he opened it to the golden glow of lantern light, "what the devil do you mean by—"

His words broke off in a startled cry, and although Anne could not see exactly what happened in the flurry of shadowy movements against the glow of light from the gallery, the sounds of clumping boots, gruffly muttered curses and commands, and violent assault gave her as much information as she needed.

"Stop that," she cried, clutching her blanket to her naked body. "Who are you? How dare you!"

One tall, shadowy figure separated from the others, spoke briefly in low tones, and then took a torch from someone in the hall. Its crackling flame lighted his face, revealing Eustace Chisholm.

"Have no fear, my lady," he said calmly as he walked toward the bed. "We have come to arrest a criminal. I am sorry if we come too late," he added in a slightly different tone.

His gaze swept over her, and his expression altered leeringly until she wanted to slide beneath the blankets and cover her head.

She did not, of course, but continued to eye him steadily as she said, "What nonsense do you speak? He is no more criminal than you are." *Much less, in fact*, a voice inside her head added.

"I am sorry to be the one to tell you this, Anne," Eustace said, stepping nearer the bed—much too near it, in her opinion. "But the man you so foolishly married today is a murderer who escaped from prison."

"You know that is not true," she said frostily.

"I know nothing of the sort," he retorted. "That young man was sentenced to life imprisonment for killing two sons of a powerful Highland laird. He was lucky to escape hanging at the time, but I doubt that his luck will continue. The added offense of his escape will most likely mean his end."

"Which you would like above all things," she snapped. "You do not fool me, Eustace Chisholm. You know as well as I do that your nephew was never tried or properly sentenced. You also know he never murdered anyone, let alone his Highland cousins, because he was completely exonerated of that crime."

The noise on the gallery faded as the other men hustled Kit away.

Eustace glanced over his shoulder at the empty doorway, then turned back with a smile. "What you think matters not," he said, "for you are but a woman, and since you can know only what Kit has told you, your word will carry no weight with any magistrate, let alone one appointed to his bench by Cardinal Beaton."

"So Beaton is in on this with you."

"Beaton is merely a friend of mine," he said. "He knows he can trust me to support him with every man I have, and to do whatever is necessary to keep Henry in England. He does not know Kit, however, and from what he has heard of him, he fears he will be as difficult to trust as Buccleuch or the Armstrongs of Liddesdale. He needs me, and he promised from the first to support my position here, that's all."

Choosing her words with care, Anne said, "I collect then, sir, that for rather a long while he has supported your desire to control Hawks Rig."

Eustace's smirk was answer enough, but he added, "He did recently do me a sad disservice, however."

"I wonder which you consider the greater betrayal," Anne said musingly, "the fact that he assured you a year ago that Kit was dead or that yesterday he decided in favor of Kit's betrothal instead of yours, thus robbing you of Fiona."

Eustace shrugged. "That hardly matters now that our Fiona has so stupidly eloped with her jester."

"Her jester is kin to Armstrong of Liddesdale," Anne said.

"Even so, she will rue the day, because the Armstrongs are likely to support Henry, and she will find herself ostracized by everyone she cares about."

"But the Armstrongs will likewise control her inheritance, whichever side they serve," Anne said, not believing for a moment that either Fiona or Willie would support an English king wanting to invade their beloved Scotland.

"That is true," Eustace said. "But Fiona's mother has money, too, you know. People tend to forget that, but her widow's portion is nearly as large as Fiona's, and she thinks well of me. And, too, there is always yourself, my dear, after Beaton annuls your marriage to my nephew or hangs him. I have no doubt that Armadale left you very well off. What would you think of twice becoming Lady Chisholm?"

The thought of being forced to marry him made her feel nauseous, but she responded in her usual calm manner, "If such a thing should somehow come to pass, sir, you would be wise not to sleep too heavily at night."

Sarcastically, he said, "Or what?"

"I have no scruples about killing vermin," Anne said with a direct look.

His arrogance turned to fury. "Your impertinent tongue has annoyed me for months," he snapped, reaching for her, "and by heaven, there is no one here to protect you now from the punishment you deserve. Beaton has already promised me the bride of my choice, and if I choose you, my lass, you will soon learn meekness, for by God, I'll beat it into you."

As he grabbed her arm, a growl startled them both, and he snapped his head around toward the sound, raising the torch higher.

A red fox with a white chest and white tip to its bushy, upright tail stood squarely on the hearthrug, teeth bared, growling viciously.

"What the—?"

Anne jerked her arm away from him. "Get out, Sir Eustace!"

He made a rude sound, looking back at her. "Faith, you do not suppose I am afraid of a fox! That stupid beast has been wandering at will all over this house for the past fortnight or more. Just see how valiant a defender it will be!" With that, he jabbed the torch in the direction of the fox, clearly expecting it to dart away.

It held its ground, watching him, ignoring the threatening flame.

"I'll show you!" Eustace exclaimed, thrusting the torch right at its face.

As Anne watched in horrified astonishment, the fox leaped straight at Eustace, somehow avoiding the torch and going for the man's throat.

With a cry of terror, Eustace threw both arms up to defend himself, dropping the torch. The braided rag rug by the bed caught fire, the flames shooting high to catch the bed curtains and the hem of Eustace's cloak. As the fire roared, Eustace grabbed the fox by the scruff of its neck and with another angry cry, flung it into the flames. Then, thrusting off his burning cloak, he ran from the room.

The door slammed shut behind him, and the flames instantly went out.

Anne blinked, and as she did, the torch flamed up again, but to her surprise, it rose onto the end of its handle in the middle of the floor. Standing steadily, it seemed brighter than before, and she decided that the burning curtains, cloak, and carpet had been figments of her imagination. Nothing was even charred.

"Ye didna dream it," a disembodied voice said as the fox sat up on the coverlet where Eustace had flung it and gave itself a shake like a dog shedding water from its fur.

"Who else is in here?" Anne demanded, although the voice seemed slightly familiar, as if it reminded her of someone she had met in the distant past or a dream.

"'Tis just me," the voice said, and the fox faded from view as a plump little countrywoman in a plain gray cloak, green dress, and black boots took its place.

Instantly, Anne's memory reminded her where she had heard the voice and seen the woman. "Maggie Malloch," she exclaimed, "I'd forgotten all about you!"

"Aye, I ken that," Maggie said, nodding as she reached into a pocket cunningly hidden in her cloak and pulled out a white implement that looked like a rounded stick with a shallow bowl attached at one end. To Anne's surprise, a glow like that of burning coals radiated from the bowl, and when Maggie put the stick in her mouth and sucked deeply on it, a thin stream of white smoke wafted upwards. Another cloud of it billowed from her lips when she exhaled.

"Mercy, what is that thing?"

"'Tis called a pipe, but we'll no talk o' me bad habits,"

Maggie said. "We ha' a far more important matter tae discuss."

"We certainly do, but what did you do with the fox?"

"I did nowt," Maggie said. "There were nae fox, only me."

"But the dogs chased one in more than a fortnight ago," Anne said. "It has been creating havoc amongst the servants ever since."

"Nay, only for a day or so, that one," Maggie said. "It left o' its own accord shortly after it got in, but I thought it might serve a useful purpose at some time or other if folks continued tae see it now and again. And so it has."

"And the flames?"

Maggie shrugged. "Most men be afraid o' fire unless they ha' good cause tae brave it. As tae that Eustace, he'll be a coward through and through, I'm thinking, talking big when he has men at his back, but no when he's alone."

"If he was so easy to rout, can you also make his horrid men release Kit?"

"Nay, that I canna do," Maggie said. "I ha' already interfered more than I should, but Eustace kens only that a fox bested him, and that fox be known in this house tae one and all. Were I tae take a hand in rescuing your Kit, I'd ha' tae use me powers where too many persons would ken that I had. I canna do that."

"But can you not simply make them forget afterward as you did me?"

"I could, but me Clan frowns heavily on such strong interference in mortal affairs," Maggie explained. "As it is, I'll likely ha' tae answer for what I did here, but since I'd sent your own guardian spirit away, I felt obliged tae see ye came tae no grief in his absence."

"I have my own guardian spirit?"

"Ye do. But now, if ye'll pardon me, I've summat tae tell ye, and ye canna fly into the fidgets when I do, for ye'll need tae keep your mind clear."

"What is it?" Anne demanded, feeling a chill of fear.

"I canna predict the future, as I told ye afore, but they do mean tae hang him, I think," Maggie said. "Another possibility exists, though, because Henry's army be closer than ye ken, and for all he said about Armstrongs, Eustace do be closer tae Henry than ye might think."

"Are you suggesting that he might turn Kit over to the English?"

"Ha' ye a better notion?" Maggie demanded. "D'ye think he'll trust that traitorous Beaton again tae do away wi' him, after he failed the first time?"

"So the cardinal did have a hand in that," Anne said. "I thought as much."

"Aye, I'm certain he did," Maggie said. "Eustace is too sure o' Beaton for it tae be aught else, sithee, and he claimed Sir Christopher's titles and property wi' uncanny swiftness. Ye'll ha' tae ask them about that yourself, though."

"But if they mean Kit to die, how could I possibly stop them?"

"He never brought ye the pistol he promised ye, but his be in yon kist," Maggie said, pointing with the stem of her pipe at a chest near the hearth.

Anne swallowed hard, saying tightly, "But even if I had the pistol . . ."

The fox reappeared in Maggie's place, but this time, the fox was black.

Chapter 19

The torch in the center of the floor had disappeared when Maggie did, but the fire had leaped into flames again, casting light throughout the room, and Anne quickly found Kit's gun tucked into the bag containing his powder, ramrod, and bullets. She also found a long black cloak among his trappings, as well as a dark shirt and a pair of dark netherstocks, but his breeches were too large for her, and when she pulled on his boots, her feet swam in them. She would need help.

A knock at the door startled her, and she froze where she was.

"My lady? Lady Anne, are you in there?" It was Malcolm Vole's voice.

With a sigh of exasperation, Anne got to her feet and clumped to the door in Kit's boots. Opening it just enough to see Malcolm, she said, "What is it?"

With a sigh of relief, he said, "Oh, my lady, I feared for your life! Sir Eustace said Sir Christopher's bedchamber had caught fire."

"As you see, he was wrong," Anne said. "I believe Sir Eustace desires only to cause trouble. Doubtless, like a child, he desires to strike back at everyone for his loss of Mistress Fiona."

Malcolm's eyebrows shot upward, but Anne did not intend to take back the words she had spoken, despite having never intended to speak them aloud. The notion had stirred in her mind, and the words had popped out before she could stop them. In any event, the steward was too busy trying to see past her into the room to concern himself further with her opinion of Eustace.

A harsh voice from the gallery said, "What are you doing there, Malcolm?"

He stiffened and turned his head, only to bow at once and say obsequiously, "Begging your lordship's pardon, but I was concerned that her ladyship might be in danger. Sir Eustace told me Sir Christopher's bedchamber had caught fire."

"One must wonder how Eustace knows that," Lord Berridge said mildly.

"He and his men arrested Sir Christopher," Malcolm said. "I assumed that in their struggle to subdue him, someone kicked a candle over or some such thing."

"It was brave of you to come alone to rescue Lady Chisholm," Berridge said with a touch of sarcasm. "Since I see no smoke issuing forth from her bedchamber, however, I warrant you can safely leave now."

"Wait," Anne said sharply. "Malcolm, go directly to the stable and order my horse saddled. I mean to ride after them."

"I cannot do that," Malcolm said in his precise way. "I should have to gain her ladyship's permission first."

"Nonsense," Berridge said. "Lady Chisholm needs no one's permission save her husband's. And since he is not at hand just now, she requires no one's permission save her own."

"I should need no permission in any event," Anne snapped. "You listen to me, Malcolm Vole. Go and do as I bid you, *now*, because I am going after them if I have to climb over the wall and chase them barefoot."

Malcolm stared at her in shock.

Berridge chuckled. "Go on and do as she commands, man, and look sharp. Whilst you're about it, you may order a horse for me, as well. I shall go with her."

"In that event, there can be no reason to forbid her," Malcolm said stiffly, hurrying away at last but with his dignity still intact.

"What a dimwitted moldwarp that man is," Berridge said, watching him go.

"Thank you for your support, my lord," Anne said, "but you need not trouble yourself over me. I can manage quite well on my own."

"You are very fierce tonight, madam, but you cannot mean to ride out at night alone, and surely not in pursuit of a band of armed men!"

"I . . . I'll take an armed escort of my own," she said hastily.

"Nay, lass, that won't serve," he said, shaking his head at her.

"Lord Berridge, you should know that he told me who you really are," she said, looking up and down the gallery to be sure no one would hear her. "I know you are an impostor, but I know as well that you are Kit's friend. You must trust me on this matter. I shall be quite safe, I promise you."

"Promise all you like, lass. You'll not be going on your own."

"I do need help," she admitted, "but you must promise not to question what I mean to do, just to help me get outside the wall. Kit trusts you, so I will trust you, too, but I do not mean to let anyone stop me or hinder my actions."

"Very well," he said. "I know Eustace's men took Kit, because my room is just down the way and when I heard the commotion, I looked out the door in time to see them hustling him away. I recognized two of them as Eustace's men, but I never saw Eustace himself."

"That is because he stayed in our bedchamber after they took Kit away. He truly is a loathsome worm, that man. He taunted me, saying that after they hang Kit, he means to ask Beaton to perform another marriage. I am to be the bride if you please, and he the groom. By heaven, I'd shoot the man before letting that happen."

Berridge smiled. "I do not think that will be necessary, my dear. We'll find Kit, but I think perhaps you should wear your own boots, don't you?"

Looking down at her feet, Anne realized that she had forgotten to stay behind the door, and that Berridge could see everything she wore. A bit sheepishly, she said, "I have only Fiona's wedding dress in here, so I took some of Kit's things, but nothing fits. I mean to startle them, but I'm afraid that anyone seeing me dressed like this would only laugh."

He chuckled. "In the darkness, the cloak will conceal everything, but you do need smaller boots. I'm not dressed for riding, either, so I must change, but if you go to your own room and fetch your boots, I'll meet you at the kitchen stairs. Kit showed me that means of escape some time ago."

"Thank you, sir." She flung the cloak over her shoulders, picked up the bag containing the pistol and its accouterments, and turned toward the stairway.

"One more thing, lass," Berridge said sternly.

"Yes, sir?"

"Don't leave without me. That would displease me very much, and if you should somehow and most miraculously succeed in finding Kit and rescuing him by yourself, I doubt that it will please him overmuch either."

Despite her fear for Kit, a shiver stirred at the image Berridge's words produced, for they reminded her forcibly of the scene in the hedged garden after she revealed that she had taken Fiona's place.

"I won't go without you," she promised.

"Good lass. I expect that if Kit told you about me, he also told you about our Willie, did he not?"

"Aye, sir, he did," she answered, fairly dancing now with impatience.

"'Tis a pity Willie's not here," Berridge said. "He might prove useful."

"He said he would ride to Dunsithe to bring help," Anne told him. "But that was before the wedding, before I knew that he meant to elope with Fiona. I warrant he has ridden as far from here as possible and has completely forgotten about Kit."

"Nay, Willie would not do that," Berridge said flatly. "If he was riding to Dunsithe, we may just pull this business off after all. Make haste, lass." And with that, he turned on his heel and hurried off down the gallery toward his room.

Anne stood for a moment, stunned that after delaying her as he had he would command her to make haste, but she quickly collected her wits. Yanking Kit's boots from her feet, she flung them back into his room, shut the door, and ran barefoot with the long cloak billowing behind her to her bedchamber, where she soon unearthed her own boots and pulled them onto her feet.

A second thought sent her to find her riding whip, but she waited for nothing more, running back to the service stair and down to the kitchen door. Certain she would have to wait at the stables for Berridge, she was astonished to find him awaiting her in the yard instead. He grinned, and she saw at once that the thought of adventure had stimulated him.

"Ready, lass?"

"Aye, sir, but are you sure you want to go?"

"I could not stay here," he said. "Kit Chisholm saved my life by helping me escape from that damned ship. I will not leave him to the likes of Eustace Chisholm and his ilk if I can do aught to save him."

Anne half expected to find that Malcolm had disobeyed her and given orders instead to prevent her leaving, but the horses were waiting and Malcolm himself stood beside them.

As she hurried up to hers, he made a stirrup of his hands and helped her mount, saying, "If there is anything else I can do to help, my lady, you have only to command me. They had no business to take Sir Christopher from Mute Hill House. 'Tis an invasion of our hospitality at best, and a criminal act at worst."

"Thank you, Malcolm," she said. "I need a holster for this pistol."

Although his eyes widened when she pulled the pistol from the satchel, he made no objection, merely signing to an underling to obey her request.

When the pistol was holstered and the satchel tied behind her saddle, Malcolm asked if there was anything more.

About to tell him she needed nothing further from him, she said instead, "How many men have we here?"

"Not enough to make an effective rescue, I'm afraid," he said.

"But enough to guard the wall and everyone inside?"

"Aye, certainly."

"Then tell them to keep strict watch and be ready to open the gates at an instant's notice. We may need to hurry back and seek sanctuary here. I've a notion that Eustace and his men are heading for the line, but if they have merely taken Sir Christopher to the nearest hanging tree, we may be able to track them quickly."

"They headed south, my lady," Malcolm said. "I was about to tell you as much, for I asked the lads here, and several watched them go. One enterprising youngster followed them down the backside of Mute Hill and saw them ride onto the ridge overlooking Tarrasdale. They appeared to be following the track towards Kershopefoot, he said."

Anne frowned. "I'm not sure I know that track, but I do know how to reach Kershopefoot from the Towers. Perhaps we should ride that way."

"Nay," Berridge said, turning his mount toward the gate. "I ken the track they took. We'll do better to follow in case they change course along the way. Moreover, if they ride the Tarrasdale ridge, they'll ride near Liddesdale. And mark me, lass, I'm guessing our Willie will have set men to keep watch there."

"Faith, is Dunsithe near Liddesdale, then?" Anne asked, following him.

"Nay, it lies west o' here some little distance, near the Debatable Land, but Willie would not have taken his lass with

him so far as that, I'm thinking. He'd take her into Liddesdale, mayhap to Mangerton, to keep her safe."

"Then he won't have had time to reach Dunsithe yet,"
Anne said.

"Never you fear that. They eloped this morning, did they
not?"

She nodded.

"Then our Willie has had sufficient time to ride fifty
miles if he had the will to do it, for he told us many and
many a time that he and his reiving band often rode that far
in a single night, and I'm thinking he'd need to ride less than
thirty today."

When they were outside the wall, making their way down
the back of Mute Hill, Anne said, "You seem to know a lot
about reivers."

"Aye, sure, for our Willie talked a good deal."

"I'll warrant he did, since that seems to be his nature,
whilst yours seems to be to keep yourself to yourself. Kit
said you never spoke much on shipboard either, at least not
about your past."

"I'm a reticent creature, that's all."

"What was the crime for which you were sentenced to
that ship?"

He was silent.

"You insisted upon accompanying me, sir. I think that
even you would agree I'd have to be a fool to be riding into
the night like this with a man who served time aboard a
prison ship and escaped, without at least knowing the crime
he committed. Kit has been exonerated of his. Have you?"

"No," he admitted. "But Willie would tell you it was no
crime at all."

"Then you also were found guilty of reiving," she said.

"I was, but we're wasting time, and I owe my freedom and likely my life to Kit Chisholm. If you can keep up, we can make up some distance, I'm thinking, for I remember this track well and there is sufficient moonlight to give the ponies their heads a bit here."

"I can keep up," Anne said, urging her mount to follow his.

"Catriona, wake up!" Maggie commanded tersely, giving her a shake.

"What's amiss?" Catriona asked, sitting up and rubbing her eyes.

"Ye were supposed tae watch them," Maggie said, moving to shake Fergus, who was curled into a ball at the hearth end of the dais in the hall. "That Eustace took your lad right out o' his bedchamber, and be threatening tae hang him."

"Oh, no!" Catriona exclaimed. "I fell asleep, and I wasn't even sleepy."

"It were that Eustace, like I told ye," Fergus said, yawning.

"More likely, it were Jonah Bonewits," Maggie said. "Did ye no say ye could feel his presence?"

"Aye," Fergus said, watching her warily. "I dinna feel it now, though."

"Nor do I feel Claud," Maggie said, realizing the sensation that had been as familiar to her in past days as her own breathing had vanished, leaving her feeling bereft. "And that Carmichael woman be fast asleep in her chamber, for I looked."

"What about me lass?" Fergus asked belatedly.

"She's gone after them," Maggie said, forcing herself to

concentrate on the moment at hand, "but she'll need our help."

"Sakes, what can we do?" Fergus demanded.

"Can ye call upon other Ellyllon tae help ye?" Maggie asked him.

"Ye ken fine that I can," he said.

"Then ye'll do that, for here's what I think we should do."

He listened carefully, his anger growing stronger by the moment. Jonah was going to win this game of his if someone did not stop him.

With his hands bound tightly behind him, Kit was having all he could do to stay mounted, because Eustace set a fast pace. When the man leading his horse suggested that, tied so, their prisoner might fall off, Eustace had laughed and said it did not matter if he did because they were going to hang him anyway.

Kit thought the two Chisholm cousins with Eustace seemed unhappy about that course of events, but they clearly lacked the strength of mind to oppose it. Still, one of them muttered the word "murder" and suggested to Eustace that such an act might preclude his inheriting the estates.

"Aye, it might were we the ones that murdered him," Eustace said, chortling, "but it won't be us, lads. We've merely arrested the man and be taking him now to Cardinal Beaton. Faith, but had the man not left for Caerlaverock in such a hurry after the feasting, we'd have turned our prisoner over to him at Mute Hill House."

"But Caerlaverock lies to the west of us," one of his men protested.

"And we'll turn west soon enough," Eustace said. "We came this way only to thwart anyone trying to follow us, but you can be sure that I mean to ride no closer to Liddesdale and the traitorous Armstrongs than we must. We'll stay west of Tarrasdale and head south toward Caulfield."

"We're going tae Caulfield? Be we going tae cross the line then, laird?"

"Nay, only to ride near it," Eustace said glibly. "We'll meet our friends long before we reach the village, I'm sure."

Kit did not have to tax his brain to determine who those friends might be, since Eustace expected to meet them so near a village practically straddling the line. Several armies roamed the Borders, to be sure, but he doubted Eustace would turn him over to any Scottish force. He had soon realized his uncle was easily swayed by anyone who promised him wealth or power, and Henry of England would promise both to any man willing to help him win Scotland and its Kirk to his rule.

"So you mean to hand me over to the English, do you?" he said grimly.

"Oh, I don't think I'll do that," Eustace replied.

"But you're meeting them. You're a traitor to your own country and a disgrace to the proud name of Chisholm."

"Don't be naïve, lad. In the Borders, one does what one must to survive. What matters which kirk one serves, or which king? They are all much the same, are they not? But Henry controls his own army, and our Jamie does not. Thus, Henry is more powerful. What's more, he puts men to death when they disagree with him. It is clear that he will win in the end, and I am no fool."

"Henry will never control Scotland," Kit declared grimly. "He may breach the line, thanks to support from traitors like you, but he will never make headway beyond the Borders, and he will never control the Scottish Kirk. Do you truly think he is more powerful than Beaton, who has the power of France and Rome at his back, not to mention that of the Scottish people?"

"What I think need not concern you," Eustace said. "You will live only long enough to let us attribute your unfortunate death to the villainous English army. You need not fear that I'll turn you over to them, though. I made the mistake once before of trusting another to see to your death. Since I mean to win Hawks Rig for myself, I won't make that mistake twice."

"The first time being when you trusted Beaton?"

"Aye, your so-powerful cardinal. He told me your death was assured, that you would be arrested for murder and hanged. But he agreed instead to let the men who captured you turn you over to the captain of his ship, a detail he did not see fit to mention to me until after you'd escaped and shown up here. Even then, he promised he would see me in possession of Hawks Rig, only to betray me again. When I reminded him of his promise, he said the law was clear on the issue of betrothals. He said also, however, that although he could not be associated with your murder, if you disappeared again or met with a sudden death, he would do as he had promised from the outset and see me safely in possession of your estates. Once that happens, I intend to marry the lovely widow and live happily ever after."

"Lady Carmichael?"

"Aye, unless you know of a wealthier widow hereabouts."

Kit grimaced, saying nothing, and the conversation ended.

When they began to ride down the steep hill from the top of the ridge, he fixed his attention firmly on staying in the saddle. Since he had no control over the horse except with his heels, he hoped it could find its way without stumbling. In any event, he could barely see the track, so he watched the landscape ahead, instead, hoping to see Willie and his lads coming to the rescue.

Instead, he saw a line of torches cresting the next hilltop, their light glinting on weaponry and armorial banners, as a company of foot soldiers streamed toward them.

"There they be, lads," Eustace exclaimed. "I recognize their banners."

Kit stared at the force streaming toward them, but then movement caught his eye, and his gaze shifted to the bottom of the hill, where another, very large rider with a torch had appeared. To his shock, he recognized Sir Toby Bell, apparently waiting patiently for Eustace.

Had Eustace seen him? Was Toby friend or foe? The answer to that last question was plain, though, because only another traitor would have known where to find both Eustace and the English army.

"I dinna trust them English," one of the men muttered loudly enough for everyone else to hear.

"I don't trust them either," Eustace said. "Nonetheless, lads, we've clearly had no time to hang our prisoner before their descent upon us, and folks will hear about that troop crossing the line. So, when someone finds the lad with a bullet in him, everyone will assume the English killed him. Haul him off that horse now and bring him to me," he added curtly. "You lads yonder, light torches so we can see."

*   *   *

"He's going to shoot Kit!" Catriona exclaimed. "We must stop him!"

"Kill Eustace, Maggie!" Fergus shrieked. "I ken he's the one. Ye'll save your Claud and Catriona's lad wi' a single stroke."

But a new idea struck Maggie. Swiftly thinking it through, she muttered, "Nay, nay, for there be only one reason now for Eustace tae kill the lad."

"He's going to shoot him because he believes the English army is at hand," Catriona said. "Fergus, stop them!"

"Nay, ye mustna do that, Fergus," Maggie said.

"Oh, what have we done?" Catriona wailed.

"Nobbut what I meant tae do," Maggie said. "Recall me warning ye that whenever a body thinks a plan must succeed, summat happens tae queer it. I ken now who Claud's mortal must be, and sakes but we should ha' seen it afore."

"Eustace," Fergus insisted.

"Nay, Olivia," Catriona said. "Isn't that right, Maggie?"

"It canna be Olivia," Maggie said. "She were sleeping earlier and I couldna feel Claud's presence in her chamber. I feel it now, though, stronger than ever, and the truth ha' been flaunting itself at us from the outset, Catriona, because what be more likely than that Claud's mortal were present when Claud disappeared?"

Catriona went perfectly still as the truth struck hard. "No," she whispered.

"Aye, Claud's mortal can be no other," Maggie said.

"But then all our plans will fail," Catriona said with a gasp.

"Who is it?" Fergus demanded.

"There be only one who were there when Jonah cast

Claud into the mortal world—only one, sithee, who be here now," Maggie said. "That be Kit Chisholm."

"But me lass loves him," Fergus wailed. "Ye canna kill him!"

"I must," Maggie said. "I'll no condemn Claud tae save any mortal."

"But ye'll be sacrificing yourself at the same time," Fergus reminded her. "At least, let Eustace kill him. If anyone deserves tae fly wi' the Host, it's Eustace."

"Nay, for if anyone else kills the mortal, Claud will die wi' him," Maggie reminded him. "There be only one resolution tae all this."

She raised her hands toward the sky.

"No," he muttered. "Ye mustna kill him, mam. Ye'll fly wi' the Host an ye do anything so daft, for Jonah be right here watching ye."

He could no longer see Catriona, only Maggie with her hands held aloft and her intentions crystal clear.

Evil laughter floated in the air around him. He knew it came either from a gathering of the Host, waiting to claim him and Maggie, or from Jonah himself, watching gleefully to see how his game played out now that he had forced all his geese into one corner. In that instant, all his pent-up anxiety and worry turned to a fury that outmatched any his mother had ever produced.

"Is that the English army yonder?" Anne asked Berridge.

"I doubt it's a Scottish one," he said. "The majority of our lads ride their own horses, and although there be many from the Highlands who likely came south on foot, their leaders are always mounted. I see no beasts with that lot."

But Anne's attention had already shifted from the soldiers to activity directly below them. She and Berridge had been following Eustace's party for some time, keeping only enough distance to avoid detection, and at first she had been relieved to see the soldiers, thinking they must be Scots who would surely help free Kit from Eustace and his men. But her realization that the approaching soldiers were more likely English chilled her, and seeing Eustace stop nearly sent her into a panic.

"Faith, but he means to murder Kit in cold blood," she said, raising the hood of Kit's long black cloak and pulling it forward to conceal her face. As she did, she caught a glimpse of Toby on horseback at the bottom of the hill, watching Eustace.

"What are you doing?" Berridge demanded.

"I'm going to stop Eustace, of course." Without another word, she pulled Kit's pistol from her saddle holster and urged the gelding forward.

"Lass, wait!"

"If you have a pistol," Anne called over her shoulder, "I suggest you draw it and follow me."

As two of Eustace's men hustled Kit toward him, a bolt of lightning streaked across the sky, followed in nearly the same moment by a deafening clap of thunder.

"The gods are angry, lads," Kit shouted to his captors. "That sky was clear when we left Mute Hill House."

"Shut up," one of them snapped, but he looked fearfully upward.

The English army was drawing rapidly closer, and Kit

saw that the rider he had recognized as Toby Bell still sat on his horse at the bottom of the hill, watching them. Eustace had not so much as acknowledged the man's presence, but it was clear enough now that Toby must have served as his spokesman with the English.

"Are you going to shoot me yourself, uncle?" Kit demanded.

"Don't be daft," Eustace snapped. To one of his own men, he said, "You there, draw your pistol and put an end to him."

"God rot ye, I'm nae murderer," the man said.

"I'll pay you fifty marks," Eustace said evenly.

"Aye, well then," the man said, drawing his pistol at once.

He took careful aim, and every man there watched him. Only Eustace and Kit turned at the sound of thundering hoofbeats on the hill behind them, and saw the dark rider bearing down on them, pistol drawn and ready.

The rider's similarity to the Black Fox of the Highlands, along with a sudden sharp tingle of electricity in the air, made Kit's hair stand on end.

His executioner held the gun to his head.

The scream formed deep within him, as all the anger he had felt for so long reached its peak in a rage so strong that it became an entity in and of itself. "Curse ye, Jonah Bonewits!" he cried, and what happened next astonished him.

Kit had time only to draw a single breath before the shot rang out, but he scarcely heard it before a double-forking flash of lightning and its simultaneous crack of thunder drowned it out, and the gun that had been only inches from his head flew out of the executioner's hand.

Cries of terror followed, and when he glanced toward the English army, he saw that where Sir Toby Bell had been sitting on his horse, only a smoking, charred lump remained.

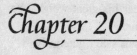

Chapter 20

Maggie, ye missed him!" Fergus cried.

Maggie stared in shock at the charred lump that had been Sir Toby Bell. "I canna ha' missed him," she whispered. "Wha' ha' I done?"

"Ye've done nowt but good, mam," a familiar voice said behind her.

Whirling, she beheld the son she had never expected to see again.

"Claud!"

"Aye, 'tis m'self, returned tae plague ye," he said, grinning.

"B-but how?"

Looking apologetic, he said, "I lost me temper."

Catriona flew to him, flinging herself into his arms.

"Easy, lass," he said, staggering. "I used up most o' me strength diverting me mam's lightning bolt tae save your lad."

"But Claud," Maggie said, worried anew, "though I dinna ken how ye managed it, ye killed a mortal when ye killed Toby Bell. Ye'll be banished forever."

"'Twas nae mortal, mam. 'Twas Jonah himself, shifted

tae Toby's shape. Sir Toby ha' been safe at Mute Hill House all along. I kent fine that Jonah were nearby, and when I saw Toby riding a horse, 'twere plain wha' Jonah had done, for ye heard yourself that Toby doesna ever mount a horse but rides in a special cart made tae bear his great weight. Ye should ha' recognized him, too, I think."

"I told ye Jonah were near," Fergus said righteously.

"Aye, and ye told us Eustace were Claud's mortal," Maggie said. "But as ye heard, 'twas nobbut Kit Chisholm, just as I said."

"Aye," Claud admitted, "and I couldna let ye kill Kit and suffer banishment for my sake. His death would also ha' meant Catriona had failed in her task, and I couldna let that happen, because the truce betwixt the Merry Folk and the Helping Hands would ha' died, and ye'd worked too hard tae build that truce."

Maggie eyed him with new respect. "I still dinna ken how ye managed it."

He shrugged. "I waited until ye grew angry, and then I compounded me own anger wi' yours, and took summat from Jonah as well, although I dinna ken exactly what. Ye're both me parents, after all. Stands tae reason I could learn from ye."

"Ye did more than learn," Maggie said gently. "Ye couldna ha' done it, did ye no ha' great powers o' your own, Claud. Ye saved yourself, and nae mistake."

Claud grinned impishly. "Mayhap even me dad will be proud o' me now."

With a wry smile, Maggie said, "I dinna think he'll tell ye so, however. Whether ye've damaged him still remains tae be seen."

"I shouted his name as I flung that bolt, so I broke his spell and all it affects."

"Ye're a good lad," Maggie said, putting an arm around him and hugging him. "Whether Jonah be proud o' ye or no, I'm as proud as I can be."

"Me, too," Catriona said, snuggling in to get her share.

Claud chuckled, reaching hungrily for her.

"Fergus," Maggie said, "it be time for me tae let the Chief ken wha' ha' passed here, and time too, sithee, for your army tae retreat."

Kit was still staring at the charred remains of Toby Bell when he heard a snarl and a warning shout, and turned to find Eustace drawing his sword.

As quick as thought, Kit reached toward the nearest man, realizing only as he grasped the fellow's sword and snatched it from its scabbard that his bindings had somehow disappeared. He had no time to wonder about that, however, because Eustace was lunging murderously toward him.

Throwing up the borrowed sword, Kit deflected his uncle's blade. As Eustace lunged again, another man leaped at Kit with sword drawn, but a second shot rang out, and the newly threatening weapon arced up and out of its owner's hand to disappear into the night.

Certain that he did not stand a chance, that the English army would be upon them in moments, Kit glanced over his shoulder, only to see that the torches on the hillside had vanished. Eustace reclaimed his attention at once, and as he set himself to disarm him, he paid scant heed to new rumbles of thunder disturbing the night.

Another shot rang out, and the voice that had warned him

before and that he now recognized as Tam's bellowed, "Hold where ye are or die!"

Eustace ignored the command, lunging again, but this time, Kit caught the blade high, and with a flick of his wrist, slid his own blade down it to its hilt and forced it downward. Closing then, he grabbed his uncle's wrist and twisted hard, forcing him to drop his weapon. When it fell to the ground, Kit put his foot on it.

"Step back, uncle," he ordered grimly. "I doubt that any man here, yours or mine, would object if I spitted you right now, after what you've tried to do to me."

Only when he heard Willie's voice and then Patrick MacRae's in the distance did he realize that substantial reinforcements had arrived, that the latest thundering had been the sound of their horses racing down the hill.

Looking over the scene, he discovered that while his attention had been riveted on Eustace, Willie's reivers and men from Dunsithe had surrounded and disarmed Eustace's men. Some were busily lighting more torches, although the moon was already peeking out from behind the heavy clouds that had gathered so quickly and mysteriously overhead.

The English army had disappeared.

A little to one side of all the others, a slender mounted rider in a voluminous black-hooded cloak held a pistol aimed steadily at Eustace.

With a last glance around to be sure that everything was under control, Kit strode toward the black-clad rider.

"You can put that pistol away now," he said, his tone low-pitched and neutral despite the strong temptation he felt to pull her from her saddle.

"Did they hurt you?" she asked, keeping her voice low, too.

"No."

She had pulled the hood as far forward as it could go, yet he knew that any man looking closely would recognize her. Glancing over his shoulder, he saw Tam a short distance away, also mounted, his pistol aimed indiscriminately at a group of Eustace's men. Gesturing to him to approach, Kit turned back to Anne, saying grimly, "I want you to ride back to Mute Hill with Tam . . . that is, with Berridge. And if you are wise, sweetheart, you'll let none of these others guess who you are."

"Ingrate," she muttered.

He nearly grinned but controlled the impulse, knowing how badly she could be hurt by the additional scandal that would arise if Eustace's men recognized her.

"I collect that the shot which disarmed my would-be assassin was yours."

"I still can't believe my bullet struck his pistol," she said. "I meant only to frighten him, hoping he would drop the thing before it went off and killed you. I'm still not certain that huge crack of thunder coming almost at the same moment wasn't what made him lose his pistol, but from the way it flew, I do think I hit it."

"You shoot better than anyone I've ever known, including my friend Patrick MacRae," he said, "but if you don't take yourself off before every man here realizes who you are, you will find out just what a poor rein I keep on my temper."

Tam was beside them now, and he said, "A remarkably fine shot, I thought."

"It was," Kit said curtly. "Now, however, I want you to take her back to Mute Hill House as discreetly as you know how. I do not want this latest escapade of hers to be the talk of the Borders by morning."

"Escapade was it?" Tam said, his eyes twinkling. "She saved your hide, my lad, and you should be showing more gratitude."

"That is precisely what I told him," Anne said, raising her chin. "I thought I made an excellent Black Fox, did not you?"

"Aye, I did," Tam said, smiling at her.

Keeping a firm grip on his temper, Kit said, "You, of all people, should recognize the danger she stands in now. Take her back to the house at once."

"I won't leave you," Anne said, giving him look for look.

"Tam, do as I bid you."

To his astonishment, Tam said, " 'Tis certainly your right as her husband to order her return, lad, but I'm thinking 'tis you who should accompany her."

"Don't be absurd. I mean to stay here and make sure Eustace and his men cause no more trouble. You are to leave immediately, however," he said to Anne, "or have you forgotten your vow of obedience so soon after making it?"

"Since I nearly had no husband to obey, I think I might be forgiven," she said, "and in any event, sir, you waste your breath. If you choose to beat me later, that is your right, of course, but I will not leave now, nor should you expect Lord Berridge to look after me in your stead."

"She has a point, lad," Tam said.

Kit was about to argue when Anne's attention shifted to a point beyond him and she raised her chin even higher. Certain that someone would recognize her, he opened his mouth to remonstrate, only to shut it again with a growl of annoyance when she reached up and pushed back the hood.

He had not been aware of the muttering behind him until

it stopped, but the silence now was as heavy as it had been after she lifted her veil at their wedding.

"'Tis a wench!" someone said. "By God, 'twas a wench fired that shot!"

Leaning forward, he snapped, "By heaven, I *will* beat you. Are you mad?"

Her gaze met his as steadily as ever. "You asked me that same question once before," she said. "I'll say again what I said then. I expect I *am* mad, but eventually someone will guess I was the one in the cloak. We made no secret of my attire when we left Mute Hill, you see, so if there is to be scandal, I can do naught to stop it, nor can you. Therefore, I thought it better to let them all see the truth from the outset." With a wry smile, she added, "'Tis of such stuff that legends are made, is it not?"

For a moment, he was speechless, but then his sense of the absurd took over, and a moment later, he was laughing. He laughed until tears ran down his cheeks, oblivious to the mutters and exclamations of the crowd surrounding them.

When he stopped laughing, he reached for her and she did not resist when he lifted her from the saddle to stand beside him. Tam was grinning, and smiles lit many of the faces nearby, but the first voice he heard was that of his uncle.

"I am glad you can see humor in such wanton behavior, nephew," Eustace said tauntingly. "If she were my wife, I'd take a stout switch to her backside for such brazenness. I see no other female here, and since she did not ride with you or with the confounded reivers, one must deduce that she rode through the night with only Berridge for company. To say that this episode will shatter her reputation by morning is but a small description of the reality."

Kit's amusement faded, for he knew Eustace was right,

but rescue came from an unexpected source when Tam, affecting the tones of Lord Berridge, said frostily, "You forget yourself, Chisholm, and if you do not want to meet your Maker this very night, you will apologize to her ladyship."

"Why should I?" Eustace sneered. "I spoke nowt but the truth."

"Aye, in part," Tam said grimly, "but 'tis plain insolence to suggest that a lady risks her reputation by riding with the man who, until her recent marriage, was her legal guardian."

Kit's jaw dropped, and a glance at Anne showed that hers had done the same.

Eustace looked as stunned as they were. "How is that possible?"

"I'm waiting," Tam said without answering the question. He had holstered his pistol, but as he spoke now, he rested his hand on the grip.

"Aye, then, if it be so, I'll apologize," Eustace said grudgingly.

"Take him away, lads," Kit said. "I'll talk with him later."

Still staring in astonishment at the man she knew best as Lord Berridge, Anne said, "Are you truly my cousin Thomas Ellyson, sir?"

"Aye, lass, I am," he said, dismounting to stand face-to-face with her.

"Then you are the new Earl of Armadale."

"I am, but my friends call me Tam," he said. "I'd like you to do so, too."

"Thank you, but why did you not tell me at once?"

"I'd intended to do that," he said. "But when I learned that Kit had stopped your cousin Fiona's wedding, and that he and the uncle he distrusted were under the same roof at

Mute Hill House, I decided he might need my help. Since I did not want to confuse matters by appearing as Armadale just then, I used one of Armadale's many minor titles instead, one I knew he had rarely mentioned."

"I see." She thought she understood something else as well. "That is why you kept silent about your past when you were aboard the ship, is it not?"

"It is," he admitted. "Your father was a proud man, and he had a temper on him that frightened the liver and lights out of me. He could not have prevented my inheriting the title, although that was not an issue at the time, but had he learned of my arrest, he would likely have shunned me and done other such things to make me miserable. My sentence was only three years, and from the start, I meant to escape if I could, so by giving my name as plain Tam Elliot, which is what I did when they caught us, I hoped to keep your father from ever finding out."

"But three years! How is it that he did not learn at least that you had disappeared?" Anne asked.

He gave a wry smile. "I served little more than half that time, and he rarely paid me more than the smallest heed. Moreover, my people are well trained to disavow knowledge of my comings and goings. Had he inquired, my steward would simply have said I was from home and that it was no business of his to expect my return. With persistence, of course, the truth would have emerged, but your father did no more than send a letter to tell me that your brother had been killed. Of course, I read that letter only recently, upon my return, and since I learned of Armadale's death at the same time . . . Well, you can see how it was, I expect."

"But who looked after things for you whilst you were gone?"

"That same worthy steward," he said. "I'm afraid I'm a lazy fellow at heart, so my people know even better than I do how to tend my estates. Things might have proved more difficult, of course, had I stayed a prisoner after your father died."

Another thought occurred to Anne. "Your letter," she said quietly. "You forbade me to marry without your permission. Will you demand an annulment?"

"Do you want one?"

Feeling heat in her cheeks, her gaze sought Kit and found him talking to Willie and two other, much taller men. He turned as if he felt her watching him, and smiled at her. The smile made her body tingle and warmed her heart.

"No," she said, "I do not want an annulment."

"Then we won't ask for one," Tam said. "I cannot imagine a better husband for you or a better wife for him."

"He did threaten to beat me," she reminded him.

His eyes twinkled. "So he did," he agreed. "I warrant he will threaten that again, lass, given similar provocation. What would you have me do?"

"I think you can safely leave us to find our own way, sir."

"I think so, too."

"You will make an excellent earl," Anne said, smiling.

"The position carries many responsibilities," he said. "I warrant I shall need a countess—aye, *and* an heir!"

"My aunt seems to like you well enough," Anne said demurely.

He winced. "I think I'll leave Lady Carmichael to Eustace if he escapes this business with a whole skin," he said. "I'd prefer someone younger and less fond of her own eccentricities."

"Do you really think she would take Eustace?"

He shrugged. "She likes men, lass, and she won't want to be without one for long. Moreover, if he gains control of her money and land, mayhap Eustace will be less of a thorn in everyone's side."

"Aye, perhaps." She glanced away only to smile when she saw Kit striding toward her at last.

He joined them, saying sardonically to the erstwhile Berridge, "Have you settled matters to your mutual satisfaction, my lord Armadale?"

"Aye, I'll let ye keep her," the new earl said, affecting a strong brogue. "Art vexed wi' me, laddie?"

"Nay, how should I be?" Kit said. "Although you might have told me."

"I did not know about the earldom myself until I reached home and found Armadale's signet awaiting me. By then, you had already stirred up a hornet's nest, and I thought I'd be more help if I did not muddy the waters by revealing my new identity to everyone. I warrant Toby would not have been so forthcoming to Armadale as he was to Berridge, and I learned a good deal from Toby."

"Do you know, just before Anne shot the pistol out of my executioner's hand and the lightning struck, I'd have sworn I saw Toby sitting on a horse just yonder at the bottom of the hill, exactly where the bolt hit."

"Well, you cannot have seen him, for I'm sure I would have noted his presence if he was riding a horse. That great lump of lard has not ridden one in years," Tam said, chuckling. "What have you decided to do about Eustace?"

Kit shrugged. "I've no liking for scandal, so for the present, at least, I mean to take him back to Hawks Rig with me. If he means to pursue Lady Carmichael, as he says he does, he can do so from there whilst I keep my eye on him. I've invited Fin and Patrick to return with us to Mute Hill tonight, but we'll make for Hawks Rig in the morning. I want to show my wife her new home as soon as I may," he added, putting an arm around Anne's shoulders.

"Is this the new Lady Chisholm?" a cheerful voice demanded as two men strode toward them from the crowd.

Kit agreed heartily that it was, whereupon Anne found herself confronting two handsome, grinning men nearly as large as her husband.

"Sweetheart," Kit said, "I'd like to present Fin Mackenzie, Laird of Kintail, and his constable, Sir Patrick MacRae. They came tonight from Dunsithe Castle."

"Then you are the ones Willie promised to bring," Anne said, extending a hand to the one called Fin and then to Patrick. "Thank you for coming so swiftly."

Fin said, "I am glad we could get here in time to help clean up the mess Kit made of all this, my lady, but you are the one he should be thanking for resurrecting *Sionnach Dubh* long enough to ride to his rescue. From all I've heard, the sight of you racing headlong into their midst, not to mention that fantastic pistol shot, stunned them all long enough to save your husband from certain death. Apparently, you also managed to rout the English army that Eustace came to meet."

"Thank you, sir, but I swear I had naught to do with the English leaving."

"For the love of heaven, Fin, don't encourage her," Kit pleaded.

Fin and Patrick laughed, exchanging glances as if they exchanged silent comments. Then Patrick said, "You must come and visit us soon at Dunsithe, both of you. Our wives will want to meet you, Lady Chisholm. Presently, they are both in a delicate condition, or they would pay you bride visits, for I believe you are distant cousins. Your mother was a Gordon, was she not?"

"Aye, she was," Anne said, pleased at the thought of meeting two new cousins who were married to friends of Kit's.

"We'll go to Dunsithe soon," he promised, "but first I want to see Hawks Rig put to rights and our people brought safely home again."

"To that end," Tam said, "may I suggest that we return at once to Mute Hill and perhaps snatch an hour's sleep before breakfast?"

Deep in the mist-shrouded High Glen, and in the cavern known as the Great Chamber, ten members of the Circle glided to their customary places around a spectral golden-orange glow that resembled a dying fire. The black-cloaked shapes of the ten stood utterly still after they had taken their places.

In the dense shadows beyond reach of the golden glow, Brown Claud sensed the presence of many others besides his mother, Catriona, and the Ellyl called Fergus Fishbait. The four of them had been summoned to the gathering at short notice, but although his previous visits to the Chamber had been unpleasant, even frightening, this time he felt calm if not entirely relaxed.

Someone shuffled feet in the blackness. Another coughed, quickly muffling the sound. Then the chief's voice sounded clearly.

"Maggie Malloch, step forward and take your rightful place in the Circle."

Claud breathed a sigh of relief at the command, for he had not known how the fickle ten would react to all that he and his mother had done, but if Maggie was to resume her seat, all would be well.

When she moved to her customary place, the Circle was nearly complete. Only one space remained empty, and that was the erstwhile seat of the wizard Jonah Bonewits, his father. Jonah's banishment had stirred trouble, for he retained friends aplenty within the Circle, and thus his position had remained unfilled.

"Ha' ye news for us, Maggie?" the chief demanded.

"I have," Maggie said. "First, we must all thank Fergus Fishbait o' the Ellyllon, for organizing his people tae pretend tae be the English army, thus aiding us in keeping the dealings o' the Clan safe from mortal ken as we dealt wi' the devilment o' Jonah Bonewits."

Fergus wriggled with pleasure at her words and the resulting applause.

"Second," Maggie said, "the lass Catriona o' the Merry Folk has successfully accomplished the task ye set for her. Thanks tae her efforts and me own, the truce betwixt her people and the Helping Hands is now permanent."

"Then ye ha' done as we asked, and we welcome ye back," the chief said. "We ha' but one more matter before us, then, tae seat our newest member."

Catriona, sitting next to Claud, leaned over to whisper, "They mean to fill Jonah's place at last, then. He won't like that."

In a wavering voice, Fergus said, "He'll be gey wroth, Jonah will."

"Hush," Claud said. "I want tae hear who's going tae take his place."

Others were murmuring too, but when the chief turned

toward them and raised his hands, the Great Chamber fell silent.

Solemnly, he said, "Inasmuch as we banished the great shape-shifting wizard, Jonah Bonewits, from our High Circle only tae see him commit many more o' his grave misdeeds, we find now that he has rendered himself subject tae final banishment from the Secret Clan. Therefore, someone new must take his seat in our Circle, and we ha' all cast our votes—all, that is, save one."

Turning slightly, he said, "Maggie, your vote will decide it, because our rule be plain. Tae seat a new member, our vote must be unanimous. The nominee be a member o' your own Good Neighbor tribe, who has demonstrated the great powers and wisdom required for membership in the Circle. With his very existence at stake, he put the welfare of others ahead o' his own, and risked all, even though he had nae reason tae believe he would succeed. His success freed many from unhappy spells, making it possible for them tae live productive lives again in our world."

"Sakes, who can that be?" Claud muttered.

"Hush," Catriona said, sitting forward so as not to miss a word. Her hand was on his knee, gripping hard, and he felt himself stir in response as he always did.

But he forgot his lust when the chief said, "What say ye, Maggie?"

"D'ye no mean tae tell me the name o' this paragon?"

"Aye, I'll tell ye," the chief said, smiling warmly. "'Tis your own son, Brown Claud, o' course. Look around ye, lass." He raised his hands again, and the blackness in the Chamber lightened, revealing a host of cheering wee folk.

Claud sat stunned, unable to think or move. Then he saw

an old friend, Lucy Fittletrot, dancing toward him with her father, Tom Tit Tot, close behind.

"Sakes, lass, I thought the pair o' ye had vanished forever," he said to her.

"We might well have," she said, "for Jonah sent me tae the distant land where he had already sent me dad tae live in a cage whilst he fiddled for folks what wear long black plaits down their backs. They were kind folk, but we couldna speak or sing, Claud, and I couldna dance anymore. I'm that glad tae be back." Shyly, she looked at Catriona, adding, "Prithee, dinna be wroth wi' me for speaking tae him."

Leaving her hand possessively on Claud's knee, Catriona smiled graciously. "Welcome home, Lucy," she said.

"Step forward, Brown Claud."

"Sakes," he muttered, "they must ha' made a mistake. I'm nobbut a dobby. Wha' I did tae Jonah were nobbut a crazy thing."

"Go on, silly," Catriona said, giving him a push. "The Circle never makes mistakes. Just look at Maggie."

He did, and the next thing he knew he was standing beside her and the chief was settling a long black, hooded robe over his shoulders. It felt heavy, and the thought of the responsibilities that came with it nearly overpowered him.

He looked in panic at Maggie. "I canna do it, mam," he muttered.

"Pish tush," she snapped. "Take your rightful place, lad, and dinna talk so much." Then, as he moved to obey her, she reached to touch his cheek, adding in a voice choked with sudden tears, "Ye've done yourself proud, Claud, and 'tis me own belief ye'll be the best o' our lot."

Chapter 21

The return to Mute Hill House was swifter than Anne had expected, for although Willie's reivers had stayed to disperse Eustace's men, there were still the men from Dunsithe to accommodate, as well as Eustace himself and Willie, the latter having insisted he had a duty to present himself to Olivia and assure her that Fiona was well. With such a large party, they had no need to move silently or by moonlight alone. Myriad torches made their path clear for all to see.

Anne rode beside Kit, with Fin Mackenzie and Patrick MacRae behind them, but they had not ridden far before Willie drew up near Kit and said, "Beg pardon, sir, but may I ha' leave tae exchange a word or two wi' her ladyship?"

Kit's eyebrows shot skyward. "Have you aught to say to my lady that you cannot say in front of me?" he demanded.

"Nay, nay, but the track be too narrow tae ride three abreast."

"Very well, but talk fast. I've no wish to share her company more tonight."

Willie nodded, but Anne noted that he eyed her warily. "Do you fear that I'll snap your head off, you villain?" she said. "You deserve it."

"Aye, or worse," he said. "I hear ye shot that pistol right out o' the man's hand when he were about tae murder our Kit."

"What have you done with Fiona?"

"I've married her, that's what," he said. "Fell in love wi' her the first moment I clapped me eyes on her, and she says she felt the same. I'm sorry we couldna tell ye, but we feared ye'd tell Lady Carmichael. I'm no looking forward tae seeing her, I can tell ye, but Fiona made me promise tae tell her all's well."

"Where is Fiona?"

"Wi' me uncle and some half dozen cousins at Mangerton, happy as can be. Me cousins canna stop staring, because o' her beauty, but she doesna pay them heed, other than tae laugh and treat them as if she'd been there forever."

"Yes, that is exactly how she is when she is happy," Anne said. "She has not an ounce of vanity in her. She said once that people never see the real Fiona, only the way she looks. I'm glad she is happy, Willie. Thank you for telling me, and thank you, too, for all the help you provided tonight."

"Sakes, I told ye, mistress. I owe me life tae Kit. I'd never ha' let him down, not even for Fiona. Nor, tae the lass's credit, would she ha' let me."

The rest of the ride passed without incident, and they arrived at Mute Hill before the sun arose. If they had hoped to go straight to bed, however, that was not to be, for Malcolm met them at the door and, taking in the increased size of their party with evident astonishment, informed them that Olivia had given strict instructions to be awakened upon their return.

Anne sighed, looking helplessly at Kit.

"I'll be glad to deal with her ladyship, if you will allow me," Tam said.

"I'll go with you," Eustace said curtly, moving to stand beside him.

"Look here," Tam said, "you don't mean to continue with that nonsense about Kit being a murderer, do you, because both Willie Armstrong and I can testify to the truth, which is that he never killed anyone."

Eustace glowered but said, "I must accept the word of the Earl of Armadale, as I am sure the authorities would, but I'll not give you free rein with Olivia."

"Her ladyship will not agree to see either of you just now," Malcolm said, barring their way and looking haughtily from one to the other. "She desires only to speak to Lady Anne."

"Then she will have to inform Lady Anne's husband," Tam said. "As for you, Malcolm Vole, I have been given to understand that you harbor inappropriate thoughts toward your mistress. Perhaps you should know that I am not merely Lord Berridge, as I told you, but also have the honor to be the present Earl of Armadale, and as such, I am head of Lady Carmichael's family."

"Can this be true?" Malcolm demanded, looking from Eustace to Kit.

Tam said sharply, "Do you doubt my word, clodpoll? Faith, but if you do not mend your ways, I promise you, you will be seeking employment elsewhere. Now, take me to her ladyship."

"Well, well, so ye've returned, have ye," Sir Toby bellowed from the hall entrance. "I warrant Olivia will make ye smart for running off like ye did, Anne."

"Lady Carmichael has no further authority over my

wife," Kit said, but Anne noted that despite his firm tone, he was staring at Toby as if the man were a ghost.

"Olivia won't let lack of authority trouble her," Toby said in his cheerful way.

"Here, now, you come with us, Toby," Tam said to him. "You and Eustace and I can have a game of Cent after I speak to Olivia. Oh, and I should perhaps tell you I was not entirely candid with you before about my identity. You see . . ."

As he hustled Toby and Eustace into the hall, his voice fading in the distance, Anne said, "What is it, Kit? Why did you look so oddly at Toby?"

"I don't know," he said. "I feel as if there is something wrong with his being here, but I cannot put my finger on what it is."

As he said the words, she had a niggling feeling that she, too, had forgotten something, but the sensation disappeared when Kit took her arm and urged her toward the stairs.

Upstairs, they found that someone had tidied Kit's bed-chamber. Candles flickered in wall sconces and in the candle holder on the bed-step table, and a fire crackled cheerfully in the fireplace.

"Malcolm must have sent someone up the moment we rode in," Anne said. "Trust that man to butter his bread on both sides."

"He's lucky he does not serve me," Kit said. "I'd most likely kick him down the stairs at least once a day and take a stout switch to his backside once a week."

"How fierce you sound," she said, smiling at him. "For my part, I do not think your temper is nearly as vicious as you have claimed, sir."

"You'll soon learn your error if you continue to behave as you did tonight," he said, putting his hands lightly on her shoulders. "That cloak is too big for you."

"It's yours," she said.

"I know."

She would have said more, but the look in his eyes silenced her. Suddenly, she was unsure of his mood, although her body remembered only his touch, and every cell in it called to him.

He reached for the strings at her neck, loosening them and pushing the cloak off her shoulders to the floor. "Are those my netherstocks, too, and my shirt?"

"Aye," she said, feeling more vulnerable now than she had with the cloak covering her, and much more vulnerable than she had ever felt in woman's dress.

"Why did you wear my clothes?"

"They were easier than my own to put on in a hurry, and . . . and I'd already decided to ride as the Black Fox," she said, rushing the last words. "I . . . I'm not sure why I did, but it seemed the best thing to do."

"I suppose I should be grateful that you did not cut eyeholes in the hood so you could wear it like a mask over your face."

His hands moved to the strings of the shirt she wore, and without speaking further, he untied the bow she had tied. The shirt opening was so large on her that he was able to push it off her shoulders the same way he had pushed the cloak. With a hushing whisper, it slid to the floor too, leaving her clad in only her thin shift, his baggy netherstocks, and her boots.

"Stand still," he ordered as he bent to one knee in front of her.

"What are you going to do?"

"Teach you to obey your husband," he said. "Lift your right foot."

Her body had come alive, tingling and aching for him, the moment he had touched the cloak strings, but now it grew wary as well. It occurred to her belatedly, as she obediently raised her foot, that although she had trusted her instincts from the outset where he was concerned, and her instincts had never led her wrong before, she did not really know this husband of hers. His temper could prove to be as volatile, unpredictable, and violent as he had said it was, and he could be about to strip her naked and beat her soundly for daring to ride to his rescue.

"Now the other one," he said gruffly.

She obeyed without a word, but when he pulled off her boot only to continue to hold her foot, stroking it lightly and gazing at it as if he had never seen a foot before, she put both hands in his thick hair and pulled hard.

"What the—!" He dropped her foot but grabbed both hands and forced her to release her grip on his hair as he rose to face her, looming over her. "Do you know what you deserve?" he demanded.

"Aye," she said, planting her hands on her hips and giving him look for look.

He opened his mouth and shut it again as his gaze moved down her body.

She stayed as she was, waiting.

He did not touch her, and when his gaze returned to her face, he said in a tight voice, "What, then? Tell me what you deserve."

"To go to bed without my breakfast," she said with a seductive smile.

He reached for her then, pulling her into his arms and holding her tight. "Anne-lassie, I think I'll keep you," he murmured against her curls.

"Take me to bed, Kit," she murmured back. "I would learn more about this business of being married."

Requiring no further invitation, he picked her up and carried her to the bed. "You still have much to learn about obedience," he said, smiling mischievously as he set her down. "Take off my clothes."

"The ones I'm wearing or the ones you are?"

He shook his head at her. "Clearly, I have much work to do to turn you into an obedient wife," he said, reaching for her feet. Before she realized his intent, he had grabbed the ends of the netherstocks she wore and yanked them off. "Now," he said, "will you take off that shift, or must I do that, too?"

"I'll do it," she said, suiting action to words. "But you are still dressed."

"Not for long," he said, pulling off his shirt.

"You should snuff all those candles before you come to bed," Anne said.

"Did you order your father around like this?" Kit asked as he stripped off the rest of his clothing.

"You are not my father."

"No, I'm not," he agreed, getting into bed beside her.

"The candles," she reminded him.

"I'll put them out when I no longer want to see my naughty wife," he retorted. "Lie back, sweetheart. I mean to feast my eyes whilst I teach you more about proper wifely obedience."

Every fiber of her body responded to the desire in his voice and his expression, and the game of obedience having suddenly become much more interesting, Anne did as he commanded.

"Put your hands at your sides and open your legs a little," he said, shifting his weight slightly and letting the candle-light reveal more of her.

His interested scrutiny heightened every sensation, and when he reached to stroke one breast, she gasped and began to turn toward him.

"Not yet," he said firmly. "Lie still. I want to take my time with this unless you fear you might fall asleep."

The thought was laughable. Gazing up at him, she said, "I should be tired, should I not? But I'm not, not in the least, so do your worst, sir. Just do not forget that last time you promised that I can explore your body the way you explore mine. I want my turn, too."

He grinned at her. "Oh, aye, sweetheart, I always keep my promises. Now, spread your legs just a wee bit more."

She obeyed, and he moved between them, stroking her breasts and body. When he bent to take one nipple in his mouth, she could no longer keep her hands at her sides but caught his ears.

"Not yet," she said urgently. "Kiss me first!"

He hesitated long enough to make her wonder how far he meant to take this business of obedience, but then his lips found hers and his tongue slid deeply into her mouth.

With a sigh of relief and increasing passion, she wrapped her arms around him and held him tight, but although he kissed her thoroughly, his hands remained busy with her body, and when he moved to kiss a shoulder, she did not try to stop him. He went on to kiss her right breast, sucking long on her nipple before turning his attention to the left one and then to her belly, and lower. By the time his mouth reached the juncture of her legs, she was lost to her own passion and to his.

The touch of his tongue and fingers was unexpected and stirred feelings unlike any she had felt before. Her mother certainly had never mentioned married people doing this, but she trusted Kit and loved him. If this was what obedience got a woman, let there be more of it, she thought wickedly, although she would never say that to him. Then her body leaped, and her mind emptied of all but her own fulfillment as sensation after new sensation flooded through her.

As she lay gasping, he moved to cover her with his body and to claim her mouth again. She could smell her own scent on his lips, and it stimulated her, so that when he entered her, she gripped him tightly, pressing against him and letting instinct take over. His eyes closed as he savored the pleasure he felt. Then his body moved faster, and as it did, he turned, holding her and lifting her so that she soon rode atop him. Then his eyes opened, and he watched, clearly delighted, as passion overwhelmed her again. A moment later, his own release came.

Quiet reigned for several minutes before he shifted her to lie beside him again and put his arm around her. "Art happy, lass?"

"Aye," she murmured, still awed by the feelings he stirred in her.

"I have never known anyone like you," he said, pulling her closer.

"I love you, Kit," she said, turning her head to look at his face.

"I know you do, Anne-lassie, almost as much as I love you."

"More," she said softly.

"Impossible," he murmured.

Contented as she had not known she could be, Anne closed her eyes.

The candles in the wall sconces guttered simultaneously and went out, leaving only the one on the little table in a room redolent now of wood smoke with a hint of lust. In its darkest corner, a shadow stirred, revealing itself as a small dark fox with a white tip to its high, bushy tail.

It gazed for a long moment at the silent couple in the bed as they held each other lovingly, and then it began to fade from sight. In the last moment, just before it disappeared, it changed to the plump figure of a little countrywoman, holding a slender pipe from which a thin curl of white smoke drifted upward.

Smiling with satisfaction at a task well done, Maggie Malloch vanished.

Dear Reader,

I hope you enjoyed *The Secret Clan: Reiver's Bride*. For those of you interested in the historical characters I included in the book, Ill Will Armstrong really existed and was hanged by James V along with Johnny Armstrong, but Ill Will's son's name was Sandie, not Willie. Sandie was the father of Kinmont Willie Armstrong, whose ballad story formed the basis for my book, *Border Fire*.

With regard to the games mentioned in the book, Poque is an ancestor of Poker, and has been played in Britain since the early fifteenth century. Both Poque and its predecessor Poch were played on painted boards, and the Victoria & Albert Museum in London has a Poque board dated 1535. Poch was first recorded at Strasbourg in 1441, which makes Poker and its ilk the oldest identifiable card game known. (See David Parlett's *A History of Card Games*, Oxford University Press, 1991.)

As for Fox and Geese, if you have played the game and wonder why Kit and company had only thirteen geese instead of seventeen, the answer is that throughout the sixteenth century and for sometime thereafter, the number was thirteen. Seventeen was considered an improvement, although if the person herding the geese knows what he or she is doing, the poor fox never has a chance.

Words for the two wedding ceremonies come from a Missal used during the reign of Richard II (1377–99), which gives the ceremony in English despite the contemporary influence of the Roman Church (which used

Latin) throughout Scotland and England. The ceremony was not significantly altered again until the King James Version of the Bible came into being in the seventeenth century.

The wheel-lock pistol that Kit teaches Anne to shoot was common in the Borders as early as the first half of the sixteenth century. As mentioned at the end of *Border Storm*, the wheel-lock is thought to have been invented by Leonardo da Vinci, the great Italian artist and engineer. It worked on the principle of a modern cigarette-lighter. For more information on the weapons of this period, see *English Weapons and Warfare, 449–1660*, by A.V.B. Norman and Don Pottinger (London, 1966). See also *Weapons Through the Ages* by William Read (New York, 1976), and *A Glossary of the Construction, Decoration, and Use of Arms and Armor in All Countries and in All Times* by George Cameron Stone (New York, 1961).

I generally end my letters to you by thanking the people who have helped me with my research or with my career, but it occurs to me that you, dear reader, are who I should be thanking each and every time. This is book number 43, and you have been in my thoughts with every sentence I have written. Therefore, I want to take this opportunity to thank you for your tremendous support, for all the letters you have sent via Uncle Sam's ponies or cyberspace, for coming out in all sorts of weather to book signings and to Scottish games, and most of all, of course, for continuing to buy and enjoy my books. So I thank you, each of you, most sincerely.

Many thanks also to my wonderful editor, Beth de

Guzman, my superb agents Aaron Priest and Lucy
Childs, and to my longsuffering family and friends, who
put up with me even when I'm at the tail end of a book
and tend to be a bit testy and forgetful (but can still put a
dynamite Thanksgiving dinner on the table!). I love you
all and appreciate you more than mere words can express.

Slàinte mhath,

Amanda Scott

http://home.att.net/~amandascott

About the Author

AMANDA SCOTT, best-selling author and winner of the Romance Writers of America's RITA/Golden Medallion and the Romantic Times' awards for Best Regency Author and Best Sensual Regency, began writing on a dare from her husband. She has sold every manuscript she has written. She sold her first novel, *The Fugitive Heiress*—written on a battered Smith-Corona—in 1980. Since then, she has sold many more, but since the second one, she has used a word processor. More than twenty-five of her books are set in the English Regency period (1810–20), others are set in fifteenth-century England and sixteenth- and eighteenth-century Scotland. Three are contemporary romances.

Amanda is a fourth-generation Californian who was born and raised in Salinas and graduated with a bachelor's degree in history from Mills College in Oakland. She did graduate work at the University of North Carolina at Chapel Hill, specializing in British history, before obtaining her master's in history from California State University at San Jose. After graduate school, she taught for the Salinas City School District for three years before marrying her husband, who was then a captain in the Air Force. They lived in Honolulu for a year, then in Nebraska for seven years, where their son was born. Amanda now lives with her husband in northern California.

THE EDITOR'S DIARY

Dear Reader,

Fate has a funny way of bringing together two people who are meant to be, whether they realize it or not. And, with a little bit of mischief and just the right amount of time, Anne Foster and Lady Anne Ellyson are about to get the surprise of their lives in our two Warner Forever titles this September.

Mary Jo Putney raves "Joan Wolf writes with an absolute emotional mastery that goes straight to the heart" and that couldn't be truer in **Joan Wolf's THAT SUMMER**. Veterinarian Anne Foster grew up in the rolling hills of Virginia horse country, helping her father train Thoroughbreds at the Wellington family racing farm and longing for Liam Wellington, the boy just out of her reach. But when a beautiful and sought-after girl in the town disappears, Anne's life is changed forever. All evidence points to Liam and his friends, but Anne refuses to accept it. Running from her own memories of that night, she leaves Virginia—and Liam—behind and vows to begin a new life. Now, ten years later, with the death of her beloved father, Anne returns to Wellington Farm and runs into Liam. Drawn into the love she could never forget, Anne is determined to clear Liam's name and risk losing her heart all over again.

Moving from the horse country of Virginia to the rolling hills of medieval Scotland, we find **THE SECRET CLAN: REIVER'S BRIDE** by **Amanda Scott** who

Affaire de Coeur has called "a master." When reivers descend upon Lady Anne Ellyson one moonlit night, she is shocked to discover their leader is none other than Sir Christopher Chisholm. Long presumed dead, Kit had been betrothed to Anne's favorite cousin Fiona before his disappearance. Now, determined to reunite them and to prevent her cousin's marriage to another, Anne must risk both her reputation and her life to help Kit overcome a false murder accusation. But dare she risk her heart? With the enchanted matchmaking mischief of the Secret Clan, the wrong heartstrings are becoming entangled and romance gets more deliciously complicated each day.

To find out more about Warner Forever, these September titles, and the authors, visit us at www.warnerforever.com.

With warmest wishes,

Karen Kosztolnyik

Karen Kosztolnyik, Senior Editor

P.S. As you try to pick out the perfect mask for Halloween, Warner Forever offers you two titles in which things aren't always what they appear to be: Annie Soloman presents a spine-tingling romantic suspense about a woman made over into the spitting image of her long-lost biological mother in DEAD RINGER; and Shari Anton makes her mainstream debut in THE IDEAL HUSBAND, a moving historical about a woman who pretends to be married to a handsome nobleman suffering from amnesia.